The Eclipse Killer

The Eclipse Killer

Rachel Funk HELLER

To Ron, for being so patient

❪1❫

Monday, August 7, 2017

KXOP News San Francisco — 5:23 a.m.

Madeline tiptoed over snaking cables on a slick floor, past stacks of monitors and an assortment of cameras, following her younger sister — a young Ariadne, leading her through the labyrinthine television studio. While they passed through the newsroom, Madeline's stomach tightened from the clacking keyboards, barking reporters, and blaring police scanners. But ahead, their destination awaited like an oasis, an island of light, the "home set," someone's idea of a bright, cozy kitchen nook set in a vast, darkened studio. "So, Cora," Madeline asked, "tell me again, these people won't bust out the pitchforks and torches when they learn I'm an astrologer?"

"Of course not," Cora replied, her darling younger sister dripping with confidence and Chanel. "This is happy, happy TV. A break between the gloomy headlines. You'll be your amazing self."

Amazing wasn't the word floating through Madeline's mind, but since Cora moved to San Francisco to intern at the station, Madeline agreed to be on live television as a favor. Because of their ten-year age difference, Madeline intended to create an adult relationship with Cora now that she was a grownup and not the cute plaything Madeline remembered when they lived back home in Hawaii.

"That lipstick looks wonderful on you," Cora said. Her petite, dark-haired little sister, who loved fashion and makeup, brought her to the edge of the cozy set.

"The makeup lady promised to make my lips 'soft and dewy.'" Madeline smacked her lips and blew Cora an exaggerated kiss. "It's got some weird name, like Corpse Flower. What's your's called?"

Cora did an exaggerated lip pucker, showing off soft petal pink lips. "It's called 'I'm a Princess and You Are Not.'"

"Fitting."

"True." Cora lowered her voice, "Don't be nervous," she said, as they arrived at the home set occupied by a dazzling blonde in full "News Anchor Barbie" drag and an astronomy Professor bespectacled, bearded, dressed straight out of the thirteenth century—all nerd, all day long. The only thing missing was the tonsure and the monk's robe.

Madeline was clueless about styling her hair. She pulled some strands away from her face and clipped them at the back. She wore her favorite slate gray silk blouse over reliable gabardine navy slacks—not much of a "look," but she always chose comfort over style. Tempted, she left the flowing scarf, bangle bracelets, crystal ball, and magic wand back at her store. "Have a seat," Cora pointed to the empty chair. As Madeline sat, she smiled at the anchor and astronomer.

"Hi Monica," Cora said to the blonde, "this is my sister Madeline."

"Nice to meet you," Madeline said as Monica's ceramic-toothed smile gleamed under the dimmed studio lights.

"It's so nice to have you, and this is Professor Joseph Pendleton from San Francisco University."

Madeline nodded to the Professor, who'd taken pains to project the solemn Professor image with wire-frame glasses and a bow tie, but his hipster beard still held crumbs from a carby breakfast.

The knots in her stomach somersaulted, her mouth dried up, and she considered bolting. Cora leaned in, her voice soothing. "Here's your mic," she clipped a tiny microphone to Madeline's lapel. Cora leaned closer and whispered in Madeline's ear. "Faster pussycat, kill, kill!"

Madeline's anxiety melted as she choked back a guffaw at Cora's use of an old catch phrase. Madeline taught it to her when Cora was, what, ten? "You're the best," Madeline said as the joke made her smile.

Cora, pleased with herself, wiggled her head. "Okay, good. Now you're relaxed. I'll be in the newsroom during your segment. Go do that voodoo that you do so well," and with a wink, she slunk back into the darkness.

"Professor and Madeline. I'm so glad you could join us," Monica said while shuffling her script. "I'll start with one or two headlines and begin the interview with the Professor."

Before either of them answered, the studio lights went from soft to thermonuclear, and the floor manager yelled, "Three, two…" He waved at Monica, who sat bolt upright. "Welcome back, everyone. We'll have an update on the Sean Muldooney trial, in a few moments, but we have some skywatchers in our studio right now. On August twenty-first, we'll bring you coverage of a total solar eclipse that will be visible here in the Bay Area. To prepare, we've invited an astronomer and an astrologer to our studio to give us the inside scoop on the event. Professor Pendleton, can you explain the eclipse to our viewers?"

Adjusting his glasses, the Professor plowed in. "It's my pleasure, Monica. The moon will cross the face of the sun, blocking it out. It will be visible in most of the western hemisphere. We're calling it America's eclipse because it will be visible from the West Coast to the East Coast."

Madeline twitched. America's eclipse. Do we have to brand everything?

Monica on her. "We've invited Madeline Merritt, an astrologer and the owner of Sirius Bookstore, for her take on the big event. Now, aren't eclipses considered a bad omen? A sign of doom and gloom?"

"Thank you for inviting me," Madeline blurted out. Catching herself, she breathed in before continuing. "Yes. In ancient times, a full solar eclipse often signaled turmoil, such as the death of a king or an invasion. We derive the word 'eclipse' from the Greek word for 'disappearance.' Astrologers interpreted the event as the sun abandoning the Earth. This historical significance of eclipses and astrology connects us to our past and helps us understand our present."

"—We're long past the days of kings," the Professor sneered, cutting her off. "Science has proven astrology to be nothing more than balmy superstition."

Madeline ignored the Professor's smug attitude, staying focused on Monica. "That's true. Most people think astrology is an old superstition or an amusement, but historically, it's the precursor to astronomy. Early scientists discovered that the planets and stars followed predictable orbits. This offered people comfort in unpredictable times because the stars don't lie. Modern astrology offers insights into our personalities and reminds us we are soul-centered creatures. Tell me, Professor, has science proven you have a soul?"

The Professor twitched his lips like a perturbed rabbit. Yes, she'd taken the shot, but he started it.

Shaking his head, the Professor's voice took on an edge. "I'm not here to talk about my soul. You can't tell me a planet that's ninety-three million miles away can predict what's happening in my life. I have free will."

Madeline smiled. "Astrology doesn't deny free will. The insights you gain from understanding your deeper motives allow you to transcend your flaws and blind spots and live a better life."

"Ha-ha! My, that's so interesting," Monica said with a flip of her hair, checking the time with a side-eye glance at the clock on the nearby monitor. "Um, well, Professor? Can you tell us how to view the eclipse?"

With his smug smile fixed, the Professor pulled out a pair of flimsy cardboard and plastic glasses. "Never stare straight at the sun. Be sure to use UV-coated glasses to prevent eye injury."

Monica beamed, "That's right. You must use eclipse glasses to prevent severe retinal damage." She put on a pair of feeble lenses. Doing stupid things on television must be part of her contract.

Madeline kept smiling while the other two prattled on about the best places to follow the eclipse. A tingle of pain shot down her left leg from sitting in the strange chair for so long. She glanced at the TV monitor just as they flashed her name. To her relief, they spelled her shop's name correctly. She looked forward to the big Leo eclipse, which promised lots of heat, which she hoped meant lots of sales.

"Well, thank you two for joining us. Now, back to Ken at the weather desk. Ken?"

The harsh lights dimmed, and Madeline unclipped the mic, stood up, and shook her leg, restoring blood flow. Monica reached out to shake her hand. "You really know your stuff," Monica said. "Do you give readings?"

Madeline pulled out a card and passed it to Monica. "I still take personal clients. Thank you for asking." To be sassy, she tossed a card across the table to the Professor. "Here, we also sell scholarly works on the history of astronomy."

The Professor ignored the card. "So, tell me why you named your shop Serious Books? That's a tad pretentious, don't you think?"

Madeline smiled. She held up her card for him. "It's Sirius Books. After the dog star? Alpha Canis Major. You knew that, right?"

The Professor flashed a fake smile. "Of course." He left the set.

Cora emerged from the shadows. "You were fantastic! — Even got a few digs in!"

"I hope it fits the happy TV bill. You want to come and watch the eclipse coverage at my store?"

"Gosh, I'd love to, but they've asked me to help with the social media coverage. One staffer is baking eclipse cookies. Thanks for the invite."

Madeline made a mental note to order Eclipse cookies. "I'm curious. I thought you majored in fashion design. Why are you interning in a newsroom?" They fell into step, making their way out of the studio.

"It was Mom's idea. Fashion is my first love, but I don't have what it takes to be a designer."

"Says who? Don't give up on your passion. You have talent, but with any art form, it takes practice."

"True. I like this place. They've given me a cool assignment. I'm researching the Muldooney-Volkov family feud. Have you followed it?"

Madeline hesitated. "Russians and Irish mobsters shooting each other in the streets?"

"Yeah, and then there's the romance. Alana Volkov marries Sean Muldooney to bring peace to the families, but now he's on trial for murder. The cops say they have a secret witness who will put Sean away for life. Hey, you think we could go out to dinner this week?"

"How about you come to the shop this weekend? I'd love to show you around. I've made some changes while Aunt Jane moved to Oregon. After that, I'll cook us dinner."

They walked past a television screen, and a show promo appeared. The headline read: "Exclusive Interview with Christophe." It included a photo of the man: crystalline China-blue eyes staring out under hooded eyelids framed by wavy blond-brown hair going gray at the temples, perfecting the air of an enlightened, thought-leader, high-performance, bro.

Madeline stopped moving. "He's going to be here?"

"Oh yeah, everyone is buzzing about it," Cora gushed. "Christophe's planning a mega event for the solar eclipse. He's coming here to promote it."

"He never does TV interviews—" Madeline said to herself. She turned to Cora and asked. "Does he?"

"No! That's why everyone is on edge. The enigmatic recluse climbing down from Mount Olympus to do an interview." Cora said. They fell back in step, walking toward the exit.

"Interesting," Madeline said, fighting to hide her nerves. "It's amazing what people will pay for products endorsed by their guru."

Cora frowned. "I don't see someone like Christophe getting his hands dirty whipping up a batch of lip balm. I'm guessing he's got Gary from the meth lab cooking up his products for his wellness centers." She winked.

Madeline laughed, delighted that her little sister appreciated sarcasm as much as she did. "No, they fired Gary he wasn't spiritual enough. Now they have Sunflower Fairy Dust working in the lab."

Cora smiled. "Well, thanks again for coming over to the dark side."

"Thanks for helping me promote the store."

"I got your back, sis." Cora reached in for a hug.

Madeline accepted the hug and squeezed Cora the way she did when Cora was a toddler, enjoying this new connection with her sister.

"Can you find your way back?" Cora asked.

"I'm pretty sure. Okay, hogs and quiches."

"All our feet are the same," Cora said and scampered off.

Madeline walked past another monitor in the hallway, repeated the promotion about Christophe's upcoming interview, and saw those disarming eyes again. What was he up to now?

❨2❩

Russian Hill, San Francisco — 6:57 a.m.

Crossing Broadway, preparing to summit the killer incline on Taylor Street, Investigator Hunter Davis gunned his decrepit Toyota, ascending the heights. He offered a silent "fuck you" to Jean Jacques Vioget—for the millionth time—for imposing a stupid grid on San Francisco's steep peaks and deeper valleys. Downshifting, the less-than-reliable transmission churned and yearned, and Hunter braced for the moment—the nanosecond when the front of the chassis went airborne. He drew in his breath as the car lurched up—only to have it clunk down with a thud. "Can't win 'em all, dude." He patted the faded dashboard and found a parking spot behind the crime scene investigator's van.

Hunter's phone chirped—Vierra's text: "Running late." He had resigned himself a long time ago to his partner being punctuality-challenged, but now it was getting worse. Hunter had been afraid of this, but who was he to tell his partner that his extra-marital affair with a mobster's wife was a less-than-ideal situation? With the ink still drying on his own divorce papers, Hunter was in no position to judge anyone's love life.

Why the delay? Where was his energy? In any other case, he'd be bounding out of the car, ready to join the show, to give orders and get answers. Something was off today. Not like any murder is ever normal. Hunter grabbed his weathered portfolio, climbed out of the car, and breathed in the early morning air. Chilly, the fog lingering, temperatures still in the sixties—a typical August morning in the city. Hunter stepped off the sidewalk into the park and took in the sweeping view before him: Coit Tower peeking through the morning fog, traffic trundling across the Bay Bridge, the financial district gleaming in the soft morning light.

He felt like a tourist in his hometown, but few tourists ever made it to Ina Coolbrith Park, a hillside lot transformed into a modest jewel. Instead of building apartments on the sheer rock face, the city planners created an oasis: a perpendicular landscaped city jewel. It featured generous landscaping, curving walking paths, and two sets of staircases running up each side of the park, beginning at the bottom of Vallejo, where it dead-ended at Mason Street. Maybe, when the case concluded, he'd return with his easel and painting supplies, but his gut told him a pleasant day of Plein air painting was as off in the distance as the Bay Bridge.

The crackling banter on the police radio scanner narrowed his focus on what had brought him here: a murdered body hidden in the park. On his left, the Royal Towers apartment building offered perfect views of the entire area. He'd order a door-to-door inquiry. Possibly, an early morning dog walker spotted something. On his right stood a smaller three-story townhouse complex. Each unit had a balcony and access to the park. The wealthiest part of Russian Hill rose behind him, a mix of multi-million-dollar mansions, remodeled Victorians, and high-rise apartments—those owners paid someone to walk their dogs. He caught a scent: bacon coming from a mansion behind him. High-quality bacon, hardwood-smoked, and no nitrates, as they were illegal in this neighborhood.

Hunter turned to the duty officer, "Good morning,"—reading the name-tag — "Officer Wong. Were you the one who called it in?"

"No, a 911 call at 6:17." Wong offered Hunter a clipboard to sign. Wong's face appeared pale from climbing up the steps. Or what he saw at the crime scene shocked him. "I was the first on the scene. I put up the tape and waited. The crime scene guys arrived about fifteen minutes ago. They're down there now."

Hunter jotted down "6:17 a.m." along with Wong's name in his portfolio. Hunter wanted Wong to be part of the team. "What's your first impression?" He asked, signing the clipboard, and handing it over.

Wong took back the clipboard and stared at it, struggling to answer. "It's a weird one, you know? The victim's just a kid."

Blood ran from Hunter's face. "Are you saying it's a child's body?"

"No, no—not that young," Wong stammered. "A teenager. Clean cut. White. God, but the crime scene. I promise I haven't lost my mind, but it reminded me of a magazine. It's beautiful."

Hunter's nerves inched up a notch. Beautiful? "Are you saying the killer staged the scene?"

Wong gave an exaggerated nod. "Oh yeah. Every inch of it."

"Got it." Hunter gulped, knowing it took a lot to fluster beat cops.

A tan Ford with the ubiquitous "Uber" sticker in the window pulled up to the curb, and Daniel Vierra, his partner, emerged, his thin, lanky frame unfolding from the cramped back seat. His blue-gray suit, cut to fit, was now rumpled and slept in. Vierra hurried to the scene without time to shower or shave. His hair, a tangle of graying curls, sprang in all directions.

"So, we're Ubering to crime scenes these days?" Hunter cracked, taking the clipboard from Wong, and giving it to Vierra.

"Well, duh. You think I'm gonna ruin my tranny grinding up Taylor Street? Jean Jacques Vioget can kiss my ass." Vierra signed the clipboard and handed it back to Wong with a quick head nod of recognition and a smile to put the cop at ease.

Hunter smirked. It didn't matter how Vierra spent his nights, although the rumor mill said Vierra was conducting an affair with Alana Muldooney, who was married to the notorious Sean Muldooney. But he never asked Vierra for details, and as long as he arrived at work with his wits sharpened, Hunter wasn't going to ask for more. "So, you couldn't find your car after too many beers or forgot where you parked it?"

"No fucking comment," Vierra said, giving Hunter's arm a playful punch and taking in the scene. "What the hell are we doing in this neighborhood?"

"I haven't seen the body, but according to Officer Wong here, we're in for a surprise."

"Perfect, I fucking hate surprises."

Hunter let Vierra start ahead of him, turning back to Wong. "Thanks for the warning."

"Sure thing," said Wong, staring off into the distance, his face still pale. "It's the third pathway on the left."

Hunter joined Vierra, and they made their way in silence down a set of stairs past the first tier of park benches.

Vierra paused and shook his head. "Jesus, that is some goddamn view."

"But why choose this place to dump a body?"

"Was the guy looking to get caught? All these apartments with a perfect view of the crime scene?"

"No sense guessing until we see it," Hunter said as they descended the last section of stairs, following the line of yellow police tape. With each step, his guts churned from the sudden rush of adrenaline. Arriving at the third switchback, they turned left.

A looping tree limb and a lush spray of periwinkle plumbago blossoms arching through the air formed a decorative canopy, framing a dark green park bench. On it sat a boy, wrapped in a multicolored quilt, with eyes closed, settled in the lotus position.

Nearby, Connie, covered head to toe in a white jumpsuit, took photos of the boy from every angle. The camera flash illuminated the boy's face, and Hunter swore it sparkled. It hit him like a sucker punch: this was his murder victim. Hunter angled in for a closer view, staying out of the crime tech's way.

"Ah, shit," Vierra said. "What did we step in here, Partner?"

"Fuck if I know," Hunter mumbled as he studied the boy: a young, mixed-race male who couldn't be over fifteen or sixteen years old with short brown hair brushed back from his face. Not a square jaw, but high cheekbones. Once he grew into them, he'd be handsome, a catch. But what brought him here? Sacrificed like this?

His body sat erect on the bench, with his head held high. Hunter's mind flashed through his mental Rolodex of crime scenes. "Wait, a minute…" Something about the posture wasn't right. He scanned behind the bench and found a metal stake planted in the dirt. "Vierra, check this out."

Vierra got down on his haunches beside Hunter. "What the fuck is that doing there?"

"The killer attached a wire to the stake, forming a shelf. The kid's head is resting on it." Connie joined the conversation.

"Hey, Connie," Vierra said. "What's your take on this?"

"Come and check out the photos."

Hunter stood with his partner, gathering to see the camera's digital screen.

"If you walked past him, you'd think he was meditating. It's only when you get close to the body you see that he's dead."

"Without the wiring, the skull would flop over," said Hunter, the murderer's intention coming into focus. "The killer staged this boy—this body—to make it … beautiful, or… or…" What had Wong said… like a photoshoot?

"Or perfect?" Vierra suggested.

"Yes. It's a strange signature," Connie said, and everything stopped.

Signature.

Hunter nudged Vierra, the word signature sizzling between them like a lighted stick of dynamite.

"Connie," Hunter said, regaining his focus, "any idea on the cause of death?"

"No," Connie said and continued taking photos. "Wait for the pathologist to get here."

Hunter studied the boy's face as Connie took another photo. The camera flash illuminated the boy's face — an iridescent shimmer of shifting colors danced on dead skin — What was the killer saying? An act of regret, adding light to death? Justifying a criminal act by beautifying the corpse?

"Connie, why is his face shining?"

Connie snapped more photos. "It's because he's wearing makeup. It's called highlighter."

"Makeup?" Vierra murmured. "This takes it up several notches on the weird scale. What's next?"

Hunter studied the blanket wrapped around the body. Thick embroidery thread spelled out words and sentences. He caught an odor. Not decay, but a perfume or spice. The aroma brought up a memory of arguing with Abby and the incense she used to burn. He'd shoved all those memories away, but then it clicked. "It's a Savvy Seeker quilt."

"Savvy Seekers?" Vierra balked. "The self-help asshole—what's his name?"

"Christophe," Hunter said. "Hey, Connie? There's some perfume in the fabric. Could you analyze it, please?"

"Will do, but I'm guessing it's Nag Champa," she said.

"Nag whatta?" Vierra asked, leaning in and squinting to read the embroidery.

"Temple incense, hot stuff," Connie replied.

"Can you read this? Does each quilt have the same writing?" Vierra asked.

Hunter searched his memory. "They're supposed to be … what did she call them? Affirmations. Stuff like, 'I am choosing happiness—Affluence is pouring into my life.'"

"No way?" Vierra balked at smelling something rotten.

"Abby went on and on about it when she started Christophe's meditations."

Vierra shuddered. "God, even his name sounds so pretentious. What's his real name?"

"Christopher Muldooney," said a soft male voice from behind them. "You know, of the Muldooney crime family."

Hunter recognized the voice of Assistant District Attorney Alistair Dunham walking down the path toward them. He dressed more like a yuppy than a prosecutor, with his shaggy, dirty-blond hair and horn-rimmed glasses. In contrast, the bespoke worsted wool suit, the glossy Italian loafers, and the chunky high-tech wristwatch screamed "lawyer."

Hunter felt Vierra bristle at the mention of the Muldooneys.

"I hate pretentious bullshit artists. What got you out so early, Mr. DA?" Vierra asked.

"And a good morning to you too, Investigator Vierra," Dunham said. "Believe me, I'm not here for the company. An office secretary woke me up and told me to get down here. Hunter, are you familiar with Savvy Seekers products?"

Hunter opened his mouth.

"Who isn't?" Vierra cut in. "The bastard advertises on the Muni buses, on billboards selling crap to vulnerable people who don't know any better. Plus, who knows what goes on in his *wellness* centers."

"You don't appreciate it?" Dunham asked, pausing for Vierra's reaction.

"No, for the record, I don't approve of exploiting people's weaknesses."

"All high priced, too." Hunter hoped to keep things from escalating by focusing on the facts. "This quilt sells for over seventeen hundred a pop. If you're willing to fork over two grand, they'll sew on affirmations that you pick yourself."

"How do you know that?" Dunham asked.

"I got into a huge argument with Abby when she bought one."

"Did you guys see this?" Connie waved them over. Using tweezers, she plucked a piece of paper tucked into the victim's lap and held it up — the size of a postcard — a thick mixture of paper and linen with deckled edges. A series of strange symbols were written on the card.

♂ 1° ♑

☿ 13° ♎

☽ 23° ♊

"These are astrology glyphs," Dunham answered. "That one might be Mercury in thirteen degrees of something else."

"First, we have makeup, and now astrology?" Vierra shot Hunter a look. Astrology. Signature. San Francisco's haunted past with the Zodiac Killer, who left a trail of bodies and taunted the police with unsolvable ciphers.

Hunter turned back to the Assistant DA. "Dunham, can you decipher this stuff?"

"I only know the basics, but there's an astrologer in the neighborhood, over on Polk Street."

Vierra smiled. "You're telling me you have a personal astrologer?"

"No, I'm saying I have a friend who's an astrologer, and she can decipher those glyphs for you. I'll text you the address," he pulled out his phone.

"She?" Vierra asked.

"We used to be neighbors," Dunham said to Hunter, ignoring Vierra and pulling out his phone. "And here's something else to consider. There's a total solar eclipse coming up in a few weeks."

"Shit. That's just perfect. Astrology and eclipses." Laughing, Vierra threw his arms out as if to say, "What else?"

Hunter captured images of both sides of the card before shifting his attention back to the victim. While observing the radiant countenance of the deceased boy, enveloped in a quilt like a contemporary monk, he sensed an unknown power at play, its presence palpable yet elusive. Were these planetary alignments causing these phenomena? Hunter squeezed his eyes tight, feeling a dull ache forming behind his temples, then turned to his partner, who was still talking to him. "…I'll call the Media Relations office. We'll go full lockdown on this." Vierra pulled out his phone and started texting. "I'll talk to all the canvas guys. No social media either. No secret photos of the body. Nothing."

"Got it." Hunter opened his map application and entered the name Alistair sent: Sirius Books, only a few blocks away. He took a few more photos of the scene for reference when writing his report. Scanning through them, he understood Wong's description: it imitated something you'd see in a luxury magazine—hell, it could have come from any of those Savvy Seekers catalogs his ex-wife had always left around the house.

At the foot of the steps leading back up to his car, Hunter turned again to assess the scene from where he first arrived. He paused, struck by the killer's ghoulish nature. This wasn't a magazine. This was a child cherished by his parents, full of potential. Then, some sicko kills him and arranges his body like a goddamn mannequin. The killer had to know it would be cops who'd see his handiwork up close. Was he toying with them?

☾3☽

Sirius Books — 10:54 a.m.

Freed from the claustrophobic airlock of Cora's TV studio, Madeline caught a Lyft, which dropped her at the alley leading to the back door of Sirius Books on Polk Street. Entering through the back door, she breathed in the familiar aroma—old leather, musty pages, years of burned incense embedded in the walls, and a whiff of ground coffee from the shop next door—the magic worked, and Madeline felt centered again.

Typical for this part of San Francisco, the store is one long, cramped rectangle split between the sales area, a workspace, and her office. The building dates back to the 1800s, and the original store layout stretched from the alley all the way to the entrance on Polk Street. Aunt Jane designed a workspace off the back door lined with bookshelves, a long worktable now covered with merchandise boxes, and a beaded curtain separating it from the public sales area. Her private office was off to the right, her personal sanctuary where she met with clients and cooked the books.

Madeline took off her coat and hung it on the coat tree outside of her office. She joined her product manager, Matthew-Tabitha, in opening up one of the latest shipments. Bisexual and with a penchant for cross-dressing, he'd shaved the ends of his eyebrows, and today, he sported bright, cherry-red lip gloss. The magenta blazer over a purple shirt and jeans told her he was in "boy" mode. Seeing him, she sighed, and the tension left her body. He'd worked in the store since Aunt Jane's time. Broad-shouldered, long black hair pulled into a tight braid, often mistaken for being a native American. The blending of his Japanese mother and Latino father created this handsome imp.

"How was the adventure in TV land? I caught the interview on my phone. Put that Professor in his place." He said, with a finger snap.

Madeline made a gesture of polishing her nails along her shirt and looking at them in admiration. "It comes naturally." They laughed as Geena, her young goth shop girl, poked her head and half her body between the beaded curtains.

"Um, Madeline? There's some guy who wants to talk to you." Geena's voice was a mix of worried excitement, all laced with vocal fry. At nineteen, Geena's effort to appear older by meeting the current Goth standard: black turtleneck over black pants hiding her anorectic frame, long hair dyed black in matching Wednesday Addams ponytails, and smudged black eyeliner. The teenager's pout and slumped shoulders proving her tough wardrobe couldn't hide her vulnerability.

Madeline nodded to Matthew-Tabitha. "Maybe, he's here for you?"

"Sorry doll, my dance card's full," he said with a wink and returned to unpacking a new shipment of astrology books on lunar and solar eclipses just in time for the solar eclipse in two weeks.

"Thanks, Geena. Tell him I'll be there in a minute, please."

Geena paused, studying the storeroom. Its shelves and surfaces overflowed with books, posters, stacks of tarot cards, tapestries of Indian Chakra mandalas, baskets filled with beads and crystals, dream catchers in all colors, blank journals, CDs of Native American drumming along with Senegalese chanting. Madeline remembered that gaze, how she'd marveled at the ancient knowledge and tools for personal transformation compiled in one place, a candy store of spiritual delights and potential.

Madeline smiled at Geena, and the girl went back into the store. What had she done with her own potential? Madeline wondered. When did these tools for incantations and magic devolve into inventory projections and SKU numbers? How long had sales figures kept her trapped back here? Every month was a crapshoot, hoping to sell enough books and trinkets to pay the rent. Then she sent up a silent "thank you" to Aunt Jane, who let Madeline live in the apartment over the store, just one flight away. A safe aviary that met all of her needs. So why was she doubting it? She chalked it up to transiting Saturn, conjunct her natal Neptune, the god of time, confronting the god of dreams.

Feeling that unwelcome heaviness again, Madeline untied her wavy brown hair and let it hang loose. Something still nagged at her, something at the edges, an unfamiliar sensation. She blamed it on the incoherent energy from the television studio suffering from the massive EMF bombardment. Madeline stopped at the ornate mirror on the wall and admitted to liking the makeup from being on TV, and she wished she'd remembered the real name of the lipstick so she could order some. She slipped through the beaded curtains and out into the sales area. At the register, Geena nodded toward a man at the door surveying the shop.

Madeline guessed his ethnicity to include something Mediterranean: dark, cropped hair with a hint of curls at the edges and pink undertones in his skin. About medium height, he wore his sales rack suit well. His worn black leather shoes were sturdy, and the tassels were clean. His posture and bearing proved him to be a regular gym rat.

Admittedly, it was a fleeting impression, yet this man possessed a profound depth that extended well beyond the surface. He wasn't a potential vendor scoping the store and checking the square footage. How he studied reminded her of Geena's gaze at all the goodies, but his interpretation was confusion mixed with apprehension. Madeline watched him squint his eyes to read a book title and then draw back, bewildered. She guessed it was his first foray into a metaphysical bookstore. His eyes followed the length of the towering bookcase, and then he fixed his gaze on the intricately patterned ceiling.

Aunt Jane had the brilliant idea and commissioned an artist who skillfully painted a mural that depicted a hole in the roof, exposing stars in the night sky — a vast swatch of the Milky Way meteors showering down around a glowing crescent moon. Among the stars, the artist emphasized astrological constellations. The man stared at the mural with his head tilted to one side.

"Admiring our trompe l'oeil?" Madeline asked, keeping her voice light, overpronouncing the impossible French phrase.

As the man turned, Madeline locked eyes with the man. Weariness filled his deep-set gaze as if he'd witnessed ugliness too often. She'd seen this battle-fatigue in military veterans and aging hippies. Still, he didn't look away, and she knew that from a cursory glance, he gleaned more information than most would after a thorough examination. Taking in a quick breath, she juggled several sensations: dread, curiosity, and perhaps a touch of delight? Sweeping the chaos aside, a truth emerged from those eyes: she intrigued him, too.

"Excuse me?" he said.

Madeline stepped forward and pointed to the ceiling. "Our optical illusion. My aunt commissioned it to make the shop seem bigger."

He examined it again and nodded in approval. "Well, it does the trick. Which constellations are those? The one that looks like a box with a neck on it?"

Madeline smiled. "That's Leo."

"And the spidery web one?"

"Virgo. My aunt is the Virgo, and my Uncle Milo is the Leo. I'm Madeline," she said, offering him her hand.

"Investigator Hunter Davis." He carried a leather portfolio and switched it from one hand to the other to shake hers.

As their palms met, Madeline experienced an inner alarm bell reverberate. "Is anything wrong, Investigator Davis?"

"No, ma'am. I just—" he dropped his hand from hers.

"Please, call me Madeline."

"Madeline. Okay, I need some information. Do you have a private space where we could talk?"

Her pulse shifted, erratic. She took it as a natural reaction when confronted by a police officer and breathed in to calm herself. "We can go to my office. Follow me."

Madeline led him through the beaded curtains, his aftershave suspended in the air. Something musky with citrus notes? Lemon or Verbena? It wasn't your typical overpowering "bro" cologne. Madeline brought him through the work area, and Matthew-Tabitha whistled.

"Investigator Davis, this is my product manager, Matthew-Tabitha." She watched her friend sizing up the investigator, a smile curling on his lips. He offered his hand to shake. "Top of the morning, officer." Matthew's voice dripped with innuendo.

Madeline knew most straight men balked at the idea of a human living outside the gender binary, but Davis reached out and shook Matthew-Tabitha's hand. "It's a pleasure," the investigator said.

Madeline shot fake daggers at Matthew-Tabitha. "Just ignore him, Investigator Davis. My office is right through here." Pulling her keys from her back pocket, she unlocked the office door and entered first, hoping to tidy the space. Random files and shipping boxes lay on the floor and on the sofa. "Come on in."

She grabbed a stack of files off an armchair, plopped them in the corner, and tossed her keys on the desk. "I apologize for the mess." The investigator stood at the door, unfazed by the clutter, taking in the high ceilings, the ancient crystal chandelier that filled the cramped space with light, and, of course, the floor-to-ceiling bookshelves on every wall.

She watched him breathe in the room and glimpsed again how he operated, looking at everything with a tilt of the head, squinting, sussing out a story, piecing together a story from the surroundings. Madeline sensed his scrutiny but waved it off as an occupational hazard. At least she felt a surge of confidence from the clothes and makeup she'd worn for the television interview.

"More books?" he asked.

Madeline smiled. "Always. A bookstore can never have enough books. Please have a seat." She offered him the comfy chair and she sat across from him at her desk.

"This is cozy," he said, settling into the chair. "Not what I expected."

"Of a bookstore owner?"

"Of an astrologer," he said with a shrug.

"You were expecting fiery torches followed by a walk down a dust-filled tunnel to a dungeon, perhaps?"

"Something like that," he said, and his face brightened.

Madeline let out a small laugh, refreshed at his open attitude. "Astrologers have embraced the modern age. We even have sophisticated software to generate charts these days. But that's not why you're here, is it?"

He heaved a sigh. "You're right. I have some questions relating to a case, but before we start, I have to ask that you keep this information confidential."

"That's no problem. I keep all my client information confidential."

"Clients?"

"I do astrological readings using birth chart information. People find it helpful when they are under stress."

"Is it something like talk therapy or seeing a shrink?"

Madeline shrugged a meh reaction. "I don't have a license to practice medicine. Let's say it isn't therapy, but most clients find it therapeutic."

Investigator Davis opened his notebook. "How does that work?"

Madeline got that he'd switched to cop mode. She gathered her thoughts, hoping to sound clear but not lecturing. "I take their birth information, which is the day, month, year, and time they were born, along with their place of birth. Using this information, I create what's called a natal chart, analyze what I see, and ask them about specific challenges in their lives to see what insight the chart provides."

He tilted his head. "What sorts of insights?"

"I could give you my Astrology 101 overview, but something tells me you are looking for help with something specific?"

He brought out his cell phone and tapped the screen a few times. "These symbols are part of my investigation. Can you explain them? One of them is a crescent moon, and the other is the sign for a male, but I don't understand what the numbers mean."

Madeline studied the photograph, grabbed a pen, and jotted the three planets in three signs on a piece of note paper on her desk. It wasn't much to work with. "So, this symbol, the circle and the arrow, the symbol for man?"

"Yes?"

"In astrology, it's the symbol for the planet Mars, and the number is one degree in Capricorn. The second line is Mercury thirteen degrees in Libra, and the final set is the moon in twenty-three degrees Gemini."

Davis leaned in. "What's your interpretation?"

Madeline hesitated, worried that she would disappoint him. "I can't give you one. I don't have enough information to draw any conclusions."

Davis drew back. "What else do you need?"

Madeline sensed his frustration. "Let's go over some basics. Let me show you what most people think is an astrology chart." She turned to her computer, searched for a file, and sent it to the printer. She pulled the paper from the printer on the credenza behind her desk.

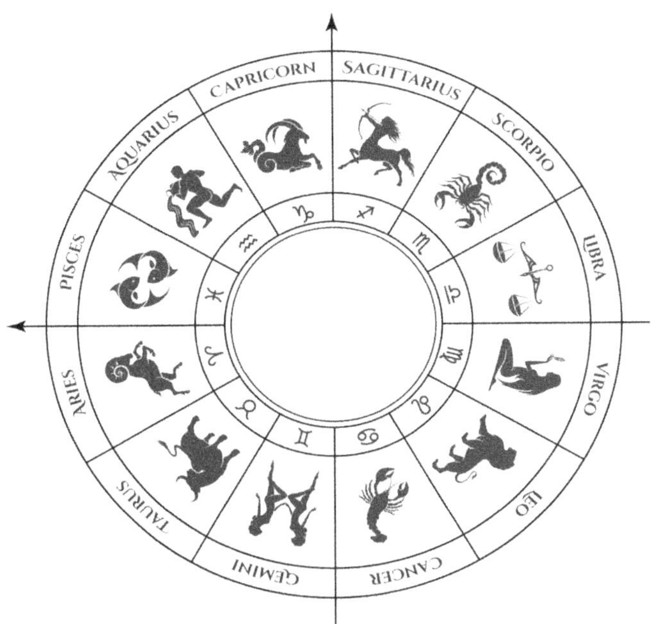

"Okay, I've seen this before, in a newspaper?"

"Yes. Let me walk you through it. It's the classic version. It's a 360-degree circle divided into twelve houses with thirty degrees each. We start with Aries on the left corner, where the sun rises in the east. This chart, in theory, is set on the Spring Equinox, with Aries at one degree. Each sign has a symbol, called a glyph, and each house is numbered and covers a specific area of a person's life such as health, career, and love life."

"Yes, but today isn't the Spring Equinox, is it?"

"Correct, grasshopper." Madeline laid the paper flat on her desk. "As time passes and the Sun and planets all move, to mark that in a chart, the sign on the left will move." She spun the paper, like turning a dial to show Leo on the left side. "It's now August, so Leo is on the left side of the chart. We call it the Ascendant or Rising sign. With me so far?"

"Oh, sure," he replied, shaking his head.

She smiled at his clever sarcasm and continued. "To create an accurate chart, I need the time, which sets the rising sign, and we need the exact location. We need to know if the chart is set in San Francisco, or Barcelona or Hong Kong, because that also influences where the planets in the sky are in relation to the earth."

Hunter blinked his eyes. "I hate to say it, but it sounds like gibberish. Can you create a chart like this from those symbols I gave you?"

"Unfortunately, I can't. I would need the exact location and time where the event took place. Without, I can't set the Ascendant."

He gave her a blank stare.

Madeline had to give him credit for getting this far. She swung her chair to face her computer. "Let me print out a chart for this morning so you can see what an event chart looks like."

"Good idea."

As she tapped the keys, filling in today's time and their location, the unreality of her situation gnawed at her. Why was this investigator, who didn't believe in anything she was telling him, so curious about what an astrology chart looked like? She pondered the three sets of planets in signs he brought to her. Something deep in her unconscious tugged at her. They had an uncanny familiarity, but that these three planets could affect her was ridiculous, given that she had crafted countless charts in her career.

She grabbed the chart off of the printer and turned it so he could see it. As expected, his eyes turned to saucers, and he shook his head. "I realize it's a lot, but there are nine planets in the sky. See all this geometry in the middle?"

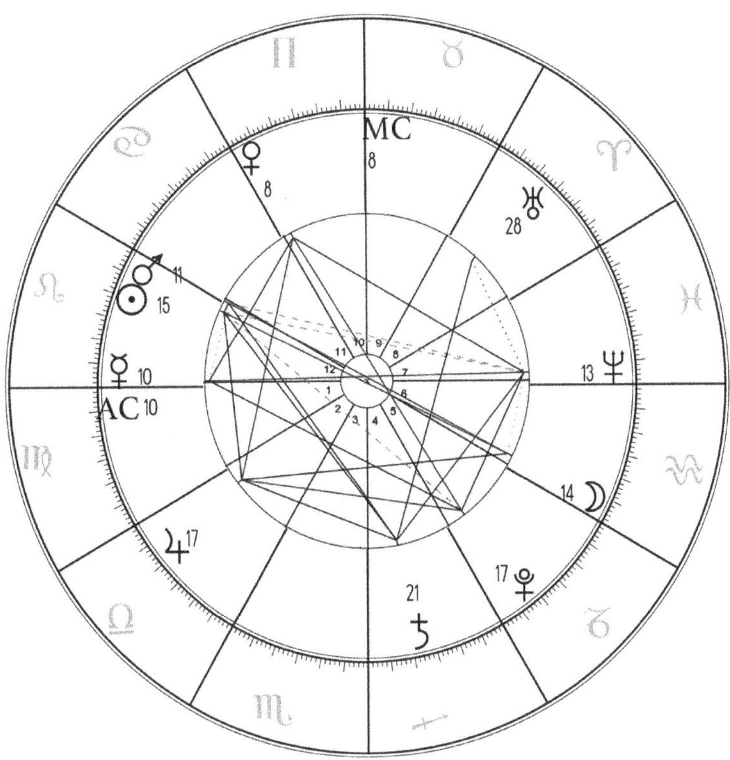

"Yes, it's like a drunk went crazy with a Spirograph."

Madeline chuckled, "Yes, all that geometry maps the relationships between all nine planets." She opened up her drawer and took out a blank chart. "Now, I'll plot the information you gave me."

Madeline drew in the sets of symbols on the blank chart. "This is what you gave me. We have Mars at one degree Capricorn, up here in the tenth house. The moon is twenty-three degrees Gemini in the third house, with Mercury thirteen degrees Libra in the seventh house." She set this chart next to the other one on the desk for him to study.

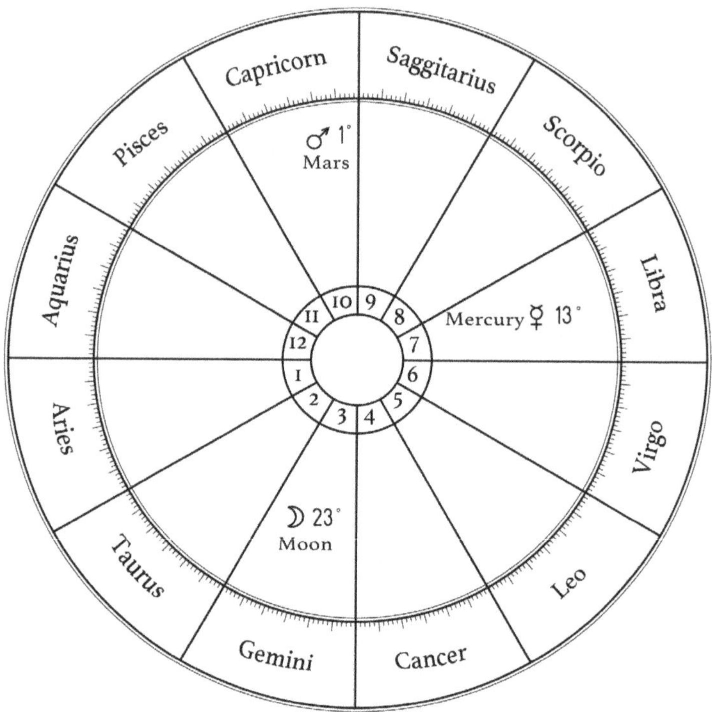

"Where did all of the drunken Spirograph marks go?"

"You can't make any, we don't have the other six planets and without setting the Ascendant we have no idea if we have them in the correct house. I can't give you an accurate interpretation."

The investigator took the chart. "Yes, so you can't identify a person from this?"

"I can't even tell you if this is a chart for a human. It could be an event. You can make charts for anything."

He sighed at her. "Even with your explanation, it's still confusing."

Madeline laid the paper on her desk. "Sorry. I tried. People study astrology for years before feeling comfortable practicing the art."

"Can we agree whoever placed this information at my crime scene is familiar with astrology?"

"O, absolutely," Madeline felt a shiver of goose flesh on her arm.

Davis touched his chin, and she sensed a similar buzz run through him. "This person plotted all of this, hasn't he? He knows the correct time and the Ascendant, right?"

Madeline understood the shudder. "That's an educated guess. Your guy has given you only three planets in signs. There are nine planets in twelve houses, so he's given you enough information to get you guessing. He's teasing you."

A loud knock at the door made them both jump. Matthew-Tabitha opened the door. "Hey, sorry to interrupt, but the grocery delivery guy is here. Want me to take it up to your place?"

Madeline grabbed her keys and tossed them to Matthew-Tabitha. "Wonderful. Thank you."

Matthew-Tabitha caught the keys but lingered a moment. Madeline knew he would tease her mercilessly later on. "Really, thanks again."

Matthew got the message. "Okay, bye," he said in a high-pitched voice and disappeared.

"Grocery deliveries?" Investigator Davis asked.

"Yeah," Madeline explained. "My apartment is just upstairs, so I often get them delivered. Saves time."

Davis nodded and returned his gaze to the chart.

Madeline felt for him, remembering how stupid and overwhelmed she was the first time she saw an astrology chart. Madeline took a chance. "Can you give me some context? What kind of crime are we talking about?"

He paused, studying her, taking an inventory of her entire persona. He heaved a long, fatigued sigh. "When I mentioned confidentiality, I really need you to promise me you won't talk about this to anyone. I mean anyone."

"Of course," she replied, hoping to sound calm and sincere.

"We found these symbols at a murder scene."

A jolt of energy ran up her spine. "A killer left you this?"

His shoulders slumped. "Yeah, and I'm sure you're familiar with San Francisco's Zodiac Killer?"

"Don't judge, but I carry at least a dozen books about it. They're best sellers."

"Right, so you understand we can't leak this to the press?"

"Of course not. But—" She hesitated. He wouldn't believe her in a million years, but she wanted to help.

"But what?"

"There are other types of charts, I could cast one for the time of death?"

Madeline looked over at her volumes of astrology lore, wondering what else to ask, and then took another shot. "How about when you received the 911 call? Technically, that marks the beginning of the case."

Investigator Davis paused, pursed his lips, and flipped open his portfolio. "What will that tell you?"

"I can compare that chart to the signs and symbols that your killer left. It might be helpful."

"You really think the time of the call has anything to do with it?"

Madeline considered his question. She didn't want to send him off in the wrong direction, but she had a hunch. "Yes, time is everything in astrology. I'm wondering if the killer made the 911 call. He wanted to make sure the investigation started at an exact time." She watched him scribble that into his portfolio.

"Hey, I have one more thing I can offer you. Hand me the chart back."

He handed it over while she pulled out a dog-eared astrology book on a nearby shelf. "Each of the signs, Capricorn, Gemini, and Libra, are further divided into decans, and there's a Tarot card assigned to each of them."

"Oh, now we're really getting into the mystical stuff. Not sure how that's going to play back at the office."

Madeline winked. "Oh, but you've come so far. You're just a blood oath away from joining the coven." He leaned back in mock horror, eyes widened, but he smiled. "So, what do the cards tell us, insightful swami?"

Madeline flipped through her text and brought a deck of Tarot cards from her desk drawer. "Hmmm. Interesting. Here we go." First, she wrote them on his chart and then pulled out the corresponding card. "Capricorn gives us the devil card; Capricorn is half goat, half fish." She pulled it from the deck and tossed it on the desk. "Libra, the scales. We get the Justice card," she placed that card. "For Gemini, we get the lovers." She placed the card next to the others and waited for his reaction.

"So, I'm looking for a justice-seeking devil worshiper who loves women?"

"Nicely done. I may have to hire you to come and give readings someday."

The investigator lifted his hands up, begging off. "No, I don't think so. May I take a picture of these?"

"Of course."

He pulled out his cell phone and took photos of the cards. "Speaking of readings, are you familiar with Assistant DA Dunham? Does he shop here, by any chance?"

"Yes, I know, Alistair. We used to be neighbors," she said. "Is he working this case with you?"

"Yes, he recommended I come see you." He shook his head and glanced up at her. "I can't believe I'm doing this, but hopefully, the spirits will approve." He pulled out a business card and scribbled on the back of it. "We received the 911 call at 6:17 am at Ina Coolbrith Park." He handed her the card.

Madeline took it and set it next to her computer. "Thank you. I'll see what comes up."

He stood up. "Thank you, ma'am—I mean, thank you, Madeline. May I take these?" He asked, holding up the charts.

"Yes, of course," she said and stood, feeling a pang of disappointment that she didn't give him much help with the symbols from his crime scene. Yet, she was intrigued at the opportunity to do the 911 chart.

Investigator Davis placed the charts in his portfolio, and he held her gaze once more. "You've been very patient and generous with your time," the investigator said, his tone filled with genuine gratitude as they walked to the door. Davis stopped in the workspace and studied her stock shelves. Was there something there that caught his attention? If it died, he said nothing. Then he turned to her. "I'm sorry I've taken so much of your time. When you've created that 911 chart, call me?""I will." She walked with him, and he grabbed the beaded curtains and held them for her. When they reached the front door, he said, "When I see Alistair, I'll mention I met you."

"Please do. Give him my best regards." She waited as he stepped out of the door onto the crowded sidewalk. Standing at the door, she couldn't help but fixate on him. A mysterious force seemed to demand her attention. Sensing her presence, he turned, saw her through the glass, smiled warmly, and waved. He walked down Polk Street, carrying the weight of the investigation like a cloak.

(4)

Buy terms divine in selling hours of dross;
Within be fed, without be rich no more:
So shalt thou feed on Death, that feeds on men,
And death once dead, there's no more dying then.
— W Shakespeare, Sonnet CXLVI

Bernal Heights House – August 23, 2001
18 days before The Ceremony 6:05 p.m.

Cocooned on the sofa in the little den, Madeline wrapped the quilt she was embroidering around her waist and set her notebook on the sofa arm. Needing time to finish the project in secret, she'd chosen the den as it was reserved as a private contemplation space away from the rest of the house. She'd lived in the group house for six months and still marveled at her luck. Nine people lived in a rundown old ranch house in Bernal Heights, where they grew their own food, cooked their own meals, and shared the same values. Christophe, their teacher, built a spiritual community by studying ancient wisdom, meditation, and expanding consciousness. Her favorite subject was astrology, and Christophe had a collection of texts that rivaled what Aunt Jane had stocked in her bookstore. Members of the household practiced by creating and interpreting charts for each other.

Madeline found contentment and solace in this simple life. To show her appreciation for Christophe, she made a quilt from various fabric scraps and planned to embroider a series of Christophe's favorite quotes all over it. She flipped through her notebook filled with quotes and notes from Christophe's lectures, looking for another quote. Madeline found one she liked: "I love you as certain dark things are to be loved, in secret, between the shadow and the soul." She outlined the words in chalk on the quilt, picked a bright violet thread, and stitched the outline for the letter "I" when, out of nowhere, an intense cramp raged through her abdomen.

She wrapped more fabric around her torso and legs, hoping the warmth would ease the pain. She remembered to breathe into her abdomen and let the pain pass. It was only August, and she planned to finish the quilt by Christmas. After the pain eased, she went back to her stitching.

Someone peeked in the door. Madeline's roommate, Victoria, smiled at her. "What's up, my darling chickadee?"

"Working on the totally secret quilt project everyone knows about, but I'm totally cramping."

Victoria, with a book in hand, plopped down next to her on the lumpy sofa. "Ung. I can relate, roomy. My period just started."

Victoria's body heat soothed Madeline's discomfort as her friend settled in while Madeline reviewed her roommate's astrology sign in her head. Being a Libra and an Air sign reflected in Victoria's fast-moving mind, which embraced Christophe's teaching of the esoteric works they studied. She was also thoughtful and always kind. Madeline's Taurus nature harmonized well with Victoria's, as their signs were both ruled by Venus, the planet of beauty. Sharing the same room, they decorated it with tapestries, soft pillows, inspirational quotes, and fairy lights. Waves of gratitude flooded Madeline's heart, and she reached over and kissed Victoria on the forehead. "Thanks, roomie." She smelled Victoria's perfume, a mix of Freesia and Vanilla that she admired so much.

Victoria kissed her back. "Speaking of roomies, or rather Rumi, the poet,"—she showed Madeline the book she brought— "I'm memorizing 'Desire and the Importance of Failure' for this Sunday's meeting."

"The entire poem?"

"Yeah ... I'm too ambitious?"

Madeline considered her quilt. "Nothing wrong with a little ambition," she said. She grabbed Victoria's book and studied the poem. "Okay, what line comes after, 'A clapping sound does not come from one hand?'"

Victoria closed her eyes. "A thirsty man calls out, 'Delicious water, where are you?'"

"While the water moans, 'Where is the water drinker?'" Lili's lilting voice caught Madeline by surprise as Lili swooped through the room, dancing and waving her arms in the air as if conjuring a spirit. A petite blonde, her hair in a perpetual ponytail, it bounced around her head, she continued: "The thirst in our souls is the attraction put out by the water itself!"

Madeline and Victoria gave Lili a polite golf clap as she curtsied. Lili was their resident Pisces, a mutable water sign who adapted to Madeline's earthy ways and Victoria's intellect. The three of them bonded within moments.

"Are we hosting a Rumi love festival?" Lili asked, eyebrows raised.

"We were being all spiritual, but we've both got cramps," Victoria blurted. "I'm renaming this the Cramping Couch."

Madeline laughed and patted the seat to her right, and Lili squeezed her tiny frame onto the sofa, creating coziness squared.

Lili nuzzled up to Madeline. "My Aunt Flow is due to arrive any day now," Lili said, leaning on Madeline's shoulder, "so I qualify."

Madeline asked Lili, "Did you memorize the entire Rumi poem?"

"No, just my favorite parts."

"Victoria's memorizing all of it before Sunday."

"Good luck, honey," Lili said with a slight note of sarcasm in her voice as she patted Victoria's arm.

Victoria changed the subject. "This cramping couch idea reminds me of the book, The Red Tent, how in biblical times, all the women's cycles synchronized, so they would hang out in a designated red tent."

"No boys allowed?" asked Madeline.

Lili giggled, "I like that idea,"

"This is working for me," said Madeline, oscillating between her two housemates. "You two ladies are the best heating pads a girl could ask for." She snuggled her head into Victoria's shoulder.

"Let's post a sign," said Lili.

"Yeah," Victoria chimed, "it should read, *Cramping Couch, for periodic use only.*"

Victoria burst into laughter at her own joke, and Madeline joined her. Lili convulsed and put her hand to her mouth to keep from laughing out loud. Madeline's body got it from both sides as if being in a massage machine powered by two women laughing hysterically.

"OMG! What's all this commotion about?" Miranda bounced in, her dark eyes and caramel curls floating around her in waves. She wore short overalls emphasizing her perfect hourglass figure. Madeline still couldn't talk, still laughing so hard, but she waved to Miranda to take a seat. Miranda pulled up the bean-bag across from them. She was a Cancer—all water, all emotional and intuitive. Madeline adored her and welcomed her into their circle of laughter. Miranda smiled, waiting for the laughter to subside.

Katia entered the room, wiping her hands on a dishtowel, and stared down at them. "What the hell?"

Madeline sobered up fast as she still struggled with Katia's energy. An Aries, the hottest fire sign in the zodiac, wore her long black hair pulled back in a bun, with various strands falling about her shoulders as if a stylist had placed every hair in place, strand by strand. From a powerful Russian family, Katia pivoted between regal elegance and noblesse oblige. Katia sank into a nearby armchair and studied the couch trio.

Then Brenda entered — the other earth sign, a Capricorn, practical as always— brought in a chair from the living room and made a space for herself between Katia and Miranda. "What's the occasion, ladies?" Brenda was of medium height with curly brown hair, and she had a soft frame. She and Madeline bonded quickly, both being hardworking and resourceful.

Lili spoke. "I'm sorry, Miranda. Hi Katia and Brenda. We're all on our periods. Victoria just dubbed this the cramping couch."

"So, no boys allowed while we each battle with Auntie Flow," Victoria added as she settled down from her laughing fit.

Katia, annoyed, crossed her arms and legs but managed a smile. Madeline sensed she wanted to join the fun, but something held her back.

"Yes, no boys allowed," Lili continued, "and we sit here and recite beautiful love poems to our lady parts."

Miranda laughed in agreement, and her laughter shook the beanbag, making it squeak. She planted her feet on the floor and spread her legs apart, bowed her head, and spoke to her lady parts: "Two loves I have of comfort and despair, which, like two spirits, do suggest me still; The better angel is a man right fair, the worser spirit a woman colored ill." She raised her head and laughed at her own antics.

Madeline loved it. Now, everyone laughed, including Katia.

"I'll take the man right fair, but give me a couple of weeks," Lili giggled.

Victoria added, "Can we also post a sign that reads: We are NOT a cult."

"What for?" Katia asked, her crossed leg swinging.

"When I'm bringing in the groceries, the hag across the street stares at me. You'd think I was carrying rotisserie babies from the scowl on her face."

Madeline understood Victoria's frustration; their choice of an "alternative life-style" freaked out the neighbors, with four men and four women living with their spiritual teacher. What other people thought about how they lived no longer bothered her. These women's physical warmth and emotional support soothed her in a way she'd never experienced before. "But with only nine of us. Don't you need at least a hundred followers to be considered a cult?"

"Didn't I read that in the cult handbook?" Brenda asked with mock credulity. You have to give up all your worldly possessions and take on spiritual names like Ariel Astrodienst and Messiah Bob.

Katia smiled. "Yes, it's the same handbook that says a real cult has a teacher from India with white robes, the works."

Madeline said, "We don't have enough people for an ashram. That makes us what? A Marsha?"

Another spasm of laughter erupted from the entire group in unison, Madeline included.

"Oh God," Brenda said through her giggles, "just like the Brady Bunch. Marsha, Marsha, Marsha!"

"That's it," Victoria squealed. "The new name for our periods! No more Aunty flow. From now on, I'm on my Marsha."

Victoria's joke sent everyone into spasms of uproarious laughter. Madeline couldn't breathe and brushed tears from her eyes. Christophe leaned in, observing them all, his posture tall and straight, with one arm draped across his chest and his hand resting under his chin. Madeline admired his trim, athletic build. He was a thoughtful Gemini with light brown hair and a distinctive cleft in the middle of his chin. Those eyes changed with the light—sometimes green, but mostly China blue. She folded the quilt to hide her embroidery and sank further into the sofa.

A thought, more like a sensation, flashed through Madeline's mind: would Christophe ever appreciate this type of female bonding?

Then he locked eyes with Madeline, sharing the moment with her, shot her a quick wink, and then he vanished. None of the other women noticed he'd even been watching them.

⟨5⟩

KXOP Newsroom — 10:13 a.m.

Sitting in the busy newsroom, Cora peeked at the Balenciaga website to catch a preview of the Spring/Summer collection. A return to massive shoulder-padded jackets did not inspire, so she returned to her assignment. She sifted through papers—piles and piles of newspaper clippings, transcripts of old interviews, magazine articles pulled from the library—as she tried to make a concise timeline of the Muldooney-Volkov battles. Amy, the assignment editor, asked her to compile it for their crime reporter covering Sean Muldooney's murder trial.

It began as an exercise in tedium, but as she followed the crimes, assassination plots, and criminal exploitations of both families, she found herself mesmerized by the saga. All around her, the newsroom buzzed: reporters working on stories, camera crews coming in and out with their equipment. She enjoyed the research project, but she felt underutilized and wanted to do more.

"Cora, come over here for a second?" Amy asked.

Cora grabbed a notepad and joined Amy at the assignment desk, a raised platform surrounded by monitors, files, walkie-talkies, dirty coffee cups, and more piles of newspapers and magazines.

Amy wore rimless granny glasses and her yellow curls in a sloppy bun on the top of her head. Cora tried not to judge her on her fashion choices, but Amy's salmon and beige striped GAP shirt over an Old Navy denim skirt did nothing for her figure, revealing all her bulges and bumps. Cora was desperate to take this woman shopping, to overhaul her wardrobe, and create a wardrobe of clothing that flattered her frame.

"Yes, Miss Ames," Cora said.

Amy handed her a list. "These are the names of some local crime bloggers. Check them out for more Muldooney dirt."

Cora scanned the list of seven different websites. "Okay, do any of them specialize in organized crime?"

"Ned over at Bayareamafiawatch does. Also, Jordan at SFCrimeblogger is well-connected. He's taking a break because his wife is pregnant. Go through and subscribe and send a personal message telling them I sent you."

Cora scribbled notes next to the two she mentioned. "Do you use these guys as sources?"

Amy returned her attention to her computer monitor when a new browser window opened on her screen. "Sometimes, because we don't have enough reporters to cover everything going on in the city or down the peninsula." Amy moused to a new screen. "Have you seen the SFPD Crime map?" Cora leaned over Amy's shoulder and examined Amy's screen; it featured a map of San Francisco with several icons scattered in different clusters.

"These icons all show a variety of crimes. The tiny fire symbol means arson, the letter b means burglary and a small s means a sex crime."

Cora marveled at the amount of information the station could access. "No, I've never seen this."

An alert popped up on her desktop, and Amy clicked on it. "Oh wow. Cops found a body on Taylor Street at Ina Coolbrith Park this morning." She clicked back to the crime map, which now showed an icon of the letter H. "The letter H stands for a homicide. That's rare."

Cora leaned in as Amy zoomed in on the H, in a neighborhood called Russian Hill. Amy hovered her cursor over the H when it disappeared from the screen.

"Hmm. That's weird. I've never seen that before." Amy said.

"What does it mean?" Cora asked.

"Well, you're here to learn," Amy said. "It wasn't a homicide, and it's being re-classified. Call the police press office and ask if it was death by natural causes or something else. Didn't you say you have an auntie who works there?"

Cora shrugged and used air quotes. "Yeah, my one legitimate source. Aunt Charlotte."

"Get moving, call up Auntie, and get the skinny on this," Amy smiled.

Cora rushed to her computer terminal and pulled up the SF crime map. "Wow. Okay, I'm on it!" She pulled out her phone and called the only person she knew in the city besides her sister, their aunt Charlotte, a secretary in the SFPD press office. "Hey, Miss Charlotte. It's Cora Merritt."

"Hello darlin', how are you?" Charlotte's voice lilted with warmth.

"I'm fine, thanks. Can you help me? I'm looking up something for my boss. She spotted a homicide listed on the crime map at Taylor Street, but then it disappeared. Do you know anything about that?"

"Hmm, let me put you on hold, baby."

"Okay." Cora heard the line click, and some innocuous music started playing. And playing and playing and playing…. While she waited, she went to Google Maps and bookmarked Ina Coolbrith Park. She did a quick Wiki search and discovered Coolbrith was a poet and a key figure in San Francisco's literary community. She copied and pasted everything into a new doc.

She almost hung up when Charlotte returned to the line. "Ms. Merritt?" Charlotte's voice was now formal and rigid.

"Yes. What's going on?"

"It was just a mistake."

Cora sensed Aunty was keeping something from her. "Okay, that's fair. Can you tell me if the police found a body but decided that it wasn't a homicide? Will they change the classification on the map?"

"I'm not at liberty to say more. I'm sorry."

Cora's internal alarms shot off. "Can you at least give me the names of the officers working the case?"

Charlotte heaved a long sigh. "No. Sorry, baby." She lowered her voice to a hush. "I'm not at liberty to discuss it."

Cora whispered back, "Even if I said pretty, please?"

After another hesitation, Charlotte spoke, her voice muffled as if she'd put a hand over the phone. "I wish I could help, but you could hunt." Charlotte's voice lifted, trying for a nonchalant effect. "You could hunt around. You could even spot a delightful view of the Vierras—I mean the Sierras. That might help. I have to go. Bye," Charlotte said and hung up.

Grabbing her pencil, Cora understood Charlotte spoke in code. Cora scribbled "Hunt," "Vierra," and "Sierra" on a piece of scrap paper. Charlotte's subterfuge intrigued her.

She opened several search engines and expanded her search to North Beach and downtown San Francisco. Pulling up the court document website, she entered her keywords from her notes. Several cases popped up, including the names of two investigators: Daniel Vierra and Hunter Davis.

What to do next? She returned to Amy's desk, guessing she'd want to give this to the police reporter." This is interesting. According to Aunt Charlotte, they took it off the map because someone made a mistake."

Amy's head popped up from behind her computer. "You're telling me the San Francisco Police Department is saying they made a mistake? That alone deserves a headline."

"What's going on?" Bob, the newsroom manager, and Cora's direct supervisor walked by and stopped.

Cora kept her voice even and told Bob and Amy what she'd uncovered. "I know it isn't in my job description, but since I discovered the names of the investigators on the case, will you let me dig a little deeper? Find out what's going on?"

Amy exchanged a glance with Bob. "What do you think, Bob? If she finds anything, does she pass it on to Ned? He needs an extra hand."

Bob nodded. "Okay, but—and I hate to sound like your dad—have you done your other homework? Have you pushed out today's stories to our social media links?"

"Yes! I have Facebooked, Twittered, and Instagrammed everything on today's rundown and linked them to the wires."

Bob nodded again. "Okay, Nancy Drew, let's go old school and pound some pavement. Get to the Hall of Justice and see what you can find out."

Cora reached out and shook Bob's hand. "Thank you, Sir! I'll do my best."

She walked back to her computer, her mind spinning. What was this sense of … elation coming from? Why can't I breathe? What are the police hiding? What in God's name have I eaten today?

Well, Balenciaga would have to wait.

❨6❩

Hall of Justice — 11:24 a.m.

Pulling back the wooden door leading to the homicide detail, Hunter took a deep breath and held it. Coming to the office was always a crapshoot—literally. He'd shown up on days when the first thing you smelled was untreated waste. The Hall of Justice was so outdated that raw sewage seeped through the walls of offices three floors below. Now, every time he walked in, he braced himself. He exhaled and took a whiff—scorched coffee and an overheated photocopier. Whew!

Seeing Vierra's empty desk, he walked down the hall and found his partner setting up the incident room. Like the rest of the office, exposed wires ran up to the walls and across the ceiling. The ancient building lacked the electrical wiring or the bandwidth for modern computers. Standing near the whiteboard on the far wall, Vierra wielded a black marker and listed the case details. Hunter pulled up a chair and slapped his portfolio on the table. They worked the crime scene all morning and faced the mountain of paperwork necessary to record their findings.

Vierra whipped his head around. "I called the Medical Examiner's office. They can't tell me when they'll do the autopsy."

"Did you ask them to put a rush on it?"

"They're backed up as usual. How did the astrology lady go?" Vierra turned back to the whiteboard.

Hunter opened his portfolio and pulled out the charts Madeline gave him. "Interesting. She said these symbols mean nothing by themselves." He held up the chart for Vierra to inspect.

"Seriously?"

Hunter nodded, looking for a magnet. "She says the killer didn't leave enough information to draw a complete chart," he explained, sticking the chart to the whiteboard. She volunteered to create a timeline for the 911 call and mentioned it could be helpful.

Vierra squinted at the chart and made a face. "And how does this help us?"

Hunter went back to his portfolio. "Her theory is the killer called it in. He wanted the body to be found at a precise time."

"That's scary. What kind of guy does all this?"

"Not your garden variety creep. I'll follow up with her later."

Vierra grabbed the pen from Hunter. "So, let's give this creep a name. How about Astroguy?" Vierra scribbled it in black on the board.

Hunter considered Vierra's suggestion. They always nicknamed the killer based on the evidence already collected. It helped them form a mental image of the criminal they were chasing. It also bolstered their focus and anger when they hit roadblocks in the case. "Works for me."

Vierra wrote "Astroguy" on the whiteboard. "So, was she hot?"

Hunter couldn't hide the blush crossing his face, so he tried sounding casual. "I don't know." He found another magnet and pinned the standard astrology chart Madeline made for him to their whiteboard. He felt Vierra smiling behind him.

"Come on, don't dodge the question. She was, right?"

Knowing Vierra would hound him the rest of the day if he didn't come up with an answer, Hunter admitted it. "Okay, she wasn't hot, hot—not like model hot. She's got long brown hair and wears it loose. More like old Hollywood hot."

"Who wears her long brown hair loose like old Hollywood hot?"

Hunter turned. Their boss, Lt. Leo, ambled in. Five-foot-five, but built like a stevedore with lean, tight muscles to go with sharp eyes and a defiant attitude.

Vierra answered. "An astrologer. She owns a bookstore on Polk."

"Oh, we're relying on the stars to solve our cases now?" Leo joined them at the table and studied the photos of the crime scene. "I invited Dunham to join us."

Vierra scoffed. "Yeah, showed up at the scene. So, I'm giving our perp the nickname Astroguy until we get more details."

Hunter sat at a workstation and logged into a computer. "Hey, boss, any news on when we can move out of this shithole?" Hunter asked Leo the same question every day.

"Yeah, the day I retire, and you take over my shitty job," Leo shot back. "So, what's the story with this kid? I've already received five texts about keeping it all under wraps."

Vierra turned to the board. "So far, we have a male Caucasian victim, young, in his teens, found in a park on Russian Hill."

Leo nodded. "Okay, and what distinguishes him?"

Vierra pointed to a closeup of the victim. "We found him sitting in a meditation position, all clean and sparkly, wrapped in a blanket covered with new-age hippy-dippy quotes. Along with a set of symbols—astrology symbols."

Alistair Dunham walked in, and Hunter noted the chill coming off Vierra as he grabbed a marker and started drawing the list of astrology symbols from the card at the crime scene on the whiteboard.

"Mr. District Attorney," Leo bellowed, waving him in, "thanks for coming down."

Leo stepped to the board, lifting his reading glasses to examine the photos. "Oh, shit."

"Yep, we stepped in it this morning." Hunter and Vierra filled Lieutenant Leo and Alistair in on the case details, including the Savvy Seeker angle about the quilt.

Leo stepped back from the board. "Hunter, what did you get on these astrology symbols?"

"Yeah, Alistair recommended I speak with Madeline Merritt. She owns Sirius Book Store. She said the symbols left at the scene are inconclusive, but she offered to make a chart for when we got the 911 call?"

"Makes sense," Alistair said while pressing down on his tie. "In my limited knowledge of astrology, you need exact times, and the 911 call marks the beginning of Astroguy's case."

Dunham turned to Leo. "This is not a good case to catch you being so close to retirement."

"What do I care?" Leo shrugged. "Hunter, where are we on an ID?"

Hunter sat at the computer and checked for updates. "I called missing persons, but teenagers are trouble because parents don't call them in as soon as they ought to."

Vierra held out his phone. "Hey, I got a text from the guy canvassing the neighborhood. Someone witnessed a white panel van on Vallejo at around five this morning."

"A commercial one?" Dunham asked. "Any signage on it?"

Vierra studied the text. "They said a white truck that looked like a delivery van. That's all." He scribbled the words "white panel van" on the whiteboard.

Hunter paused, thinking about the geography involved. "Wait, so if the killer parked a van on Vallejo, he'd have to hump the body all the way up those stairs to the second pathway? Wouldn't it make more sense to go the way we did? From Taylor Street?"

"Guess our Astroguy works out," Vierra added.

"Well, you'll ask him when you haul his ass in here." Leo studied the whiteboard. "You guys head over to the Savvy Seekers and check their sales records for the quilt." Leo crossed to the door. "And get the lab guys to examine it. Every single stitch. I want photos of the whole thing."

Hunter picked up on Leo's line of thought. "Are you thinking Astroguy might've hidden some message or code inside the affirmations?"

Leo pursed his lips. "I don't want to get caught flat-footed on this one. With astrology involved, you know someone's bound to ask the Zodiac question."

"Did you ever work on that one, Leo?" Vierra asked.

Leo shook his head. "No, but the old-timers still talk about it. So far, this one seems tame, but if we receive unsolvable ciphers in the mail, well, then we're up shit's creek." Leo left the room.

"Your astrology friend seems to know a lot about this stuff," Hunter said to Dunham. "Madeline says 'hello,' by the way. Can you vouch for her?"

"She's one of the best in the city," Dunham said, locking eyes with Hunter. "Call me if you need a warrant for Savvy Seekers. Christophe will get his public relations team to cover for him. I'm gone."

"Will do," Hunter said, relieved when Alistair left the room. He joined Vierra back at the whiteboard, studying the closeup of the victim.

"Is it just me, or did our assistant district attorney change the subject when you asked about his astrologer friend?"

"I doubt he'd admit to having a personal astrologer."

"Or were you testing the waters? You think Dunham has a crush on your girlfriend?" Vierra said.

"Enough with the girlfriend stuff. Let's grab lunch on the way to Marin. You're buying."

☾7☽

Sirius Book Store — 12:15 p.m.

Madeline stood in the front window, adjusting the elements in her solar eclipse display. It was coming together nicely, filled with planet-shaped ornaments, eclipse-themed jewelry, and a couple of pairs of the eclipse glasses she snagged at the TV station. Geena worked the front counter, and Madeline was impressed to see her spend twenty minutes with a customer, a high school girl, helping her pick out a book on astrology houses and rulerships before escorting her to the counter for Matthew-Tabitha to ring up the sale. As the customer left with her purchase, Madeline felt a flush of pride. Through the glass door, she saw Vicky, promising young drag queen, approaching the store. Madeline extracted herself from her display to greet her.

"Hello, Miss Vicky!" Madeline said warmly as she opened the door to welcome the diva.

"Hey girl, hey," Matthew called, waving. "Show me today's ensemble."

"For you, anything," Vicky said and blew Matthew a kiss as she twirled. She wore a sateen purple mini dress over sequined fishnet stockings and chunky black Doc Martin boots. She wore her long black hair in a loose, graceful chignon, and her makeup glittered.

"Spec-ta-cu-la-di-da!" Matthew-Tabitha cooed.

Vicky gave Matthew-Tabitha a seductive wink and spotted the eclipse display. "OMG, all of these goodies—I love it. I am totally into this Solar Eclipse. Tell me, it's in Leo, right?"

"Oh yes, it is," Madeline replied, fanning herself with her hand to emphasize the point.

"That's a lot of heat. Maybe it's a good opportunity to burn these last few pounds off my fat ass?" Vicky crooned as she bumped her hips back and forth.

"That ass is divine, my dear," Matthew-Tabitha proclaimed. "Maddie, I'll grab those books I unpacked today and set them up in the window." With an air kiss to Miss Vicky, Matthew-Tabitha disappeared through the beaded curtain.

Geena stood frozen, unsure what to make of Vicky, as she tidied the front counter, her dark brown eyes wide with shock at Vicky's brazen bump and grind.

"How can I help you today, my friend?" Madeline offered.

"So, I'm researching a subject for a mini documentary. Ever heard of Sister Boom-Boom?" She asked, this time with a smaller hip check on each "boom."

"Of the Sisters of Perpetual Indulgence?"

"Yes!" Vicky squealed and jumped. "Tell me, did you know her?"

"Sure. She shopped here all the time. Sister Boom-Boom and Aunt Jane were friends."

Vicky leaned in. "Do you have any contact information for the people she worked with? I want to set up some interviews."

"I know someone who ran an AIDS charity. Let me see if I still have it." Madeline scrolled through her contact list on her phone. The store bell rang, and Cora came in, carrying a white bakery box. Madeline waved her over. "Hey, Cora, come meet a friend of mine. This is Miss Vicky."

Vicky offered Cora her hand, murmuring "Enchanté" in a perfect French accent.

"Uh, hi," Cora said, balancing the box and shaking Vicky's hand.

Madeline held up her phone. "I have the contact here. I'll text it to you."

"Perfect!" Vicky sang.

"My pleasure. Sister Boom-Boom deserves a comprehensive documentary."

"Right? Thank you. I'll let you get on with little sis. Looks like she brought some goodies."

"Kindergarten rules enforced by our mother. If you want to indulge, be sure to bring enough for everyone."

"I'd do the same, but then I might get busted for drug trafficking," Vicky said with a wink and a chortle before twirling around and sashaying out the door.

Madeline turned to find Cora and Geena staring at her, waiting for an explanation.

"Did I hear that, right? A documentary on a Sister Boom-Boom?" Cora said.

Madeline chuckled at them both. "Yes, she was a fixture in San Francisco's gay community. Sister Mary Boom-Boom wore huge fake breasts, a nun's habit, and black fishnets. So, what's in the box?"

Cora smiled and opened the box. "They're canelés from La Patissier. They baked them only on Monday, so I bought a dozen. Here, try one."

"I will, but let's not eat them on the floor. Come on back behind the counter."

Geena scurried behind them. "What's a canelé?"

Cora placed the box on the small table behind the counter. "It's the most amazing French pastry. It's like burned caramel on the outside and custard on the inside." Madeline passed around some napkins she kept in a drawer below the register. Cora opened the pastry box, and the aroma of vanilla filled the space.

"So, why are you blessing us with these delights?"

Cora bit into the pastry and swooned. "I'm celebrating my first proper assignment."

"This is amazing," Geena gushed after taking her first bite. She kept chewing and held up the canelé. "Matthew-Tabitha, try one. These are mind-blowing."

Mathew-Tabitha set down an ornate mirror on the side of the counter. "Don't mind if I do," he said, scooping out a canelé and devouring it.

"Congratulations, Cora!" Madeline said after swallowing her bite of the pastry. "What's the story? Something to do with mobsters?"

Cora chewed the last bite of her canelé. "No, cops found a body on Russian Hill yesterday."

Madeline stopped mid-bite. She exchanged a quick glance with Matthew-Tabitha. He raised an eyebrow and continued to eat, adding nothing to the conversation.

"I tried my sources—well, my source. You know Aunty Charlotte? Who was sorta helpful." Cora babbled, gesturing with her second canelé. "No one in the SFPD wants to talk about this case."

Madeline put her pastry down. "I'm sure they have their reasons."

"I saw an opportunity and jumped. Show the boss you have some drive. I mean, Dad taught us that. I found out the names of the investigating officers. A Hunter Davis and Daniel Vierra. I'm going to the Hall of Justice to see if they'll tell me more."

"Hey, one of them was here," Geena said through a mouthful of custard.

Everyone stopped chewing and stared at Geena.

"What do you mean?" Cora asked, looking confused.

Geena pointed to Madeline. "Yesterday morning, one of those cops asked to see Madeline."

Cora's eyebrows flew up. "What did he want?"

Madeline kept a stone face, but she already sensed her sister's anger stirring. "I promised Investigator Davis to keep our conversation confidential. So, I can't tell you anything about it."

"Even though it would help your sister's career?" Cora barked as she grabbed another canelé.

Madeline cocked her hip. "Your career? Are you serious? It's an internship. Don't blow it out of proportion."

Geena followed the entire exchange, nibbling her second canelé and watching, eyes wide. Matthew-Tabitha didn't hide his amusement.

"It could be a career," Cora pouted. "It's a competitive business. Every little tidbit counts."

"Calm down, sis. There'll be other stories," Madeline said.

"Not like this one! Come on, please!" Cora whimpered, switching gears, hoping to coax it out of Madeline. "Can you at least give me a general idea of what the cop wanted? Pretty, pretty, please?"

"No. I can't give you anything. Stop digging."

Cora heaved a sigh and grabbed the pastry box. Geena snatched another canelé before Cora shoved the lid down. "Fine, I get it. You're afraid that one of your weirdo customers is doing something illegal." Cora tucked the pastry box under her arm. "Thanks for nothing, Sis."

Madeline took a few steps toward her sister. "Cora, don't do this."

"You're not my mother," Cora said with a childish pout. She spun around and marched out the door, closing it with a loud bang that set the mounted bell clanging back and forth.

"Whoa, she's got a temper," Geena said as she wrapped her third canelé in a napkin.

"That she does." Madeline lost her appetite, so she grabbed a napkin and wrapped her canelé.

"Tinkerbell is fierce. I like her," Matthew smirked before retrieving the sun mirror and returning to the window display.

"So, what did the cop want?" Geena asked.

Madeline shrank back. "Not you, too? If he didn't ask me to keep my mouth shut, I'd tell you. I hate having to keep other people's secrets."

Geena tilted her head. "That's not true."

Bewildered, Madeline faced Geena. "What do you mean?"

"Your private clients," Geena replied, opening the napkin and picking at her pastry. "You keep their secrets. I see them coming in, looking all sheepish."

"That's different. They want me to give them insights into what's going on in their lives. I don't ask for details, not unless—" She stopped herself. Her clients shared their deepest secrets with her. They confessed details they wouldn't tell their closest friends. She kept many, many secrets. "You're right. Keeping secrets is an occupational hazard."

"No wonder your sister is angry. Reporting the news is all about exposing messy details. Funny how you two are on opposite sides of the same thing."

Funny was not the word Madeline would use to describe the situation. "Do you have any siblings, Geena?"

"I had a turtle once," she said as she ate another bite and walked away.

Madeline had to kick Matthew-Tabitha's ankle to keep him from laughing as hard as she wanted to.

⟨8⟩

Savvy Seeker Compound — 1:45 p.m.

Hunter rode shotgun as Vierra drove. Fighting back a yawn, Hunter asked, "Should we have stopped for caffeine on the way, Malcolm?" He hoped to break the tension by using his nickname for Vierra. Vierra shook his head, keeping his focus on the road. "I'm already swimming in it. Audrey."

Hunter smiled, enjoying the role reversal. Over time, to maintain their sanity during lengthy investigations, they created alter egos named Malcolm and Audrey. These personas were based on an imaginary couple who avidly watched forensic cop shows on TV.

Hunter noticed the gradual transformation of the surrounding neighborhoods, starting from quaint single-family homes and progressing into ostentatious junior Mcmansions, until finally giving way to vast wooded areas concealing grander estates. Hunter's thoughts returned to his heated arguments with his wife, Abby, about Savvy Seekers. She pestered him, getting him to meditate, but he didn't see the point of it, and her interpretation was that if he rejected meditation, it meant he also rejected her.

They drove in silence until the Google Maps lady called out the turns and the street names. They went up to Tiburon, known for its exclusive and secluded addresses.

"Damn, they must sell a lot of essential oils," Vierra remarked as they drove down a winding driveway surrounded by thick forest on both sides. The driveway led them to a tall and intricately crafted iron gate with zodiac signs adorning the top edge and a sun in the center, its rays made of gleaming metal.

Vierra drove up to the intercom and pushed a button. "Investigators Davis and Vierra. We have some questions."

The intercom clicked, but the gate took forever to open, putting Hunter's nerves on edge. Who was watching them? They drove into the compound and entered a vast parking lot, which was a surprise. With only about a dozen cars parked, even though the lot could accommodate hundreds. "They invite friends over on the weekends to watch the Niners?"

"Perhaps they hold a meditation Olympics that we don't know about?" Vierra parked the car. "It's all very flazéda."

Hunter got out and inspected the property. In front of them, the compound's terracotta roof peeked out above a high bamboo fence. In the center of the fence, covered by a portico, another double gate, crafted from the same wood with the matching sun design in the middle, extended a couple hundred feet in both directions, blocking the view of the compound buildings. A gleaming white SUV parked a few feet from the gate.

The top of the portico featured words carved into the wood. Hunter read them out loud: "'Remember you come here having already understood the necessity of struggling with yourself—only with yourself. Therefore, thank everyone who gives you the opportunity.' Wow, by some guy named Gurdjieff."

Vierra shook his head. "Jesus. So, spouting off bullshit like this qualifies you to be a self-help guru? I should make a career change."

"Looks more like a help-yourself-first guru," Hunter scoffed, yet he took out his phone and snapped a picture of the quote.

As Vierra moved to knock on the gate, it opened, and a woman stepped out. Somewhere in her late thirties, with blazing dark eyes, long black hair, and a stern expression. With a walkie-talkie in her hand, she exuded the energy of someone highly disciplined. Hunter guessed her ethnicity as Eastern European or Russian. She wore an immaculate dove-colored pantsuit made of soft, buttery fabric tailored to her shape and stood with her arms crossed in front of her. He expected Granola Girl but found Ms. Executive Suite instead.

"Yes, gentlemen. You are from the police?" She kept her voice businesslike as she crossed her arms over her chest and studied them with her head tilted to one side, which made Hunter squirm, like being x-rayed by a mean girl.

"Yes, we are," Vierra stammered, and his face paled as he produced his badge from his coat pocket. But he recovered with a quick throat clearing, and he continued with renewed authority. "I'm Investigator Vierra, and this is my partner, Investigator Davis. We have some questions regarding a quilt sold by Savvy Seekers. What is your name and position here, please?"

"My name is Katia, and I'm the Operations Manager. You should have called our customer service department."

"We did, ma'am, and no one answered our call."

Katia sneered. "I'm sorry, Officer Vierra, but we value our privacy. You must come back with a warrant."

Hunter stepped toward her. "We respect your privacy, but I found one of your quilts at a crime scene. We'd like you to help us track down the person who ordered the quilt so we can question them."

"A crime?" She asked, still blocking the entrance like a petite bodyguard.

"Yes," Hunter added, an edge to his voice.

Hunter observed her as she examined them, contemplating her choices. "I apologize. I recognize that you are carrying out your duties. However, we have a strict confidentiality agreement with our customers. We treat them as if they were part of our own family. And we do not disclose family matters to the public. Return with a warrant, and we will resume this discussion with our internal legal team."

Hunter glanced at Vierra, who stood off the side of the open gate. "Looks like we have to head back." Vierra pointed back toward Katia, who made way as a man in a white suit and sunglasses emerged from behind the gate and walked straight to the white SUV. "Are they still there?" A woman's voice came over Katia's walkie-talkie. Hunter crossed his arms over his chest, holding his portfolio, prepared to hold his ground. Katia turned away from him to speak into the walkie-talkie. "Just give me another minute."

"We're already late," came the female voice.

Vierra stood shoulder to shoulder with Hunter, emphasizing their determination to stay until they got what they wanted.

The chauffeur opened the back door to the SUV, and Katia pulled the gate open for the entourage coming out of the compound. A caramel-skinned woman dressed in a flowing blue-green gown emerged, heading toward the car, but stopped when she spotted Hunter. Her long black hair bounced around her shoulders, and she smiled at Hunter, her bedroom eyes squinting, but she gave away nothing as she took in the rumpled policemen.

Hunter spotted the next woman in the lineup. She was medium height with a round frame. She carried herself with authority in an expensive mauve suit. She wore her brown curls cut close and bangle gold earrings. She wasted no time and got up in Hunter's face. "I'm sorry, officer, but you have to leave. We're already late, and Christophe doesn't want you here."

"He doesn't?" Hunter said, faking incredulity. "I thought he loved meeting new people. Don't lowly police investigators deserve an audience?"

"No, only members of our inner circle and significant donors receive that honor. You've stated your business, so get moving so we can do ours."

"Brenda don't be rude to our guests," Christophe's voice carried toward them as he exited the gate. Brenda's expression changed; her lips curled, her eyes furrowed, and she stepped away from Hunter, feeling the sting of her guru's chastisement.

"Good morning, investigators," Christophe, taller than Hunter expected, sported with a fit, athletic build. He wore an immaculately tailored shirt in an exotic silk over tan linen pants and Italian shoes that cost a small fortune.

"Good morning. I'm assuming you are Mr. Christophe, is that right?" Hunter offered his hand, and Christophe shook it while keeping his eyes locked on Hunter with a sliver of a glance at Vierra.

"Christophe is fine." He pointed toward Katia, who came and joined him. "My operations manager has answered your question, hasn't she?"

"She did, but she's sending us back to the office for a warrant."

"As well she should. She's also married to one of my attorneys. You should follow her directions."

"I'm sure you hate to have your time wasted, Christophe. We're in the middle of a murder investigation and need to know how one of your affirmation quilts wound up at our crime scene. I'm sure you don't want to make us drive all the way back to the city, wasting precious time, do you?"

Christophe considered his options and turned his gaze to Vierra, who maintained his composure, but Hunter sensed Vierra's energy, holding in his frustration, begging for a reason to clock Christophe. Props to him for keeping his cool.

Christophe flexed his shoulders, releasing pent-up energy, and leaned into Hunter. "Go get that warrant, we don't want to cut corners, now do we?" He stepped toward the SUV.

Yet, Hunter wanted more, so he approached the SUV, blocking Christophe. "Interesting color choices, white? I thought for sure you'd pick a sleeker ride?"

"All our vehicles are white. I chose white for a reason: white contains the entire light spectrum, representing a higher vibration, and black is the absence of light. I work hard to keep my vibration high, so it makes sense to carry that choice into my car." Then he pointed toward Hunter's car. "You might think about that when you finally replace your clunker."

Hunter stepped away, allowing Christophe to climb into the back seat. His chauffeur slammed the door, sprinted toward the driver's side door, hopped in the car, gunned it, and headed out of the compound. Hunter turned back to see Katia closing the gate behind her.

Hunter turned to Vierra, "At least we learned one thing, Malcolm."

Vierra nodded. "All of their vehicles are white. Got it. Now let's get the flazéda out of here."

(9)

Ina Coolbrith Park — 3:31 p.m.

Madeline took advantage of the afternoon lull to have some me-time. With no direction other than "south of Polk Street," she hopped on a bus, and it dropped her off at North Beach. She strolled up Vallejo Street, spotting Ina Coolbrith Park in the distance. She recalled how she and her aunt Jane often stopped at the park and took in the view. Why not today? Yes, if she were honest with herself, she would admit she thought about Hunter Davis and the crime scene. Walking up the hill toward the entrance, her mind wandered to her other relationships with men over the years. Images of faces flashed through her mind, and she swiped them away, clearing out the negative residue from her past mistakes. But then, what was she left with?

Her heart warmed, knowing she had Matthew-Tabitha in her corner. He was an exceptional product manager and a dependable friend. They often went out together for a break from the shop and to enjoy each other's company. He is that "safe" gay man who wouldn't break her heart. She walked up the steep incline on Vallejo Street toward the park entrance, stopping to catch her breath.

From Vallejo, the park still resembled a rugged cliff, now tamed by city engineers, with stalwart staircases running up both sides and a serpentine path in between. An urban marvel, like so many other San Francisco gems, Madeline appreciated how the city took the old, ill-used, discarded, and crafted an urban delight.

She watched her step entering the park, avoiding the trash scattered on the first few stairs. Something shiny caught her eye, and she kicked some leaves away and spotted an old-fashioned brooch. Picking it up, she turned it over. The bar pin had broken off, and uncaring feet had tromped on the Laurel leaf pattern done in silver, resulting in dents in places. An image of Matthew-Tabitha appeared in her mind. This pin was the kind of thing he loved: oddball treasures found in the trash. She stroked the gem clusters, lifting the dirt, unveiling the stones' inner sparkle, streaks of purple fire, and a multicolored opal set with tiny pearls. Madeline tucked it away in her pocket, planning to clean it up once she got home.

Madeline chose the staircase along the right side of the park, and as she climbed it, she admired the mixture of ferns and ornamental grasses in the long shadows of the Coast live oak tree in the center of the park. After walking up a few more flights, she turned, now parallel with the line of apartments alongside the park. Looking over their rooftops, she breathed in the view, beginning to doubt her decision to come here.

After Investigator Davis left her shop, she entered the time and place for the 911 call into her computer and generated a chart. It revealed a bright, energetic victim who met sudden and fatal violence. But what intrigued her the most was the chart revealed the killer to be a woman. Madeline knew her inner voyeur wanted to experience the place for herself. She walked along the switchback trail for a while, and as she ascended the heights, the view became more dramatic. It was a refreshing break from her Polk Street routine. She took a moment to ground herself and to check in with the elementals. Facing east, she breathed in the air. Under clear skies, it felt bright and inviting, with no lingering fog.

She acknowledged the earth she stood on, feeling its specific vibration, different from the crowded city streets. The place invited leisurely walks and unhurried exploration. What energy did the apartments and houses surrounding the park emit? Safety? No, it was a certain satisfaction in wealth and ownership in such a special city. Looking down the hill, Madeline sensed the shift from well-heeled Russian Hill mansions to a transitional neighborhood, not Chinatown, but not North Beach either.

What about Fire? She didn't see any fire hydrants, but in the distance, Telegraph Hill and Coit Tower, which was a monument to the volunteer firefighters. Looking toward the financial district, she tried picturing in her mind the old tents, shacks, and shanties consumed by flames. And then dynamite to blow up the remaining homes to deny the fire more fuel.

As for water, that was easy: the bay surrounding the city. But there must be a closer source. She walked along the next switchback, examining the landscaped sections, knowing the city installed native indigenous plants in the parks. She spotted manzanitas, some coyote berries along with bee plant, California fuchsias, and red elderberry mixed in with swaths of blue plumbago. In the park, she could not spot a sprinkler system. As she walked up to the next turn, she remembered seeing gardeners hooking hoses to hand water the plantings. Madeline heaved a satisfied sigh, pleased with her energetic check in. The elementals blended well in this space.

Moving further up the path, Madeline halted as a wave of nausea filled her body. Madeline noted a set of dark green park benches up ahead. She took a few steps up the path but stopped, unsettled. In order to calm her body down, she took in several deep breaths. She expected to encounter unbalanced energy at a crime scene but didn't expect it to be this brutal, but this was murder. She turned around and breathed in the view's beauty, the colorful patchwork of buildings, the various colors, the styles, often called the cool gray city of love. She adored it.

With the antidote of a fresh view, the nausea abated, and she understood the true reason for coming to the park: Hunter. Madeline admitted being attracted to him and wanted to understand his world. After sensing the energy at the crime scene, his world was a sharp contrast to hers. Where she looked at something as abstract and ephemeral as an astrology chart, he mucked around in the trenches of human carnage. Yet, he preserved his humanity. He'd been kind, curious, and willing to listen.

An image popped into her mind, the Tarot card she'd pulled for him, the Justice card. The image of a man sitting between two pillars, a sword in one and a scale in the other. Confronted with violence, the instinct was to restore balance and seek justice. How far would Hunter go for justice?

❨10❩

Homicide Division — 4:17 p.m.

Cora gobbled down two more canelés after leaving Madeline's store, and the lumps of flour and fat sloshing inside her made her feel bloated and ashamed. She dumped the rest of them in a trash can and ordered a car on her phone. Why did she lose her cool in front of Madeline and her shop girl? And for what? *A news story that I think will not even be a story. How would she be a reporter if she couldn't interview her sister without losing it?*

And how fabulous was Miss Vicky in her ensemble?! The image would not leave her mind: the elegant eggplant-colored cocktail dress—a vintage store classic, so well preserved—paired with the fishnets scored a ten in her book. But the clunky Doc Martin commando boots? Why not a cute pair of Mary Jane's or black kitten heels? What about Madeline's goth shop girl, Geena? What was her story with the dyed hair, the goth makeup, and those fake brown contact lenses? She half expected spiders to come crawling out of the girl's hair, creepsville.

"Focus, Cora!" Now was no time to worry about some random kid's fashion choices. The car turned onto Bryant Street and parked. She paid the fare, emerged from the car, and beheld the massive Hall of Justice looming over her. When she first arrived in San Francisco, mom had insisted she meet Aunty Charlotte, who was nice enough to give her a tour, but she had paid little attention, not expecting ever to return. Getting out of the car and adding a tip on her phone, she took the elevator to the seventh floor. She found a sign that read "Homicide."

Tapping her foot, knowing she had no business being here, she couldn't decide whether to knock or what. Even if she managed to find one of these investigators, they'd send her back to the press office. She refused to leave empty-handed. And she needed to suss out what Madeline was hiding. Did the cops want to speak to one of her customers? Cora knew Sirius Books harbored a freak show of customers, from conspiracy-theory weirdos to folks who talked to angels. Visiting Aunt Jane had frightened her when she was a kid.

Mustering some courage, Cora raised her hand to knock on the door when it flew open. A hefty man in a tracksuit with a buzz-cut missed plowing into her.

"Excuse me, can I help you?" he asked.

Bulldozing ahead, she blurted, "Yes! I need to talk with Investigator Davis or Vierra."

Buzz-cut must have pegged her as harmless — he nodded toward the hall. "It's your lucky morning." He pointed to a man walking toward them. "Hey, Mr. Aqua Velva, one of your groupies is here."

Groupie? Cora scoped out the investigator as he got closer—tall, thin, and exhausted. His suit was off the rack, but his tie, a maroon silk that matched his skin tone, not a total troglodyte. He yelled at Buzz-cut, "Okay, Mr. Social Secretary, I'll take it from here."

"No problem. Catch you at Murph's tonight?"

"You better be buying," the investigator said with an endearing grin. Buzz-cut waved him off as he swaggered away.

The investigator—Vierra? She guessed—heaved a sigh. "What do you want? I'm in a hurry."

Cora vomited out her prepared speech. "I'm Cora Merritt from KXOP. I'm doing some research. Did you find a body in Ina Coolbrith Park this morning? I was hoping to … talk to you about it?" Her voice trailed off.

He took a moment, rubbing his hand along his chin. "You know what I'm gonna say, don't you?"

Cora lifted her shoulders and chest to show some backbone. "Please don't send me back to the press office. I'll only get the runaround. Again."

"Don't you think we have a reason for that? How freaking old are you? Bet you don't have your learner's permit?"

"Sure, make fun. I'm impressing my boss, so he'll let me work on hard news stories and not just monitor social media channels. I have to start somewhere."

For a second, Cora thought it worked, that he considered helping her, but he shook his head. "No dice, I can't say anything, though I appreciate your enthusiasm. I do. Listen, I gotta go." He strode to the Homicide division door, but Cora moved with him, not ready to give up.

"I was young once, too, but this is…"

"What? This is over my pretty little head?" Cora jumped in. It was worse than talking to her sister. Aha! What about her sister's store? "Well, I've got confirmation that Investigator Davis spoke with an astrologer about this case. Do you know what kind of headache you'd have if I sent out that gem of a tweet?"

"What's your name again?"

"Cora Merritt. Why?"

"Okay, Ms. Merritt. I'm Investigator Daniel Vierra. Nice to meet you." He offered to shake her hand, which Cora took, and he nearly squeezed the life out of hers.

"It's very nice to meet you, too," she managed through a wince.

Vierra took a deep breath and pressed his hands together in a prayer motion. "I was ambitious once, too. We don't release information on active cases. If you're determined to track down this tidbit and work up a social media mess for us, I ask you this. How on God's green Earth is that helping the poor people who lost their child?"

She considered the dark eyes staring at her. Was he messing with her? If so, why had he confirmed they found a child's body? "I get it. No one would want to contribute to a parent's grief, but doesn't the public need to know there's a killer on the loose?"

"I understand the public's right to know, but what will they do? They're all just going back to their Taco Bell and cable TV. I'd love to continue this conversation about police work and media relations, but I have a freaking job to do. If I see anything on social media come out of this conversation, you can bet I'll call your boss and read him the riot act. That won't help your career, will it?"

"No," she said, "it wouldn't." Cora paused. "Thank you for your time." She wanted to look confident and offered her hand again.

He locked his eyes on hers, "points for trying." He shook his head and opened the door without saying another word.

She walked back to the elevators. Her stomach churned again, and it hit her. He didn't deny Hunter Davis's interview with Madeline. He hadn't shot it down. What in the world did her big sister, the astrologer, have to do with a dead child?

***

Homicide Division — 4:45 p.m.

Hunter sped through his emails, clicking on one from the crime lab when Vierra stepped up to him.

"You will not believe this, but a chick named Cora Merritt from a TV station just asked about our case," Vierra said.

"Merritt? Like Madeline Merritt, the astrology lady?" Hunter asked.

"How many Merritt women are running around in the city?"

"Beats me, but I got the audio file for the 911 call. Take a listen." Hunter clicked the file: "Uh … yeah," the woman's voice started, sounding nervous. "Yeah, I think I just saw a body … Yeah, on a bench in the funny park on Taylor, on Russian Hill? I think. I don't know but send someone. He's like, dead."

"Wow, he's like dead. That's original," Vierra said with a yawn.

"Well, like totally." Hunter replied, "Come on, give the girl a break. She never saw a dead body before."

"True."

He played it over again. The woman kept her voice calm, monotone. "What do you think? A nurse walking home from a late shift? An early bird watcher strolling in the park?"

Vierra ran his hands over his face. "Could be, or it could be Alice in Wonderland looking for the rabbit and found our victim instead. I'm beat, my brain is full. How about we take this up in the morning?"

Hunter scanned his email list and felt a wave of exhaustion hit him in the chest. He couldn't blame his partner for needing a break, but he was taking more of them. "Go ahead, let me plow through more of these. See you tomorrow," he said while looking at his computer screen.

"Have at it," Vierra said on his way out.

Hunter turned away from the emails and played the audio file again. The voice bothered him, and he wasn't sure why.

∙∙⊶⊷∙‹ **11** ›∙⊶⊷∙∙

TUESDAY, AUGUST 8, 2017

Sirius Books — 9:03 a.m.

After a predawn meditation, Madeline's energy improved, her body no longer carrying emotional stress from the energy at the crime scene. She dressed and readied herself for the day. As she walked down the stairs from her apartment to the store, the three planets in signs flitted at the edges of her mind, seeking connection, but nothing fit. Needing to do something productive, she headed down to her office to catch up on paperwork. After that she worked on the chart for the 911 call, eyeballs deep into horary astrology books, when she heard raised voices outside her office, followed by a knock. She opened the door to find Geena panic-stricken.

"We have some nutty lady out here. She insists on talking to you," she said and swiped a lock of hair off her face. Madeline didn't know if Geena was on the verge of tears or ready to explode from the tension now filling her tiny frame.

"Sure thing."

Madeline let Geena lead the way through the work area.

"She said she ordered a copy of some alien abduction book," Geena explained in a tense whisper. "I checked the holds shelf, and I can't find it. She insisted on seeing you."

Following Geena into the shop, Madeline recognized the customer. Mrs. McKenzie, one of her regulars, a tiny spit of a woman, not even five feet tall. Her ancient Chanel suit clung to her bony frame.

"Hello, Mrs. Mackenzie. What can I do for you?"

Mrs. Mackenzie spun around like a startled animal, but she relaxed upon seeing Madeline "Oh! Oh, Madeline. I'm so sorry. But who is this girl? I don't know her."

Madeline sensed Geena prickle at Mrs. McKenzie's bluntness. She took a deep breath, hoping to ease them both. "Mrs. McKenzie, this is my wonderful new shop assistant. Her name is Geena."

"Oh, I say, it's nice to meet you, Geena," Mrs. McKenzie said, now relaxed. She turned back to Madeline. "But you told me Hill's newest edition arrived, and I'm so desperate to read it."

"Yes, it arrived late yesterday, but I forgot to put it on the hold shelf. It's my fault, not Geena's. Let me get it for you."

Madeline ducked into the storage area and grabbed the book, hoping the encounter would teach Geena about customer service.

When Madeline returned, Mrs. McKenzie took the book and clutched it to her chest as if it held magical powers. "Thank you! Thank you so much. Well, now I must go home to read it. Thank you, Madeline. I apologize, Miss Geena."

Madeline stayed with Geena after Mrs. McKenzie left the shop.

"I'm sorry," Geena said, "I didn't expect her to freak out when I couldn't find the book. Does that happen often?"

Madeline sighed. "No. She's one of my unusual clients. About ten years ago, she lost her son in a car accident, and six months later, her husband died of a broken heart."

Geena withdrew into herself. "Oh. That's awful."

"Agreed. She came here and bought books on grieving, but she found a book on alien abductions. She latched on to the idea her son and husband are still alive, only living on another planet."

Geena's brow knitted. "You order alien books just for her? That makes you an enabler."

"You're right, but if thinking about aliens helps her cope with the devastation in her life, I'll keep ordering them. You did the right thing by asking me."

"Okay," Geena said. "I don't know. Those aliens weird me out."

Madeline sensed something from the girl. It wasn't contrition but ambivalence. Geena had little experience interacting with elderly people and couldn't grasp the concept that Mrs. McKenzie had once been a nineteen-year-old, ready to take on the world. And if aliens weirded her out, what was she thinking working in a metaphysical bookstore?

The bell at the front door chimed, and Madeline turned. Her heart jumped at seeing Alistair Dunham walking toward her, exuding his easygoing charm. His hairstyle was a series of cowlicks turning gray at the edges. His vest and tie were worlds away from the natural cotton tunics and pajama pants he wore back in the Bernal Heights house. He'd often stop by on weekends, and they'd go out for coffee. But the comfort of seeing her old friend turned to trepidation, as she sensed this wasn't a social call. "Alistair, so good to see you." She greeted him with a hug.

"Hey, Madeline. I hope you don't mind me stopping by."

"I don't mind at all. Come on back to the office." Madeline turned to Geena. "I won't be long. You're doing a magnificent job." A genuine smile crept across Geena's face, and she bent her head to the side, an endearing gesture.

As Madeline and Alistair walked through the storage area and into her office, she recalled the day he stumbled into her shop, and they renewed their friendship. She sat at her desk while Alistair pulled up the chair opposite her.

"I wondered if Hunter Davis came to visit you. Did he show you some astrology symbols?"

Madeline re-arranged some files on her desk, as she sensed something off-putting about this visit. "Yes, he did. I told him that without a time or a location, I couldn't give him an interpretation."

"That's what I thought," Alistair said and leaned back. "I was at the crime scene when they found it. I sent him here to hear it from my favorite expert. And…"

"And what? Spit it out?"

"And I wanted you to know about the case because who knows. If the killer is an astrologer, he shopped here?"

Madeline felt a sharpness in her gut. She considered the idea that one of her customers was involved but thought it could never be true. "Do you think so? I'm not the only metaphysical bookstore in town. Plus, there's so much information available online these days."

Alistair nodded. "You're right, but I've seen some interesting people hanging out in the stacks."

"True, I inherited them from Jane, but I think by only giving three planets in signs the killer is messing with the cops' heads, don't you? That it's a big-time waster?"

"It's a reasonable theory. Did he tell you what else they found?"

Madeline held up her hands. "No, and don't tell me. No details," she protested, lifting her index fingers to form a cross.

"Okay, okay. So, what about the planets in signs? How did Hunter react?"

Madeline shrugged. "He tried to digest it, but it felt like initiating an unsuspecting Muggle into the world of the dark arts."

"Oh yeah, I'd forgotten the long learning curve." Alistair tilted his head and smiled. "And with only three planets to work with." Alistair's phone chirped. He checked the screen. "Sorry, I have to grab this. It's our Muggle."

Madeline glanced down at her desk, moving folders around, pretending not to listen to Alistair's call.

"Yeah. What's up?" Alistair said as he stood up, turning away from Madeline.

Madeline puzzled over the idea of a killer browsing in her store. Every few months, she'd get a wannabe dark magician. Mostly lonely guys, asking if she carried grimoires or books on black magic. She'd show them her history of magic section, the history of alchemy, and the books on sacred geometry. The thought of studying advanced geometry, chemistry, and calculus sent them on their way.

"I'm away from my office, but I'll have my secretary send it over. Okay?" Alistair nodded toward Madeline with an expression that said he was wrapping it up. "No problem. We'll see what turns up. Bye." He clicked off his phone and started texting. "You will not believe this. Hunter needs a warrant for—"

"—No details, remember?"

"Sorry. This case is so bizarre." He finished his text and sat down. "Hunter mentioned you might do up a chart for the 911 call?"

"I have it here," she said, picking up the chart and placing it on her desk.

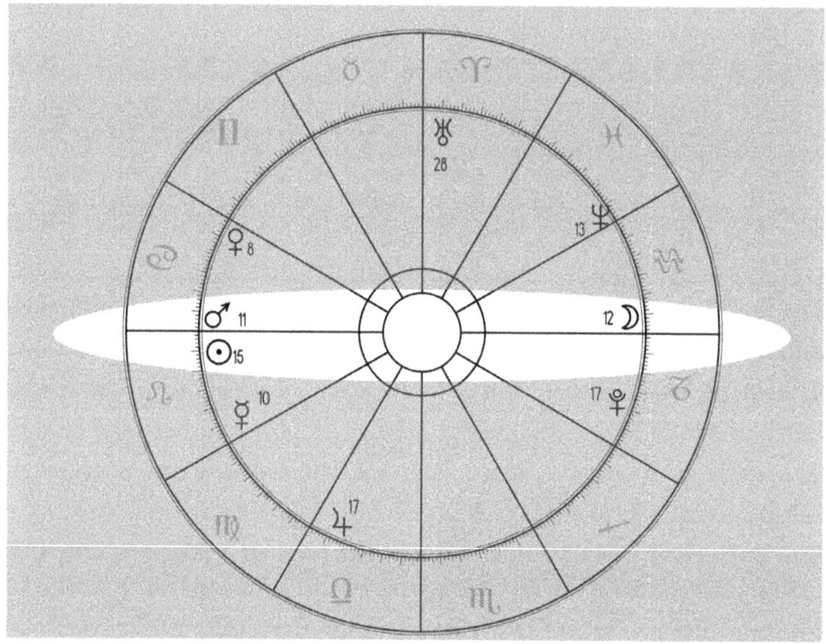

"We have the Sun rising in the first house—that's our victim, bursting with amazing solar energy rising at daybreak. But it runs right into Mars, which signifies sudden violence. Poor guy didn't have a chance."

Alistair pointed at the chart. "And opposite the victim is the moon in Aquarius. Does this mean a female killer? The moon is feminine, right?"

"Matthew-Tabitha and I think so, but Saturn rules Aquarius in the fifth house of children and romance." She let the chart fall to her desk. So, how do I explain this to the police without sounding like a witch doctor?"

Alistair grinned. "Don't worry, Hunter's a good cop. He'll be open. It's his partner, Vierra, who's the real skeptic."

"Investigator Davis didn't mention his partner. What's he like?"

Alistair leaned back in his chair. "Oh, you know, your average bro. He can be an asshole most of the time, but he's a solid investigator. Too bad he's in a world of trouble."

"Go on, tell," Madeline sensed he wanted to gossip.

"Have you been following the Sean Muldooney case on the news?"

"The mobster on trial for murder?"

Alistair nodded and leaned forward. "Yeah, well, Vierra's sleeping with Muldooney's wife Alana, the princess of the Volkov crime family."

"You're kidding me?" Madeline shivered. "And how is this affecting a Muldooney brother we both know?"

"He's still keeping his distance from the clan. Have you seen any of the others? Like Brenda or Lili, perhaps? Or, God help me, Miranda?"

"No. I've kept my distance from the Savvy Seekers," Madeline blew out a heavy sigh. "And I lost track of Lili. I used to see her and Luna every once in a while."

Alistair squirmed in his chair. "Interesting. When are you going to show the 911 chart to the guys?"

"Not sure. Investigator Davis asked me to call him when it's done."

"And it's done." Alistair bent closer to her, his fingertips resting on the desk between them. "Why are you waiting?"

Madeline concocted a convincing lie. "I thought I might run it again, add some fixed stars too," she said and stood, hoping he'd catch on that she didn't want to talk about it anymore.

Alistair remained seated. "Yeah, super weird. Have dinner with me tonight? We can work on your presentation." He flashed his charming smile, and it worked.

"Not tonight," she said and motioned to her computer. "I have Tobias Silva's presentation. But thanks for asking." She walked around her desk to open the door. "But will you come to the meeting with Investigator Davis? I'll feel better with a friendly face in the room."

Alistair smiled and stood up. "Sure thing. I know muggles can be a pain."

"Thank you." Madeline walked out into the shop with Alistair. As they approached the sales area, they heard Geena raising her voice.

"I told you, she's busy. You'll have to be patient." Geena stood at the front counter.

"But I gotta see her now. I have to tell her." Madeline recognized Sluggo, another regular. He stood in the middle of the shop, scanning the space, agitated. In and out of treatment centers, homeless, he made Sirius Books as his "safe place." His shaved head, weathered skin, and emaciated body told of his life as a homeless man. His eyes found Madeline. "Oh, there you are. We have to talk, I" — He spotted Alistair, and he ran into the stacks to get away.

"What did I say?" Alistair asked in a mocking tone.

Madeline turned to Alistair. "Sorry, I have to handle this. We'll talk more?"

Alistair walked to the shop door. "Sure thing."

Seeing Geena still upset, Madeline smiled. "Don't worry. Just breathe, I'll send him out the back, okay?"

"Yeah, thanks."

Moving through the store, Madeline found Sluggo where he often hid, sitting on a step stool in a corner between the books on energy healing and Quantum Physics. He hugged his torso tight to keep from shivering. "Hey, Sluggo," she kept her tone soft, as if speaking with a frightened child.

Seeing her, he leaped up, his eyes wide and his body shaking from anxiety. "Oh, thank the goddess. It's the Masons. They're at it again."

Given Sluggo's constant obsession with California's Freemasons, Madeline should have realized that after a full moon, he would be upset. "What are they doing this time?"

Sluggo rambled. "It's the fire. They're getting ready to do it again. They have an entire network behind them, and they're serious this time. It's going to be bad, like terrible." Waving his arms, he put his hands on his head. "I told you. They started the 1851 fire on purpose, right? I'm serious. I was at the public library, and I found the references. They say it was some pyromaniac. But that's a cover story, right?"

"Why would they do that?"

"Because of the Ohlone massacres, man. The energy. It's still in the city, bad mojo from killing off those poor innocent people. You know the Masons were colonists. It's global. It's what they do."

Madeline needed a tactic to stop mania. Taking a deep breath, she said, "I tell you what, Sluggo. I have work to do. How about I take you next door for a cup of coffee?"

"Yeah, okay. But don't blow me off. They have Know-sis this time."

It was the first time she'd heard him use the term. "Gnosis, as in the gnostic gospels?"

Sluggo's eyes bulged as he waved his arms like a football referee waving off an incomplete pass. "No, it's K. N. O. W. S. I. S. Christophe got it. He's scheming with the Masons."

Hearing the name sent an icy chill through Madeline, but she wasn't sure what it meant. She shrugged it off, seeking a way to soothe Sluggo. He was always tying Christophe to the Freemasons, even though Madeline knew Christophe wasn't concerned about the organization. "Okay, if that's true." She put her arm on his shoulder and steered him to the front of the store. "I'll get you some coffee and some money. You return to the library and bring me some photocopies, okay?"

"I can't get you a copy of Know-sis. It's all hush-hush."

"That's fine. Bring me the information on the Mason's setting for the 1851 fire. Can you do that?"

"Oh, you betcha," Sluggo nodded his head, and his crooked smile revealed, for a moment, a coherent mind shining through the haze.

12

*"In a world where death is the hunter, my friend,
there is no time for regrets or doubts. There is only time for decisions."
—Carlos Castaneda, Journey to Ixtlan*

Bernal Heights House–August 21, 2001
20 days before The Ceremony 9:32 a.m.

Madeline checked Christophe's hand-drawn Tree of Life diagram: ten circles with lines connecting them, along with the names of the house members scribbled in his loopy handwriting. Alistair joined her in figuring out how to transfer this diagram onto the living room carpet, making a map for the ceremony Christophe would conduct. While Alistair studied the map, she couldn't help but stare at his hair—how his curls flowed down his back to his shoulder blades. When he turned around, his hair swirled, framing his handsome face.

"What are you looking at?" he asked, touching his chin. "Do I have something on my face?"

"No, no. I … It doesn't matter." She stammered, hiding her embarrassment. "I don't know. You think the ancient Sumerians ever held their ceremonies in a Bernal Heights ranch house living room?"

"Not, but as adepts in the magic arts, we adapt," Alistair said with a wink as he evaluated the carpet. "But we need something to mark off the Sephirot. Any ideas?"

Alistair placed his hand on Madeline's shoulder, which made her melt. They'd muscled all the furniture to the back of the room, including the enormous sofa and various chairs, to maximize the space. At the left end of the room, near the front door, Madeline had set a small table for Christophe. It would allow him to face the entire room. Using scarves, they'd created a pathway for participants entering the room to find their place.

"When performing magical ceremonies on a budget, you improvise. I'll go down to the basement. I think there's some fabric stuff the previous owner dumped there."

"Okay," Alistair smiled again. Which lit up Madeline to the core. Grinning, she walked down the hall to the door leading to the unfinished basement.

Once down there, she moved past piles of abandoned wood framing where the previous owner had started construction on an apartment but ran out of money. The room's only light source, one bare bulb, pierced the gloom, but the stench repulsed her. The guys had set up some dumbbells and a lifting bench down here, and she caught Jethro in the middle of a workout, and his sour body odor made her gag.

"Well, hey there, little sister, did you come down to see me?" Jethro put his barbell on the rack. Shirtless, with a sheen of sweat on his chest and a protruding belly. A former chemistry student with massive "jewfro" who stood over six feet tall, with an ego the size of Florida, he was the one person in the house that got on her nerves.

"No." Madeline pouted, "I came down to get something." She marched to a shelf stacked with aged cardboard boxes filled with junk the previous owner had left behind. She opened one and then another, searching for something to use in the ceremony. Of course, Jethro had to join her. "Ugh, could you at least put a shirt on?"

"I still got more reps, baby." He pulled his arms up in a powerlifting pose. "So whatcha looking for?"

"I thought I saw an old box of placemats down here. I need them to set up the ceremony. I'm working with Alistair." Saying his name brought that smile back, but, of course, Jethro picked up on it.

"Ooh, Madeline's playing with the handsome Alistair," he teased. "You know Christophe is pairing him off with the bodacious Miranda. Sorry, sweetie."

"Yeah, I heard. Doesn't mean I can't enjoy working with him."

Jethro grabbed an overhead pipe, showing off his biceps, imitating Sylvester Stallone from that scene in "Rocky." He grinned at her. "I bet Christophe is going to pair you with me. Two earth signs, me Capricorn, you Taurus. You know, the horny signs of the zodiac."

Madeline stared at him, disgusted. "Oh, please. I'd rather sit on the sidelines."

"Aw, baby. Don't be a buzzkill. Besides, I'm gonna drop a hit of acid before the ceremony. Can you believe it? We get to fuck our way to enlightenment." He gyrated his hips back and forth, nodding his head, a shit-eating grin on his face.

Disgusted, Madeline walked past an ancient gun safe and a broken China hutch, and on a shelf found a box filled with tablecloths and placemats. She then marched toward the stairs. "You're just being gross. I'm outta here."

"Aww, don't leave mad, baby. We were just getting started," Jethro shouted with glee as she stamped her bullish feet on each stair tread, marching out of there.

Madeline carried the box back into the living room, rejoining Alistair, doing her best not to scowl. "These will do." She placed the box on the floor and pulled out several round placemats, orange and brown colored, woven from some heavy string. "They're flat and should be unobtrusive."

"Excellent choice," Alistair grabbed several of them. "What took so long?"

Madeline shivered. "Oh, that ogre in the dungeon. Jethro was being a pill. Let's get back to work."

Following Christophe's map, they re-created The Tree of Life using ten placemats to stand in for the ten Sephira in the tree. Christophe assigned each member of the household a specific Sephira to stand on. Following the map, they placed name cards where Christophe wanted everyone to be for their part of the ceremony.

"All we need now is for Christophe to sign off on it," Alistair said, smiling at her.

"Let's review the diagram again. Make sure we have everyone's name in the right place." Madeline said. "According to the design, Christophe stands at Sephirot one, Kether."

"Got it. Sephirot two and three are William and Katia, our King and Queen of Wands."

Madeline cooed, "And at Sephirot four is the Inimitable King of Cups, Alistair Dunham." He extended his arm in the air and bowed. Madeline answered his bow with a curtsy, and they both laughed.

"King of Cups … or Queen of Drama? Miranda's right next to you," Madeline said with a wink.

Alistair frowned. "Ah, the darling girl. All emotions all the time. Not my type."

"Be kind," Madeline ribbed. "Moving on, at Sephira Seven is Victoria, Queen of Swords, and at Sephira Eight is her dance partner. Oh."

"What?"

"It's Christophe. He's put himself at Sephira One and Eight? Does that make sense to you?"

Alistair checked the diagram. "None of this makes sense to me. I can see Victoria as the Queen of Swords. Christophe should be the King of Swords, but he has listed himself as Prince of Swords. And where does Edgar fit?"

"Edgar is with Brenda. They are the King and Queen of Pentacles. They are at Sephira nine. You're right. Christophe should be King of Swords or at least the Prince of Swords. He is a Gemini. All that Air."

"Has Christophe told you what will happen after the ceremony?"

"No. Christophe put Lili at the unseen Da'at and me at Sephira Six with Jethro," she said while exaggerating a shiver of disgust.

"The whole thing sounds sketchy." Alistair waved the map in the air.

"Why are you guys doing this now?" Katia demanded, entering from the kitchen with William right behind her. Everyone in the house dressed casually except for Katia, who wore a pale cream silk blouse over dark-hued palazzo pants.

Madeline cringed. "We wanted to test Christophe's diagram."

Katia crossed her arms and sniffed as she examined their work. William glanced at the design. "I spoke with Christophe, and he wants to make changes. He wants Lili at Sephira ten and to pair her with Jethro."

Madeline exchanged a glance with Alistair, both shocked at the change. "Lili's a Pisces. Why pair a water sign with a Capricorn?" Madeline tried not to whine but failed.

"Duh," William piped up, "Capricorn is half goat and half fish." He gloated.

One of the more intellectual members of the group, William, projected a rock-n-roll, bad-ass posture: Glossy black hair, dark eyes, and a goatee stressed his oval-shaped face. Black T-shirt over black jeans, lots of silver chains and rings, pouts, and posturing. Madeline hated herself for acknowledging that it worked, and his depth of arcane knowledge rivaled her Aunt Jane. She let out a deep sigh. Learning she wouldn't have to be with Jethro was a relief. "Okay, you're right. I was wrong." She turned back to Katia. "When did you hear this?"

Katia leaned into William. "We were out in the garden chatting with Christophe just now."

Alistair nodded. "Okay, but that leaves Madeline without a partner."

Madeline caught Katia's glance at William — they were hiding something.

"I wouldn't worry about it, Madeline," said Katia as she slunk over to the sofa. "He won't exclude you. You're too much of a teacher's pet." Katia's voice dripped with scorn.

"Teacher's pet? Excuse me? I'm here to do the work just like you are."

"No one doubts your sincerity, Madeline," William said. "But it's annoying how you stare at him during his lectures."

That hurt. What did it matter how she stared at Christophe? And what were they doing watching her staring at him? It was like being back in high school. "I don't care what you think of me."

"Don't get them in a bunch," Katia sneered. "But I'm sure you noticed he's partnered with Victoria?" Katia's voice went up at the end, teasing her.

"Fine, you can play these games—I'm finished." Madeline picked up the diagram and walked to her room. Why did she allow Katia to un-nerve her? She stopped at her bedroom door, humiliated because she knew they were right. She was too much of a teacher's pet. As much as Alistair made her feel admired, she wanted to be seen by their teacher. Was that so wrong?

⊷⊶ 13 ⊷⊶

Manny & Jennifer Acosta's home, Corte Madera — 10:15 a.m.

Hunter suppressed a yawn while Vierra drove through Corte Madera, another enclave of the well-moneyed. They spent most of Monday night following up leads and filling out paperwork when Hunter received a call from the Missing Persons department: they identified their boy as Jonathan Acosta, and they drove to his parent's home.

Vierra pulled into the driveway of a modest 1970s single-family home already suffering from neglect: a sagging shingle roof, a tired paint job on the exterior, and uneven paving stones leading from the street. An unexpected eyesore in an otherwise expensive neighborhood. After Vierra parked, Hunter exited the car, knowing they were going to make the pain worse. As they approached the house, another inconsistency tugged at him. "We're a long way from Russian Hill, Audrey. How did our victim end up so far from home?"

"I'm stumped. Teenagers are ubering to crime scenes, too." Vierra sighed.

At the front door, Vierra rang the bell, and they both heard fast-moving footsteps on the hardwood floors. The front door swung open, revealing a small woman with unwashed blonde hair. She took several moments to focus, her crystal blue eyes rimmed red from crying. And in the next moment, she knew.

"Mrs. Acosta?" Vierra asked.

"Yes." Her voice cracked.

"I'm Investigator Daniel Vierra, and this is my partner, Hunter Davis. May we come in?"

"Is this about Jonathan?" She asked, her voice a high-pitched squeak.

"Yes, ma'am."

Hunter caught the sigh underneath Vierra's standard cop voice. Mrs. Acosta put her hand to her mouth, but even in her grief, she remembered her manners and opened the door wider. She ushered her guests inside like a proper hostess, but her mis-buttoned blouse and inside-out yoga pants told another story.

In the entryway, Hunter witnessed the realization crash through Mrs. Acosta. She staggered, unbalanced, toward a nearby chair, her knees crumbling beneath her.

Hunter kept her from falling and shuffled her to the chair. "I'm so sorry, ma'am. I realize how terrible this is. Please, take all the time you need. But, when you're ready, we need you to come and identify … to identify Jonathan."

Still unbalanced, she slid off the edge of the chair onto the floor, pulling an old, faded blue baby blanket down with her and burying her face in it. She needed more than a moment.

Hunter scanned the room. The entryway led to a remodeled kitchen; the counters filled with food and spices, cereal boxes, and snacks. An open living room and a window with a million-dollar view. Hunter's chest ached. These were ordinary people living the life they could afford in a neighborhood that didn't know what to do with them.

"I … I need to tell my husband," Mrs. Acosta gulped. "Can he come too?"

"Of course. We can drive you down, and he can meet us at the Medical Examiner's office if that's easier." Vierra said.

Hunter found a tissue and gave it to her. She cleaned her face. "I'm so sorry, I … he's our only child. He was our miracle," she sobbed into the tissue.

Hunter checked out the mantle with all those happy family photos. Mrs. Acosta, the petite, fair-skinned blonde next to her tall, rugged husband, sporting dark hair and green eyes, but Jonathan didn't look like them. He had dark brown hair, almond-shaped eyes, and pale skin. Hunter pointed to the photo. "Did you and your husband adopt Jonathan?"

Mrs. Acosta, more alert. "Yes, we tried on our own for years. None of the treatments worked, and we'd given up on having a family when we got the news."

"Did you use a private agency?" Vierra asked.

"No, we worked with a family attorney my husband…" The tears returned. "Oh god, I have to call Manny."

Hunter noticed a cell phone on a nearby counter. "Do you remember the attorney's name?"

"Oh, it was so long ago, I know it was Polish sounding."

He brought her the phone. "Take your time."

Mrs. Acosta took the phone in both hands and gathered her courage.

"While you speak to your husband, may we look at Jonathan's room?" Hunter asked.

"Yeah," Vierra added, "it will help our investigation if we get to know more about Jonathan's life."

"It's the first door down the hall," Mrs. Acosta pointed the way.

"Thank you, we won't be long. Take all the time you need to speak with your husband." Hunter said as he and Vierra crossed the living room toward the hall.

Hunter entered Jonathan's room, assaulted by the pungent scent of boy - a mixture of dirty gym socks, a faint whiff of airplane glue, and a hint of perfumed body wash. Comic book art, posters, and astrology artwork lined the walls, but over his bed, a giant poster of a Tarot card titled: "The World."

The tarot card left Hunter clueless, not understanding how to interpret it. He pulled out his phone and took a photo of the image: a woman floating in the air, a purple scarf around her nude body, surrounded by a green wreath. Four smaller images in each corner included a man with a blond head, a bird, a lion, and a bull. Madeline would explain it to him if she were here. Jonathan gazed at this poster every day. Did he put it there because he thought the world was his to conquer? Did it excite him, make him think his world was filled with possibilities?

Then Hunter noticed a small stuffed elephant sitting on a table. Hunter picked it up, and he felt Jonathan's unspoken hesitation in crossing the threshold into adulthood.

"Where do you want to start?" Vierra asked.

"All these kids live on their computers, I'll start there. You take the closet and the dresser?"

"You got it."

Hunter put on latex gloves and sat on Jonathan's rickety old chair. Picking through the cluttered desktop, he found school notebooks for algebra, civics, and English. He pulled open the desk drawer and rooted around until he found a small black notebook.

"There's nothing unusual in the closet. He's got way too many socks but no hidden weed or C4," Vierra said, joining Hunter at the desk.

"What? No young-terrorist kit? Any supplies for a homemade bomb?" Hunter flipped through the pages.

"Don't tell me a fifteen-year-old already uses a little black book? Don't they keep everything on their phones? We didn't find a phone at the crime scene, did we?"

"No, I didn't see one. Connie found it when she unwrapped him." Hunter flipped through more pages. "Ah, this isn't a black book for girls. It's his password keeper." Hunter turned on Jonathan's computer and waited for it to boot up.

"Let's bring the computer in and let the tech guys crack it open?"

"Okay but let me try something." Hunter spotted a list of crossed-out passwords and entered the last one on the home screen. It worked.

"Hallelujah for small favors," Vierra said.

Hunter opened a folder on the desktop labeled "Christophe Master File."

"Oh shit," Vierra said. "Do I want to see this?"

Hunter scrolled through the multiple text, audio, and video files. "Jonathan is a big Savvy Seeker fan."

"Man, what is all this stuff?" Vierra asked. "We gotta bring it to the lab."

"Agreed but look. He's got a vlog folder." Hunter opened it and found the most recent entry. He hit play.

Jonathan's face filled the frame. "So, I have to say," Jonathan began, his voice animated as he gestured with his hands. "I'm thinking the Hammarskjold quote is the key to the entire code. 'Our work for peace must begin within the private world of each of us. To build for man a world without fear, we must be without fear. To build a world of justice, we must be just.'" Hunter paused the video.

"What the hell? This kid is fifteen, for Christ's sake," Vierra said. "This kid should be scrolling porn sites and playing video games, not worrying about building a world of justice."

Hunter found himself drawn to the earnest expression on Jonathan's face. A sudden pang hit him. What man would Jonathan have become?

"What's going on? I heard Jonathan's voice." Mrs. Acosta rushed into the room, wiping tears away with a tissue. Hunter stood up.

"I'm so sorry, Mrs. Acosta," Vierra said, facing her. "We found a video Jonathan made. Did you know about these?"

"Yes … He wanted to start a YouTube channel. He hoped to get Christophe's attention."

"Do you know why?" Hunter asked.

"I didn't understand any of it. Something about taking Christophe's meditations and turning them into a video game…" She shook her head. "Well, not a game so much as a puzzle. I wanted to encourage him, but I wanted him to focus on his schoolwork, too." She stared at the frozen image of her son on the computer screen.

"Thank you," Vierra said. "I am sorry, but we'll have to take his computer to our lab. It might have information on it that links to his killer."

"What?!" She sat down at the computer. "It's his personal life. He had everything on it." She touched her son's digital face on the screen.

"How about we leave it here for now?" Hunter said. "I'll send a lab technician to make a duplicate of his hard drive. Is that okay?"

"Yes, if you don't mind. I promise I won't touch any of the files."

"We trust you. We'll return it to you as soon as possible."

"Yes. That'll be fine, thank you." She kept gazing at the screen.

"Mrs. Acosta, what else can you tell us about Jonathan? Anyone new come into his life? How are his grades?" Vierra asked.

She kept staring at the computer screen, at her baby. Then she tilted her head and stared into space.

Hunter felt they were losing her again. "Mrs. Acosta? Are you okay?"

She waved a hand in front of her face. "Please, call me Jennifer. I remember something. Last year, a man came to visit Jonathan."

"Did you know this guy?" Vierra asked.

Jennifer kept puzzling over it. "I'm not exactly sure … He and Jonathan were talking when I came home. He introduced himself, but I can't get the name. It was Chinese." She turned to Vierra. "The man was Chinese. Jonathan's adoption was closed, but he had one of those DNA tests done, and he has a lot of Chinese from his birth parents. He got all excited and started looking into Chinese social clubs. You know? The ones that teach Kung Fu and do all the lion dances?"

"Of course," Hunter said. "Did the gentleman recruit Jonathan for a club?"

"That's what he said, but after he left, Jonathan went and sulked in his room and never mentioned it again."

"Can you describe the man?" Hunter asked.

Jennifer tried to remember, then turned to Hunter. "He was a couple of inches shorter than you. Stocky but muscular, and he had long black hair tied in a tight knot. But he had a kind face. That's all I can remember."

"If you can come up with a name, we'd appreciate it," Vierra said.

She reached out and touched the image of her son's face on the computer screen.

Hunter put his hand on her shoulder. "Why don't you come with us. Okay?"

Jennifer Acosta's chest caved. Although she nodded, she still kept her hand on the image of Jonathan's face, unable to let go.

14

KXOP Newsroom — 10:25 a.m.

Cora carried her quadruple espresso and hurried back toward the newsroom. At the coffee shop, she spotted a couple of alternative newspaper racks, which made her wonder about other sources of crime reporting in San Francisco. Back at her workstation, she checked on Amy's list of blogs. Most sent a pre-programmed "thank you for subscribing" note, but not much else. Using some creative word searches, she found other Bay Area crime bloggers, a community-based TV show, and an alternative newspaper or two. She bookmarked several of them, subscribed to a few, and followed a couple on Twitter.

She scrolled the news sites, looking for anything about the Russian Hill murder, when she spotted an old headline: "Investigator Vierra alleged to be involved with a mobster's wife." She scanned the article but glanced over at Amy at the assignment desk. "Morning, Amy."

"So, what happened at the Hall of Justice yesterday?" Amy asked.

Cora's shoulders drooped, and she tried to keep some enthusiasm in her voice. "I met Investigator Vierra. He didn't deny he and Investigator Hunter Davis are on the Russian Hill case. And Davis spoke with my sister, Madeline, the astrologer from yesterday morning. But she won't tell me what they talked about."

Amy's lips curved into a small, impressed smile. "That's an interesting angle. The police released the victim's name—Jonathan Acosta," she said, reading it from the computer screen. "It's a kid from up in Corte Madera, but that's it. Bob told me to toss the story back to Ned. He'll add it to a crime wrap-up."

Cora wasn't ready to let it go. "So, was the boy murdered? And isn't Corte Madera way up in Marin somewhere? What's he doing getting killed on Russian Hill?"

Amy leaned back in her chair. "That's a good question, but that's one for an experienced police reporter to answer."

Cora got the inference. "But—"

"No buts. You've done a bit of sleuthing. Now you have to let the grownups take it from here." Amy picked up a piece of paper from her desk. "But I need you to run something into studio C for me." Amy leaned toward Cora. "It's my famous Zucchini Bread recipe. Give it to Cheryl. She's been asking for it."

Confused, Cora accepted the page. "Okaaaay?"

Amy chuckled. "Hey, I know it sucks to be an intern. This is one perk I can offer you. They're interviewing Christophe in Studio C in about thirteen minutes. Head on down and give me the scoop later."

Cora couldn't believe her luck. "Wow, thank you." She said and held the Zucchini Bread recipe to her chest, treating it as a blessed, holy document.

Cora rushed from the newsroom and put on her best innocent intern face as she arrived at the studio door. People gathered on both sides of the hallway, hoping to glimpse the reclusive self-help guru. She peered in the studio door and found Cheryl, a tall black woman wearing a matching fawn suit and trousers. "Hi, are you Cheryl?"

"I am, aren't you one of Amy's?"

"Yeah, I'm Cora. She asked me to give this to you?" Cora handed over the recipe.

Upon seeing it, Cheryl grinned. "Yes! She finally got around to it. Thank you. You gonna stick around?"

"Weeell"—Cora drew out the word — "I'd love to watch the interview."

"Your timing is spot on," Cheryl said, with a wink. "Here he comes."

Cora turned as the people in the hall pressed themselves to the wall as the entourage barreled through. Leading the group, a tall man with black hair and goatee, wearing a gorgeous Italian worsted wool suit. Cora stepped further back as a flashing-eyed Latina woman with high, arching eyebrows moved past her. She styled her hair in a gorgeous updo and wore a flowing silk dress—an abstract pattern of golds, greens, and coral shades that blended beautifully with her caramel-colored skin and blonde highlights. Christophe followed her.

Sensing the energy coming from Christophe, Cora gained a new understanding of the phrase "star power." The energy came off him in waves, and she and everyone crammed in that hallway knew it. But the man himself seemed oblivious to the impact he made on the crowd, or at least pretended to be. He wore what Cora thought of as "guru casual." Faded blue gabardine trousers, a little worn at the knees but tailored for his exact frame. He also wore a pale blue chambray shirt. She read an Esquire article on chambray shirts, which had to be the most expensive on the list. His entire ensemble accentuated his dazzling China-blue eyes.

The Latina woman halted before Cora and tapped Christophe's shoulder to get his attention. Christophe shifted his gaze and halted upon seeing Cora. As he glanced in her direction, his eyes shone with a fierce brilliance, making her feel exposed with nowhere to run. The Latina woman offered Cora her hand. "Hello, I'm Miranda, and who are you?"

Cora opened her mouth, but Bob made a quick introduction. "Yes, Christophe, this is one of our interns, Cora."

Cora found her voice, "Hi. It's a pleasure. I'm Cora Merritt."

Hearing her name, Christophe, and the woman both exchanged a curious glance. Cora looked at Bob. Had she done something wrong?

"Did you say, Merritt?" Christophe asked, his voice a soft hush.

"Yes," she squeaked.

Miranda whispered in Christophe's ear, "The sister."

Christophe nodded, his condescending smile resembling an adult who humors a clever child. "Nice to meet you," he said, extending his hand. Cora shook it, surprised at the firm grip, and felt as if he read her life story in one handshake. He dropped her hand and joined his people as they entered the studio. Once Christophe finished examining her, Cora realized she had been holding her breath.

"Mind telling me what all that was about?" Cheryl asked.

Cora shrugged. "I'm just as clueless as you are."

"What was Miranda talking about?"

"Haven't the foggiest. They think I'm cult material," she said, filling her voice with sarcasm to keep Cheryl from asking more.

"Well, since you made such an impression, come watch the interview from the control room," she pulled open a heavy door.

"Wow, thank you." Cora followed her into the darkened room, lit only by a floor-to-ceiling wall of TV monitors. A handful of people sat at a long desk filled with lights, sliders, and flashing gadgets. Cheryl pulled over an office chair, and Cora took a deep breath and sat down. What did Miranda mean when she called her, "The sister?" Cora knew they must be referring to Madeline, yet Madeline never told her anything about meeting Christophe. How were they connected?

Cheryl pulled up her own chair at the expansive control panel, gathered up her script and, in hushed tones, spoke with the show director. The banks of monitors showed the program on the air, along with shots from all the studio cameras. Cora watched as Christophe came onto the set, a simple arrangement of two chairs and a table between them, all set up on an oval-shaped platform.

Christophe, a microphone clipped to his lapel, made himself comfortable in the chair. He scanned the cameras and took in the studio as if he were on television all the time. The interviewer, a guy named Patrick, one of the regular news anchors, took his place and spoke to Christophe, going over his plan for their interview. Cora texted Amy about being invited to watch the interview. Amy texted back, telling her to enjoy it.

The air in the control room shifted as the director spoke up, saying they were about to start. The floor director counted the hosts in, and the interview was live. Patrick introduced Christophe and thanked him for coming. After a few softball questions, he switched it up: "So, tell us, Christophe, you have mentioned on your website that Savvy Seekers is planning a spectacular event for the city of San Francisco on the day of the total solar eclipse. Can you tell us about it?"

Christophe paused half a beat. "With great pleasure." Another momentary pause, where he made eye contact with Patrick. "We are a global company, and we're forging relationships with farmers and artisans all over the world. And in our travels and here at home, we have experienced the devastation of colonization. We're still suffering the effects of the first missionaries who came to Yerba Buena before it was called San Francisco."

Cora noticed Patrick leaning in, mesmerized by Christophe's voice, with its husky edge and hypnotic cadence, enunciating every word. No wonder he made a fortune on guided meditations. "But that was over two hundred years ago. What are you proposing to do about it now?" Patrick asked.

Pausing again, Christophe continued, "On August twenty-first there will be a total solar eclipse with the sun in the astrological sign Leo. Leo is a fire sign, and in our practices, the fire element is one of cleansing and purification."

"Are you going to purify the city somehow?" Patrick couldn't hide the skepticism in his voice.

Christophe dismissed Patrick's attitude and pulled up taller in his chair while never losing his focus. "In a few words, yes, we are. We have all witnessed how our beautiful city suffers from low vibrational energy. Homeless people are running amok in parts of Market Street and the Tenderloin. This low-frequency vibration was caused by the massacre of the Yelamu tribes who used to flourish in those same areas."

Patrick couldn't suppress his reaction but did his best to be impartial. "So, you're saying that somehow, during the total solar eclipse, you're going to solve the city's homeless problem? Excuse me, but that sounds farfetched."

"Ah, Patrick, but remember. San Francisco was once the city of flower power and free love." Christophe said, smiling. "Our plan is simple. Our students are learning how to work with energy, and we will have over five hundred of them starting at Grace Cathedral, positioned around the Cathedral, and going all the way down to Market Street. As the eclipse begins, they will perform what are called energetic passes. And they will continue to do so during the entire eclipse. Yes, to the uninitiated, it sounds insane, but it's time for another energetic renaissance in the city by the bay, the city we love so much."

Cora noticed Patrick nodding, taking in the plan, imagining it in his own mind. Cora saw it, too, not hundreds, but thousands of people moving in unison. It was weird. But intriguing at the same time.

"That's going to be a spectacle, for sure. Over 500, what are you calling them, dancers?" Patrick asked.

"Meditators," Christophe replied. "They will be in a state of deep meditation when they begin. You will be covering the event, and we are offering a live stream from the Cathedral and expect thousands of our students from all over the globe to join in. The energy will be palpable."

Cora's phone vibrated. A text from Amy asked her to come back to the newsroom. Cora thanked Cheryl and headed out of the control room. She couldn't wait to tell Amy about Christophe's plan and hoped she'd have the chance to watch the live coverage. But what about Madeline? She tucked that thought away until the next time she saw her sister.

····⊷·‹15›··⊷····

Office of the Medical Examiner — 12:45 p.m.

Hunter leaned back, one leg against the wall, holding a cold cup of coffee. He was across from Jonathan's father, Manny, who sat in a chair in a small waiting room at the Medical Examiner's office. They identified Jonathan's body and agreed to answer more questions. Manny bore a strong resemblance to Vierra — they shared the same skin coloring, and short, curly black hair going gray at the temples. Jennifer sat next to Manny, who put his arm around his wife's shoulder, each doing their best to be strong for the other. The grieving couple tried to remain present, but Hunter felt the heartache eating at their souls. Jonathan's autopsy was scheduled for tomorrow, so they didn't know how the boy had died.

Vierra took the lead. "Again, we are so sorry for your loss, but we have some important questions."

Manny squeezed his wife's arm but said nothing. Sitting across the room from the couple, Vierra made eye contact with Hunter, who nodded, signaling Vierra to nudge the conversation.

"When was the last time you saw Jonathan, Mrs. Acosta?"

"Again, please, call me Jennifer." She sat up straighter, adjusting a strand of hair from her face. "He went to a party Saturday night. He said he might spend the night at a friend's house afterward."

"Did he often stay out over the weekend?" Hunter asked.

Jennifer shook her head. "No, he was a homebody. Everything he loved was in that room. His computer, his books. Every so often, he'd go to a friend's house after school, but he never slept over."

Manny nodded in agreement. "Yeah, he was the best kid. We trusted him to let us know where he was going."

"Sounds like a responsible young man," Vierra added.

Jennifer nodded and rubbed a soggy tissue to her eyes as fresh tears came.

Hunter grabbed the box of tissues from a side table and placed it next to her. "Can you tell us where the party was?"

Jennifer wiped her hand away. "Oh, with those kids, you never know. They go from one party to another. He sent me a weird text about spending the night at Frank's house. Which was unusual. When he didn't come home, I called all his friends, but nobody knew what happened to him. I didn't know who Frank was. I told the police when we filed the missing person's report."

Hunter read the report, and according to the officers handling the case, neither Frank nor any of the partygoers knew when Jonathan had left the party or whether he'd left alone or with other friends. "Did he have regular friends he hung out with? His gang, so to speak?"

After a pause, Jennifer nodded. "Everybody liked Jonathan. He always made friends. Mostly, he hung out with Lance and Electra—he'd known her since elementary school. And Stellan came over a lot. They'd be in Jonathan's room for hours. Talking and making their weird videos, but then Stellan disappeared. He made other friends, so it was surprising when Jonathan asked to go to a party with Stellan."

"Did he give you an explanation?" Vierra asked.

Jennifer shook her head. "I didn't ask. I figured it was time to quit hovering so much, you know? Let him decide for himself. Now I wish I hadn't."

Hunter saw the emotion swell in her. They couldn't keep this up much longer, so he changed the subject. "Can you tell us more about the adoption process?"

Manny and Jennifer exchanged a glance. Manny leaned back, pulling his arm away from Jennifer's shoulder. Hunter picked up on it and glanced at Vierra, who spotted it too. Jennifer answered. "It was unusual. A family friend recommended a lawyer. As I mentioned, it was a private adoption."

"Were there any … problems?" Vierra asked.

"No, not at all," Manny said, "other than being expensive … we were desperate. I got the call one night, and everything happened so fast…. We met the lawyer outside of a church in Bernal Heights. Saint Anthony's, if I recall."

"But don't get us wrong," Jennifer interrupted, waving her hands. "It was a legal adoption. We signed all the papers in the lawyer's office but when we picked him up …. We felt kind of like criminals, like it was a drug deal or something."

Hunter jotted the details in his portfolio and nodded at Vierra, telegraphing to him this needed investigating.

"But we brought him home," Jennifer continued, "and he's been our delight ever since." Her voice cracked on the word "delight," and she wept. Manny leaned over and helped her to stand.

"One last thing." Hunter asked. "Do you remember the lawyer's name?"

"Something Polish? Grudzinski. I will check our records to be sure," Manny said.

Hunter noted that the lawyer's name might be important, but they couldn't push these people too hard.

Manny held his wife to him and glared at Vierra and Hunter. "You're gonna get this bastard, right?"

"Yes," Vierra said, "yes, we are."

Hunter could only nod in agreement, and scribbled another random note, hoping the Acostas wouldn't pick up his sense of doubt. Watching them leave, he felt the solution getting further and further away from him.

16

Hunter's Point — 6:36 p.m.

"God, I hate coming here," Vierra said for the five-hundredth time as they arrived at the Hunter's Point crime lab. The day was ending, and Hunter's mood matched the gloomy lab location. Vierra was toast, yawning every fifteen minutes.

The SFPD crime lab was built on a federal Superfund waste site at the Hunter's Point Naval Shipyard, and visiting the lab was a dicey undertaking. If the rumors about the place were true, no one should be there. The SWAT team was also housed there, and lots of the SWAT guys complained about exposure to toxins.

Walking past a row of date palms at the entrance, Hunter could only imagine what kind of toxic chemicals were in the tree sap. The complex gave him a major case of the heebie-jeebies, which lasted as they passed through the building to an evidence examination room. Connie waved them inside. Several massive tables took up the center of the room, all covered in plastic sheeting. The quilt from Jonathan's crime scene lay unfurled on the tabletop. Connie rigged up a camera wired to the computer that stood over the quilt for closer examination.

"Miss Connie, please tell me the killer embroidered his name in giant letters on this thing. Make our job a little easier?" Vierra asked as he pulled up a stool near the table.

"No dice. Sorry." Connie said as she examined her computer screen. Out of her PPE, she'd pulled her pale blonde hair back in a loose ponytail. She scrunched up her slender frame on her chair, perched like an owl on a branch. "Okay, I have the camera set so we can examine the quilt close up on the screen."

As Hunter leaned over, he couldn't help but marvel at the meticulous stitching and attention to detail on the quilt, which was stretched out to its full size. In the center, the embroidered lines of text radiated out as if each track were a ray of light coming from the center of the sun. Made of a mosaic of tie-dyed fabric, the colors in the quilt transitioned seamlessly from light yellow and orange in the center to various shades of green in the middle section and finally to blues, violets, and ultramarines at the edges. All very hippy-dippy, like something you'd see in a shop in the Haight—or in Madeline's storeroom. Hunter's thoughts floated back to her, but he reeled them in. Focus, pal.

"So, what are we looking at with all these aphorisms?" Vierra said, twisting his head to read them.

"*Affirmations*, asshole," Hunter bristled, too tired to find humor in his partner's ignorance.

"These aren't affirmations," Connie said. She turned on a projector, and Hunter looked up at a screen on the opposite wall, now filled with an image from the quilt. "You can read them better this way."

Connie zoomed in, bringing one line of text into sharp focus. Hunter moved closer to the screen and read the line aloud: "Failure is the key to the kingdom within - Rumi."

"What? I thought affirmations were positive. And if failure is the key, I should be king by now," Vierra said.

"Weren't you listening?" Connie chastised Vierra. "These are quotes from enlightened thinkers." She moved the camera once again so they could read the next one:

Buy terms divine in selling hours of dross;
Within be fed, without be rich no more:
So shalt thou feed on Death, that feeds on men,
And Death once dead, there's no more dying then.
—W Shakespeare, Sonnet CXLVI

Hunter felt his gut tighten up. "'Feed on Death that feeds on men?' What the hell, Connie?"

"Fuck, don't tell me our Astroguy has embedded a cipher in this?" Vierra added.

Connie came around, lifting her safety glasses. "No, I don't think so. There are twelve of them from a variety of spiritual teachers. There's Carlos Castaneda, Pablo Neruda, Dag Hammarskjold—"

"Dog, what?" Vierra couldn't help himself.

"Don't you read?" Connie's annoyance was showing. "He was Secretary-General of the United Nations until his plane went down in Africa."

Vierra held up his hands in appeasement. "Sorry, no, my collection of United Nations Chairman action figures is far from complete."

Connie shook her head. "But that's not the important thing. These quotes are the backbone of Christophe's meditation and lecture series. It's called *The Masters Speak*. It put him on the map. Look it up."

While Vierra grabbed his phone and did a quick search, Hunter studied the lettering on the quilt: very precise, all evenly spaced. "This doesn't look hand-made. Is it?"

"No, it's machine embroidered," Connie said as she moved the camera, searching for another quote. "Savvy Seekers doesn't sell this one anymore. Their catalog says one of his early fans came up with the idea. It looks like Astroguy, as you are calling him, wants to get Savvy Seekers' attention."

"Is there any kind of stock number or bar code here?" Vierra asked.

Connie shook her head. "I haven't found one. I could rip it open and look inside, but that would ruin it. I've seen the real ones, and they embroider the stock number along one corner, along with the owner's name."

"Here, I found it," Vierra said and read from his phone in a smarmy radio DJ voice: "The Twelve Masters Speak, a twelve-part lecture series by Christophe. Enter the minds of the world's greatest teachers as Christophe delivers his land-mark lecture set. On CD or digital download. It cost three hundred and fifty dollars?" Vierra's eyes widened.

"And worth every penny, if you ask me," Connie said as she threw her shoulders back, bracing for Vierra's next retort.

"You? Seriously, Connie?" Vierra asked.

"You don't have to buy the complete set. You should try them. They include guided meditations. They helped me get off my anxiety medications."

Hunter turned to her. "Anxiety—you?"

Connie popped her head forward and drew her shoulders back in a 'duh' gesture. "I work at a toxic waste dump site. Of course, I have anxiety. Plus, I have to put up with boneheads like this one."

Vierra opened his mouth and mimed being offended. "Okay, while I still have a brain cell to work with, can we look at the big picture? What is Astroguy saying here? Is he warning us about death, like he's got more planned?"

"You got me," Connie said. "That's your job, genius. I process what I find at the crime scene."

"But you are familiar with this guy Christophe's work," Hunter said, keeping things from going sideways. "Why does he talk so much about death?"

"But they aren't all about death." Connie went back to the camera. "Here's one that's my favorite."

The self-confidence of the warrior is not the self-confidence of the average man. The average man seeks certainty in the eyes of the onlooker and calls that self-confidence. The warrior seeks impeccability in his own eyes and calls that humbleness. The average man is hooked to his fellow men, while the warrior is hooked only to infinity. It's from Carlos Castaneda."

Hunter read the words, but the meaning floated above his head, circling in a pattern — impeccability, humbleness, self-confidence. He tried to pull them down and digest them, but instead of providing inspiration, the quotation meant more work.

"You're gonna have to buy me a couple of rounds of scotch before I can wrap my head around this one, Connie," Vierra said.

"How about this? I'll type these all up and email them to you. You can read them when you're at the bar."

"Yeah, you, me, Hunter, and the dog guy. We'll all meet up at Café Macaroni. Hunter's buying."

Hunter turned to Connie. "Ignore him. Can you send me the link to the meditations, along with photos of these quotes?"

"Of course. And I mean it, don't knock the meditations. They work."

Hunter smiled at her. "I don't doubt you, but the day I start meditating…." He stopped. The weight of the day, the mountain of work ahead of him tomorrow, and the weariness penetrated him. "Is the day I start meditating," he finished in defeat but stopped, examining the embroidery again. "Hey, Connie, do you know what this is?"

Connie and Vierra joined him. He pointed to a strange piece of embroidery at the lower right corner. A line drawing of an "X" with two lines making the right side of the letter into an arrow. From the center of the "X" ran a long line that had three short lines crossing it.

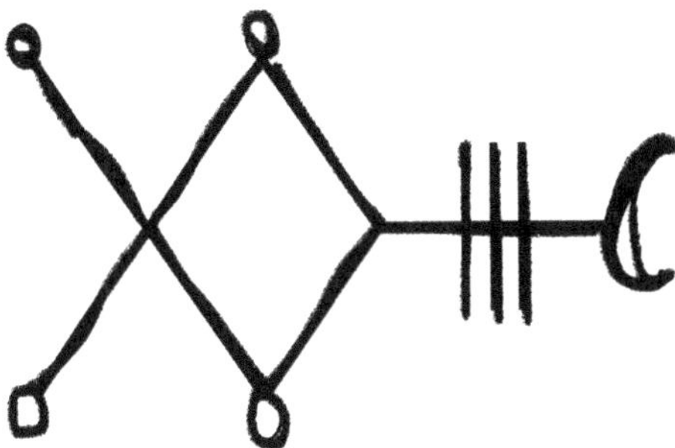

Connie zoomed in and the image filled the screen. "Not sure, I missed it the first time."

"It isn't another astrology symbol or something?" Vierra asked, squinting at the fabric on the table.

"Not that I know of. But I'll poke around and see if anything comes up."

"Thanks, Connie," Vierra said and yawned. "Sorry, guys, but I have to get going. Hunter, in the morning?"

Hunter knew where Vierra was headed but was too tired to argue. "Yeah, tomorrow, get some sleep," and his partner was gone.

"Is he still seeing the wife?" Connie asked.

Everyone wanted to gossip. "Sorry, Connie, it's all above my pay grade." She watched him, anticipating more, but he focused on the quilt. "Seriously, Connie. Why would Astroguy do this? Is it all just blowing smoke? Tell me about that quote you like. What do you think it means?"

Connie stood up and stretched. "Christophe puts it all in context. But the line about the warrior seeking impeccability in his own eyes—it's about setting a higher standard for yourself, no longer caring what other people think."

Hunter heard the conviction in her voice. "I get that, I do. But the killer wrapped this around the body of a teenager. A teenager. He wasn't a warrior. He wasn't anything yet, just all hormones, being a pain in the ass to his parents, and potential..." Hunter didn't need to share his frustration with her. "What's Astroguy saying with all of this?"

Connie crossed her arms over her chest. "That's why I'm not an investigator. I just process this stuff. You guys come up with the conclusions. I'm not your girl for this, Hunter."

Hunter nodded. "I'm sorry for bugging you."

"No, it's fine." Connie reached for her phone. "Hey, I gotta go check on something in the other lab. You okay here?"

"Yeah, let me hang for a minute, then I'll be on my way."

Connie smiled at him and turned to go, letting out a long sigh.

Hunter wasn't sure what the sigh meant. Relief from having to deal with him, or was it something else? Should he consider Connie's familiarity with Christophe's meditations a red flag? What was it about that guy that seemed to appeal to so many women? He knew he should leave, but he kept looking at the quilt, letting the colors and the shapes of the fabric dance before him. His eyes lingered on the peculiar symbol tucked away in the corner. He froze, feeling a chill run through him. He'd seen it before and knew where to find it.

17

Sirius Books — 9:26 p.m.

"On that kind note, I'll bid you all a splendid night," Toby Silva said to the audience gathered in the shop, applauding his lecture on the Templar knights. Madeline joined Toby at the little podium she'd set up for him. "Thank you so much for sharing your groundbreaking research with us. Everyone, another round of applause for our intrepid author." This time, the crowd stood, and Toby clasped his hands in front of his chest and bowed in appreciation.

Madeline steered her guest speaker to a small table with copies of his book, pens, and a glass of water. Those who wanted signed copies lined up, and he took a seat and dove in, meeting his readers with smiles and handshakes and listening patiently to their autograph requests. Madeline drew back, saying goodbyes to the shop regulars. The event worked its magic, a reminder of why she kept running the store. Seeing readers connect with a favorite author made her ever so happy. The evening had been a success: Toby had a loyal readership, and they did lots of shopping before the lecture started. Madeline took her place at the front counter in case of any last-minute purchases. She wondered if Toby would ask her out for a late-night drink again after she closed the store, and she wondered if she'd turn him down again, or not.

The last of Toby's fans wandered off. Madeline thanked the last of the attendees and locked the front door, leaving her alone with the author.

"Gosh, thanks again, Madeline. It's so nice to discuss this topic with a well-read group."

"Oh, the pleasure's all mine, Toby. Thanks for agreeing to do this."

Toby glanced up. Something at the door behind her had caught his attention. "You've got a last-minute straggler."

Madeline turned and gasped, spotting Hunter standing outside the shop, studying the sign that hung over the entrance. She paused, taking a deep breath, and willing her pounding heart to slow down. She made her excuse to Toby. "It's someone I know," she said, just as Hunter looked at her through the glass. "Hang on a sec."

She unlocked the door and opened it. "Hunter? This is a … surprise."

Madeline caught Hunter exchanging looks with Toby, so she pulled the door open and waved for him to enter. "This is Tobias Silva. He gave a lecture tonight. We were wrapping things up."

Hunter hesitated, but decided to come in. The two men shook hands with awkward energy, like prize fighters acknowledging each other, ready to engage in combat once the bell rang.

Madeline closed the door behind him, knowing this might throw a proverbial wrench into Toby's night. "Investigator Davis is a police officer working …." She stopped short, recovering. "He's an investigator."

Taking his cue, Toby gathered his coat and a copy of his latest book. "Oh my. Well, carry on. I don't want to interrupt police business, but here's a copy of my latest book. The Templar knights were the coppers of their day."

Madeline watched Hunter accept the book and nodded to Toby. "Thank you, that's very kind."

Madeline smiled at Toby and gave him a quick hug. "Thanks again."

"Brilliant. Good night then." Toby threw his jacket on and wandered into the night, looking less peppy than he had a few minutes earlier.

Madeline watched Toby walk away, steeling herself to face Hunter. When did she think of him as Hunter and not Investigator Davis? She went to the center of the shop and started closing the folding chairs. "What can I do for you?" she asked.

"May I help with those?" he asked as he joined her folding up the chairs.

"Oh, please. Don't bother. I can get it." He ignored her and soon had the rest of the chairs in a stack.

"Where can I put these?"

"We can stack them up here," Madeline said, joining him in the task and carrying a chair to a space between the shelves. "Matthew-Tabitha will help me put them into storage tomorrow." It only took them a few moments to finish the job, followed by awkwardly standing in the middle of the empty store. Hunter turned his attention to her, and she experienced that discomfort again, of being evaluated.

"Sorry," Hunter said, perhaps sensing her unease, "I didn't mean to interrupt you and your … friend—"

"It's all right. In fact, you saved me from hearing about his latest trip to New Zealand. I love the stories, but he tends to tell too many. Now, how can I help you, Hunter?"

"I won't keep you long. I have a quick question." He walked over to the window. "On your shop sign, there's a logo with a strange symbol? It looks like an X with a long tail and extra hash marks?"

Madeline felt a twinge of disappointment and realized she'd had this ridiculous idea that he came to the shop just to see her. She shoved that thought away and focused on his question. "That type of symbol is called a sigil. This one is for the star Sirius."

"Do all stars have one of those sigils?"

"The stars identified in ancient Mesopotamia do, but as for stars identified in this century, not. This is an ancient symbol from the early stargazers. Sirius is bright enough to be seen without a telescope."

"Does this one have any special meaning?"

Madeline smiled. "No. It's my Aunt Jane's little joke. She liked calling the store Sirius because those unfamiliar with the star would wonder why she sold serious books."

Hunter half snorted. "Oh, I get it. Serious."

"What brought this up? Why so curious?"

Hunter shifted his stance and scanned the store, taking time to form his answer. "I hate to repeat myself, but it's about the investigation. Sorry."

Madeline understood his reluctance to share more. "Sigils, astrology symbols … You are awash in clues."

He nodded with a shrug. "Running low on some, overwhelmed with others. Listen, I don't want to sound like a jerk, but I hope you don't mind me stopping by so late."

"Not at all. Your timing was perfect. Toby is one of those people who often takes forever to say goodbye. Here," she pulled out two of the folding chairs from the stack, "You look tired. Why not come and take a seat?"

Hunter took his chair, and they sat at right angles to each other. "So, has your sister asked you anything else about the case?"

Madeline remembered Cora's scene in the store. "No, we haven't talked. She's still mad at me."

Hunter changed his tone, leaning back. "Oh, I'm sorry, it's nothing to worry about. But would you mind explaining to your sister that we need to control what information we give to news outlets? It's tough enough as it is, without us getting calls from the neighborhood crackpots."

"Crackpots, like my customers? Conspiracy theorist and assorted crackpots?"

Hunter cracked a smile. "Hey, I didn't say that."

"But you were about to. I admit, we're a magnet for those folks." Madeline would not mention Alistair's visit. It didn't feel right to bring it up.

"Forgive my assumptions, and no disrespect to your sister. I'm sure she's a fine journalist."

Madeline crossed her arms and her legs. "No, she's not really a journalist. She's just an intern. But, if she plays by the rules, she has the tenacity for it. Once she goes after something, she's worse than a dog with a tennis ball."

Hunter smiled at her reference. "We should lure her to the dark side, make her a cop."

Madeline chuckled. "Not her cup of tea. She hates uniforms. She should report on fashion shows and pop culture, not hard news."

"Let me tell you, I have days when I wish I had that job. Is Boy George still a thing?"

Madeline relaxed. This was a good guy sitting across from her. "I have that chart for the 911 call ready if you'd like to look at it."

Hunter smiled but put up his hands. "Don't think I don't appreciate it, but I don't think my small brain could take in anything that complex. Can we save it for a day or two? When can you brief my partner and my boss?"

"Of course, that's fine. Would they both come here?"

"You should come to the Hall. I'll arrange for a driver if you need one?"

Madeline swallowed and smiled. "No, I can get there. That's no problem." But it was a problem: she didn't know how to act in front of police officers, especially when explaining an astrology chart, but she didn't want him to notice her panic. She focused on Hunter while he studied the books in the shop, puzzling over the titles. What did he need?

Hunter waved his arm toward the books. "This will sound weird, but I want to know more about all of this. You joked about conspiracy theorists but tell me more about your customers." Hunter stood, walked over to a shelf, picked up a book on shamanism, and flipped the pages. One page caught his attention. He held the book open to a photo of a shaman deep in trance, his eyes rolled back into his head. "I'm sorry, but this looks like he's on a trip to crazy town."

Madeline repressed a grin, recalling one of Aunt Jane's remarks about books finding their reader even if the reader rejects the book. "Or is it a trip to deep spiritual communion? Who knows?" She sensed a combination of wonder mixed with frustration from him. "But that's not a topic that interests you, is it?"

He shrugged, tilting his head from side to side. "It's not a topic for everyday conversation, but how far do you go? Look at my ex-wife. She got all caught up in the guy, Christophe, from Savvy Seekers. You must have heard of him?"

Madeline let out a long sigh, hoping he wouldn't read too much into it. "We get his customers all the time. I'm sorry about your wife. Did she buy all the meditations? The lip balm? Did she go a little overboard?"

He stepped away from the bookcase. "In a word, yes. She listened to his meditations every day and went on about how enlightened he was." He reached for a book off a shelf but returned it. "I don't even want to tell you how much she spent on his stuff. She started taking supplements, went to classes at night. She told me she was growing and that our marriage was holding her back. It went downhill from there." A sudden agitation got him pacing the room and examining the books again. "But that's not it. I mean all these books."

Madeline stood and took a chance. "You want answers?"

Hunter nodded vigorously and smiled. He exaggerated his desire, raising his arms as if pleading to the heavens. "Yes, I'd like some answers!"

Grinning at his antics, Madeline waved him toward another part of the shop. "Okay, grasshopper, follow me." Hunter followed her. "You're not alone. Everyone who's ever stepped foot in this shop wants answers."

"Damn, and here I thought I was special."

She led him to a set of bookcases from the floor to the ceiling. "This is the astrology section. These books represent millennia of people wanting answers.

Will I land the dream job? Should I move? What's in my future?"

Hunter stood opposite her and leaned against the bookshelf. "So, what answers do they give you?"

Madeline straightened a book and wiped off imaginary dust. "Do you want my genuine answer or the Hallmark version?"

"Let's start with Hallmark."

"Okay. Here it is. You already know the answers. For the important questions, your instincts will tell you what's right."

Hunter shook his head, still smiling. "Damn, I should have seen that one coming. You mean I can already identify the killer?"

"Not consciously, no." She paused and tapped a book on horary astrology. "There is an astrology technique that lets you ask important questions, but it is very complex and takes a lot of work. The results can get convoluted if you don't know what you're doing. So, I'd say no, but I can conclude that your killer has studied these books and somewhere, somehow, he or she decided murder was the answer to their problem."

He traced his fingers along the spine of a book and nodded his head while allowing the silence to fill the space between them. "You've got that right. And he or she bombarded us with a mountain of clues. I confess I'm in overwhelm mode."

She touched his shoulder. "But you've been at this a long time. I bet you follow hunches all the time." She felt his energy soften and kept her hand there a moment longer. "How long have you been on the job?"

Hunter gazed at the floor, tapping his foot against the bookcase. "I don't know. I lost count."

Watching him stare at the floor, Madeline sensed his regret, a regret he was unwilling to share with her, so she prattled on. "And in all those years, you've seen people come up with crazy answers to solve their problems. This person is no different. He had what he thinks is a perfect reason for killing your victim and for toying with you. Why do criminals take that risk?"

Hunter looked up. "They want attention. To be taken seriously."

"There you go. This guy thinks making you jump through hoops will solve something."

"And he's watching Vierra and me flail around. Frankly, it pisses me off."

Madeline wasn't sure what to say, so she stayed mute.

Hunter looked at her and caught himself for getting too worked up. "Hey, let's turn this around. Here's an idea. Can you do my chart? That way, I can see if this woo-woo stuff makes any sense?"

She had not expected that. A challenge filled with delight and trepidation. "All right. But do you trust me with your personal information?"

The corner of Hunter's mouth curved up, and he raised an eyebrow. "As long as you don't use it to hack my bank account?"

"Of course, I would never. But I can't vouch for my evil minions," she said with a wink.

Hunter smiled. "Then let's go for it. What do you need?"

She walked over to the front counter, and he followed her. "I need the date, time, and place where you were born." She grabbed a notepad and a pen.

"Hunter Davis, born on December 17, 1971, at 2:15 p.m. in Hunter, Nevada."

She stopped scribbling and stared. "Seriously?" She asked, scribbling his info down. "What's the story?"

"The family legend says Hunter is a ghost town. My parents were driving from Elko on their way to Reno, and my dad checked out the site. The town itself died back in the 1870s. My mom was pregnant, and while Dad was a tourist, she went into labor."

"You're kidding me?"

"Nope. And since they didn't know if they could get to a hospital in time, Dad busted out blankets from the trunk, all the water they'd brought, and I made my earthly debut," he bowed and mimicked doffing a hat.

Madeline chuckled at the image his story created. "I bet your mom tells that story all the time."

"No, it was my dad who told it. Until everyone got tired of hearing it." His phone beeped. "Hang on. Yeah?"

Madeline saw his shoulders slump down as he turned away from her. The fun was over.

"Okay, thanks, Al. We'll put it on the top of our list to do in the morning. Okay. Goodnight." Hunter stood up and pocketed his phone. "Sorry to cut this short, but... work."

Madeline had been enjoying their conversation, but insecurity crept in. "I'm glad you came by. I'll put your digits in the computer, and we can go over this some other time."

Hunter squared his shoulders and locked eyes with her. "I'm looking forward to that. And as for the 911 chart, how about I text you, and we can figure out a time for you to come to the office?"

Madeline smiled, "Absolutely. I'll have it ready for you."

"Great. Again, sorry for keeping you up late. Take care."

She hesitated and stood at the counter instead of walking him to the door. It felt safer having the counter to lean on. "You too," she said as he dashed out the door. Madeline didn't go to the window to watch him march down the street, hoping for another wave, hoping for a last moment of connection. Instead, she returned to the two folding chairs in the middle of the room. She sat down in her seat and let the encounter sink in.

⁓✷18✷⁓

WEDNESDAY, AUGUST 9, 2017

Polk Street — 8:24 a.m.

Madeline woke up tired; thoughts of Hunter's investigation filled her mind and played out as she popped into the corner coffee shop for her peppermint mocha. Someone left a copy of the San Francisco Chronicle on a nearby table. Most days, she'd leave it there, not wanting to waste her mental energy on the daily news, but her curiosity won the battle, and she flipped through the pages and stopped at a story about the boy found on Russian Hill. As she read the five paragraphs about Jonathan Acosta from Corte Madera, the details intrigued her, prompting her to follow up on the name. Acting on instinct, she grabbed her phone and snapped a photo of the page.

A text message popped up from Kess, one of her jewelry vendors. She'd forgotten that they planned to meet at the store. Grabbing her coffee and tossing her purse over her shoulder, she left the coffee shop and spotted Kess walking toward Sirius Books.

"Morning, Kess. It's good to see you. I can't wait to see what you have." She unlocked the store's front door. They both stepped inside, heading into the workspace behind the beaded curtains.

"Good to see you, Madeline. I got you some special charms for the upcoming eclipse. I hope you like them," Kess said. An older gentleman who still rocked the hippie vibe with his torn jeans, motorcycle vest over a white T-shirt, placed his battered leather case on the worktable. "I figured you'd get some interest in them." He unfurled the sleeve, revealing a series of rings, pendants, and bracelets, all with various sun and moon symbols in various combinations. The bracelets featured gold suns and silver moons with faces, with the moon on top of the sun's face, and they appeared to be kissing.

"Oh, I love these," Madeline said. "I'll take three of the full sets, a ring and pendant, and some extra bracelets. They are popular these days."

"Sure thing," Kess pulled out the jewels and placed them in plastic sleeves.

Madeline remembered the brooch. "Hey, can you do me a favor?" She dug into her purse.

"Of course, what do you need?" he asked as he continued to bag the jewelry pieces.

She pulled out the broken pin from her trip to Ina Coolbrith Park and brought it to the workroom. She held it up to the light for Kess to inspect. "I found this the other day. It's dirty, and the pin broke off and needs replacing. Could you spiff it up for me?"

Kess lifted the jewel up to his eye, examining the break. "Of course, no problem. I'll bring it by next week?"

"Perfect, and be sure to add the repair to my invoice?" she asked.

Kess winked, "I got your invoice right here," he pointed to his cheek.

Madeline smiled and gave him a quick peck. "You drive a hard bargain."

"It's a rough world out there, sister. Here you go." He handed her the jewels she requested, rolled up his leather pouch, and they both walked to the front door.

She said her goodbyes, then took the new jewelry pieces and added them to the eclipse display. Looking at the jeweled faces under the display lights, her thoughts returned to Jonathan. She couldn't help herself. Returning to her office, she sat at her desk and pulled up her customer database on her computer.

She scanned her subscriber list, found nothing, and then studied the online purchases. Because astrology was all about pattern recognition, she searched for any identifying patterns in customer purchases. Scrolling through the first page, she spotted *The Secret Language of Birthdays*, *The Only Astrology Book You'll Ever Need*, and this one always made her smile, *Astrology for Dummies*. Scrolling further down the list, a name jumped out at her: Acosta, Jonathan.

A jangling vagus nerve spasm shot through her. What the heck? He'd bought: "House Rulerships," "Predictive Astrology," and several academic texts on Tarot cards.

Madeline flashed to the 911 astrology chart and pulled it up on her screen. The Sun. This boy, brimming with potential, is brutally murdered. The weight of his death gathered on her shoulders.

"Oh, the shark babe has some teeth, dear," Matthew-Tabitha's basso profondo rang through the empty store as he came through the back door.

"MT, I'm in the office," she hollered.

She heard Matthew-Tabitha move through the work area and opened her office door. Matthew-Tabitha was in "boy" mode, wearing a multi-patterned western shirt over jeans and shit-kicker books. "Oh, mistress of destiny, I'm at your service."

"Come here," she waved him to join her at the computer. She turned the monitor for him to read the screen. "Do you remember this customer? Jonathan Acosta? Look at what he ordered?"

Matthew-Tabitha focused on the screen, eyebrows squished, he smiled, "yeah, a sweet man-child. He made me open the locked Tarot bookcase. You could tell he wanted to buy every single box. He finally settled on Thoth Tarot. Why? What's going on?"

Madeline pulled out her phone and found the photo she had taken of the news story. "That murder? Over in the park on Taylor. He's the victim."

Grabbing the phone, Matthew-Tabitha zoomed in the photo to read the print. "No. No way. Not that sweet kid?"

"I never met him. Was he nice?"

"Yes, a total sweetie pie," Matthew-Tabitha drew a chair over and sat. "He spoke with Geena, and they seemed to hit it off, although he seemed a lot younger than her. Damn."

Madeline sat back in her own chair, the bleakness of Jonathan's death simmering in her heart. What more could she do? She wished she'd had Jonathan's birth information. She could search his natal chart for answers. The aroma of warm cinnamon wafted in the room; Geena poked her head through the office door, carrying a small pastry box in one hand.

"Hi, I was hoping to bring some canelés from La Patissier, but they didn't have any. I brought some cinnamon rolls."

"How about you put them on the worktable in the back? Thank you, sweetness." Matthew-Tabitha said.

Geena paused. "Did you guys see Christophe's interview yesterday?"

Madeline froze. Her eyes darted to Matthew-Tabitha, but he shook his head and switched his attention to Geena. "No, what did he say?"

Geena twirled her hair around a finger. "He's celebrating the total solar eclipse by setting up like five hundred meditators around the city." She made air quotes with her hand, "To raise the energy so the city can heal. Sounds bogus. I'll put these in back and get some napkins," she said and slid out of the room.

Madeline stared at Matthew-Tabitha. "What the actual hell? Is she right about Christophe?"

Matthew-Tabitha threw his arms in a "bless me" manner. "Oh yeah. You should listen to my brothers and sisters at the Rosicrucian group. They are working themselves up something fierce."

"Why?"

"They didn't think of it first, and because he's going to draw energy from the Freemasons' ley lines."

"Which one?"

"That big tanker coming right off Mount Diablo, straight up to Grace Cathedral to the Masonic Temple next door. They have to be involved with this. Knowing that Christophe is involved, there's got to be some shady angle to it all."

Madeline considered Matthew-Tabitha's explanation. What was Christophe hoping to gain from this?

❖19❖

**"All the world knows that beauty is beauty, and this is ugliness.
—Lao Tzu**

Bernal Heights House – September 7, 2001
3 Days before The Ceremony 7:34 p.m.

Madeline kept reading the same passage but couldn't derive any meaning from it. She got off the bed, left Victoria studying her text, and headed out of their shared bedroom. She passed the dining room, where Miranda and Edgar studied a Tarot card spread. On her tippy toes, she snuck into what they called "Kitchen Gorgeous," another inside joke among the house dwellers because the room was, in fact, hideous.

Christophe had bought the rambler-cum-prairie-cum-tear-down-nightmare house in a foreclosure. With no money for remodeling, they managed with the outdated separate living, dining, and bedrooms without an open plan in sight. The kitchen was the worst, with its outdated 1950s plan and 1970s decor of burnt orange appliances and red brick detailing. Its saving grace was the size. Lili took over one side of the kitchen table where she made her special recipe lip balm, measuring the gooey concoction into cute, itty bitty glass jars.

On the opposite side, Katia washed the dishes at the sink, with a window that had a view of the backyard garden. The aroma of cinnamon and raisins filled the air as Brenda pulled a batch of oatmeal cookies from the oven and transferred them to a cooling rack. Pulling off a sheet of paper towel, Madeline grabbed two cookies, winking at Brenda, and then headed through the hall back to the room she shared with Victoria.

"Cookie?" Madeline offered one to Victoria, who lifted her head and breathed in the aroma but shook her head and returned her attention to her book, *Greek Metaphysics*, shook her head, and went back to studying. Madeline sat at her desk and took up her sonnet analysis, munching on a warm cookie. They all needed to finish their assignments before the ceremony, scheduled to take place in only three days.

As she gulped down the first cookie and moved on to the second, the mystery of it all continued to gnaw at her. The uncertainty of not knowing her place in the ceremony — if there even was a place for her. The worst part was being so intimidated by Christophe that she couldn't build up the nerve to ask him for an answer. Victoria had done her best not to gloat, but anytime they talked about the ceremony, Victoria's secret smile revealed her satisfaction that Christophe had chosen her as his partner.

Swallowing the last morsel of cookie and sipping the tea she'd prepared earlier with chamomile and lavender from the garden, Madeline focused on the poem in front of her. The same poem Lili had quoted to her lady parts during the laugh-fest on the cramping couch:

> **Two loves I have of comfort and despair,**
> **Which, like two spirits do suggest me still:**
> **The better angel is a man right fair,**
> **The worser spirit a woman coloured ill.**

The classic interpretation was Shakespeare's struggle with the love triangle: himself, the Dark Lady of the Sonnets, and another young man. The esoteric interpretation claimed it spoke of the struggle between opposing forces within us: our "better angel" of reason, intellect, and rightness going up against our worst selves, our base desires, our lust, and our greed.

> **To win me soon to hell, my female evil,**
> **Tempteth my better angel from my side,**
> **And would corrupt my saint to be a devil,**
> **Wooing his purity with her foul pride.**

Why were women always painted as evil? She'd acknowledged her own female evil, that part of her that yearned to be seen as worthy in Christophe's eyes. How she wanted him to recognize *her* power and make her a key player in the ceremony! But where was her power if she couldn't even face the man? The one rule they all agreed to while living in the house was to practice self-control and self-awareness. To master the base emotions, to learn humility, and to accept the teacher's decisions. Of course, she was failing. Failing miserably.

Looking back on the sonnet, here was the section that puzzled her the most:

Suspect I may, yet not directly tell;
But being both from me, both to each friend,
One angel in another's hell.
How do you guess one angel in another's hell?

Madeline pondered the last line when a knock at the door brought a moment of relief. Madeline turned to see Lili come in.

Victoria put her book down. "Hey, you, what's going on?"

Lili pulled up the stool next to Madeline's desk. "Oh, William's deciding about going to law school along with Alistair. Katia's throwing a fit because she thinks the evil patriarchy will swallow them up and turn them into corrupt capitalists."

"What does Christophe have to say?" Victoria asked.

"He's on his Sufi kick, reminding them that the Sufis held day jobs and blended into society and then did their spiritual practices in secret."

"Sounds about right," Victoria said and closed her book, sitting up and stretching her arms up over her head.

Madeline swiveled her chair around to face her friends. "Why is everyone talking about careers? I hate to sound like I agree with Katia, we're all doing fine. We all pitch in our share of living expenses by working part-time jobs. Isn't that enough?"

Victoria tilted her head, thinking. "It's a valid question. I dropped out of business school and have no interest in going back, but I would like to do more than just work at a grocery store. What about you, Lil?"

Lili was doodling abstract swirls in Madeline's notebook. "I loved my software design courses, but if I pursue that path, it means dealing with the toxic Silicon Valley work culture."

"We agree to make that our focus for the ceremony. To toss aside our old ideas of success and let spirit guide us to the proper outcome," Victoria said. "That we each ask for clarity. What is our greater purpose?"

Madeline looked at Lili, and for a nanosecond, they locked eyes. Madeline felt from Lili the same anxiety that ran through her own mind and spirit. Lili tossed down the pencil and sat back, pulling up her legs and wrapping her arms around them. "Yeah, but it's three days away, and Christophe still hasn't explained why I have to be paired with Jethro or what Madeline's role will be."

Madeline sensed Victoria's need to be supportive, but as Victoria already knew her role in the ceremony, Victoria had little to say. Madeline was about to say something when Victoria stood up. "Let's get this situation resolved. Let's just go ask him." Victoria marched out of the room.

Madeline looked at Lili, and they both scrambled to follow Victoria down the hall into the living room. Victoria got there just as Christophe stood up from his wingback chair while Katia, William, and Alistair sat on the sofa and now looked up at the women.

"Christophe, we have a question for you?" Victoria demanded.

Madeline felt her heartbeat quicker as Christophe smiled and opened his arms, turning his head to one side. "Yes, my darling. What do you want to know?"

Victoria held Christophe's gaze, and Madeline felt the energy between them: an adoring kindness, sweet yet tinged with something darker.

Victoria broke her gaze with Christophe and turned to Lili and Madeline. "We'll be celebrating the ceremony soon, and you have yet to tell our dear Madeline what role she's going to play. She deserves that clarity, don't you think?"

Christophe turned to Madeline, and she felt as she always did when he focused his attention on her, as if her chest would burst wide open if he looked at her for too long.

Christophe turned to the others, clearing his throat. "Yes, of course." He glanced at Madeline and winked, which set her heartbeat racing. "Forgive me for keeping you in the dark. I ask with deep respect and admiration if you would be so kind as to serve with me, to help me prepare the space, to light the incense and the candles, and to bear witness to the energies that gather around us as our loving family comes together. What do you think?"

The lump in her throat expanded, choking her, but then she glimpsed William mouthing the words: "teacher's pet."

Ignoring William, Madeline gazed at Christophe, and words burst out of her. "Thank you, Christophe. It would be an honor." Then she caught the smile on Alistair's face as he nodded to her.

"Wonderful, that eases the tension," Victoria said. "Now, I'm going back to my studies." She blew a kiss to Christophe and left the room, followed by William and Katia. Alistair came over to Madeline and pulled her aside for a chat, but something caught Madeline's attention. Christophe embraced Lili for a moment too long and he inhaled the scent coming off her hair. Closing his eyes, he melted into her embrace. Watching his face sent a shiver up Madeline's neck. What was going on?

"Okay, you'll be serving at the teacher's hand," Alistair said. "That's an important step up."

Madeline looked back at her friend, regaining her focus. "I hope so. But he didn't explain anything about Lili and Jethro. The oddest pairing of the group."

"Well, he seems to know what he's doing."

Madeline wasn't so sure. "Yeah. I gotta get back to my books, too." She walked down the hall, elated that she'd be helping Christophe. And yet ... What? Jealous? Was she jealous of the hug he'd given Lili? And why couldn't she get over her longing for Christophe? She struggled with the deep love she felt for her spiritual leader, as he had helped her to understand herself better, and yet, as a man, after seeing him hug Lili, she knew he would never love her, never take her as his partner in life. The lump in her throat returned as she went back to her room to consider the sonnet once again:

> **Yet this shall I ne'er know, but live in doubt,**
> **Till my bad angel fire my good one out.**

That's what the sonnet meant, that to get over this feeling of being rejected by Christophe, this feeling was her "bad angel." That her good angel would see the situation differently. She should be happy that he included her at all. Being selected as his assistant was a great honor and allowed for a deeper understanding of his group plan. At that moment, she decided her intention for the ceremony: How can I learn more? How can I become better? How can I become more worthy of his love?

⁂20⁂

Office of the Medical Examiner — 11:18 a.m.

Hunter shuffled down the hall, delirious from the lack of sleep. He had made the mistake of reading the first chapter of Tobias Silva's book on the Templar Knights, then dreamed about knights on horseback battling with the Moors. The images were so vivid; it felt as if he'd been awake the entire night, getting no rest at all.

The authorities had planned for the San Francisco Office of the Chief Medical Examiner to move from the Hall of Justice into a gleaming, multimillion-dollar facility later in the year. But until that day came, Hunter tolerated his visits to the antiquated green-walled, linoleum-tiled autopsy suite with reluctance, which always gave him a good dose of the creeps. It just did. He had to be a law enforcement professional, knowing how vital this information was to his case, but all the logic and clinical distancing would never dissuade him from the raw feeling that he stood in a brutal abattoir. Vierra leaned back with one foot against the wall, checking his phone, oblivious to his surroundings.

Forcing himself to look at the table where Jonathan Acosta's body lay, Hunter noted the familiar autopsy "Y" incision running across his chest and down through the abdomen. He worked up the courage to look at the boy's face just as the suite door burst open, and Dr. Carl Booth, a onetime NFL linebacker, entered, carrying a manila folder. He pumped iron as if he was still on the team. The doctor's massive chest and biceps bulged out of his lab coat. "Okay, gather round, children. I have the results on Zen Boy." His deep voice boomed through the eerie space.

"Is that what the lab guys are calling him?" Vierra asked as he put his phone away. "Our guys are calling him Quilt Boy. We're calling the perp Astroguy."

"Totally original, dude," Booth chuckled. "The lab techs who had to unfold him dubbed him that. Rigor had set in, so it was a tug of war to unbend the body. Here's the basics. Your victim died from a gunshot through the left ear at close range."

Hunter hadn't expected that. "Shot in the ear?" He bent over, examined the ear, and saw a faint burn just inside the ear's inner fold.

Booth checked his report. "Yes, small caliber, a twenty-two slug, intact. We sent it to ballistics."

"Was he shot while he was meditating?" Vierra asked, also bending to check out the ear.

"No. We found Fentanyl in his blood. That means he was unconscious when they killed him."

"A mercy killing?" Hunter theorized with a look over at Vierra.

"Or the cleanest human sacrifice you can think of. What else?"

Booth read more from the file. "Time of death was somewhere between midnight and four in the morning. His last meal was tortilla chips, guacamole, and bean dip. There was blood pooling in his lower trunk and legs, knees, and his butt. This tells me the killer placed the boy in a seated position shortly after death. And possibly kept him in cold storage until staging him at the crime scene."

"Any signs of a struggle?" Vierra leaned in to look at the boy's hands.

"None that we could find. Nothing under the nails. There were no cuts or contusions. Someone must have slipped him a mickey. One bullet through the ear killed him. They turned him into a pretzel and wrapped him up. Your Astroguy is one cold-hearted SOB," Booth said, and handed Vierra the file.

Hunter let it sink in. A lot of work had gone into this. "Assuming Jonathan was drugged somewhere other than the park, which is probable, someone had to carry him in the middle of the night, either dead or unconscious, down to the staging area where we found the body. No easy task to accomplish single-handedly."

Vierra shook his head. "What? Astroguy has a crew of evil devotees?" He jabbed at the file in his hand. "It says the kid only weighed a hundred and twenty pounds. A big guy could toss him over his shoulder and hump it into the park and up those stairs."

"Look, I know the doctor over here could bench press him to the park," Hunter quipped, and as if on cue, Booth brought up his arms, flexing his biceps in a classic muscle man pose. "But I couldn't." They all enjoyed a bit of mirth, and then Vierra handed the file to Hunter, who opened it and saw the crime scene photo of Jonathan on the bench. He looked over at Jonathan's body, cold and pale on the table, and then back at the photo. In his mind's eye, he could see shadows circling Jonathan, preparing him, staging the scene. Shadows. Two? Three? He couldn't make out any more detail. He saw the scene as if a thick veil of fog obscured it.

"But seriously, though," Booth said, "if Astroguy went to this much trouble, my guess is this is just the beginning of something bigger. Did I hear something about astrology signs?"

Vierra shot Hunter a side-eye glance, and Hunter blinked. The shadows were gone.

"Everyone's supposed to keep a lid on this case," Vierra said with a frown.

"Good luck with that," Booth responded with a shrug. "I barked at my lab techs not to take selfies with the body, but who knows if they listen. Everyone looking to post shit on social media."

Vierra cursed under his breath. "Tweedle-Creepy and Tweedle-Tasteless?"

Booth shrugged again. "We do what we can, but you know this business attracts misfits. You're a perfect example of that," he said and smiled at Vierra, who just shook his head.

Hunter's phone chirped. He checked it and felt a wave of relief. "It's from Dunham. The warrant's ready."

"Outstanding." Vierra reached out and shook hands with Booth. "Thanks for your hospitality, big man. But we've got some stones to look under, whether the designer-granola-bitch likes it or not."

"Are you talking about the Savvy Seeker quilt?"

"Yep. We've already been once, and they stonewalled us. Thanks for your help, Doc."

"Just don't bring me any more like this," Booth said.

"Smug bastards," Vierra remarked from the door. "I know they're hiding something up there, and I want to get my hands on it."

✦21✦

KXOP Newsroom — 1:03 p.m.

Hunkered down at her computer, sipping her coffee, Cora suppressed a giggle from reading Anna's private message: *What is it about these Russians? They sure can come up with some hot hotties.* Up popped a photo of Vlad, the youngest of the Volkov sons. Dressed in Armani, Vlad oozed "dark and brooding," with long black hair, dark eyes under hooded eyelids, and just a hint of baby fat in his cheeks. Cora typed back: *Yeah, he's a ten on the Prince of Darkness scale.*

Hannah: *Don't get too carried away. The man's wanted for murder and extortion.*

Cora: *Will do. Got anything on the Muldooneys?*

Hannah: *I'll dig some up later. It's the young one, Finn. He's a total dreamboat.*

Cora: *Sounds yummy, gotta run.*

Cora let out a contented sigh, enjoying her chat with Hannah. Cora reached out to all the crime bloggers on Amy's list; Hannah messaged her back, explaining that her brother Jordan ran the @SFCrimeblogger site, but he was taking time to be with his newborn daughter. She was charming and loved talking about true crime. Cora did some quick investigating on social media and found Jordan and Hannah's profiles on Facebook, which featured lots of family photos of a newborn baby girl on Jordan's page, and Hannah's profile showed her mountain biking in Mount Diablo State Park. It all checked out. Cora told Hannah about her assignment on building a timeline, and Hannah provided tons of information.

Hannah: *Have you guys got anything new on Sean Muldooney's trial?*

Cora: *Lemme check.*

Cora checked the browser window for the station's official feed and scanned for any updates but saw nothing new. She messaged Hannah back: *Sorry, no updates.* Then a question popped into her head, and Cora messaged back: *U know anything about Monday's murder on Russian Hill?*

Hannah: *Check this out.* She sent a link.

Cora flushed with nervous excitement. She clicked on the link, and it took her to @SFCrimeblogger's website. The featured photo showed the entrance to

Ina Coolbrith Park, with yellow crime tape blocking off the way in. She scrolled down to another photo, this one blurry and out of focus, showing a teenage boy wrapped in a blanket, sitting cross-legged on a bench. She scrolled further and found one last photo on the page. The photographer used a flash, which cast enough light to reveal the boy in more detail. With his eyes closed, he appeared to be meditating, but his skin was pale gray. Cora gasped upon realizing what she was seeing. Her heart thundered; this boy was dead. She was looking at a dead body.

Cora: *Is this Jonathan Acosta? The police released his name earlier.*

Hannah: *That's him. Creeps me out. One of Jordan's buddies works in the crime lab. SFPD isn't releasing any information because they think they have a serial killer on their hands.*

Cora reread the words: serial killer. What was she supposed to do now? She needed a minute and sent a quick reply: *Hey, my boss is calling, gotta answer. I'll be right back.*

Hannah: *K*

What to do? If Cora told Amy and Bob, they'd take the story away from her, but did she even want it? An energy was pulsing through her that no amount of espresso could replicate. Yes, she wanted this. She grabbed screenshots of all three images, stored them on her phone, and sent them to the printer. She closed her browser window, hiding her discovery, and scurried down the empty hallway. Luckily, no one was there. She got to the machine as it spat out the three pages. The images were blurry, but at least they had a time stamp on the pages. She would take these to Vierra. Then he'd have to give her something she could bring to Amy.

Back at her workstation, she clicked her computer monitor on, but the screen reverted to the website's home page. She tried the link again, but the page disappeared. She messaged back. Cora: *Why did you take the page down?*

Hannah: *It's for your eyes only. I need to know I can trust you. Cops have to wait for another body to confirm their dealing with a serial killer. Once it's confirmed, you'll have a scoop on your hands.*

Cora: *Why me? Why not the regular crime reporters?*

Hannah: *Because Ned Mullinex is a boring douche who never gives my brother credit.*

Cora: *Good to know. Thank you, Hannah. This is an intriguing story. I look forward to seeing your updates.* She hoped she sounded sincere.

Hannah: *I got your back. We have to stick together. I gotta run. The day job calls.*

What to do? Cora dug around for a used manila folder for the photocopies. Despite being thrilled to receive these from Hannah, Cora couldn't keep them to herself. Shouldn't she go to the police? She needed to confirm that this was the victim. And she was still eager to uncover the connection between Madeline and the case. What other options did she have? But first, she needed to finish her task list for the day. She'd work through lunch and leave early. Putting the manila folder in her bag, Cora hunkered back down, a new sense of purpose and determination blossoming inside her.

❖22❖

The Savvy Seeker Compound — 2:32 p.m.

"Okay, my fairy princess, we've returned to flazéda land."

While riding shotgun as Vierra drove, Hunter relaxed, "resting his eyes," as his father used to say. Now, blinking awake at Vierra's quip, he glanced across the vast parking lot to the compound buildings, and his anxiety flared up. "Damn. All this from meditation videos and blankets?"

Vierra got out of the car. "Don't forget the lip balm. Balmy is as balmy does, Malcolm."

Hunter smiled. "Okay Audrey, you want to take the lead on this?"

"Well, if these seekers don't give us some answers about that damned quilt, I'm going to hurt someone. You ought to do the talking."

Hunter nodded. "Sure thing. You do the skulking and the giving of bad cop attitude."

"Got it."

Emerging from the car, Hunter resolved to get definitive answers from these people. He pulled out the warrant from his portfolio as they walked toward the portico with the Gurdjieff quote. Upon arriving at the gate, the doors swung open, revealing Katia dressed in a splendid navy pantsuit. Hunter glanced up at the cameras embedded in the portico. Katia must have been watching them as they approached.

"Morning, gentlemen. I see you've returned. Is your paperwork in order?"

Hunter held up the warrant. "Yes, it is. May we come in?"

Katia retreated and let a tall man in an expensive suit join her at the gate. Dark-haired, he wore a precision-cut goatee and trimmed mustache, his demeanor as sharp as the edges of his sideburns.

"Gentlemen, this is one of Christophe's attorneys, William. And he is also my husband."

"One?" Vierra retorted. "How many lawyers does one guru need?" he said as Katia ushered them inside the gate and closed it behind them.

William smiled through tight lips. "We are a multi-national company with offices and factories around the globe. We make it company policy to obey the laws in every country in which we work. Including this one."

Hunter picked up on the pandering to the dumb cops and let it slide for now. "I'm Investigator Davis, and this is Investigator Vierra." He handed the warrant to William, who flipped through the pages, pretending to read it. William pointed something out to Katia, who inhaled, then shot an icy stare at Hunter. It made him shiver. He made a mental thank you to Alistair for getting a warrant that allowed them to search the entire compound if necessary.

William handed the warrant back. "You're just wasting time with this," he said as another woman emerged from behind the gate and joined them. "Investigators, this is Victoria. She is our Business Manager. I invited her to join us on our tour of the embroidery hut, where the quilts are prepared for order fulfillment."

Hunter felt her gaze as she sized them up. Dressed in a tailored suit, similar to Katia's, this one in forest green accentuated her sparkling green eyes and long auburn hair. Victoria exuded a soft grace, but Hunter guessed underneath there lived a shrewd yogini, as the company was worth millions.

"Gentlemen, it's a pleasure," Victoria said.

"Let's get started," Katia said.

Hunter and Vierra stepped through the gate doors and discovered the property was much larger than it looked from the outside. Off to the left was a sprawling mansion that had to be worth millions. Katia turned to move down the path, but Hunter stopped her. "Excuse me, but before we begin the tour, I have a few questions."

All three sets of eyebrows arched as Katia, William, and Victoria stared at his impertinence.

"Go on," William said.

"Yes," Hunter started, as Vierra stood next to him, watching all of them for their reactions. "Could you tell me where each of you were on Monday morning? From around four in the morning to say just after five thirty?"

William sniffed. "Are you asking us for our alibis, investigator?"

"Yeah, that's exactly what he just did," Vierra snapped.

Hunter had his portfolio open and clicked his pen, waiting for an answer, keeping a smile on his face.

Victoria approached with a smile. "You're thinking we're out back in our dungeon, sacrificing small animals in the wee hours of the morning?" Keeping her voice light, full of humor.

Hunter smiled back. "I don't know. Were you?" He raised his pen, ready to scribble a note.

"My apologies, this is serious business, isn't it?" Victoria continued in her light tone. "I left at 3:45, because I wanted to beat the traffic, so I left super early. I arrived at the Orchard Garden Hotel with enough time for an early morning meditation on their beautiful terrace and went to my meeting. You could check the hotel has security cameras that recorded my movements."

Hunter wrote the name of the hotel on a clean page and turned to William. "And you, sir, where were you?"

William glanced at Katia while crossing his arms over his chest. "Oh, bloody hell. At that hour, I was still in bed. I don't do my morning meditation until six. We, too, have a closed-circuit camera system on the grounds, but not at our private residences. You'll just have to trust me."

"Can anyone corroborate your statement?" Hunter nodded to Katia.

Katia blew out a long sigh, hunched her shoulders up her neck, and pulled out her phone. "I hate to say it, but my lazy husband is correct," she pulled up a menu on her phone. "Monday, I'm up at four thirty to hit the gym and check emails. He was snoring away in bed. I'm sorry, gentlemen, but I thought you were here to find out about our quilts. Is that still on the program?"

"Absolutely," Hunter said. "Carry on." He winked at Vierra letting him know his skulking was on point.

Katia stepped ahead. "Since you're so curious about us, I might as well orient you. "To your left, the largest structure is our main house. It holds our business offices and our meeting rooms, and we have a fully functional television recording studio in the basement. Just ahead, there are our social and meeting areas. We have a café and a cafeteria for all of our paid workers and our visitors to enjoy."

Hunter took notes while William and Victoria appeared bored, but Katia continued. "On the other side is the embroidery hut. Beyond it is our botanical garden and a lab where we derive plant essences for our essential oil line.

We also have a dormitory for visiting meditators and private apartments for key personnel."

Vierra nudged his partner and rubbed his thumb and fingertips together: money, money, money. Hunter breathed in the lush atmosphere and marveled at the planter beds, filled with a dense collection of shrubs, and flowering plants, bursting with color. Among the native plants were exotic tropicals. He imagined they must spend a fortune to keep these plants watered and pay the army of gardeners necessary to keep it all so perfect.

Then Hunter felt a sharp heart flutter as if some strange energy had pierced his body. Attempting to pinpoint the source of his discomfort, he saw nothing but brilliant sunlight illuminating a meticulously designed campus. Yet, without understanding why, he knew in his bones that underneath this manicured pretense lived secrets. Lots of them. And he was going to wrestle a few out into the light.

Katia marched on ahead of them. "The embroidery hut is further down. It's not too far to walk."

"Do you sew the quilts from scratch?" Vierra asked.

William answered. "No, we have a factory in Vietnam that cuts and sews the quilts. We ensure the workers receive a living wage and work in a safe and clean environment. They ship the quilts here, where we embroider the customer's exclusive affirmations. Can you tell me what affirmations were on the quilt you have in evidence?"

Hunter glanced at Vierra, who picked up on his cue without missing a beat. "No, not off the top of my head. Do you only embroider affirmations? Do you ever put anything else?"

"Like what?" Katia asked.

"I don't know, a bible quote, a poem?" offered Hunter.

"No, we only add affirmations to the quilts." Katia stopped and turned to face them. "We invite our customers to select a list of affirmations to use in their meditations. Once we receive them, our staff and volunteers embroider them onto the quilts. The intention is for the customer to follow up their meditation by physically wrapping themselves in the higher frequencies those powerful sentences carry."

"There are plenty of scientific papers proving the use of affirmations is an effective tool for self-actualization." William's voice dripped with sarcasm. "She's not just giving you a line, Investigator Davis."

"I didn't think she was," Hunter replied with a smile, and they all continued on.

"Here we are," Katia said as they approached a building designed to resemble an Asian temple, constructed of dark bamboo with sliding rice paper doors, open now to let in the air as the day was warming up. Hunter appreciated the architecture. At the front door was a rack filled with shoes.

Katia stood at the door. "Don't worry, gentlemen. You may keep your shoes on. Do you have the manufacturer number for the quilt? It's embroidered along the bottom right corner. I can match it to the quilts we have on file inside."

Hunter knew the answer but flipped through his portfolio for show. They must already take him for a fool, so why not play it up? "There's no mention of one in the lab report."

"Oh dear, I'm sorry, investigator," said Katia, her voice filled with enough syrup to trigger a diabetic coma. "Your criminal used a counterfeit quilt. You came all the way out here for nothing."

"Counterfeit? Could one of your quilts walk out of here?"

William cleared his throat. "We trust our staff and our volunteers, Investigator, but we can't be held responsible for people who steal our product. Our customers receive their confirmation number before we ship them the quilt. We ensure they get what they pay for. And we keep that information confidential."

"Do I have to show you the warrant again?" Hunter asked.

"No," William snapped. "You don't."

Hunter felt his temperature rise. William's smarminess made his skin crawl. He glanced at Vierra, who picked up on his cue.

"Is counterfeiting a big issue for you?" Vierra asked.

"Unfortunately, it's the price you pay for success," William sighed. "We found some workers in our first factory were stealing quilts and selling them on the black market. Now we work with a more reputable firm with much tighter security."

"Is that why the quilts are so overpriced?" Vierra asked.

"Overpriced in terms of fabric to keep your body warm," Katia said, "But for those seeking a deeper understanding of themselves, self-knowledge which will set them free—that, gentlemen, is priceless."

Victoria stepped up. "Why don't you come to watch our volunteers as they do the embroidery," she said and ushered everyone through the door of the hut, and then she greeted a couple of volunteers whose eyes brightened at seeing their mother hen.

Stepping inside, Hunter found his gaze drawn up to the ceiling of the room, which had multiple bamboo fans and Asian-styled drapes to buffer the sound. Opposite the door was a wall of floor-to-ceiling windows, bathing the room in natural light. A series of posters explaining each step of the embroidery process covered the wall to his left, and a dozen people sat at worktables filled with multicolored quilts, spools of thread, scissors, and task lights with magnifying glasses for working with dark thread against a darker fabric.

Hunter flipped back through his portfolio. "Are all the affirmations quilted by hand? Do you ever use an embroidery machine?"

Victoria shook her head. "We never use a machine—look around, we don't have any."

Hunter scanned the room, as did Vierra. All they saw were worktables, but there were a series of locked cabinets large enough for sewing machines.

A female volunteer carried a completed quilt toward Victoria, offering it for her inspection. Victoria stepped over, greeted the volunteer, and examined her work. "Oh, my Stephanie, you've done a beautiful job. Excellent." The volunteer beamed with pride, then carried the quilt over to a shelf and tucked it away.

On the wall opposite the posters, a row of quilts hung from bamboo poles. A quilt at the far end was mounted under glass. Something about it drew Hunter toward it. "What's the story behind that quilt on the wall?" He asked out loud, not caring who heard him.

Victoria steered him toward it. "Oh, this is one of Christophe's treasured items. I'm so pleased you noticed it." She drew him over to it. "One of our early volunteers made it," answered Victoria. Turning, Hunter observed her gaze at the quilt with an expression he couldn't read: was it admiration or a hint of jealousy?

He turned back to the quilt on the wall and stepped closer for a clearer view. As he read the words, the hairs on his neck stood at attention. This quilt featured the same quotes Connie had back in the lab: quotes from Carlos Castaneda, Rumi, and, of course, Dag Hammarskjold. In fact, it looked like the same one found at the murder scene.

"I'm sure you've heard the legend," Victoria continued. "Christophe based his award-winning meditation series on these quotes."

Vierra had joined Hunter and shot him a quick nod before opening his mouth. "Hey, what's this one mean?" Vierra asked Katia, who looked at the investigators with disdain. "By this Dog Hammer fella?" When Vierra played stupid, he played it to the hilt. Hunter held back a smile.

"One of my favorites," William responded from behind them. Hunter and Vierra both turned to face him. "Our work for peace must begin within the private world of each of us. To build for man a world without fear, we must be without fear. To build a world of justice, we must be just."

"And are you just?" Vierra asked, gravitas entering his voice.

Hunter watched William lean into Vierra. "You know, I get it. I've been dealing with skeptics like you for years now. You think what we do is bullshit. That we make expensive garbage, line our pockets, and sit back and laugh at gullible dumbasses … such as yourselves."

"Dumbasses? Did you hear that, partner?" Vierra's voice was calm, but Hunter knew he was boiling inside.

William continued unabashed. "I am still an officer of the court, and I understand you need answers to solve your case. But you don't care about understanding our work. I get it. For me, it's like explaining what an onion tastes like if you've never tasted one. And because you've never studied Christophe's approach, you don't appreciate that we are truly in the business of helping people lead better lives. Are we done here?"

Hunter smiled. "Let me grab a few shots of this enlightening quilt." He took several photos with his phone, getting close-ups of the quotes, and then ice hit his veins. In the lower right corner, the Sirius star sigil. He'd spotted it on Jonathan's quilt and on Madeline's shop sign. He snapped several shots, then examined them on his phone. Had Madeline ever mentioned Savvy Seekers? He scoured his thoughts, recalling his conversations with her. He was about to ask for the name of the volunteer who had made this quilt when his blood went from ice to fire.

"Oh my, look at you," Victoria spoke to someone behind him. "How far along are you?"

"Hunter, is that you?"

The voice he'd known forever. A voice he'd cherished for years. Hunter felt his guts collapse as he realized at that moment that not hearing that voice every day had been one of the hardest adjustments he'd ever made. Abby. He took in a full breath of air before turning around. And there she was, her face bright, cheerful. Not like the last year of their marriage, when she'd worn a permanent scowl.

Abby had a scarf draped over her bouncy brown curls. She'd changed her hairstyle and wardrobe after she'd read Christophe's books. She stood wearing a long pale blue dress of some airy fabric, nothing like the designer suits she used to wear. Glancing at her midsection, he spotted it. A bump. She was pregnant. He should congratulate her. Say something, asshole, but he couldn't. He felt Vierra by his shoulder, just behind him.

"Hi, Abby. So, you work here now?" Vierra jumped in, allowing Hunter a moment to recover.

"Hi, Daniel. Yes, I volunteer here a few days a week. Good to see you."

"Likewise."

Hunter finally said, "Hi, Abby." By instinct, he shot a vicious look at Katia, standing just behind his ex-wife, with her arms crossed in front of her chest, glowing with self-satisfaction.

Hunter pulled it together enough to reach over and hug Abby. "You look good, and…" He gestured toward her body, unable to form any further words through his shock.

Abby smiled and caressed her belly. "Yes, I'm five months along. Kalyan and I are overjoyed," she laughed.

Hunter nodded, knowing he should say something supportive. "I'm glad for you. You really are into this place." He waved to the room, knowing he was looking like an idiot.

"Yes, I met Kalyan here. And—oh, it's a long story. We should have coffee sometime. When you have time between investigations."

He smiled, knowing she didn't mean it, so, he lied, too. "We should. Before"—he nodded to her state — "because afterward, you'll have your hands full."

Abby beamed. "I can't wait. Call me when you have some time. I better get back to work. The boss lady over here is watching." She shot a smile at Victoria, who laid her arm across Abby's shoulder.

"Yes, these investigators have to get back to their work, too," Victoria said.

William stepped in. "I'll walk you out, gentlemen."

The walk out of the compound was a blur. Hunter listened to William and Vierra exchanging barbs, but he tuned them out because of the deafening pounding in his head brought on by seeing Abby.

"I don't care if the quilt was a counterfeit. I don't like these people," Vierra said as they got to the car. "That stunt with Abby was pure bullshit. Come on. You were too good for her. And what the hell kind of name is Kalyan, anyway?" Vierra said and unlocked the car.

Hunter appreciated Vierra's effort to cheer him up. He wondered if Katia had arranged Abby's visit to throw him off the scent because she had something to hide. At least they'd made a dent by getting their alibis, weak as they were. Again, the persistent feeling that there were secrets here kept gnawing at him. Hiding in the landscaping, in buildings, and even in the plants. Organic, plant-based, spiritual secrets.

❖23❖

Acosta Home, Corte Madera — 3:05 p.m.

Madeline kept her plan to herself, keeping Matthew-Tabitha in the dark, knowing he'd convince her not to do it. Seeing Jonathan Acosta's name on her customer list had sparked a new sense of responsibility and the urge to do something. She needed more accurate information, which is what she explained to Jennifer on the phone. That's what she told herself as she stepped up to the Acosta home. Now, standing outside the door, filled with trepidation. Her intention was to be helpful, and yet she worried the woman will overreact and yell at her for invading her home.

Jennifer opened the door and stumbled as she looked at Madeline.

"Mrs. Acosta, it's Madeline Merritt. Thank you again for seeing me."

Jennifer left the door open and shuffled away. As Madeline entered the home, a wave of negativity engulfed her, causing her body to tremble instinctively. The wreckage of grief filled the living room: shirts tossed on chair backs, an ironing board set up along with a basket of laundry, but the clothing remained un-ironed. Mail piling up on a side table, unopened. The room smelled musty as if no air had circulated, with a faint odor of uneaten, take-away Chinese food.

Near the door, a tie-dyed kid's backpack, decorated with colorful pins, and a bunch of keychains hanging from the zipper, which was open, most where Jonathan had tossed it when he arrived home. For the last time.

Jennifer trudged toward the living room and sank into a sofa, staring at the ground as if that was all the energy she could exert.

Looking around, Madeline pulled over a chair from a side table and then reviewed the mantle filled with family photos. The photos of Jonathan grabbed her attention with his bright eyes and crooked smile, gleaming with vibrancy. Then, in the family group photos, Jennifer, her husband, and Jonathan. Madeline noticed the boy's Asian ethnicity.

"Sorry, I'm not much for company," Jennifer's words were heavy and slurred. Was she on medication? Madeline pulled her chair over to be closer to the unkempt woman.

"Mrs. Acosta, once again, thank you so much for seeing me." Madeline kept her voice soft.

"Call me Jennifer. I haven't been called Mrs. Acosta this many times since." She didn't finish the thought but waved at the air. She lifted her head, focusing on Madeline. "You're that shop lady, right?"

"Yes. I own Sirius Books on Polk in the city. Jonathan ordered some astrology books from my store and—" She wasn't sure how to approach this. Jennifer stared at her with the expression of a small child, looking to a grownup for an answer.

"Did you meet my boy? He loved all that Tarot cards and occulty stuff. You never know, do you? What your kid is going to get into."

"That's right, you don't. But since he was showing an interest in astrology, I want to cast a chart that I think will offer some insight into what happened to your son."

"You can do that? I just thought it was birthday stuff or how to find a girl-friend." Jennifer's torso swayed forward and back, a self-soothing mannerism.

"Yes, you can create lots of different charts, but the key is knowing the right time. That's why I'm here. One piece of information, and I'll leave you alone."

"Oh, okay. You're nice. You don't have to worry about leaving me alone. What is it?"

"Can you tell me the last time you heard from Jonathan? The time he called you?"

Jennifer turned her head. "Oh, he didn't call, but he sent me a text." She got up and patted the pockets of her bathrobe, "now, where is my cell?"

Madeline worried that in her state, Jennifer may have left the phone anywhere, whether it be in the dishwasher or in the dryer. The poor woman grew more delirious, her eyes glazed and unfocused.

Jennifer shuffled to a side table and picked up a greasy cell phone, then plopped herself down on the sofa again. "You know it was a funny thing, I tried telling the cop. The missing people cop." She took in a deep breath to gather her thoughts. "I'm sorry. I told the police officer when I made the missing person's report."

"Okay, what did you tell them?" Madeline had her own phone out, ready to note down whatever Jennifer forced her mind to remember.

"I told them it didn't make any sense for Jonathan to spend the night."

"You mean Jonathan wasn't one for sleepovers?"

"No, even as a little boy, he always felt awkward staying at his friends' houses. So, when I got this, it didn't sound like him." Jennifer found enough energy to scroll through the phone, finding Jonathan's text messages. She held out the phone for Madeline. It read: "staying at Franks CU morning." The time stamp read 2:01 am. Madeline used her phone to take a photograph of the text.

Madeline scanned the previous texts. Jonathan included happy face emoji when messaging his mother. But this message was bare. "This is the last time you heard from him?" In a heartbeat, she registered her mistake.

Jennifer held the phone up to her face and began rubbing it across her skin. Her mouth opened, and a horrible gurgling sound emerged. Madeline offered her hand to Jennifer, who cringed back, holding the phone with both hands as if she thought Madeline was taking it from her.

"Jennifer. Oh, Jennifer, I'm so sorry." Madeline felt her own tears streaming down her face. "I'll just go. I'm sorry."

Jennifer let the phone drop to the floor, then clutched at a gold cross on a chain around her neck, then curled into a ball on the sofa. Madeline tried to touch her somehow, but the woman flinched, wanting her solitude. Madeline got up and cautiously pushed the chair back into place before silently slipping away as the moaning began. As she approached the door, she caught sight of Jonathan's backpack resting against the wall. Unable to resist, she looked inside. She found a notebook and flipped it open, scanning its pages. — Along the top, she saw the words: "Know-sis: Enlightenment for all." Feeling like a thief, she took a quick photo. What had Sluggo said? Christophe had stolen it.

✦24✦

**"I Love you as certain dark things are to be loved,
in secret, between the shadow and the soul." - Pablo Neruda**

Grace Cathedral - August 26, 2001
16 days before The Ceremony –2:31 p.m.

Madeline couldn't be happier. On a glorious, cloudless day in San Francisco, traipsing through Huntington Park with Christophe and the people she loved. After a tantalizing brunch in the city and a quick shopping spree in her Aunt Jane's store, they arrived at the park to soak up the sun and discuss their new books. Madeline admired Christophe's plan. Everyone needed a break from their intense study schedule, so a "field trip" did the trick.

Madeline couldn't help but wonder why Aunt Jane kept watching Christophe while he browsed the store shelves. Her aunt recognized him, but Madeline hadn't asked how she knew him. Madeline made a mental note to bring it up the next time she visited the store.

As they walked through the park, Christophe stopped, looked up at the surrounding buildings, and shook his head. "Can you imagine what this place must have been like before any of these buildings were here? When the native tribes lived here?"

"What do you mean?" Victoria asked, stopping next to Christophe.

He pointed to the skyscrapers that surrounded the park. "Just think, without the mansions or the Fairmont hotel blocking the view, this must have been one of their sacred sites. I mean, you can feel the vibe coming through the earth. I'm sure that's what influenced the park designers." He turned to face the other direction. "But of course, the churches grabbed up the most sacred spaces," Christophe pointed at Grace Cathedral and sat down on a section of grass; the others followed his lead. Madeline sat next to Victoria. Lili sat on her other side while the others all clustered near Christophe to hear him.

"The glorious relic that is Grace Cathedral, a medieval anachronism in our Baghdad by the Bay. I'm amazed it's still standing."

"Well," William said, as he stretched out on the grass, Katia snuggling next to him. "Every major city needs a Cathedral. In fact, builders constructed most of the European Cathedrals next to the marketplaces, as churches have always followed the money. San Francisco is no different."

"Touché, dear William," Christophe winked. "Can you believe how far the church fathers went to control people, using fear of a vengeful god who kept tabs on everyone's behavior? It's barbaric when you think about it."

Alistair sat near Christophe, looking at his leader. "But there have always been powerful organizations that looked to control people. It used to be the church. Now it's politics."

"Coming from the senator's son," Katia jibed.

"But it's a legit question," Alistair fought back. "It's no longer the fear of God that keeps people motivated. It's the fear of lack. Lack of money, lack of abilities. If we are about helping people become more self-aware, how are they going to use it in everyday life?"

Christophe turned to Alistair and pointed a finger at him. "You are going to make an excellent lawyer someday."

Alistair waved his hand, dismissing the idea.

"No, I mean it. Becoming a lawyer is one way we help foster self-awareness. You can't just tell people what to do." He pointed to the Cathedral again. "That's what broke the churches. People were tired of being told what was right and what was wrong. In our hearts, we all know ethical behavior. And for those of us on the path, our job is to live it. Not preach it but apply the truth and live up to a higher standard. Look what's next to the Cathedral: The Freemasons. They've re-branded themselves as a club focused on building character, not about forming buildings out of stone."

"Oh, enough talk!" Victoria leaped up and grabbed Lili's hand. "While the men jabber about power and self-awareness, the women will celebrate!" Madeline caught on to Victoria's energy and joined hands with her friends, and the three women danced in a circle.

Lili shouted out, "On this glorious summer day, how can you just sit around and talk?" She opened the circle as Miranda laughed and joined them. Brenda and Katia stuck close to their men and grinned at the antics. Victoria led them over to the cement circle filled with water, where they found the statue known as "the dancing sprites." In the center, three children stood, their hands linked, their faces beaming with pure joy.

"Ah, leave it to our beautiful women to know how to celebrate," Christophe exclaimed, a smile spreading across his face as he rushed toward Victoria and seized her hand. He then turned to Madeline, his grip on her hand strong yet tender. The touch of her guru's hand sent a rush of emotions coursing through Madeline's heart, threatening to burst it wide open. The family all gathered in a circle around the statue, running and laughing, not caring what anyone else thought.

··«‹**25**›»··

Thursday, August 10, 2017

Mill Valley — 11:33 a.m.

During an early morning briefing with Leo, Hunter updated Vierra on the important parts of his meeting with Madeline, and how he had asked her about the sigil and explained the meaning behind it. Vierra couldn't hold back the jibes about Hunter wanting to meet up with his "girlfriend" again. They bandied ideas back and forth: Is some crazy freak from Madeline's store behind this and framing her for Jonathan's murder? Was "astroguy" piling on more useless information to burden them with busy work? They went round and round, but the discussion went nowhere.

Leo got them back on track by focusing on victimology. If they gathered more facts about Jonathan, they'd have a better shot at nabbing his killer. They decided on a visit to Jonathan's school, and Vierra drove them to the campus. Once there, Hunter admired the modern buildings made from space-age materials with lots of chrome and miles of windows. A shimmering-metal creation resembling an alien starship destined to land in Silicon Valley but ending up in Mill Valley instead.

The suddenness of Jonathan's death had hit the campus hard. This evidence was apparent in the central courtyard where students had erected a makeshift altar. Adorned with a photo of Jonathan, it featured an array of flowers, photographs, teddy bears, and various mementos. Surprisingly, and there were a couple of Tarot cards and a picture of Christophe.

Hunter and Vierra walked down the hallway, following the sound of music, until they reached Mr. Erickson's media arts room. He was a Black man. Hunter guessed he was in his early forties, the deep sadness at Jonathan's murder etched on his face. Erickson confirmed Jonathan's interest in Tarot cards, offering to screen yet another video Jonathan had created. Erickson hit play on a remote, and Hunter and Vierra watched as the video monitor lit up and the screen filled with Jonathan's bright face, so animated as he spoke on camera: "What we know to be the modern Tarot cards originated as simple playing cards during the renaissance." Jonathan spoke with his hands, whose energetic motions matched his enthusiasm for his topic.

Hunter flipped through his portfolio and noted the Tarot cards Madeline had mentioned: The Devil, Justice, and the Lovers. He scribbled a note to himself to search Jonathan's computer for any reference to these cards. The video continued with close-up shots of several cards, including The Magician and the Tower card. "Many sources cite Tarot as simply being a card game with no mystical or fortune-telling aspect until—"

"The rest of the video is much the same," Erickson said as he pressed pause, and the room fell silent. Hunter caught the teacher's visible distress as he scanned the video screen, his discomfort palpable.

Vierra leaned back in his chair. "What is it with teenagers and occult stuff? It's an interesting approach."

Erickson nodded. "Who knows? He started this project during a summer enrichment program with his buddy, Stellan. Jonathan showed it to his history teacher, hoping to get extra credit."

"A multitasker?" Vierra said.

"He did all the research. No reason he shouldn't get credit for—" Erickson stopped and stared at the screen. "I still can't believe he's dead. Can you tell me anything about how he died?"

Hunter wanted to give the teacher some comfort, but he couldn't. "We can't. I'm very sorry. We're keeping a tight lid on the investigation. Can you send us a link to his other videos?"

Erickson responded with a wistful smile. "Of course. I'd be happy to, if it's going to help you find Jonathan's killer."

"Yes, it will," Vierra answered. "Can you tell us more about Stellan?"

"Sure, he wasn't enrolled in our school, but I have his contact information. He tried to convince Jonathan they should start a blog about this stuff, but Jonathan wanted to stick with video." Erickson tapped at his keyboard and scribbled information on a piece of paper. Hunter reached for it as Vierra grabbed his phone, looked at it, and said, "Excuse me, I'm so sorry, but I have to take this." Hunter shot his partner an evil stare, but Vierra ignored him and walked out of the room.

"My apologies, Mr. Erickson, we're working on several fronts here."

"As long as you catch the bastard who did this, "Erickson handed Hunter a piece of paper.

Hunter accepted the paper with Stellan's info from Erickson. "You mentioned a couple of Jonathan's friends are available to talk to us?"

"Yes, I texted Electra. She'll grab Lance and be here in a moment."

"Hey, partner." Vierra jerked his head for Hunter to join him by the door. "Can you interview the kids on your own? They're talking about a development in the Muldooney trial. It doesn't sound good."

Not that Hunter couldn't interview two teenagers alone, but Vierra was the one good with kids; Hunter always felt uncomfortable around them. But what could he do? "Go, take care of business. I'll be fine."

Vierra tapped Hunter's shoulder and disappeared. Moments later, two teenagers entered the room.

Erickson greeted them. "Thanks for coming in, guys." He ushered them to a table and chairs. Hunter pulled up a chair, joining them.

Lance, a tall boy standing around six feet, moved awkwardly in his lanky frame. He hunched his shoulders, creating a protective barrier around himself. His dark complexion had Hunter guessing that his people were from India. He had curly black hair with matching dark brown eyes. Hunter sensed the boy's reluctance to be there.

The girl's downcast gaze and slouched posture revealed a sadness that mirrored her friend's somber mood. Her appearance revealed her diverse heritage, with her glossy black hair and captivating almond-shaped eyes reflecting her Asian roots. She wore a long-sleeved blouse over loose jeans. Hunter wished she wasn't in this room, wished this lovely girl was running down the school hall, chasing after her friends, sharing a laugh at something that popped up on her phone. But no, it was his responsibility to examine a wound that was just forming a scab. Silently cursing Vierra for bailing out on him, he forced a smile at the teenagers, hoping to radiate an ounce of sincerity.

"Okay guys, this is investigator—" Erickson stalled.

"Davis," Hunter said and tried to look reassuring.

Erickson shrugged, a gesture of confusion. "Investigator Davis, thank you. He's going to ask you some questions and please do your best. I know it's rough, but he's going to find Jonathan's killer with your help." Erickson looked at Hunter. "I'll just step out for a bit."

Hunter noted the skepticism on Lance's face and the bewilderment on Electra's. He would start with her. "Hi, Lance. Electra. Thanks for sitting down with me. Let me just say that I've spent some time with Jonathan's parents, and from everything they told me, he was a sweet kid. Electra, can you tell me more about him?"

Electra self-consciously crossed her arms over her stomach and shrugged, avoiding eye contact. "I don't even know where to start."

"Whatever comes to mind," Hunter said. "Have you known him a long time?"

Electra shrugged again. "We've been friends since, like, second grade. I don't know. He was like the brother I never had. He was family," she finished, and then covered her mouth with her hand, on the verge of tears.

Lance jumped in to save her from having to go on. "I still can't believe it. I mean, there are those kids who drive too fast and skateboard in stupid places. You expect bad things to happen to them, but not Jonathan."

"What makes you say that?" Hunter leaned in.

"Because he was super safe and polite as fu" — Lance held back an expletive — "as nice as anyone. He wanted to help people."

"Your teacher showed me Jonathan's Tarot project. Did you see it?"

Lance slumped, "Of course. You couldn't get him to stop. He used us all as guinea pigs. He tried giving readings, but I don't think he knew what he was doing half the time."

"Did he read cards for you too?" Hunter asked Electra.

"Yeah, I thought it was silly. Until…"

"Until?" Hunter perked up.

Electra sat up straighter. "Until he started getting things right. It was freaky."

"In what way?"

"Okay, so I had this beef with a girl in gym class. Some stupid argument. Jonathan picked out three cards. I can't remember the others, but one card, the Empress, came out upside down. Jonathan said it meant this person was jealous of me. I mean, what total crap, right? But then later on, I overheard this girl talking to a classmate, and it came out she was jealous because I hung out with Lance all the time." Electra smiled at Lance. "She likes you."

Lance shook his head, showing his disinterest. "Whatever, but that won't help the cops find Jonathan's killer."

Electra shrugged. "Yeah. What else can we tell you?"

Hunter, scribbling a note in his portfolio, danced around the edges, but now he got to the point. "I need information leading up to the murder. We learned Jonathan was at a party on Saturday night. Were you there?"

"Yeah," Electra answered.

"Who threw the party?"

"Frank's. Frank Nguyen. He goes to Tamalpais High."

"Do you have his address?"

"Yeah, fourteen Via Vandyke. I got there around nine-thirty." She turned to Lance. "I didn't see you at first."

"I was down in the basement," Lance said. "Frank's dad set up a bunch of video game consoles, it was pretty sweet."

"More like a bunch of guys smoking weed," Electra said, smirking.

Lance elbowed her. "Dude, not in front of the cop."

"Oh yeah. Sorry."

Hunter smiled. "Don't sweat it, Lance. We've all been there. Where were you, Electra?"

"Up in Frank's sister's room. A bunch of us girls messed around putting on makeup…" She shot a look at Lance, who responded with an eyebrow raise. "And smoking weed. Guilty as charged, officer."

Hunter appreciated their honesty. "Hey, if you hadn't been smoking weed at a party on a Saturday night, I'd wonder if something's wrong with the two of you."

They exchanged broad smiles, and the mood lightened. Hunter continued. "Where was Jonathan?"

Lance leaned in. "He'd been hanging downstairs for a while, but the Norwegian heartthrob showed up."

Hunter played at flipping through his portfolio. "Would that be Stellan?"

Lance rolled his eyes. "Yeah, he kept bugging Jonathan about something."

"I saw him too." Electra crossed her legs. "He brought some other kids, a couple of chicks, and some other dude. They hung around and drank too much, raiding the liquor cabinet."

"Did either of you see Jonathan leave the party?"

They both shook their heads no. "I offered him a ride home, but Jonathan told me to buzz off. They had some conspiracy going on. So, I took Electra home. That was the last I saw him."

"Did any of you take any photos that night? Did anyone post anything on social media?"

Electra pulled her phone from her purse. "I shot some stuff with the girls." She started scrolling. "I got one with Jonathan."

"Would you mind sending those to me?" Hunter passed her his card.

"The ones with Jonathan?"

"Please send all of them, just in case?" Hunter tossed a card to Lance. "You get one too."

Lance took the card. "No problem. But how is this helping?"

"We need to know how Jonathan went from a party in Mill Valley to Russian Hill, where he was found. The party was the last place Jonathan was seen alive."

In perfect unison, Electra and Lance shook their heads, the weight of Hunter's words settling on their shoulders.

"Wow, man," Lance said under his breath, and then looked up at Hunter. "It's like you just never know."

"No. You never do. Thanks, and please send those photos. I would appreciate it."

Lance pocketed Hunter's card. "My phone is in my locker."

Electra tapped on her phone. "I'll send you a reminder text."

"Thanks, E."

"Okay." Electra looked up at Hunter. "I just sent you all the photos. I took the last one at around eleven."

"Thank you." Hunter reached out to shake her hand and then Lance's. "I know the next few weeks are going to be tough. Please, if you can think of anything, call me."

Just as the kids were leaving, Vierra returned, nodding as he passed them.

"I'll catch up with you, E." Hunter heard Lance say to Electra as she walked away. Lance turned back to Hunter just as Vierra returned to the media room. "Umm, I didn't want to say this in front of Electra, but Jonathan was being followed."

"What do you mean, followed?" Hunter asked. Vierra reached out and closed the classroom door.

"It started back in March. Jonathan said he kept seeing this weird-ass black car parked on his street and outside school."

"Did you check out the plates?" Hunter opened his portfolio with renewed interest.

"Of course. It was a blue and red diplomatic plate." Hunter scribbled it down.

"Did it say which country?" Vierra asked.

"No, so Jonathan bought a portable GPS tracker off eBay, and I helped him install it on the car one day after school."

Vierra blanched, "How did you manage that?"

"It was pretty freaking easy. We spotted the car parked outside of the school. I kicked my skateboard and sent it 'accidentally' under the car's chassis. When I grabbed the board, I planted the device under the car. Then Jonathan started tracking the car on his computer. The dude was from the Russian consulate over in Pacific Heights. The weirdest part is we were studying the whole Russian involvement in the 2016 election in our social studies class. Here's his license plate number." Lance showed them a picture on his cellphone.

Hunter scribbled it down in his portfolio. "Did you get a good look at the driver? Was it always the same person?"

"Yeah, it was this burly Russian dude. Black hair always wore a dark coat. Totally creepy."

"Did Jonathan ever mention this guy to his parents?"

"No, he didn't. I kept telling him to, but—" Lance's shoulders collapsed. "I should have insisted on it. Damn."

"Why do you think he was being followed?"

"He had this crazy idea he called Know-sis that he thought this guy wanted to steal it from him."

Hunter scribbled it down. "What is that?"

"It's some crazy mash-up between a video game and a meditation helmet with astrology stuff in it. Totally off the wall."

"What's it supposed to do?"

"He tried explaining it. You wear this thing on your head, and it measures your brain waves, and if the stars are not in your favor that day, it makes you more mellow. I don't know."

Hunter put his hand on Lance's shoulder. "This is very helpful. Thank you."

"Yeah, okay. I'll send you those photos, too." Lance said and left. Hunter looked at Vierra. "While you were out, they mentioned this guy Stellan was at the same party as Jonathan."

"Next stop on our hit parade, Malcolm?"

"Sure thing, Audrey."

··«‹**26**›»··

KXOP Newsroom — 11:47 a.m.

The crime scene photos in Cora's bag nudged at her mind for most of the morning, making it difficult to focus, but she monitored the latest in the Muldooney trial, speculation about who would come forward to testify against the vicious mobster. She'd resisted calling Madeline, still bothered at her sister's reluctance to help her with the investigation. She hesitated, then glanced up just in time to witness her boss, Bob, approaching her desk.

"Hey, Cora, it's intern time," Bob said and waved to her.

She pointed a finger at her chest. Yeah, she was an intern, so what gives? "Yes, what's going on?"

"I need you to go to conference room D. The solar eclipse coverage team needs an extra hand."

Cora's face squished — she didn't know a darned thing about eclipses.

"Don't give me that face, Bob laughed. "They'll sort you out. Grab a notebook and get down there. Renee Baptista will tell you what she needs."

Following orders, she grabbed her purse, phone, and notepad and shot a quick look over at Amy, who rolled her eyes but didn't argue with the boss.

Then Cora remembered Christophe and his grandiose plans for the eclipse at Grace Cathedral. Upon arriving at the conference room, she glanced inside and found a group of six people huddled around a table. Maps of Grace Cathedral, the Mason temple, and the roads encircling the area adorned several whiteboards throughout the room.

At the head of the table, a stunning blonde woman captivated the attention of the others, her navy-striped suit stressing her impeccable style. Once Renee caught Cora at the door, she stopped speaking.

"Are you Bob's intern?" Renee asked, and all eyes in the room turned to Cora, who choked out a "yes."

"Great! Grab a seat. We've already started. I'm Renee, and you'll meet the team in a minute. What's your name?" Her voice — a nanosecond slower than an auctioneer's. Cora did as she was told and grabbed a seat at the table while Renee picked up where she left off.

"We've begun work on the binder, and Shelly, I'll need you to get the updated route specs from the San Francisco Entertainment Commission. We'll have to set up scouts along the routes. These meditators are all up and down Jones Street to Market, same with Taylor. Ken, I need you to liaise with our camera department and find out how many drones we can have in the air to cover it all."

Cora scrutinized the map and found it on the whiteboard. The scope of Christophe's plan dawned on her, and this was how the station was going to handle covering it all.

"I'm sorry, intern, what's your name?"

Surprised, Cora mumbled, "It's Cora, hi."

"Cora, Dora, the explorer. Sorry, I'm shit with names. I may end up calling you Dora until things settle down. My apologies for making you dive into the deep end. I need you to help Jo Anne with the binder."

A petite woman with springy black hair and glasses waved from the other side of the table. "Hi, welcome to the madhouse," Jo Anne said.

Cora waved to her and waited for Renee to fill her in.

"Right, the binder is the bible for the event. We shove in every bit of information we can think of for the entire coverage team, with special inserts for the anchors. Because you never know what kind of questions they might have. If someone jumps out of a cake during a meditation, we need to know who baked it. Are you with me?"

"Absolutely."

"Good on ya. Now, I have to run but come sit with Jo Anne, and she'll get you started." Renee stood and, in an instant, was on her cell phone marching from the room. Cora kept out of her way and then went to where Jo Anne sat at the table. The others were moving about the room, adding information to the whiteboards.

"Hi, Jo Anne. It's nice to meet you. So, what can I do to help?" Cora asked.

"Hey, Cora. Welcome to the team." Jo Anne's voice was soft and accommodating, a drastic change from Renee's. She pulled over a massive three-ring binder for Cora to examine. "This is the binder, as Renee mentioned. We have various sections, from route logistics to camera setups and the names of the insurance companies covering the event. What I need you to do is help me build up the section on the Savvy Seekers. Are you familiar with Christophe's company?"

"Sorta. I poked around their website, looking to buy some face cream."

Jo Anne smiled. "I'm a Clinique girl myself, not sold on the airy-fairy products. But can you pull together bios of the company's major players? I need Christophe and other staff members just in case they are at the event and if one of our roaming reporters can grab an interview with them."

Cora nodded. It sounded like an interesting project, although not as interesting as the investigation into Jonathan's murder. "That sounds reasonable. Can I still do this while I'm in the newsroom, or do I work someplace else?"

"Stick to working in the newsroom. You'll be easy to find. As you can see, it's like setting up coverage for the Super Bowl, with lots of moving parts. Amy can help you if you run into any snags. Start with the company website but check out all of their social media channels. We need photos, and be sure to enlarge them, make them easy to spot, got it?"

Cora jotted down some notes, her excitement building, though the haunting images of the crime scene photos lingered in her thoughts.

··❬❮27❯❯··

Cascade Canyon — 1:17 p.m.

"So, what do we have on this Stellan?" Hunter asked Vierra as they wound their way through yet another above-his-pay-grade neighborhood. They'd stopped for lunch at some El Taco greasy spoon off the highway, and his frazzled brain was begging for a siesta.

"First off, I want to know why someone from this neighborhood—and let's face it, Jonathan's kind of charity case—what does a rich kid like this want with our victim? I mean the Acosta's house doesn't measure up to this." Vierra drove Hunter's Toyota up a serpentine driveway, through old-growth trees along the gracious curves toward another secluded property.

"This Stellan was looking for a leg up. He spots Jonathan's talent and piggybacks on Jonathan's work to improve his grades?" Hunter asked.

"Or a romance thing? We never asked his parebnts if Jonathan was straight or gay, did we?"

"You think Jonathan's sexuality is a factor here? The killer put makeup on him...."

"Yeah, nowadays, all these kids watching drag queens on TV and talking about gender fluidity—who knows?"

Hunter found himself in front of another magnificent mansion, this one tucked away in a lush, wooded canyon. Standing at a height of three stories, the building caught the eye with its sleek combination of high-tech materials and stained wood.

A young man with blond hair stood spraying a light coating of foam onto a gleaming cherry-red Lamborghini that was parked in the massive courtyard. Hunter noticed the tension on the kid's face upon spotting their car. Vierra turned the Toyota around, facing it down the driveway for a quick exit. Or was Vierra showing off his driving skills to the rich boy with the fast car? Hunter took his time getting out of the car while Vierra walked over to the boy, badge in hand.

"Excuse me," Vierra said. "We're looking for Stellan. Is he home?"

"That's me." Stellan turned off the hose and put the sprayer down.

Hunter joined Vierra, showing his badge to Stellan, who hovered over both of them. He had to be at least six foot four, light blue eyes peeking through his wispy blond hair. A loose white T-shirt over khakis. The boy carried himself like a rich man's son, a certain bearing that reminded him of someone.

"Nice car. Yours?" Vierra asked.

"Don't I wish." Stellan took his latex gloves off and tossed them near the cleaning supplies. "It's my dad's. If I want to drive it, I have to wash it. He's old school that way."

"Good for him," said Hunter. "We have a few questions for you if you don't mind."

"Not at all. Do you want to come inside?"

"No. Out here's fine," Vierra said. "We want to ask about Jonathan Acosta."

Stellan nodded, a mournful expression crossing his chiseled face. "Sure thing. He was a unique guy. I miss him." Stellan let out a heavy sigh and turned away for a moment, as if collecting himself.

"We talked to his parents, and they told us you and Jonathan were tight, at least for a while?" Hunter had opened his portfolio, pen in hand.

Stellan dipped his head. "Yeah. We started working on a project together."

"Mr. Erickson showed us a clip. Why Tarot cards?" Hunter asked.

"My sister gave me this book on Tarot and astrology. It had lots of detailed graphics. We thought we'd make an animation out of them and post it on YouTube."

"Astrology? Do you believe in that stuff?" Vierra asked.

"Sure. I mean, look how the moon affects the tides on Earth. Why can't all those other planets affect us? Ya know?"

"Sorry, I don't know," Vierra said, frowning. "So, what happened?"

"Jonathan just kept on playing with the editing software. He didn't care too much about getting the graphics right."

"And you wanted it done right, not slapped together?" Vierra asked.

"Yes. If there's one thing I learned from my dad, the devil is in the details. Like this car. But then I paid attention in physics class and learned about quantum entanglement. My teacher said stuff like there's a potential in the quantum field for me to have a car like this. I'm working on my manifesting skills."

"Good luck with that. Do you need to finish cleaning this one?" Vierra asked.

Stellan shrugged. "No, I can let the foam sit for a while."

"When was the last time you saw Jonathan?" Hunter asked.

Stellan thought for a moment. "Saturday. A party at Frank's house. I didn't expect him there. Jonathan usually avoids those people."

"Going to parties was unusual for him?" Hunter asked.

"Going to parties where kids were getting stoned, yeah. I mean, Jonathan was a total nerd. This was a full on the-parents-aren't-home, let's-get-drunk party."

Vierra nodded, remembering his youth. "More your style?"

Stellan flashed a smile. "The girls at this party were smokin' hot—and I don't mean weed," Stellan said to Hunter. "Know what I mean?"

"Sure. Did any girl catch Jonathan's eye?"

"I think so. He started spending more time with Electra. Lance wasn't too happy about it."

"Are we talking serious love triangle or just flirting?" Vierra asked.

"Not sure—. But it was weird. I mean, we used to all just hang out, you know? Then, it was like they were both impressing her. Jonathan was just figuring it out, being what he thought she'd be interested in. It's tough. Girls are … I don't know."

"Yeah, it never gets easy figuring out how to talk to girls," Hunter said.

"Do you remember seeing Jonathan leave the party?" Vierra asked.

Stellan bent to pick up the hose. "No, I don't think so. I was down in the basement, smoking weed with some buddies. I must have passed out. When I got ready to go, I couldn't find him."

"What time was this?" Hunter was taking detailed notes.

Stellan turned back around. "I think around 3 am? I dragged myself home and went to bed. Didn't give it much thought."

"Well, you finish up with that Lambo." Vierra fished his card out of his wallet. "Here's my card. If you think of anything that will help us, call. And if you figure out how to manifest your own Lambo, you better call."

Stellan smiled, "Okay." He shoved the card into his back pocket. "Do you think it's too early to talk to his folks? They're such nice people, I feel terrible for them."

"Give them a few days," Vierra said. "They'd like to hear from Jonathan's friends," Vierra responded. "Helps keep him alive."

"Yeah," said Stellan, and his voice went down an octave. "Wow, they … they just adored him, you know?"

Hunter and Vierra both nodded, all of them standing in silence. Stellan's body shuddered, a wave of grief that was too heavy for someone so young.

"Okay, thanks for your time," Hunter said, concluding the interview.

Stellan knelt to pick up the hose and turned it on, then stood aiming the spray at the car, and the foam slid off the Lambo, revealing the dazzling red paint job sparkling in the afternoon sun. Hunter walked toward Vierra, who sat in the Toyota's passenger seat. The car, dejected, had a distinct case of Lambo-envy.

"So, back to the office and re-group?" Vierra asked Hunter.

"Yeah," Hunter said. "Follow up on this Russian guy and see if there's anything in the party photos from Electra. How about I swing by the Federal Building after we get back to the city?"

"It's worth a shot. Your turn to drive," Vierra said, stifling a yawn, and tossed the keys to Hunter, who had to twist to make the catch.

As Hunter turned to grab the keys sailing through the air, his eyes caught Stellan watching them momentarily before the boy shifted his focus back to scrubbing the car. It was in that moment that it hit Hunter - Stellan bore a striking resemblance to Christophe. "Hey Stellan, one last thing, tell me about Jonathan and that guru guy Christophe?"

Stellan flinched but tried softening his reaction with a teenager shrug. "Jonathan was impressed with the guy, but frankly, I couldn't get into all the meditation stuff. The astrology, sure, but I draw the line at guru dudes."

"Thank you." Hunter got in and started the car but sat for a moment, watching Stellan polish the stunning paint job with his head down, his bangs covering most of his face. "According to Lance and Electra, Stellan wouldn't leave Jonathan alone at the party. Something doesn't add up."

"Well, Malcolm, it sounds like everyone was pretty tipsy, so…"

"So, it could be a simple matter of confusion. Okay, Audrey. Either way, this party was the last place Jonathan was seen alive, yet no one remembers him leaving."

··◄◄28►►··

Phillip Burton Federal Building — 4:41 p.m.

After suffering through late afternoon traffic and making a dent in their mountain of paperwork, Hunter and Vierra hoofed it to the Federal Building. Hunter embraced the cool weather and enjoyed the walk to relax. Vierra was equally subdued. The stroll through the emerging "South of Market" neighborhood was a pleasant change, seeing new buildings rising out of the old warehouse district. But once they made it to the Civic Center, with the homeless encampments sprawling along the sidewalks and in the alleys, Hunter's mood darkened.

Images from the case floated around his mind: the quilt, Jonathan's room, seeing Abby in that embroidery hut, and Madeline's eyes.

"Have you met this Consuela person?" Vierra asked, scanning his phone. He'd called ahead to the FBI field office and arranged the meeting.

"No, the only run-in I've ever had with the "Famous But Incompetent" was on an organized crime bust back in my uniform days."

As several agents passed them on the sidewalk, Vierra paused and turned aside, looking down as if seeing something on his shoes. Hunter let him have his moment and kept walking to the building entrance. Vierra soon followed, and they passed through security by showing their badges, then took an elevator to the FBI field office.

With closing time approaching, the sound of chatter and footsteps filled the office as secretaries and other workers bid each other farewell and made their way toward the elevators. As Hunter scanned the area, a petite Filipina caught his eye. Dressed in a snug navy dress and jacket, along with a fierce attitude, zeroing in on them. This had to be Consuela Amihan.

"Investigators Davis and Vierra?" she asked.

"That's us." Vierra offered his hand, as did Hunter.

Consuela lugged an enormous black leather purse stuffed with so many notebooks and files that it dug deep into her shoulder. "I'm sorry you guys came all the way down here," she said, ignoring their hands, "but the answer is no."

"We haven't asked the question?" Vierra balked.

"You did. The minute you texted me the license plate number. Anything to do with foreign consulates is a no-go at the moment."

"But this is a murder investigation—"

Consuela shut him down with a wave of her hand. "I know. I pulled up the case file and checked my sources, and this guy isn't involved with your murder."

Vierra jerked his head in disbelief. "Your sources? I thought the FBI was supposed to support local law enforcement. How on Earth can you tell us this guy has nothing to do with our case? He was following the victim."

"I feel your frustration, but our counterintelligence unit checked their data. You're gonna have to trust me on this."

Hunter placed a hand on Vierra's chest, preventing him from unloading on this woman. "And if we find any physical evidence or information that points to the driver of that car, will you share your data with us?"

Consuela bit her lower lip. Finally, she said, "If the evidence is overwhelming, I'll let you know." Looking at Vierra, she added, "But it won't be. You can contact me again if anything else turns up. I'm sorry, gentlemen, but I'm late for another meeting. Thanks for stopping by." She marched off to the elevator and waved to a colleague who let her in, and she was gone.

"Jesus, talk about stonewalling," Vierra said.

"More like steamrolling. She could have just sent a text instead of having us come down here. So now what?" Hunter asked.

Vierra continued staring at the elevator banks. "Fuck me if I know. How about we take the night off, get some sleep, and dive back in tomorrow?"

"We could do that." Hunter paused, waiting.

Vierra slumped his shoulders as he turned to face his partner. "Yeah, but you have some other great idea?"

Hunter shuffled one foot as if kicking a stone out on a country road. "Well … we could take up Madeline Merritt's offer to show us the astrology stuff?"

Vierra threw his hands up like a giddy cheerleader. "Ooh, yeah. Let's. Let's all hold hands and have a séance. In the middle of the freaking FBI field office, you mooncalf."

"Oh, don't overreact. She says it might shed some light on the killer's mindset. I'm inviting her to come in tomorrow." Hunter pulled out his phone as Vierra headed for the elevators.

"Wonderful, just tell her not to forget the freaking Ouija board and incense sticks. Let's do this thing right."

··✦❰ 29 ❱✦··

Madeline's Apartment — 5:42 p.m.

After returning home from her visit with Jennifer Acosta, Madeline sat on a stool at her kitchen island in her apartment over the shop. Unable to remove the images of Jennifer's grief from her mind, she skipped working in the shop and came home. But now, with her laptop set up, she entered the information Jennifer gave her and created a chart for the time Jonathan sent his last text. She entered the information on all the pull-down menus and watched as the chart took shape.

It confirmed her worst fears. In setting up the chart, she'd included the fixed star, Caput Algol, which was twenty-six degrees Taurus. According to all the horary astrology books, it meant murder and violence, often to the victim's head. Other interpretations said Jonathan had been kidnapped and then murdered.

She felt a strange sensation filling her mind, an odd sense of responsibility that she'd contributed to Jonathan's murder in some esoteric, tangential way. Was it that Jonathan shopped at her store, and she never got to meet him in person? That he held the promise of potential and a full life, and now it had been erased? Sure, she'd admit her initial attraction to Hunter was a factor, but her intuition said there was more, that something else was pushing her toward it.

"Yoo-hoo, special delivery!"

Ah. Just what she needed. She flew to the door, and in burst Matthew-Tabitha decked out in full Harajuku drag: a full face of makeup, a blond wig, a tight pink bodice, a ruffled pink skirt held up by massive layers of crinoline festooned with pink silk roses, and white lace. Dozens of fabric roses are embedded in the crinoline, making the blossoms fill the skirt like a ballerina's tutu. On her feet were black platform sneakers that were at least five inches thick, and she carried two grocery bags.

"Ah, saved by the drag queen. Come on in, Tabitha," Madeline said.

"Don't mind if I do. I snagged the groceries from your delivery person. They are growing some cuties down at the co-op these days." Matthew-Tabitha carried the groceries to the kitchen island, depositing the bags on the counter.

"And what have I done to receive a visit from Her Majesty?" She asked while putting her purchases away.

"To kick you out of that funk you've been in all day," he pulled out a stool from the island and sat down. "Did the new boyfriend let you down already?"

"Oh please, don't use the BF word for him." As she finished putting away the groceries, she filled Matthew-Tabitha in on her visit to Jennifer Acosta and the new chart.

Matthew-Tabitha pulled her head back in shock. "N to the O to the N. O. You went to see the boy's mother?"

"I know, I know," Madeline said as she leaned her elbows on the countertop. "Like a total shmuckasaurus."

"As well you should. But come on, I didn't get all dressed up just for you." Matthew-Tabitha did a twirl, showing off her frock.

"And what is the inspiration for today's ensemble?"

"It just arrived from Japan. Last month, I was chatting with Grandma Hatsue and, wouldn't you know it, she sends me this Harajuku masterpiece."

"Way to go, grandma." Madeline smiled as she thought of an idea. "Hey, why don't you wear it to Christophe's big meditation eclipse? That ought to be fun?"

Matthew-Tabitha shook her head. "Oh no. I already have my *Mars Attacks* space suit for that clusterfuck."

"You think it's going to be that bad?"

Matthew-Tabitha shook his head. "Gimme that laptop. Let me show you something."

Madeline turned the computer around while Matthew-Tabitha pulled up a stool and sat down. "Why? What's going on?"

"One of my fellow Rosicrucians shared this on our group page." He tapped some keys and swung the computer around. It showed a map of San Francisco, and Matthew-Tabitha zoomed into the area surrounding Grace Cathedral and the Masonic Temple. "Remember how we talked about this spot?"

Madeline let out a sigh. She hadn't thought about Christophe and Grace Cathedral for a long time. "I thought he held all of his events in his swanky compound?"

"Yes, he surely does. Now look at this." With a keystroke, a series of blue lines appeared on the screen. A large circle enveloped the Cathedral with thick blue lines emanating from the front of the entrance, and several lines went all the way across the heart of the city. "This circle is for the Grace Cathedral vortex. This circle draws energy all the way from across the bay."

Madeline leaned closer as he zoomed in and moved the map past San Francisco straight across the East Bay to Mount Diablo. "And this is the energy tanker you mentioned?"

"What's super creepy is the ley lines are manmade."

"What do you mean? I thought ley lines occurred naturally, that they were magnetic energy coming from the earth's core?"

"Yes, because the top of Nob Hill has a natural vortex, but someone, and I'm not saying who, built the lines that connect to Mount Diablo. Probably to draw power to fuel their secret ceremonies."

Madeline looked up at Matthew-Tabitha, waiting for her to spill the beans. "And what kind of people have the juju to set up a line like this?"

Matthew-Tabitha zoomed the map back to Grace Cathedral. "Oh, I don't know, possibly those pesky next-door neighbors. Our dear friends, the Freemasons. I mean, seriously, why do you think they built their meeting hall across the street from a Cathedral?"

She nodded. "So, what are you saying that Christophe is going to tap into this energy? I thought he said on the news that his group would raise the energy?"

"Yeah, and he's going to post meditators running all the way down to the Civic Center to bring up enough energy to clear out all the old negative vibes left over from the massacre of the Ohlone? That's a mighty big draw. I don't think he really knows what he's doing."

A shiver ran through Madeline as her thoughts raced to the map Christophe designed for their ceremony. He had confessed not knowing what he was doing back then, either.

··»◦ 30 ◦«··

FRIDAY, AUGUST 11, 2017

Homicide Division Conference Room — 1:27 p.m.

Standing before a projection screen filled with the three planets in signs the killer left at the crime scene, Madeline breathed air deeply into her lungs and focused on her heart, hoping to hide her nervousness. Regretting, for the seventeenth time, the third Mojito Matthew-Tabitha insisted she drink the night before, the alcohol still swirling in her intestines.

She'd tried on several outfits while dampening her gnawing anxiety. Matthew-Tabitha convinced her to go with a gray gabardine pantsuit matched with a floral silk scarf and pulled her hair up in a tasteful chignon, hoping to achieve at least the appearance of a professional, someone with authority. Madeline spritzed on some Chanel number five, but it gasped and paled in competition with the aftershaves and bro-colognes clogging the small room.

Hunter set up the meeting in an anonymous conference room inside the homicide section of the Hall of Justice. She finished explaining the placement of Mercury, Mars, Moon, and the three corresponding Tarot cards.

Her eyes met Hunter's as he sat across from her, pen poised over his portfolio, his neutral expression masking any personal bias. His partner, Vierra, sat further from the table, legs crossed, with a permanent scowl. To her surprise, Hunter's partner turned out to be a tall, lanky guy with a wild jewfro. It was unexpected, but then again, she would never have guessed that Matthew-Tabitha, a transgender occasional cross-dresser, would be her product manager.

Their boss, Lieutenant Leo, a short man with a paunch, nursed his coffee while Alistair hung back, looking for a neutral space to support her but knowing he needed to protect his reputation with his colleagues.

"Summing up, the three planets in signs your killer left you are meaningless without a location and a time to cast the chart." Madeline clicked a key on her laptop to change the slide on the projection screen behind her. The first three planets in signs disappeared.

She noted the blank stares from Leo and Vierra while Alistair smiled. Hunter smiled, his eyes softened, but the tension in his clenched jaw revealed his anxiousness. Taking a deep breath, she continued her presentation.

"I mentioned to Investigator Davis that a handful of astrologers practice a technique called forensic astrology."

"Excuse me?" Vierra piped up. "Forensic astrology? That's some joke, right?"

Madeline steadied her nerves. "Not for the practitioners. They use a classic form of horary astrology. It provides symbolic information about the relationship between the victim and the perpetrator. I asked Investigator Davis for the time the 911 call came through." She clicked on the next page of her presentation. "Here is the chart I created."

Vierra sat back and shook his head like a skeptic at a magic show. Hunter and Leo both leaned in.

"I realize this is all gibberish, so I'll walk you through the key elements. On the right side of the pie chart is the rising sign. Here, we have Leo, ruled by the Sun, which is in the first house. This symbolizes your victim. Please remember that I have no specifics about this case. Investigator Davis only gave me the symbols and the time of the call. Are we all clear about this?"

"Sure thing, Star Doctor," Vierra said. "So, what does it mean the Sun is our victim?" Feeling the skepticism coming from Vierra, Madeline kept her composure and moved forward. This was her area of expertise, time to take these guys to school.

"It means potential. The Sun is the life giver—a clear, radiant energy. But here's what's interesting. The Sun rises in the east but runs right into the planet Mars, which is also in Leo."

Vierra's eyes darted toward the other guys, a mix of surprise, and perhaps he felt slighted as they showed interest in her presentation. "And so, like men are from Mars and chicks are from Venus?" Vierra's joke got a few soft chuckles, diffusing the tension pulsing through the air since she'd arrived in the room.

Madeline relaxed a few degrees. "Spot on. Mars is the god of war, and it's in Leo, a fire sign that makes it explosive. Based on my understanding, your victim was a vibrant and promising individual in the wrong place at the wrong time. He encountered an enormous force of violence, which led to his unfortunate end. In horary astrology, Mars is associated with men, danger, combat, strife, and weapons of all kinds, especially guns." Vierra's accusatory stare locked onto Hunter, who recoiled in response. As Alistair and Lieutenant Leo locked eyes, a silent conversation passed between them. She must have hit a nerve.

"Why guns?" Hunter asked, trying his best to keep his voice steady.

Madeline placed her hand on a horary reference volume she brought to back up her claims. "Yes, from the horary books I consulted, Mars often shows death by gunshot."

Lieutenant Leo squinted at the chart. "Okay, but you're telling me this chart shows you a young victim being harmed by a weapon of some sort. It could be a knife or something else, right?"

"Yes, that's right," Madeline agreed. "But whatever weapon the killer used, death came fast and violent. And remember, this is all symbolic. I'm offering it to help you focus your investigation, to help you find the facts." She glanced at Alistair, his face looking grim.

"I'm aware none of this will hold up in a court of law. But if it helps you sift through a mountain of clues to find this killer, then I've done my job." She waited for a moment, but Hunter wouldn't meet her eyes, and she sensed the tension building between him and Vierra, so she kept going. "The next important symbol is what's on the opposite side of the chart. This gives us insight into your killer. And here, exactly opposite the Sun by two degrees, is the Moon."

"Is this rare?" Leo asked.

Madeline motioned to the entire chart. "All of this is rare. All of this is specific to this exact time in this exact place. This chart will never show up again for another 250,000 years." That caught everyone's attention. All four men leaned in, captivated. She'd witnessed this before when teaching her astrology classes. Deep within each person, this information resonated with their hearts, but convincing their egos proved challenging.

"In astrology, the Moon," she continued, keeping her voice calm and confident, "is thought to be a feminine planet, and my interpretation is your killer is a woman."

"Really? A woman?" Leo asked, his tone revealing his disbelief.

"That's what the chart is telling me. Now, the Moon is also within fifteen degrees of Pluto, symbolizing death and transformation. It may sound cliché, but the forces of darkness are helping the Moon, so to speak."

"So to speak?" Vierra shook his head, physically denying what she said, and his frustration with her came to a head. "This stuff is B.S. What's your hustle here, lady? What are you pulling?"

Alistair jumped to her defense. "She's not here to pull anything. She's studied this stuff for years. You should thank her for helping you."

"I'm sorry, but this is all supposition based on superstition. Who fed you details about our crime scene? I want to know who is leaking your information?"

Madeline stepped back to take herself further out of the range of Vierra's frustration. Alistair was about to defend her again, but she cut him off. "Investigator Vierra, I understand your frustration with what for some is total superstition, the feeling that we have science now, so we don't need astrology. "But, as I explained to Investigator Davis, it doesn't matter if you take me seriously," she said with a hint of frustration. Your killer takes this seriously. And she or he is messing with you by only giving you the three planets in signs and not an entire chart."

"But why? What's his or her reason for all of this?" Hunter asked before Vierra could jump in.

Madeline kept her gaze focused on Hunter. "He or she has given you three symbols." Madeline tapped the computer key to bring back the first graphic. "There are nine planets to consider, plus hundreds of fixed stars and asteroids astrologers use in charts. The killer gave you three. Does he plan to give you more? Will they show up at another crime scene? How many crimes have to be committed before you understand this reality?"

"We're already considering it," said Vierra, and sat back in his chair. "Are you saying you can use this little chart to tell us what the killer's gonna do next?

Because that would be helpful." He finished with mock sincerity, but at least he'd calmed down.

"Astrology is all about patterns in place and time. You found the first body on a Monday at six in the morning under a full Moon. What if it's as simple as Mondays? Next Monday morning, the moon will be at its last quarter before going dark. On the following Monday, there will be a total solar eclipse. It's just a thought. But I have one more chart to show you before I go." She found her fingers shaking as she clicked on the next screen.

"This chart is for 2:01 on Sunday morning. The location is Corte Madera. I got this time and location when I spoke to Jennifer Acosta." She braced herself.

"You did what?!" Vierra blasted as he stood up. Lt. Leo shook his head, and Madeline felt Hunter shrink as if he'd been punched. Even Alistair's energy shifted.

"I'm sorry, Ms. Merritt," Lt. Leo started, "but that is uncalled for. Talking to the victim's mother? The woman's grieving, for god's sake."

The shame rushed through her body as images of Jennifer's pained face flashed through her memory. "Please hear me out." Madeline held her palms out in front of her as if to push back the spiking energy from their reactions. "I scanned my customer database and discovered her son Jonathan Acosta ordered books from my store." Madeline paused, and everyone's eyes popped out. Any sympathy they had for her vanished, but she kept going. "I informed Mrs. Acosta about this and asked her permission to come and speak with her. I wanted to know when Jonathan sent his last text so I could cast this chart. She told me she received a text from Jonathan at 2:01 a.m."

Vierra shook his head. "This is unbelievable. What the actual fuck! This woman just lost her only child, and you show up selling her your crap!"

"And her son bought four astrology books from me," Madeline continued. "So, Jonathan didn't think astrology is crap, and neither did his mother. I understand your frustration, but I'm only helping."

Lieutenant Leo heaved a sigh as he sat back in his chair. "No one here doubts your sincerity, but we need evidence. Hard facts. And adding to this woman's emotional turmoil. Well. That's. That's just." He shook his head, unable to finish.

"I understand you, believe me. I won't approach her again. But I suggest you go back and speak with her. She thinks there's something strange about the text. She doesn't think Jonathan sent it."

Silence lingered in the room, and Madeline worked up the courage to look at Hunter.

"Why did she say that?" Hunter asked.

"She said Jonathan never much liked sleepovers, even when he was little. And the language of the text didn't sound like him at all. My guess is the killer hacked his phone. And this chart, this fixed star called Algol at twenty-six degrees Taurus, tells me they kidnapped Jonathan before they killed him."

Hunter and Vierra shared an exchange - Vierra facepalmed and shook his head.

"Well, you've given us a lot to think about." Lieutenant Leo stood up, signaling they'd all heard enough. "But let me confirm: Jonathan shopped at your store. Do you remember him?"

"No, I don't. My Product Manager does. I can get you in touch with him."

"Okay, pass that on to Hunter. Thank you for coming in." He offered his hand, and Madeline shook it.

Hunter stood up, "text me the information, and I'll let Alistair show you out. Thanks."

Madeline noted a sudden softness in his demeanor and knew he supported her, but his loyalty was to his guys.

"Thanks for taking the time to listen." She turned the projector off. "I have copies of the chart for you." She passed them to Hunter, who accepted them with a smile. Vierra ignored them and pulled out his phone to check a notification.

"I'll help you with your equipment," Alistair said, joining Madeline at her laptop. "I'm sure Vierra and Davis have work to do."

"Yes, we do. No offense, Ms. Merritt," Vierra said and turned to Hunter, mumbling, "I gotta step out for a minute. Catch you back in the incident room in ten," and raced from the room. While Vierra's exit captured her attention, unbeknownst to her, Hunter had been silently observing her. She sensed his hesitation, as if he had something to say to her, but opted for silence, not wanting to speak in front of Alistair. He stumbled over his words briefly before blurting out, "Yeah, thanks again," his cheeks turning red. "Your work is impressive. We'll be in touch," he said, his words lingering in the air, and then he left her with Alistair.

Madeline's knees quaked, and the encounter was more stressful than she'd imagined. Once Hunter left, she breathed out a long sigh.

"You rattled them," Alistair said and unplugged the projector. "I mean to the core."

Madeline unhooked the cables. "I'm sorry, but that's what the chart showed me."

"Come on, let me walk you out."

Madeline finished packing her gear, and her nerves settled. They left the room to find Hunter waiting outside in the small foyer. "Hey, I wanted to, you know, apologize. My partner can be…"

"A tool?" Alistair asked.

Madeline let out a sigh of relief and smiled. "Not at all. I've seen worse reactions. This hits a nerve for some folks."

"Yeah, so," Hunter said, waving at her while Alistair was texting. "I'll call you, okay."

"Drop by the shop anytime," she said, pretending to sound casual, even though she rehearsed that line all afternoon.

Hunter's genuine smile illuminated his face, the same one she felt spreading across her face. And then he turned and disappeared around the corner.

Madeline walked with Alistair to a bank of elevators. "Talk about a tough room," she said when the elevator arrived, and they got in. "But I didn't expect so much pushback from Vierra."

"Don't sweat it. You made your point. You did your job, and I'm hoping they'll catch this killer before he—or she—strikes again," Alistair said. They rode in silence to the lobby. After an awkward pause, Alistair turned to Madeline. "Let's go grab a cup of coffee," he said.

It took her a split second, but she decided, why not? Alistair came to her defense, and she needed some caffeine. "I'd like that," she said.

***

Cora stood on the sidewalk across the street, unable to believe her eyes.

Madeline, her sister, stood outside the Hall of Justice talking with the assistant D.A. Were they flirting? He had a hand on her shoulder, and they went down the sidewalk together. What the actual heck? Cora accepted the fact that Madeline bewildered her. She had no idea who this woman was. Then she considered the photos in her folder, photos of a dead boy wrapped in the quilt, and knew somehow that her sister had become entangled with this murder, and the whole situation really pissed her off.

If her sister wanted to keep secrets, Cora could to. Following her instincts, she crossed the street and walked up the steps. As she entered the Hall of Justice, she considered seeing Vierra again. Maybe she would have the chance to meet his partner and get her burning questions answered.

···»◇**31**◇«···

Incident Room — 2:46 p.m.

Hunter stared at a printed version of Madeline's chart for the 911 call and thought about her prediction: the next body might show up on Monday morning. It shocked him to think the "astroguy" planned his kills this far in advance, but he recollected the first crime scene and the meticulousness of the staging. It made perfect sense that the killer worked from a timeline, but why? What was he gaining from this? Making the cops look like fools? Terrorizing teenagers into staying home nights?

Vierra bounded into the room. "What the fuck was that all about?" Vierra slammed his hand on the worktable where Hunter sat.

"Cool the hell down. Weren't you listening?" Hunter stood, appalled at Vierra's behavior toward Madeline and now at this outburst.

"Yeah, I listened to your girlfriend pull a fast one on us. She called Jonathan's mother. Went to her house?"

Hunter added the astrology chart to the whiteboard, experiencing an unknown anger toward his partner. "She's not my girlfriend, so back off."

"Yeah, well, you want her to be. I can't stand this cutesy crap."

Hunter's right arm itched to punch his partner in the face. "Hey, no one's giving you shit about what you're doing with your girlfriend."

"Hey, you lovebirds, cut me some goddamn slack," Leo said, bursting in on them. "Vierra, if the killer left clues in Swahili and we brought in a translator, would it make you this upset?" Leo asked. "Hunter, your astrology lady is charming. And face it, she's got a fifty-fifty chance the killer is a woman."

Vierra whined. "Ah, lieutenant, please, don't tell me you're taking her side?"

"I'm not taking anyone's fucking side. Let's examine the fucking facts and leave the fucking emotion out of it," Leo barked. "Okay?"

Hunter breathed in, tamping down his anger. His boss was right.

"Okay. Fact one," Vierra pointed to a photo on the whiteboard. "This sigil embroidered on the quilt from our crime scene matches Madeline's shop logo."

"But does that connect her shop and Savvy Seekers?" Leo asked and pointed at Hunter. "Did you ask Madeline if she's connected to Christophe and his gang?"

Hunter paused in a slight panic. He reviewed their conversations. "I asked her, but she didn't answer."

"That's a legitimate line of inquiry," said Vierra, his voice sharp with sarcasm.

"Yeah, and fact two," Hunter fired back, "we spoke with Jonathan's teacher, his friends, and that Stellan kid. We confirmed Jonathan studied astrology, and Madeline confirmed he shopped at her store. She didn't hide it."

Vierra pointed at Hunter as a secretary approached him and murmured in Vierra's ear. Vierra nodded his response, and the secretary walked out of the room. Vierra threw his hands in the air. "And fact number three," said Vierra, his face full of intrigue, "Madeline's little sister is here to see me."

Hunter's jaw dropped. "You're kidding?"

"No, I'll bring her to the conference room."

***

Hunter walked back to the small conference room where they had listened to Madeline's presentation, intrigued by the sight of Vierra bringing in a younger version of Madeline, dressed in a tailored black suit, an ivory silk blouse, and high-heeled boots.

"Ms. Merritt, I'm investigator Davis," Hunter said, shaking her hand. "Your sister Madeline mentioned you were in San Francisco." He motioned for her to take a seat and sat across from her while Leo and Vierra took seats around the table.

"Call me Cora," she said, sitting. "I'm sorry, but my sister hasn't told me anything about you. You'll be happy to hear that she upheld your request for confidentiality."

Hunter liked her. That dash of spunk went well with her fashion choices. "I'm sure you understand our need to keep information about this case from leaking to the press."

"And this is our boss, Lieutenant Leo," said Vierra, taking over. "Now, I've been told you have something important to show us related to the murder on Russian Hill."

Cora cleared her throat and placed a manila folder on the table. "I've been in touch with one of the city's local crime bloggers. I checked with my boss—this one is a legitimate source of information. The reporters at the station can't be everywhere in the city, so they rely on sources like bloggers for hot tips and—"

"—Got it," Leo interrupted. "Our press office deals with them on a regular basis. So, what's in the file?"

Hunter studied Cora and couldn't help but imagine Madeline at this age. Young and curious, Cora doing her best to sound authoritative.

"This morning, my source sent me these." Cora opened the folder and spread three pages out on the table.

As Hunter processed the crime scene images, his heart dropped into his stomach, leaving him feeling defeated. Their efforts to keep information from the press were in vain, as it eventually leaked. Cora spread out five photographs - three captured the Ina Coolbrith Park crime scene, while the other two focused on Jonathan. One is a closeup taken with a flash, which must have come straight from Connie's camera. The other two showed Jonathan's body wrapped in the quilt with its bright colors and embroidered quotes.

"Are we going to see these splashed on tonight's news?" Vierra asked in a confrontational tone.

"Not at my station," Cora was quick to answer. "I promised my source I'd keep them to myself. But I realized you needed to see these. Who would have access to photos like this other than the killer or someone on your team? And I can't imagine why the killer would share photos with the media. Could someone in your department leak this information? Or the killer wants some recognition for his work. Ooh, yeah, that could be it. He wants attention, credit, glory—"

"—You did the right thing," Hunter said, interrupting Cora's unsettling train of thought. "Thank you."

Cora sat back, self-conscious about taking things too far. "I asked my source where they got the photos, but they said they got them from an anonymous source. I also asked why they did not post these on their blog, but they said they wanted to see what happens next. My source thinks it's the work of a serial killer. Is that true?"

Vierra sighed and squeezed the bridge of his nose to manage his frustration.

"I'm sorry, but we can't discuss the case with you. But tell me, what's your sister's background? How did she become an astrologer?"

Hunter wanted to kick Vierra under the table but focused on Cora, who thought about Vierra's question.

"My sister is nine years older than me. We were both born and raised in Honolulu. Madeline applied to colleges here to study mathematics when I was still a kid."

"Mathematics? In college?" Vierra said.

"It qualifies her as a total freak show from the start. We weren't close, and then Mom told me one day that Madeline had moved in with Aunty Jane. When Jane moved up to a cabin in Oregon, Madeline agreed to run the shop, and she moved into the apartment upstairs."

Hunter leaned in. "So, did she get into astrology after working in the store?"

"No clue." Cora sighed and continued. "Our folks weren't too happy about it. But Mom said she took wonderful care of Aunty Jane when she got sick."

Vierra stood, signaling he'd heard enough. "Okay, thanks for coming by, Ms. Merritt. I'll walk you out."

"You did the right thing, young lady," Leo said as he shook her hand, turning over his shoulder to Vierra. "Make sure you give her your card. In case this blogger gives you more information about our case."

"Thank you," Cora stood, taking a deep breath before asking, "And remember me when you need someone to break this thing. If I bring an exclusive to the station, it will do wonders for my career."

Hunter sat back as Vierra ushered Cora from the room, impressed with her gumption to make a case for herself. She stood her ground like Madeline did in this room an hour ago.

Leo pulled the pictures toward him and pursed his lips. "The astrology stuff is a little too up in the atmosphere for me. But the older sister's suggestion about Mondays—that sticks, you know?" Leo rubbed his chin. "Perfectly legit, but where? Do we put extra cops back on Russian Hill?"

Hunter shook his head, thinking. "I found nothing in Jonathan Acosta's background to connect him to any place on Russian Hill. He's from Corte Madera, and his school is in Mill Valley."

Vierra returned to the room, shaking his head. "No. This is just. NO. Let's look at the bigger picture here. What if, and Hunter, I know you don't want to hear this, but what if Madeline is actually our killer's partner?"

Hunter's body trembled, and his hand clenched up without realizing it. Vierra held a hand before his face as if to fend off Hunter's anger. "Now, hear me out. We listened to her entire show, right? And what if it's just that, a show? The killer setting up the symbols. Even calling Alistair in?"

"But that's ridiculous." Hunter's stomach turned itself into knots.

"Is it? What did Alistair say? A secretary called him. Not *his* secretary. Let's think this through. What if 'astroguy' called Alistair, knowing he'd send us to Madeline? She's saying the symbols at the crime scene are meaningless but, then comes in, and we spend what an hour looking at some other astrology chart when we could be running down other leads?"

Leo stood up. "But you've followed up on every lead, and there's just too many moving pieces. Okay, it's Friday. If Monday is the day, "Astroguy" has already lined up his next victim. If Madeline is connected to this killer, and if she's throwing all this symbological stuff at us, I want evidence for both our sakes."

Hunter agreed with his boss and his partner. "So where do we go now? What's the plan, action man?"

Leo pointed to the photos on the table. "I want the two of you to follow Madeline this weekend. I'll get the captain to approve a budget item to get you some help. Old school stakeout, forty-eight hours. Do it."

Hunter acknowledged the plan to follow Madeline made the most sense, but thinking about it made him feel like a lovesick stalker, and it gave him the creeps. "Is that the best option we have?"

"Look at it this way. We'll also spot her if she does something stupid, like going to the crime scene and holding a séance to ask Jonathan who killed him. You hear me?"

"Loud and clear," Hunter said.

⟨·32·⟩

Sunday, August 13, 2017

Polk Street — 9:43 a.m.

Hunter parked his car on Polk Street, which offered a direct view of Madeline's shop and upstairs apartment. Their exacting surveillance plan turned into a bust: Madeline didn't go anywhere. Not to the movies, not to a bar, not to see her sister—nowhere. It had to be the weirdest stakeout he'd ever worked on. Leo recruited a couple of investigators to take the night shift, and they thanked him for the easiest overtime they'd ever earned. Madeline worked in her store and went home at night.

Now, early Sunday morning, a sense of frustration and anger grew within him, fueled by Astroguy's wasting their time. Despite everything appearing normal, a nagging feeling in his gut told him Madeline was hiding something, but what? What if this wasn't the work of a serial killer? What if there wasn't going to be a body dumped tomorrow morning or ever? What if it was a one-off?

The blue curtains covering Madeline's window parted, and he caught a flash of purple fabric. Hunter leaned forward and caught her looking out her front window, checking the weather as she shrugged her purple jacket over a long-sleeved blue shirt. Was she getting ready to go out? He saw her grab a scarf, and he quickly took inventory of his clothing: he'd remembered his good walking shoes and a dark brown jacket to blend in; he had a hat stuffed in a pocket and cash in his billfold because you never wanted to be stuck. He waited, and then she walked out of her front door on Polk, heading toward California Street.

Hunter got out of the car and stayed on his side of the street, keeping Madeline in sight several yards ahead of him. When she turned down California, he stopped to peer in a shop window, waiting for her to walk a few steps ahead. He thought about texting Vierra but decided it was easier to handle it himself. Hunter kept a solid pace as Madeline walked with purpose, but it wasn't the walk of the career criminal. No, she drew her shoulders back, her stride long and loose. She took in her surroundings, a happy city dweller enjoying the morning.

***

Madeline breathed in the fresh air and enjoyed the chill as it spread through her lungs. She'd resisted the voice. After leaving Cora several messages about their weekend plans and getting no response, Madeline accepted that her sister didn't want to see her, which darkened her mood. Her apartment, usually a sanctuary, felt suffocating and cramped. And she was desperate for a break from the shop, yearning for a change of scenery.

She'd gone downstairs and performed her regular Sunday morning ritual: at six a.m. on the dot, she'd taken her sage bundle and her set of Tibetan bells and smudged the store, going into every nook and cranny, waving the healing smoke while jingling the tiny, tinkling bells to clear the energy and shoo away any mischievous spirits still lingering in the space. A ceremonial nod to fire and air always calmed her nerves. But not today. Still recovering from Vierra's adverse reaction to her presentation the day before, she needed fresh air to clear her head. At Hyde Street corner, a cable car waited to depart, but she chose to keep walking, taking comfort in her familiar neighborhood.

She promised not to indulge in the idea of Hunter, in the possibility of him—the man—separate from his job. But she couldn't help herself. She'd created Hunter's birth chart from the information he gave her on Tuesday night. A double Sag. Both Sun and Moon in Sagittarius, with Taurus rising, which matched her Sun in Taurus—that accounted for the ease she experienced with him.

Madeline studied the chart in her mind as she walked. His Sun in a Fire sign explained his drive to find the facts, so the abstract quality of astrology didn't fit in his wheelhouse. Saturn in the first house explained his becoming a police officer, as Saturn was the "bad cop" of the galaxy. But his Jupiter balanced that out in the eighth, which accounted for his ease in dealing with death and also his genuine understanding of human nature. Walking past the Top of the Mark, she waved at the doorman, her mind filled with the idea of inviting Hunter for drinks there, even though she knew it was a fantasy. Despite the professional boundaries, it would be refreshing to see him in a relaxed atmosphere where he could let go of his "cop" persona.

***

Hunter relaxed his stride. Now that Madeline was deep in thought, he could take the vigilance down a notch. She turned right and headed down Powell. He jogged across California Street, staying behind her. Hunter drifted through several tourists, keeping her purple coat in sight, and felt irritated; he felt cheated. He should be out enjoying Sunday in the city, not following—no, he'd guessed it right, stalking—Madeline. Seeing her brought a mix of comfort and unease. He'd be more productive if he were at the office, digging through Jonathan's computer files or analyzing the autopsy report, but watching her hair float around her shoulders as she strode with such confidence gave him hope. Genuine, kind people still exist in the world.

She walked past Union Square, which was filled with tourists clogging the sidewalks on both sides of the street. He watched her purple coat and noticed her pulling out her cell phone. He angled his body away from her and checked his phone when she turned toward him. Had she spotted him? He was relieved when he realized she was taking a photo of the Dewey Monument, its female statue holding a wreath and a trident glittering in the morning sun. His anonymity was still safe.

***

Madeline checked her photo of the statue, one of her favorites in the city. As she pocketed her phone, it hit her: she couldn't afford to think about Hunter, and yet, when she tried to think of something else, her mind zeroed in on the store and that Jonathan shopped there. She remembered the title on the notebook in Jonathan's backpack:

"Know-sis: Enlightenment for All." An ambitious idea for a teenager.

Looking down the street, she realized she needed to talk to Sluggo. Sometimes, he hung out down at the Ferry Building. She was already on her way there. Then she remembered she needed to call Matthew-Tabitha. Madeline needed him to check the backroom and their stock of books on horary and evolutionary astrology. She wanted to add them to the window display dedicated to the solar eclipse, so she called and left him a long message also asking him to look for posters of the sign Leo and other lion-related things to fill in the display.

***

Hunter kept an easy rhythm as they continued past the shops along Powell Street, wondering if she'd stop in any of the stores. But she moved through the crowds as Powell hit Market Street at the cable car turnaround. Unfazed by the tourists, the homeless people, and the insistent Sunday hucksters, she kept going. He braced himself, as it was an unpredictable crowd, and he checked around to spot any officers on patrol.

In his early days on the force, he'd taught a self-defense course for women, and he felt a growing panic as he witnessed Madeline do everything wrong. She waved at bus drivers, stopped to speak with strangers and pet their dogs. She admired the crazy lady's mismatched display of stolen bric-à-brac set out as a makeshift sales stall on a dirty blanket. Madeline did everything he always warned women not to do. She didn't walk defensively. She wasn't worried about projecting confidence. Madeline didn't hold her purse tight to her side to dissuade thieves. She didn't scan the area for potential threats—she enjoyed walking through the dangerous crowd on Market Street. He wanted to run ahead and stop her, but he couldn't. How did she do it? What was her secret? Why wasn't she afraid?

He tried to picture her as a killer, stalking her prey, setting a cunning trap, and going in for the kill. Impossible. Then a vibration in his gut exploded as an idea: What if she was just the decoy? What if the killer was one of her customers? What if he blackmailed her into this? Could "Astroguy" set her up to be the focus of the investigation? He dismissed the ideas and chalked it up to hanging with Vierra for so long. It seemed implausible but not impossible.

Madeline walked down Market Street through the empty financial district, and Hunter understood her destination as she crossed the Embarcadero to the Ferry Building. He rushed, keeping up with her, not wanting to lose her in the busy marketplace along the ferry docks. Did she plan on grabbing a ferry? Where was she headed? If she crossed the bay, he'd have to follow. She entered the building near the ice cream shop, and he quickened his pace so he wouldn't lose her in the crowd.

Upon entering the grand hall, the enticing aroma of freshly brewed artisanal coffee, warm baked bread, and a subtle whiff of sea salt from the nearby ferry dock overwhelmed him with a longing to enjoy the space, instead of stalking Madeline. He looked to his left—no sign of her, then right—and spotted her in a stall that sold soaps, herbal concoctions, and frilly lacy things. She stood before an ornate framed mirror, admiring her reflection. Just as she turned her head, she glimpsed his reflection in the mirror. Their eyes made contact. As he watched, he saw her eyes light up with a flash of recognition reflected in the mirror. Hunter's heart sank as a million shitty opening lines played through his brain, but he couldn't. The job wouldn't let him, so he turned, pretending the moment hadn't happened, and he escaped into the crowd, finding a pillar to hide behind.

As he eavesdropped, the saleswoman asked Madeline if she needed anything. As polite as ever, she said no. When he peeked out, he saw her scanning the area, searching for him. After a moment, she gave up the search for him and heaved a sigh, defeated. Hunter also let out a sigh. He'd been burned, and there was nothing to do but watch her walk—no, shuffle—down the hall, staring at the floor.

***

Madeline questioned her senses, but there was no mistaking that she had spotted Hunter in that mirror. It brought a moment of elation, of hope that he'd stop, and they could have another conversation, one that had nothing to do with killers and corpses, but he'd bolted with no explanation. She wandered down the hall. Normally she'd shop in the gourmet stores, but her heart wasn't in it anymore. It was uncanny how she had just been thinking about him, only to have him appear out of nowhere and freak out and leave.

Mid-thought, she paused, knowing in an instant Hunter was following her. She pulled away from the crowd and stood for a moment. His decision to follow her implied she'd gone from a consultant on the case to a suspect. Did he believe she had any involvement with the killer? Then, the deeper cut: no matter what happened with this case, she was just another suspect, another source in a long line of investigations. That's what he did. It's who he was. Someone who sifted through the mess that murder left behind. She was just another part of the job for him, nothing special.

Madeline exited the building, abandoning the thought of searching for Sluggo, and surveyed the farmers' market on the concourse. Usually, she'd take her time, lingering at each stall, hoping to find exciting products, new vendors, something to tease her tastebuds. Instead, she would pick up some vegetables and head home. The morning couldn't get any worse.

***

Hunter stayed behind the pillar long enough for Madeline to get further down the hall. He pulled out the beanie in his jacket and mashed it on his head in case she turned around. But he knew she wouldn't, as her entire body language had changed from happy-go-lucky to defeated. She walked with her head down, ignoring the bright shop stalls, and left through the exit. Deflated by his cowardice, he criticized his decision. Why hadn't he stopped to chat with her? Make it appear like a casual meeting. He had the skills to make it happen, right?

He followed her outside, navigating the farmers' market stalls. At a produce stand, she grabbed a shopping basket and filled it with bunches of fresh spinach, some garlic, and onion, and she reached for a bag of white mushrooms. He got hungry, thinking how she'd chosen his favorites. All they needed was some red wine and a hefty steak to go with it.

Hunter imagined them sitting at a candle-lit table -- when the high-pitched wail of an infant shattered his reverie. He spotted the mother with a baby carriage behind Madeline. The woman leaned over to pick up her screaming bundle, and as she bent over the stroller, Hunter observed Madeline's face contorted in sheer horror. Madeline spun so fast that her shopping basket slammed into a pile of tomatoes, knocking several to the ground. Madeline stared at the baby, now soothed in its mother's arms; a wave of hopelessness washed over her face.

The stall owner, a kind man in an apron, approached Madeline, and she snapped out of her dazed state. And she saw the ruined tomatoes at her feet. Squatting down, she threw them into her basket and insisted on paying for all of them. She gave the money to the vendor, apologizing for the mess. He tried to comfort her, saying it happened often. However, Hunter knew he'd failed her and it led to a loss of trust, ruining her bright day. He felt insignificant and small as he watched her walk away, letting her go alone. Madeline crossed the Embarcadero and disappeared into the crowd. He no longer had the stomach for the job.

❨33❩

M‍ONDAY, A‍UGUST 14, 2017

Madeline's Apartment — 5:44 a.m.

Madeline rose before dawn, craving her morning meditation, seeking solace from the fiasco at the Ferry Building. Checking her daily horoscope, she spotted the issue: her Mars was opposite her Sun, a difficult transit. She'd done her best to salvage the day by making an appetizing Bolognaise sauce from the tomatoes she'd knocked over at the Market. She ate her dinner at the kitchen island instead of her usual seat by the window, assuming either Hunter or some other cop still had her under surveillance, waiting to see if she planned to dump a body somewhere on Monday morning. It was unbelievable how her prediction and her effort to help the police had pushed her to the top of their suspect list, which resulted in the mess at the Ferry Building.

After a deep meditation, she felt grounded and more at ease. She couldn't blame Hunter and Vierra for clutching at straws; she knew she was innocent, but overthinking the situation would only cause more stress. From her front window, she spotted Hunter sitting in his car across the street, his hand tapping on the steering wheel, staring off into the distance. She picked up her phone and placed an order at the downstairs coffee shop. Because she hated ambiguity, because she knew he had a demanding job, and because the temperature had dropped overnight, she pulled on her coat and went to the café. Armed with a cup of coffee and takeout bags, she marched down the sidewalk toward Hunter's car.

After a moment, he clocked her approaching him. As she met his gaze, her heart raced. With nowhere for him to hide, she watched his reactions play on his face. A second of surprise, followed by a nanosecond of recrimination. He emerged from his old Toyota, hands in his pockets. He stared at the gray cement sidewalk while waiting for her. Being cautious, Madeline approached, and as she got closer, their eyes met, causing her to halt, maintaining a safe distance of a few feet. Just as he was about to say something, she interrupted him and handed him the cup. "I figured you could use some coffee since you've been here at least 4 in the morning."

Hunter took the cup, letting its warmth permeate his stiff hands, astonished that she'd already blown his cover as early as four in the morning. Was that normal? But even as he asked himself the question, he already knew the answer: she was anything but ordinary.

Madeline gathered her nerves, and words tumbled from her mouth. "I don't know what you like in your coffee, so you'll find packets of sugar, aspartame, and stevia in this bag. Also, a few little creamers, just in case."

Hunter accepted the small white paper bag, unable to suppress a smile as he tore off the coffee's cover and took a sip. It was exactly how he liked it: black and bitter. He suppressed a smile and let her continue her speech.

Madeline drew her shoulders back, steadying herself. "And I thought you might be hungry, so here." She handed him the larger brown paper bag. "Again, I didn't know what you liked, so I got an everything bagel with cream cheese and a plain toasted bagel with butter."

Balancing the coffee on the roof of his car, Hunter accepted the bag of bagels and opened it, never taking his eyes off her.

Madeline checked her watch and kept talking, unable to stop the tension filling her voice. "And so, it's 6 a.m. on Monday, and as you can clearly see, I'm not killing anyone—unless you think I poisoned your coffee—which I didn't — sorry, that was a stupid thing to say, never mind. What I mean is, I am obviously not dumping a body in a nearby park."

As Hunter chewed on the plain bagel, he consciously tried to stifle his laughter, not wanting to hurt her feelings or seem like he was mocking her. When she stopped, he swallowed and cleared his throat. "Madeline?"

She crossed her arms before her chest, preparing for the worst. But at least she'd made her peace.

"Madeline, I know you aren't a killer. I've known that since I met you. I've followed career criminals, and you do not fit the profile. Trust me."

Madeline averted his eyes, unable to muster the courage to look at him. "But yesterday…?" She asked, her voice trembling."

Hunter cringed, feeling like a yutz all over again. "Yesterday was my mistake. As you figured, we've been watching you since Friday. Leo ordered us to do it."

"Oh. It's the just-doing-my-job excuse." She heard the sarcasm in her voice and cringed, wishing she had given him a chance to explain.

"Unfortunately, yes. You are the only person we have with a direct connection to both victims. And we're clutching at straws. But as you said, now we have proof you didn't do it. But we also know the killer wants us to pay attention to you." He grabbed his coffee and took another sip.

Madeline nodded. "I get that."

"And I apologize for yesterday. When you spotted me, an old habit kicked in, so I turned around. I could have done better." He sipped his coffee and paused, needing to be sincere. "I should have acknowledged seeing you. I could have made up some excuse about being there by chance. But it would have been a lie, and you'd have spotted it immediately."

Madeline let that seep in, knowing he was right. She knew that if he had lied to her, she would have felt it, which would have been painful.

Hunter softened his tone. "If I hadn't been working and this situation was different, I'd buy you a bagel. Or one of those designer grilled cheese sandwiches from the gourmet shop in the Ferry Building."

Madeline's right hand flew up over her mouth.

Hunter continued. "And I'd suggest that we go out to the dock and find a quiet bench to watch the ferries come and go on a lazy Sunday afternoon."

"You enjoy watching the ferries?" She whispered through her fingers, her eyes fixed on his as if they were watching them together.

"Yeah," Hunter said. "I used to do it with my dad. We'd jog down from the Presidio, have a bite, and hang around the docks before heading home. He liked that you could buy a ticket, hop a ferry, and go on an adventure."

Hunter picked up his coffee and took another swig. "And for the record, I take my coffee black. Too many years on stakeout trained me to drink it that way. And while I appreciate the everything bagel, a plain toasted with butter is my favorite."

Madeline beamed, but her throat choked up, and she didn't want to speak for fear of crying in front of him after he'd said … what he just said. She turned to go but stopped, thunderstruck, when he reached out and took her hand.

A low whisper broke the silence. "Madeline," Hunter's voice said her name. "This case is going to drag on. I've known it since we found the first body, and I don't know when we'll find the last one. That's all up in the air. You can see it in some chart somewhere, but I'm certain there will be a time when we can watch the ferries together. Okay?"

Dazed, Madeline kept her head down, pondering the road ahead. Peeking up at him, she murmured, "Okay." Then, giving his hand a quick squeeze, she turned and ran back to her apartment, maintaining as much dignity as possible until tears fell from her eyes.

Hunter watched her return to the apartment. He grabbed the bagel and took another bite, leaning on his car. "Great," he said to himself. "She brings you coffee and bagels, and you make her cry. Way to go, jerk."

Madeline returned to the safety of her apartment, out of breath, and sat down hard on the sofa near her front window. She watched as Hunter got back in his car and drove off. She could no longer keep the energy building in her heart at bay, but she allowed it to move through her. Still and deep, like standing at a mountain lake where you can't see the bottom. She stood on the shore and, in her mind, allowed the ripples of the waves to fall onto her feet, but she would not dive in. The last time she did, it nearly killed her.

(34)

Incident Room — 11 : 39 a.m.

After finishing his bagels, Hunter got to the office early and filled out the paperwork needed to complete the surveillance detail. And boy, didn't that make him feel like a jerk all over again as the memories of the Ferry Building fiasco came rushing back, filling his mind with regret. He'd just grabbed his third cup of burned industrial blend coffee, thinking Madeline's coffee tasted so much better, when Vierra stumbled into the incident room carrying a white pastry box.

"I know it's too many carbs, but we'll need them." He plopped the box down in the middle of the table. Hunter peeked inside. Vierra had gone to the Mission, to Dianda's bakery, and brought in their famous Almond Torte. Its sweet aroma filling the room. Hunter went to a nearby cupboard and grabbed two paper plates and a knife while Vierra pulled out the torte. Hunter cut a slice, tossed it on a plate, and handed it to his partner. "Talk about too many carbs. Madeline brought me bagels this morning."

"She what?" Vierra laughed through a mouthful of torte.

Hunter set his slice on the table and slumped into his chair. "Yeah. She came out at exactly six in the morning, proving she wasn't the killer. And she brought me two kinds of bagels because she didn't know what I liked."

Taking a seat across from Hunter, Vierra tried to suppress a smile. "Okay, I get it. She's a conscientious astrologer. And we are back to square fucking one."

"Unfortunately." Hunter bit into the pastry. The cake, with its springy texture and almond-infused sweetness, was a delightful surprise. The additonal layer of raspberry jam provided sweet, fruity goodness, offering him an unexpected opportunity to relax. But taking the next bite, he breathed in some of the thick coating of powdered sugar on the top of the pastry which made him cough.

"God, this is good," Vierra said, dusting crumbs from the stubble on his face and handing Hunter a napkin.

Hunter chewed his torte and pondered the whiteboard, which displayed the extensive scope of their investigation. He zeroed in on Jonathan's face. The boy's connection to Christophe popped into his mind. What did it mean? Did he discover something about Christophe that he wasn't supposed to know? And that's how he ended up wrapped in one of their quilts? "I know this might sound a little farfetched, but what if this murder is connected to the Muldooneys somehow?"

Vierra leaned back and put his fork down. "The only Muldooney connection is Christophe being Sean's younger brother. Why?" Vierra got up to get more coffee.

Hunter chewed the last of his torte. "Jonathan's connection to Christophe bothers me. He had a *Christophe Master File* on his computer, and we found him wrapped in that damned quilt. That can't be pure coincidence."

Vierra returned to the table. "Yeah, it bugs me that a great, conscientious kid like Jonathan was interested in Christophe's malarkey. Did you ever get those photos from one of the kids at the party?"

"No, nothing from Lance, but you know, not all teenagers are conscientious." He tossed his paper plate in the trash.

"Yeah, okay." Vierra finished his pastry in two large bites, grabbed a paper towel, and wiped the powdered sugar off his hands. "You're thinking about the Muldooneys. But what about Christophe's chosen family, the people he works with and lives with? His business associates. His followers?"

Hunter sighed, knowing there were so many angles to look at. "Have we heard from ballistics yet? Do you think Christophe-er owns a gun?"

Vierra scoffed, "Jeez, what are you? Some cop or something?"

"I don't know. I mean, he grew up in a crime family. Don't they give out guns when you turn thirteen or something?"

"Who the fuck knows?"

"Any news on Sean's trial?" Hunter asked as he pulled out his phone. Vierra did the same.

"This isn't good," Vierra read from his phone. "Seems the prosecution's key witness didn't make it to court this morning."

Hunter found the same headline on his phone, "Jesus. All the work Sid and Andy did to bring Sean in? This stinks." Hunter saw Vierra's face darken, the muscles in his neck tighten as he rocked back and forth. "Do you need to go make a call?"

Vierra placed his phone on the table "Not now." But the scowl on his face contradicted his actions and Hunter felt the tension rising in his partner's body. Vierra's phone chirped, and he snatched it back up again. "Here we go, it's from Connie. The lab nerds sent us a link to check out the GPS tracker that Jonathan installed on the Russian dude's car."

Hunter swung a chair around as Vierra sat in front of the computer. "How is the data organized?"

"It's all here by date. When did Jonathan go to the party?"

Hunter checked the whiteboard. "Saturday, August 5th."

Vierra searched through the dates and opened a file. "Okay, the guy parked at Jonathan's house in Corte Madera and drove up to Via Vandyke."

Hunter grabbed his portfolio and flipped through it. "That's the address Electra gave me. That's where the party took place. Are the plates listed on the app?"

"YA0898."

Hunter studied the computer screen over his partner's shoulder. "How long was the car at the party?" Hunter scanned the screen; it showed a series of digital maps with the car's route highlighted in blue.

Vierra searched further into the record. "He hung around until 2:57 a.m. on Sunday and drove to Alameda. There's no activity after that until two in the afternoon."

"Maybe he gave up and drove home? What about Monday morning, the day we found the body?"

"Let's see, Monday the 7th. Our guy leaves Alameda and goes to Pacific Heights—that's got to be the consulate. Then, he drives back to Corte Madera."

"Nothing showing him near Ina Coolbrith Park?"

Vierra shook his head. "Nope, he parked outside Jonathan's house and stuck around." Vierra checked his watch, "Until we got there. Shit, if this isn't our killer, then why was he following Jonathan?

☾35☽

KXOP Newsroom — 6:48 p.m.

Sitting at her desk, Cora chewed the cardboard edge of her coffee cup. With multiple browser windows open, scanning Twitter, Facebook, Instagram, and other news station feeds, watching the saga unfold. Running around, fueled only on a morning muffin, she'd clocked out for the day just as she received a text from her @SFCrimeblogger friend Hannah telling her to check the hashtag #deadgirlmeditatingSF on Twitter. The Police had found another victim, this one in Washington Square Park in North Beach. Some freak posted photos of the body on Twitter, and Cora stood dumbfounded, watching in real-time as people on Twitter retweeted the photos with the hashtag #SFwhoisthis. "Hey, Dave, are you watching this?"

Dave, the night shift assignment editor, stared at his computer screen, mouth open, his lanky body draped on his computer chair with his legs resting on the desk, grunted. "I'm watching a lot of things. What gives?"

"That body in Washington Square Park. Her photo is all over social media."

"Why is this important?" Dave droned, uninterested, without looking up.

Cora did her best to keep the overwhelming irritation she felt out of her voice. "Because her friends are retweeting the photo."

Dave's legs hit the floor a few seconds later as he stumbled to sit up properly. "The dead girl's friends are tweeting about her?"

"Yes! Here. Someone tweeted out: "Her name is Sasha Randall.""

Dave focused on the computer screens on his desk, confirming the announcement.

"And there, another photo. It's a closeup. I'll search for her on Facebook." Cora clicked on another tab and searched for the name. Up popped several choices, but the third one featured a girl with long dark hair, an exact match to the dead girl in the park photo. "This has to be her. The dead girl in North Beach is Sasha Randall."

Cora scanned the girl's social media profiles. Popular, with a fair number of followers, she posted selfies and photos with school friends. Sasha's selfies revealed her ability to use makeup to enhance her radiant skin, captivating dark eyes, and rosy cheeks. She was always smiling in her posts. A couple of photos verged on the "no-one-understands-my-pain" variety. Cora flipped back to the live Twitter feed, and the comments came fast and furious. She checked Sasha's page. "According to her feed, she's posted nothing in two days. And by the looks of it, she's the type that posts something every day."

"I'm on it," Dave said from the assignment desk. "I'll call Bob about this."

Cora texted Hannah: *OMG, they've identified the body on Twitter.*

Hannah responded in a flash: *Sasha's body was staged just like Jonathan's.*" Two photos popped up on their message thread, one of Jonathan and the second one of Sasha, both wrapped in the same quilt.

Cora couldn't believe her luck: *Nice catch. Are you posting these on your blog?*

Hannah: *Now that we've confirmed it's the work of a serial killer, YES! You can do the same, then sit back and watch the shitstorm!*

Cora typed: *What shit? Why a storm?*

Hannah: *Say the words serial killer in San Francisco, and everyone assumes it's the heir of the Zodiac Killer.*

Serial killer? Was the story that big? Was this really happening?

She stood and went to Dave. He was on the phone, listening, and then said, "Yeah, will do," then he hung up.

"So, what did he say?"

"He said don't jump the cops. We have to wait for an official identification. If we get it wrong, it could mean lawsuits."

Cora returned to her computer and checked Sasha's Facebook page and scrolled through it. She found a photo of the girl's parents. Her father, tall with a ginger mullet, and her mom, a lanky brunette with fair skin, neither parent showed any ethnic resemblance to Sasha. Cora clicked on the link to the mom's Facebook. Nothing in the past few months. She kept her content restricted to friends. She kept searching and found out that her father had a Twitter account. "Oh, shit. I found her father's Twitter feed."

"What now?" Dave yelled.

"People have posted messages identifying her." She sent the link to Dave.

"Holy crap, what a horrible way to find out your daughter is dead!"

Cora walked over to Dave's desk. "That alone makes it a story."

"We have to wait. We have to take the liability issue seriously."

"Okay, you're the boss." Cora stalked back to her desk, thinking about their missed opportunity. Seeing Sasha's dad on her computer screen, she got an idea. Cora grabbed her phone and went to the other side of the newsroom. As soon as she was out of earshot from Dave, she called Vierra. It rang a few times, but he picked up.

"Vierra."

"It's Cora Merritt."

"Hey, princess, I don't have time for this."

"It's about Washington Square Park," she blurted.

"Okay, I'm listening."

"Your victim's photo is circulating all over social media. People have identified her as Sasha Randall—they're retweeting it to her parents."

"Are you telling me you know this girl's name?" Vierra barked.

"Yes. The victim's friends have identified her as Sasha Randall. Call her parents before some idiot does, telling them their daughter is dead."

❨36❩

Washington Square Park, North Beach — 7:33 p.m.

Hunter faced the young girl's body, determined to ignore all the surrounding noise: Vierra outside the privacy barriers barking at the officers to maintain the perimeter, reporters yelling questions from across the street, and the click-click from Connie's camera. He closed his eyes, blocking out the cacophony, and when he reopened them, a yearning for the truth washed over him.

From the moment they received the call at six in the evening, he knew this had to be the work of Jonathan's killer. But this time, instead of arriving at a serene "photoshoot" on Russian Hill, he and Vierra raced to a busy farmers' market in the middle of North Beach. In contrast to Jonathan's body, staged to be ignored in the early morning hours, here, among the crowds at the popular market, the killer made sure the body would attract attention before the police arrived on the scene.

Seated like a vendor at a bustling market, the victim, a teenage girl with delicate features, showcased a wide assortment of herbal concoctions on her display table. She wore a pale dress adorned with delicate golden lace, her upper torso held in a fixed and posed position, and her head gracefully tilted to one side. Her long, glossy black hair cascaded down one side of her face and over her shoulder, adorned with delicate flowers woven into her curls. Golden eyeshadow shimmered on her eyelids, and a gentle pink blush graced her cheeks—a vision of a modern bride envisioning her future husband. But the gray pallor of her skin revealed the truth that she'd been frozen and set in this place by madness. Instead of a bridal veil, an affirmation quilt covered her shoulder, and one edge spread out onto the table. Her arm and hair framed a quote in beautifully rendered embroidery:

**I love you as certain dark things are to be loved,
in secret, between the shadow and the soul. –Pablo Neruda**

The final touch: a profusion of flowers—giant magnolia blooms, purple orchids, dazzling pink and white azaleas, and a smattering of white roses, accented by tiny red spider blossoms—an explosion of life surrounding the maiden of death. All accessorized with boughs of myrtle and ivy, and sprays of large, round eucalyptus leaves, accented by twisty stalks of dried wood sprinkled with glitter.

A sweeping black velvet curtain draped the tent's back wall, which concealed, along with the flowers, the complex rigging used to hold the victim's pose. Hunter suspected the killer meticulously prepared everything in secret, only to unveil their masterpiece at the last moment before disappearing into the bustling crowd. And in that moment, he knew. In his gut, in his mind's eye, Hunter saw her. A woman. A cold-blooded killer who wanted everyone to witness how powerful and masterful she was.

"Hey, Hunter," said Connie, breaking the spell. Dressed in crime scene PPE, she stood up from behind the table, holding up with tweezers a white card with telltale deckled edges. "Another set of astrology symbols."

Hunter examined the card and sighed. The killer left another set of three planets and symbol combinations. He took out his phone and snapped a quick photo. "Anything on the other side?" Connie turned it over, and they both flinched back, exchanging a tense glance. Two words: "She knows." Hunter snapped another photo, and Connie put the card in a plastic sleeve, but Vierra burst in before he could process the impact of this new message. "You won't believe this, but Cora says there's an entire Twitter thread on our victim with photos of the body. And they've ID-ed her. Her name is Sasha Randall."

"On social media?"

"Excuse me, gents," said a patrolman popping his head behind the screens, "but a woman here from our press office would like your attention. She says it's urgent.'"

Vierra nudged Hunter. "That's you. You're a gent."

Hunter said nothing, but they both stepped out from behind the privacy screens. Several TV vans competed for parking space on the nearby street, with technicians setting up lights for their reporters. Hunter turned his attention to the nervous woman in front of him. About medium height, mixed-race, with a round face and pointy little nose, her lips pursed and shoulders so tight her upper torso was toad-like. She was scanning the area wide-eyed and nervous. He'd seen her once or twice at other press briefings.

"Hi, are you the investigators in charge of this case?" she asked.

"Yes, I'm Investigator Hunter Davis, and you are?"

"I'm Trish from the press office. Sources on Twitter are identifying the victim as Sasha Randall. And I just got a call from her dad, a Johnston Randall, wanting confirmation?" She asked with her eyebrows raised, with a major nostril flare.

Hunter leaned in toward Vierra. "What if we meet him at the ME's office? He can give the official identification. We get her down there as soon as we can?"

Vierra smiled at Trish, and she relaxed an iota. "Okay, I'll stick around and finish up here. You go meet the father. Okay, Trish?"

"I'll call Mr. Randall back and set it up. Thank you." She smiled at Vierra, looking relieved, and then turned to make the call.

Hunter turned to go when Vierra put a hand on his shoulder. "Did the killer leave another calling card?"

Hunter said nothing but took out his phone and showed Vierra a photo of the astrology symbols on the card. Then he swiped to the next photo and saw his partner's eyes widen. Reporters were yelling at them both, asking if San Francisco had a new serial killer. Somewhere from the crowd floated the name Sasha Randall. Vierra breathed deeply and looked at Hunter with an expression Hunter knew all too well -- as if they were each saying the same thing: "What the fuck had they stepped into?"

❪37❫

Sirius Book Store — 7:41 p.m.

"Holy shit cycle, this is so wrong," Matthew-Tabitha said, shaking his head while he scanned the laptop. Madeline sat across the worktable in the workspace, feeling the rough, scratched wood surface beneath her hand as she tried to process the images flashed on the computer screen. She'd been organizing the solar eclipse ornaments she'd ordered when Matthew-Tabitha raced into the workspace, told Madeline to switch on her laptop and they planted themselves in front of it. Watching the drama surrounding Sasha's identification on Twitter was a dizzying, exhausting rollercoaster. Then Matthew-Tabitha followed links that showed a gallery of photos. Then Madeline saw it: the quilt.

"Whoever this killer is, she's got some ovaries," Matthew-Tabitha said, looking at Madeline for agreement. "So, if you make another chart, do you think Mr. Hot Investigator will ask to see it?"

Madeline suppressed a laugh, "Oh, as you might say, hell to the no." However, she found herself warmed by the memory of seeing Hunter that morning.

"I'm sorry." Matthew-Tabitha raised an eyebrow.

"Don't be. It's a lot to take in. Why don't you head home? I'll close up."

Matthew-Tabitha reached for his backpack. "Are you sure?"

"Yeah, get out of here, leave the computer on. I want to check on inventory." She got up from the table and hugged her friend.

"All right, take it easy, lemon squeezy." He floated from the room.

Madeline waited until she heard the click of the back door lock before building up the nerve to return to the computer again. Stepping back to the table, she felt a sharp pain in her left leg. Madeline performed a quick calf stretch and then went to the computer screen. The photo of Sasha held her gaze, its beauty tinged with an undeniable sense of doom. But then she worked up the courage to study the quilt that flowed around the dead girl. She zoomed in as far as the site would let her, hoping to read the words embroidered on the colorful fabric. Could it be? The unfamiliar fabric bore a striking resemblance to the quilt she had crafted for

Christophe all those years ago. She'd read somewhere that Savvy Seekers offered an affirmation quilt but refused to look at them, knowing the idea had come from the one she'd given to Christophe. But this killer had wrapped Jonathan and Sasha in versions of her quilt. Why?

Madeline searched the social media posts to the beginning of #SFwhoisthis thread. She scribbled down the time of the first hit and pulled up her astrology program to cast the chart. Then another thought crossed her mind: would Hunter arrive with yet another set of astrology symbols? She choked down her dread and got to work. Entering the information into the computer, she felt a shiver run down her spine as the chart appeared, and it turned out to be even worse than she expected. On the left, for the victim was Pluto, the god of death and transformation, one degree from the ascendant, which meant it doomed this poor girl from the start. Sasha's killer was shown on the right side, as Venus, the planet of beauty and femininity, exactly conjunct with the descendant within a one degree of orb. The shining star, representing beauty and love, left a lasting impression on her vision.

She no longer questioned herself as she did before. This time, Venus stood in for the killer, confirming that the killer was female. But why had this woman wrapped her victims in a facsimile of Madeline's quilt? Looking at it again, Venus opposite Pluto, it often meant difficult relationships and—

"Oh my god," she whispered as an icy tingle shot up the back of her neck. How did the killer know this? How did the killer know Madeline had this exact configuration in her own birth chart? Just to be sure, she pulled up her own chart. The planets were in different houses, even so, with the same opposition and energies at war with each other.

Looking at both charts, the impression was downright diabolical. She closed the laptop as if slamming it shut would dampen the noise from the ideas racing in her mind: the symbols, the quilt, the crime scenes? Tying them together, she concluded this woman killer must have seen Madeline's own chart, but how? The killer was speaking to her through astrology. But why her? What did it mean? Was it a threat? Or a warning?

❨38❩

Office of the Medical Examiner — 9:22 p.m.

Despite the creeping exhaustion in Hunter's neck and shoulders, he put on his best cop face as he sat with Johnston Randall in the lobby of the medical examiner's office. Randall, a redhead with the physique of a bodybuilder, sported intricate tattoos on both arms curling down to his hands, but this physically imposing man quivered, on the verge of breaking. He held a rumpled paper napkin and wiped the fresh tears away.

Hunter did what he could to keep the exasperation out of his voice. "I know we just met, and this may not mean much, but I am genuinely sorry for your loss. Most of all, I'm incensed that you learned about your daughter's death through social media. I'm sorry. I can't fathom how callous people can be." Hunter hoped he sounded sincere and not defeated.

Randall nodded at Hunter. "Thank you. It means a lot."

"You need to be with your family, but I have some crucial questions."

"Go ahead. I'm too riled up to stay at home. My wife — I gave her a tranquilizer, and she's out, but tomorrow...." His voice trailed off.

Hunter opened up his portfolio. "When did you last see your daughter?"

"Like I told the guy from Missing Persons, I'd gone down to Monterey for a car show. I'm a Ferrari mechanic, and a client wanted me to check out some cars he was considering buying."

"Your wife kept an eye on Sasha?" Hunter asked.

"Well..." Randall half shrugged. "It's a job keeping an eye on a girl at this age. They're like tornadoes. You have kids?"

"No sir, I do not."

"The girls, you think they'd be easier to raise, but not our Sasha. She's a whirlwind. Every day it's some new concert or school event or a party. You try to keep them focused on schoolwork, but there are too many distractions."

"How old is your daughter?"

"Fifteen. She's only fifteen." Mr. Randall's voice broke, and he needed a minute to continue. Randall blew his nose into a soggy napkin, and Hunter handed him the box of tissues from the table.

"My wife, Lauren, told me Sasha made plans to stay at her girlfriend's house for the weekend. Lauren said Sasha texted her last night that she was coming home from school today. That was the last we heard from her—if it was her— God, in my mind, all these different scenarios play out. Was it her last text? Is the killer texting with Sasha's phone? It's enough to drive you insane, man."

Hunter scribbled a note to himself to ask Connie if she found Sasha's phone at the crime scene. "It's a possibility that we're going to investigate. Every detail you give us is valuable."

"Why didn't I call her when I got home? I wanted to, you know, but we give her space. She posts more on social media than she ever discusses with us in person. When she didn't come home from school today, and her cell phone went directly to voicemail, we called the school, and they said she was absent. We called her friend Ashley, but she said Sasha had canceled plans with her, and she hadn't seen her all weekend. We called the police. I got on social media, reaching out to her friends, and that's when I saw those photos. My baby girl. I'm sorry." Sasha's father shook his head as grief overwhelmed him once again.

Hunter wrote it all down, reminding him of what Jonathan's parents told him. Another kind, responsible child, trusted by her parents to live her life. And they're taken away in a blink. After Cora called Vierra about the photos from the crime scene trending on Twitter, Hunter scrolled through Sasha's photos on her Facebook and Instagram, searching for links to Jonathan, and he realized what they might have in common.

"Mr. Randall, is Sasha adopted by any chance?"

"Yes, she was." Randall tossed his soggy napkin in a trashcan. "Everyone comes to that conclusion when they compare Sasha's dark looks to her mother's blonde curls and my ginger hair."

"Did you go through an agency?"

"No, we worked with an attorney."

"And the attorney's name?"

"I don't remember, it was ages ago. Something Polish, I think…"

Hunter flipped open his portfolio. "Like Grudzinski?"

"I can't be sure, sounds right. I'm sure we have the records at home." Mr. Randall sighed, and Hunter knew he had to move things along and let this man go home.

"One last thing, Mr. Randall, was Sasha interested in astrology or Tarot cards, that occulty stuff?"

Randall's face lightened for a moment. "Yeah, she and her friends liked all that stuff—planets and energies. They did yoga and ate tofu, were all new agey."

"Are you familiar with most of your daughter's friends?"

"Sure, some of them. But these girls post their whole lives on Instagram. They're easy to find."

"Did it bother you, her putting so much of her life online?"

"It's crazy. I told her not to post photos online when we went to Hawaii in the spring. You don't want to tell the entire world our house is empty making it a target for thieves."

"How did she react?"

"She threw a fit and said her generation was different. Hey, do you think the guy who killed her studied her posts?"

Hunter closed his portfolio. "Our tech guys will analyze the data, and look for any leads. And we'll contact you tomorrow. We'll need to speak with your wife and search Sasha's room if you don't mind." Hunter stood up and reached his hand out to Johnston Randall, who stood as well. "That's the best I can offer you right now."

"It's not much," Mr. Randall said, shaking Hunter's hand with a grip that crunched Hunter's knuckles together. "But I know you're just doing your job."

Hunter watched Randall leave and agreed with him. It wasn't much.

《39》

Sirius Books — 11:46 p.m.

Hunter walked up Polk Street toward Madeline's store. He'd texted her from the Medical Examiner's office, and she agreed to meet him. Seventeen hours had passed since she brought him coffee and bagels, so he hoped her good-will was still … good. He found her standing in front of Sirius Books.

"Hi," Madeline said as he approached. "Wow, I hate to say it, but you look beat."

Hunter stopped before her and caught a hint of her perfume, which lifted his mood. "It's been a long day. I just came from talking to the father of the latest victim. He found out about his daughter's murder on Twitter. I can't imagine what he's going through."

"That's awful. No, I can't imagine. But it's the same killer, isn't it?"

"Unfortunately."

"And did the killer leave any new planets in signs?"

Hunter sighed. "Unfortunately."

"Okay, let's see what the stars have to say." She pointed to the door next to her shop. "I hope you don't mind if we go to my apartment. I've set the alarm for the shop, and once it's set, it's a bear to undo."

A series of internal alarms went off in Hunter's chest: Her apartment? No, turn around, run. But he ignored the alarms. "Sure, that's no problem." He waited while she unlocked her front door, his senses on high alert. The door opened to a staircase.

"It's up one flight." She walked ahead, and he kept his gaze on the stairs, one tread at a time, not wanting to study the backs of her legs as she walked in front of him. Once he reached the top landing, a sparkling chandelier caught his eye. It resembled a mobile crafted from mirror glass and crystals, reflecting rainbow-patterned light in the otherwise dark staircase. "I take it that you like shiny things?"

Madeline smiled. "Yes, I salute my inner magpie. One of my clients made it for me so I would never come home to a dark staircase. Here we are." She led him into a foyer. Lights from the wall sconce cast a warm, welcoming glow. Several watercolor paintings of seascapes and dense forests adorned the walls. Exuberant flower arrangements filled side tables and her kitchen island. The foyer opened up into a living room. To his left, he recognized the blue curtains he'd stared at the entire weekend while on stakeout. In front of the window was an inviting seating area: a plush loveseat and chairs upholstered in soft blue and purple hues flanked by a rectangular glass table; a multicolored, thick Persian rug ran the width of the room. "It's cozy in here," he said, keeping his voice casual.

"Thank you. It's a mix of my aunt's furniture and a few things I picked up from various yard sales and street corners."

In the middle of the table sat an ornate, Islamic-styled wooden cabinet, its drawers all open with bottles of cleaning solution and rags piled around it. Madeline moved around to the other sofa and motioned for him to sit. His exhaustion begged him to sit, but if he did, it would take a herculean effort to get up again, so he stood and pointed to the chest on the table. "What's the story behind the cabinet?"

"Another one of Aunt Jane's pieces. It's from Morocco, I think. If I have cabinets, I fill them with useless stuff."

"Yeah, when my wife and I split up, we discovered all sorts of junk squirreled away." He caught himself. "I'm sorry."

Madeline smiled and waved her hand, dismissing the subject, which helped him relax.

"I'm sorry I can't stick around. It's been a long day, and I'm getting loopy. I need to give you these symbols and grab some sleep."

"I understand." Her voice lost a little of its glow. "I can't imagine the stress you two are under to solve this."

"Thanks," he said, his words trailing off. Then he showed her his phone. "I took a photo of the planets in signs. Did I get that right?"

"Yes, you're getting the lingo already. Hang on a second."

She got up from the sofa and dashed over to the kitchen which was done in dark gray slate and sparkling glass tile. He tried to avoid exploring the photos on her fridge or finding out what kinds of crackers lived on her counter. Her kitchen was so much cleaner than his, but he didn't want to be thinking about that either. Madeline returned and held up a piece of paper.

"I remembered I'd printed a copy of the chart I made for you."

"Oh, okay," was all he managed to say. Madeline sat across from him and moved the Moroccan cabinet aside.

"Please, make yourself comfortable," she said, pointing to an armchair.

He did the polite thing and sat in the chair. The moment he did, he felt an immediate pang of regret. The soft chair enveloped him in comfort, too much comfort. With her chart in front of her, she motioned to his phone, and he held it up for her to read the symbols.

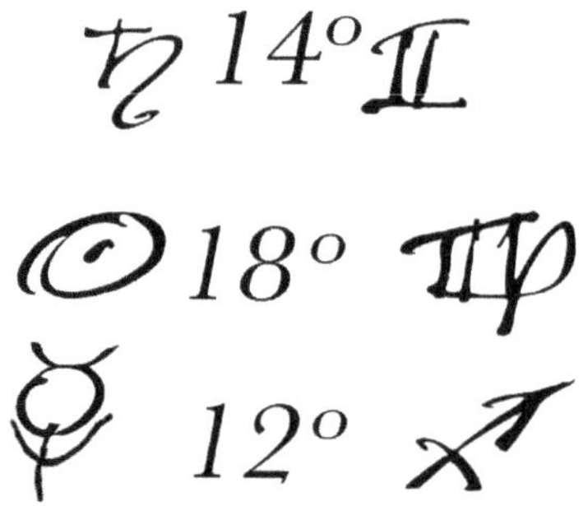

Seeing them, Madeline's brow furrowed, straining to recall an elusive detail, only to dismiss it by shaking her head. She offered him a bright smile and wrote the symbols on the chart. "Saturn at fourteen degrees Gemini, the Sun at eighteen degrees Virgo, and Pluto twelve degrees Sagittarius."

"Please tell me it's enough to go on?"

She let out a sigh and showed him the chart. "Unfortunately, it isn't."

Hunter sunk back lower in the chair. "Astroguy is toying with us again." Hunter caught her eye for a moment, holding her gaze.

"Seems that way," Madeline stood up and dashed to the kitchen. "I'm so sorry. I've forgotten my manners." She motioned to the refrigerator with the chart in her hand. "Do you want a drink? I've got sparkling water, tea? Or I could make coffee if that would help?"

Unable to ignore the flat note in her voice, he forced himself out of the chair. "No thanks, I can't stay," he stammered. What had gone wrong? Why the awkwardness from her? He walked to the door, and she followed. "Thanks again for seeing me this late at night. I'll see myself out. Will the door lock on its own after I step outside?"

She cleared her throat and kept her gaze on the floor. "Yeah. Yes. It will. Again, I'm so sorry the chart still isn't complete. If you like, I can research the corresponding Tarot cards?"

After the mess he caused over the weekend, her continued desire to help solve the case touched him. "Why not? Send it to me when you can."

"Okay, you got it," she said.

"Great." Hunter lingered at her door. It occurred to him he should take the chance and ask if she was connected to the Savvy Seekers. His brain flashed the words "she knows" from the crime scene. Despite his desire to ask her, he couldn't bring himself to. He couldn't overcome that mental barrier. The exhaustion fogged his mind. "I'm sorry. I really need to get some sleep." Madeline finally locked eyes with him, and he knew she wanted to say something, too, but couldn't. He'd have to leave it alone.

"Yes, get some rest. Goodnight, Hunter," she said as she closed the door.

Hunter took the stairs two at a time and, once outside, breathed in a chest full of cold, clear air. He walked to his car, parked in the same spot he'd parked in earlier that morning. The question gnawed at him: What was she hiding, and when would he find the nerve to confront her about it?

***

Madeline leaned against the wall and gazed at the foyer where Hunter stood moments ago. She heard the front door downstairs slam, and then she returned to the sofa and studied the chart. Why did she do it? Why didn't she tell Hunter the truth? Because she wasn't ready to live through that nightmare again.

Using her pen, she filled in the rest of the chart: Uranus—Pluto—Saturn, the ascendant. All of it. Exactly the way they were all those years ago. "God damn you, Christophe! And the horse you rode in on!" She screamed to herself.

····∗∗∗∗∗⟨∗⟨**40**⟩∗⟩∗∗∗∗····

TUESDAY, AUGUST 15, 2017

Madeline's Apartment — 2:37 a.m.

She launched herself through the darkening landscape, clutching her abdomen, heaving from nausea, her left leg exploding in pain with every stagger. Somehow, she escaped and now stumbled through the shrubbery, fueled by adrenaline. She couldn't see two feet ahead, and her right foot hit a stack of rocks, which sent her flying.

All the air burst from her lungs as she landed hard in the dirt and tall grass. She beat a fist on the ground. Why? Why is this happening to me? The question screamed through her mind. Hadn't she followed all the rules? Hadn't she gone along with the program? Fucking Pluto conjunct Neptune!

Another wave of nausea swept through her. She gagged, but nothing came up. It was so much easier to lie here with the pain, her face to the earth, so much easier to sink into the ground, to let it swallow her up.

Poor soul, the center of my sinful earth,
Fooled by these rebel powers that thee array,
Why dost though pine within and suffer dearth,
Painting thy outward walls so costly gay?

"Oh, shut up," she mumbled. She didn't have time for a sonnet to churn through her consciousness. The dizzying nausea threatened to pull her down, and the internal bleeding would do the rest, but she muttered aloud, "No. Get moving... come on."

Placing both hands on the ground, she pushed herself up, and the pain galloped down her left side. She collapsed, wheezing for air, crippled by pain.

Why so large cost, having so short a lease,
Dost thou upon thy fading mansion spend?
Shall worms, inheritors of this excess,
Eat up thy charge? Is this thy body's end?

"Is this thy body's end?" The words swirled through her, cascading.

Is this thy body's end?

Is this thy body's end?

Is this thy body's end?

It beat in her mind with the beat of her heart. This would not be her end. Lifting her head, she searched through the darkness. She found the new tree, a sapling they'd planted only two months ago, on a beautiful day. A day when everyone had been so full of light, so happy—NO! She couldn't lose focus. She crawled to the tree to give herself leverage.

Fighting the sickening pain, she pulled up her right leg and balanced on one knee. The left leg, useless now, sizzled with every nerve firing, snaps of electric torture. Before deciding what to do, she heard a sound, distant at first but forming a regular pattern. Footsteps. Like an animal, she sniffed the air. Unable to move, she hovered on one knee, then lowered down to the soil. Playing dead was her only choice.

The footsteps grew closer. She smelled him as the bile threatened again, her head swimming. She waited till the last moment to stop breathing and make it look convincing. He searched the grounds but stopped. She held still. She felt him above her—the man she'd trusted with her life, the man she loved. She sensed his hesitation, and then her anger boiled to the surface. You coward! Why did you let this happen?

The steps receded. She breathed out, all those years of training coming into play, and finally, she took a slow sip of air as the retreating footsteps turned to a run. She refused to stay here. Now fueled by the anger burning in her belly, she pulled herself up once again.

Then soul, live thou upon thy servant's loss
And let that pine to aggravate thy store;
Buy terms divine in selling hours of dross;

Within be fed, without be rich no more.

"Within be fed, without be rich no more," she whispered over and over as she dragged herself forward. Finding the tree trunk, she pulled her body up, standing on her right leg, using the tree as a temporary crutch. Shock waves erupted along her spine and down her leg, and she thought she would faint. She returned to the ground. She'd have to crawl.

Tears streaming through the dirt and blood stuck to her face, she sought her anger once again. But it left her. Everything faded except for the stars. She leaned against the tree; looking up, she spotted Mercury, the messenger of the gods, when a shooting star fell across the sky, a tiny speck of dust burning up in the atmosphere. She closed her eyes and felt the darkness pulling her … down… then a low rumbling in her ears…

The sound grew louder. And light?

She opened her eyes, but dark spots obscured her vision. Closer. Two beams. A car driving up the lane!

Leaning on the tree, she hopped on her right leg, turning to catch the light in time. She waved and heard the car slow.

So shalt thou feed on Death, that feeds on men,
And Death once dead, there's no more dying then.

Madeline bolted awake, her left leg searing and knotted, contracting her muscles so intently that she had to stand up and walk around, easing the contorted leg. The dream, or nightmare, was so fresh in her mind she saw the car's headlights in her mind's eye. The spasming eased, and she sat at the end of her bed. It hadn't been this bad in years. Pulling herself up, she walked to the kitchen island, where she picked up the chart she'd made the night before.

What she should do is call Hunter and set up a meeting to explain everything that happened in the Bernal Heights House. But before she could humiliate herself in front of him like that, she had to find Lili.

❨41❩

What we speak about becomes the house we live in – Hafiz

Bernal Heights House - The day of The Ceremony
September 10, 2001 – 8:30 p.m.

After a full day of fasting and chanting Om Namashivaya, Madeline fought back the exhaustion that made her legs wobble and her head spin. Christophe explained how the process stifled the ego and opened the practitioner to new levels of spiritual awareness. Madeline couldn't think, and all she wanted to do was sleep. Sunset arrived, and Christophe gathered everyone in the living room.

Everyone donned their silk satin gowns in all the colors of the rainbow—each couple wearing the same color to achieve a harmonious vibration. Christophe entered in a dark blue-black robe, with its hood covering the top of his head. He wore a headpiece, a thin metal strip with a silver star in the middle of his forehead, symbolizing his open third eye. Soft music played on the stereo, and the scent of Nag Champa incense, Cinnamon, and Sandalwood filled the air.

Madeline resigned herself to the position Christophe assigned to her. Since she had no partner, she wore a simple white silk tunic over blue silk pants. She sat cross-legged to the side, to Christophe's right, to help him guide the ceremony. Everyone sat in their places on the symbols she and Alistair mapped out. The couples turned to each other. Alistair is across from Miranda. Brenda looked into Edgar's eyes. William and Katia were already deep in a trance, while Victoria sat in the center facing Christophe, and Lili and Jethro hummed together, harmonizing their mismatched energies.

Christophe kissed Victoria and stood. He gestured to Madeline, and she joined him at the small altar at one end of the living room. Christophe picked up a metal chalice and held it to his heart. Earlier, Madeline helped him mix the concoction in the kitchen. He measured the ingredients, not telling her what all the herbs and powders contained; she mixed it all into a bowl with water.

Christophe spoke to the group. His voice filled the space. "This, this is our night. We have arrived. When the day slips into night's arms, the time of the sorcerers is upon us. My family, my urban witches, and mages, we gather to share in libations and to share our deep and abiding love. Love for each other, love for this planet, and love for the observer, observing us into life."

His words filled Madeline's heart, and tears of joy fell from her eyes. Gratitude overwhelmed her, stirring her very soul. Gratitude for having found her true family, gratitude for having applied the wisdom of the ancients to her life. In her mind, she flashed to the faces of her birth family: the stern face of her father, the unforgiving mother, and Cora, their perfect child, the perfect child that Madeline never was. Madeline banished those thoughts and focused only on the people in this room; they alone mattered. She smiled, seeing Miranda staring into Alistair's upturned face. He listened to every word from Christophe's mouth. She felt her heart open toward Jethro as tears fell down Jethro's face, staining his silk gown.

The music changed from soft synthesizers to steady drumming and chiming bells. Madeline's body stirred with an impulse to move with the music. Christophe, like the priests of old, held the chalice up for the group and blessed it. "From this vessel, we will drink. From this chalice, we seal our bond. Our bond of heart to heart and spirit to spirit. Each of you take a healthy sip and, with it, bring into your body the true plant medicine that will heal our bodies and set our spirits free."

Christophe nodded to Madeline and handed her the chalice. She took up a piece of red cloth and brought the chalice to Victoria, who took a long drink. Madeline wiped the chalice with the soft cloth before offering it to Miranda, who drank, and Madeline offered it to Alistair, who smiled at her before drinking. Madeline went to the others, going around the room as Christophe continued his blessing. "After all the years studying the stars and the sacred geometries, I've been waiting for this moment. This auspicious time when all the planets align in such beautiful, powerful aspects. I sit in wonder and amazement at the divine order in all things. And stand here in deepest humility, asking spirit to reveal itself to us. Madeline and I are your humble servants tonight. We are here to serve you all, to care for your bodies, and invite the spirit to join us."

After everyone drank from the chalice, Madeline handed it to Christophe. He sighed and shot her a quick wink. She expected him to drain the rest, but he offered it to her. Madeline paused. They agreed earlier she would not drink the potion to remain conscious in case anyone needed help. For whatever reason, Christophe changed his mind, and he watched as she drank a sip of the sweet brew. Christophe took the chalice from her hands, put it to his mouth, and drank the rest.

Madeline took the cup from him and placed it on the table. She settled in her spot next to the altar, grateful to serve alongside Christophe and witness the magic. The potion took effect quickly. Victoria and Miranda's faces glowed, and they smiled with closed eyes, their bodies swaying with the music.

Madeline swayed, too. The drum beat increased, growing louder, beating faster. She sensed the energy in the room shifting like water had surrounded her body, and the tide shifted from moment to moment. Christophe leaned back and sat down on the floor hard, eliciting a laugh from him that sent giggles around the room. Laughter erupted from everyone, from the women, and soon the men too were guffawing. The sound took on a hysterical quality, as no one seemed to control themselves anymore. Had some cosmic punch line hit home? Christophe's body joined in the laughter, bobbing up and down.

In a moment, he stood, unstable on his feet, and stepped over to Lili. He couldn't hold up his body, and he stumbled into her. She caught him, and Victoria caught him, all three in a loose embrace, still laughing. Christophe kissed Lili full on the lips, which made Victoria laugh harder. Jethro stroked Victoria's hair as the energy shifted again, and soon all the couples kissed and embraced.

Madeline assumed everyone would fall into a trance and fall to the floor; she hadn't anticipated laughter or kissing. By now, she couldn't keep her eyes open. The incense and energy made her eyes grow heavier. Still, she saw Miranda grab onto Alistair and thought she saw Katia stand, dancing to the tribal beat, her body moving with ease, the energy building in her body. Madeline tried to stand, but all her body wanted was sleep. The sounds in the room amplified as someone moaned, and then a piercing shriek filled the space.

Madeline fell to the ground. No longer concerned about the sound, she rolled on her side to sleep. Then a hand ran along her leg, someone lifted her up, and she disappeared.

····ᐳ›‹42›··ᐸ····

House on Sutro Heights — 7:16 a.m.

Madeline walked toward the house on 48th Avenue, on the border between Sutro Heights and Vista del Mar, as memories flooded her mind. Memories of helping Lili find the house, moving in, and caring for beautiful Luna. They created a Friday afternoon ritual: the three of them sitting on the wall, watching the ocean, listening to it crash out in the distance. Each of them processed their Bernal Heights experiences in their own way. Lili found solace in raising baby Luna, while Madeline focused on her astrology studies and working in the store.

The A-frame house, three stories tall, dated to the 1920s. Lili had the basement apartment. Outside the front door, a small garden space featured roses climbing among the "rust art" of an old wrought-iron chair, a Victorian-style gate, and a rusting chandelier balanced over a multi-tiered plant stand. Once Luna was old enough, Lili returned to school and got a degree in software engineering with help from her family. Sometimes, Madeline would pitch in and babysit Luna when Lili was deep into her final projects. Luna was born before her due date, yet she was a bright, beautiful, healthy baby.

Madeline knocked on the door. While she waited, she scanned the area for signs of toys or beach things but realized Luna would be a teenager by now and had outgrown toys. No sound came from the apartment, and Madeline worried about what to do next.

"Yes," an older man called to her from the upstairs door.

Madeline stepped toward the stairs as the man emerged from the house. "Yes, good morning. I'm sorry to disturb you, but I'm looking for Lili Todd. Does she still live here?"

"I'm sorry." The man reacted to hearing the name as if hearing something from his long, distant past. He shook his head. "She used to live here, but golly, she moved out nine years ago."

Madeline walked up the stairs. "Did she leave a forwarding address?"

"No, she was in a rush to move on. It had to do with her little girl. Oh, what was her name?"

"Luna?"

"That's right. She was the sweetest thing, but I think there was some issue with her learning ability—some developmental problems."

A shiver ran through Madeline. "Can you explain?"

"There were days when she would stand up on the deck and stare at the sea for hours. Now, she was only five, but she'd stand stock still, just staring. Strangest thing."

"Was she in some kind of trouble?"

"No, not at all. But one day, she was out with her mother, and Luna turned and looked at me. Stared into my eyes. I'll never forget it. It's like she was looking into my soul. Then she turned around and ignored me."

Madeline felt a swish of cool air brush through her. "Okay, well. If you ever think of anything, could you call me?" She handed him one of her cards.

The man looked at it, "Sirius. Like the dog star?"

"Yes, few people get that."

"I studied astronomy back in the day. Okay," he pulled his door open. "I might have a card for the realtor who helped her move out. If I come across it, I'll call you. Funny, but you're the second person to come and ask after her."

The hair on Madeline's neck raised up. "Oh, can you describe the person?" she asked, thinking it might be Alistair. "An older man with shaggy hair and glasses?"

The man shook his head. "No, a younger man. Tall. Blond. But when you're old like me, you can't tell people's ages anymore. I could say he looked like seventeen, and he could really be thirty. Who knows?"

"I understand. Thanks for your help. Have a good day."

"Thank you."

Madeline turned to go down the stairs but glanced at the deck and the roiling ocean in the distance. What had Luna searched for?

Turning around, she glanced up over the hill at Sutro Park, tempted to go for a long walk but knowing she had to get back to the store. How on earth was she going to find Lili now?

••••••••◦•‹43›•◦••••••••

**"Go against the world in all things
you shall come to love by the quickest way." — Jacob Bohme**

Bernal Heights House- the day after The Ceremony — 7:12 a.m.

With her eyes plastered shut, Madeline struggled to open them. She lifted her head off the floor, but moving her body was painful. It felt as if they had buried her underground, and she had to shovel dirt out of her body and mind to regain consciousness. Finally, after several tries, she opened her eyes, discovering she lay sprawled on the living room floor, but someone had placed a pillow under her head and covered her with a blanket. All the placemats, decorations, and silk robes lay scattered as if a tornado had moved through the house.

Hushed voices coming from the kitchen caught her attention, making her sit up. She was alone in the living room, and the smell of the incense lingered in her nostrils. Pulling herself up from the floor took more effort than she expected—her body craved more sleep—but she got to the kitchen and found William and Edgar huddled around a small TV on the counter. Christophe hated television and wouldn't allow them to have one in the main living room. Miranda had insisted on at least a small one for watching cooking videos.

Madeline yawned. "Oh, you're awake. I was about to wake you," Edgar said. She studied his face, dark black hair, and Asian features. They often chided him, calling him the house Buddha, but his customary serenity had been replaced with fear. "You've got to see this." Noting the urgency in his voice, she hurried over. At first, she thought she was watching a clip from a disaster movie. "It started a few hours ago," William said. "I went down to the market because we were out of coffee. I saw it on a TV set in the store. It's unbelievable. The country is under attack. I have to wake up the others."

Attack. The word bounced around Madeline's mind but didn't land, and she couldn't take hold, even as she watched it play out on the screen. A jet plane flying into the World Trade Center. First, the North Tower and then the South Tower were both destroyed. The panicked voices of the announcers filled the kitchen. No one had any idea what was going on. Video of people running for their lives. Then, an announcer came on to say another plane had crashed into the Pentagon.

In a moment, Miranda was there, along with a barely conscious Victoria and a disheveled Alistair. They all gathered around the small screen. William came back with his laptop and pulled up another news station. More of the same information.

"This is a joke, right?" Victoria slurred.

"No way, this is the real thing," Edgar said. I've been watching it for half an hour. First, one plane hit the North Tower, and then another. Brenda has family in New York, but she hasn't been able to reach anyone." Brenda was sitting in the corner with the house phone, making call after call.

"I wonder who's behind this," Miranda said quietly, intently watching the small screen.

"They say the government has grounded all airplanes flying in the United States. I can't wrap my head around this." Edgar paced the room but kept jerking directions like a defective wind-up toy. "Hey, has anyone seen Jethro?"

William, ignoring Edgar's question, looked up from his laptop. "We need a bigger TV. I can't see what's going—" A booming voice cut off William and the rest of their chatter in the cramped kitchen: "We don't need a TV at all. What are all of you doing?" Everyone parted the way as Christophe pushed past them to the screen. "After the ceremony we conducted last night to create positive energy, you indulge in the news. Have I taught you nothing?" As he spoke, Lili scampered in behind him and huddled with Madeline and the girls by the table, where Brenda had stopped making calls but still held the phone in her hands. Lili wore one of Christophe's shirts.

"No, but Christophe," Edgar said, taking hold of the tiny TV to prevent Christophe from damaging it. This is an enormous story. Terrorists have flown airplanes into the Twin Towers in New York."

"Oh, that's some bullshit joke," Christophe said, his voice filled with disgust. "No one can do that."

"No, it's real," William insisted. "It's all over the internet, too. They think Osama Bin Laden is behind it all. They had planes aimed at the Capitol and the

White House. It's crazy."

Madeline struggled to breathe. She waited for Christophe to say what she knew only he could say. The words of love and strength that would bring them all together. Christophe threw his arms in the air. "I don't care what you say. That is a reality that I don't want to waste any time on. Give me that." He shouldered his way toward Edgar, who finally let go and backed away. Christophe grabbed the set and yanked it from the wall.

Then he turned to William, who slammed his computer shut and put it on a different counter. Madeline's gut churned. Oh God. None of this made sense. She stared at Christophe, who glowered at all of them. "This is what we are fighting against. That life out there is not our life. Last night, we made a bond. We took a vow with our bodies and our souls. We devoted our full attention to Spirit, to the Divine. Not to this warmongering bullshit."

"Christophe, this is not some Hollywood concoction." Alistair had stepped forward, which Madeline thought was very brave with Christophe in this state. "Thousands of people are dead."

Christophe shook his head. "I don't care. Thousands die across the planet every minute. If you spent time counting all of them, you'd drown in a sea of sorrow and lamentation. That is not what I want for us. How many times do I have to say it? The only important thing happens here," he pointed his finger into his chest, "in our hearts and souls. This is tragic, yes, as tragedies go. But don't focus on it. Remember last night? Remember how we all had Spirit come into our bodies? It changes our vibration, the very chemistry of our cells. Rejuvenated, reborn. We cannot waver from the focus of our lives. We will live our days the way we always have. Now, who has kitchen duty this week?"

Victoria raised her hand. "Miranda and me."

Christophe took Victoria's hands. "All right then, let's all get out of here and let our soul sisters prepare a small breakfast, two hours after which we'll meet for meditation."

Madeline felt the energy leave the room as Christophe marched down the hall, leaving them alone. Everyone looked around at each other.

"Christophe is right," Victoria said after a moment of silence. "We need to stay focused on what is important. Now go on, get out of the kitchen."

As the household members drifted off, Madeline watched Miranda and Victoria go about gathering things to make breakfast: avocados, bread from the bread box, and tomatoes from the garden that had been ripening on the windowsill. Victoria looked at her and smiled. "Go on, Madeline, get moving. We'll take care of this."

Her friend's voice broke the spell, and Madeline nodded and left the kitchen. Looking around the living room, she cleaned up the detritus from the ceremony. She gathered the robes and put away the incense burner. Then the chart, Christophe's astrological chart cast for the ceremony. The two beautiful grand trines of Saturn opposite Pluto had exploded through their lives in a manner no one could have predicted.

Incident Room — 9:34 a.m.

"It's all over the news! We need to get ahead of this story." Leo stood over the table in the crowded incident room. Hunter hung back at the whiteboard with Vierra, making room for the staffers Leo had gathered, all sipping their coffee and avoiding eye contact with their boss. Leo grabbed a newspaper from the table and shook it for everyone to see. Other papers featured side-by-side photos of their teenage victims on the front pages. "Where's that little reporter, that Madeline miny-me?" Leo asked Vierra. "Didn't you warn her to keep a lid on this?"

"My reporter?" Vierra balked at the accusation.

Hunter held up his hands to soothe Leo's anger. "Boss, with the whole social media angle, the press invaded the park last night. It's impossible to keep it under wraps." Hunter did his best to be the voice of reason, but his head pounded from lack of sleep.

Toady Trish, from the press office, stood at Leo's side, brandishing an extra-large smartphone and stylus. "KXOP was the first news outlet to use the term serial killer." She was there to help manage the shitstorm. "They were the first media outlet to run photos of both victims. No one else had the photo of the first crime scene."

"More press means more noise. Copycats, false tips, distraction." Alistair spoke up from his corner of the room.

"Why thank you, Detective Dunham," Vierra quipped, his scorn on full display. "We hadn't thought of that."

"Investigator Vierra," boomed the deep baritone voice of the man entering the incident room, "that is no way to speak to a member of the court." The voice belonged to Commander Emilo Watts. Everyone in the room came to attention, and even Alistair stood taller. The commander found a rickety office chair near the door and transformed it into his throne; straightening the razor-sharp crease in his trousers, he surveyed the team. Hunter witnessed the man scan every face, photo, and piece of evidence gathered in the room. Then, withholding any sign of judgment, he rested his shrewd eye on Leo. "Go ahead lieutenant, you were saying?"

"Thanks for joining us, Commander Watts. As I said, with this intense media pressure, I have to keep Hunter and Vierra focused on the investigation. Trish, I need you to handle all of the press inquiries. We'll schedule a formal press conference once we have an official identification of the latest victim and not some social media speculation. Keep the media swarm away from my investigators." Hunter didn't take for granted his boss's support, knowing that this second victim had turned the pressure up on all of them, including the commander.

"Ahem, Leo, there's one detail that's causing a big stir." Trish inched backward from the Commander's sightline, but now Leo had stepped aside, making her the center of attention. A sheen of perspiration glistened on her cheeks, which only made her appear more amphibious. "It's the two quilts, sir. The photos are plastered on all the social media sites and crime blogs. The Savvy Seeker connection is spreading like wildfire."

"Connie," Leo said, snapping his head around to find her hovering by the door, feeling naked being outside of her lab. "Tell us about the quilts?"

Connie straightened some flyaway hair from her face but could do nothing to hide her dark circles and sallow skin as she crossed over to the whiteboard and tapped a photo of each quilt with her pen. She must have pulled an all-nighter to be ready for this meeting. "They're exact replicas. Twins. And they're knock-offs with no serial numbers, but Trish is right. Images of the quilts are flooding the social media channels. It's doing a lot of damage to the Savvy Seeker brand, which I'm sure Christophe doesn't appreciate."

Hunter noted how she stood up for Christophe, and admitted she followed his work. But could the person who leaked the photos be working with the killer? Did they both want to hurt Christophe and Savvy Seekers? "But who would go to such lengths just to mess with some rich guy's bottom line?" Hunter asked.

"Who would go to such lengths to do any of this for any reason at all?" Commander Watts spoke from his perch. "Someone is executing an elaborate and deliberate plan with more moving pieces than I can count. Teenage murder victims wrapped in meditation quilts and both victims were adopted." He targeted the whiteboard with a lift of his finger— "Astrological charts? A gunshot wound in the ear. A Shakespeare quote?" The Commander's voice resonated. "Have you connected *any* of these dots yet?"

Hunter held his breath. No one dared say a word.

"No, I didn't think so," Commander Watts said, piercing one face after another with his sharp gaze.

Hunter spoke up. "Sir, but now that we have two victims, we know more about the killer's pattern. It's a lot to sift through, but we'll get there." He felt the need to stand up for his team.

The Commander turned, "Then you better get your butt moving." The Commander crossed to the door and then stared at Leo. "I'll be waiting in your office, lieutenant, when you're ready," he said and left.

"One more thing, sir." Hunter risked the Commander's ire.

"Yes, Investigator Davis?" The Commander's tone indicated that the question had better be important.

Hunter crossed to the whiteboard and pointed to the license plate number YA0898. "We have data on Jonathan's computer proving he was being followed by someone driving a car with this diplomatic plate. We checked with the FBI but were stonewalled. Could you ask Agent Amihan to help us out? Give us a name?"

The Commander held onto the door. "I'll put in a call." Then he walked out, letting the door slam behind them both.

Hunter felt the collective sigh at seeing the Commander leave, but the tension in the room was still thick. The Commander hadn't arrived to review the minutiae of the evidence gathered. He came to tell them they were under heavy scrutiny from the upper ranks.

"Nice catch, Hunter," Leo said. He crossed the room to join Hunter and Vierra. "What's your next move?"

"I better talk to my little reporter friend again, after all," Vierra said. "Find out where mini-Ms. Merritt got those crime scene photos of Jonathan. The ones she brought us a few days ago?"

"You might be onto something, but first things first. The Randalls need to tell us about that adoption attorney," Hunter said. "If it's the same guy, this is a real lead. Anyone could have leaked those photos for a million different reasons."

"Randalls, adoption lawyer, leak," Leo said. "You've got your marching orders. Now all of you get outta here and do your damn jobs."

As they filed out of the incident room, Hunter heard Leo say under his breath, "And let's hope I still have mine by the time you get back."

⋯⋙⋗⟨**45**⟩⋘⋘⋯

Grace Cathedral — 11:32 a.m.

Her failure to find Lili and Luna, the bombardment of nightmares and memories from her past sent Madeline to Grace Cathedral, seeking solace. During her time with Aunt Jane, Madeline studied the history of Labyrinths. The most famous was the one at Chartres Cathedral. Grace Cathedral started the modern Labyrinth movement. Madeline guessed this resulted from the famous Bill Moyers interview with Joseph Campbell, which took public television by storm in the late 1980s.

The Cathedral had two Labyrinths, and Madeline favored the one outside, set away from the Cathedral entrance, with a view of the park. Standing at the circle's entrance, with paths leading into four equal quadrants, Madeline calmed her mind and stepped on the path, moving at a leisurely pace, watching her breath. In the first section, she focused on releasing. Images of her quilt on the news flashed in her mind, and she let it go. But an image of sitting in her old room, stitching the fabric, engulfed her, bringing a wave of sadness. How she'd poured through the books and chose the perfect set of passages, obsessed with making each stitch perfect for Christophe.

She batted at the air, sending the images away, focused on her breathing. What a fool she'd been. Naive, trusting, never doubting her teacher's abilities to guide them and create the perfect life. Then came the anger, and she would not indulge in that destructive energy. She'd come so far from those nightmare days. Looking down, she noticed she'd made it to the center of the circle, where, according to custom, she should find peace and answers to her prayers.

She sank to her knees and rubbed her face, the agitation in her heart multiplying. Giving no thought to being in a public space, she closed her eyes and steepled her hands below her chin, turning her thoughts to light, to peace. But the thoughts raged, old scenarios playing out, accusations and recriminations tumbling together. An image formed in her mind's eye — the Sun, its rays of flames shooting out of its dense, roiling center. Then a black and silver Moon engulfed the Sun, the celestials engulfed in a battle for power, with the Moon appearing to squeeze the Sun. In response, the Sun shot out streaks of flames into a darkened sky. A tiny silver ball appeared out of nowhere, orbiting the Sun and Moon, and Madeline swore she heard the planet giggling, laughing at the herculean efforts of the cosmic superpowers.

Madeline opened her eyes and stood up, purging the image from her mind. Abandoning the rest of the Labyrinth, she turned to her left and walked toward a bench in front of the Cathedral offices. When she heard the laughter again, she froze and recognized the voice. She sat on the bench and stared as Miranda exited the church office, laughing, with Edgar following her. Madeline turned away, not wanting them to see her. Could this really be happening? Unable to stop, she turned back and watched Christophe emerge from the office and close the door behind him. Madeline stood as if a magnetic force compelled her to move toward her old teacher, but she forced herself to stop.

The fifteen years hadn't harmed him. In fact, the gray hair and his bearing gave him an air of gravitas. Unable to move, she watched him step away, and then, in an instant, as if hearing someone call, he turned and spotted her. She clenched her hands and stared into those China-blue eyes. Shocked, Christophe opened his mouth as if to speak but stopped. Madeline willed all of her power and stood her ground, fighting against that side of her nature that begged to run to him, to force him to make things right.

As if hearing her plea, his lips pulled up in a sneer, and he shook his head, his face filled with scorn, and he walked away. Madeline staggered from the assault and sat on the bench, her breathing forced, gasping for air. Then, as if watching a digitized screen, the images from her vision shuffled and reformed themselves. She understood. The plans Christophe put in place for the total solar eclipse, him and his army of meditators harnessing all of that power, would lead to nothing less than disaster.

⠶⠶46⠶⠶

Alameda — 1:55 p.m.

Hardly an hour passed before Hunter received a call from Consuela Amihan. She set up a meeting with her contact at the Russian consulate, who was named Ivan. No last name. Very hush-hush. Vierra returned to Connie's lab to review the evidence from Sasha's crime scene while Hunter drove out to Alameda to meet the mysterious Ivan. Hunter couldn't remember the last time he'd crossed the East Bay to Alameda, an island between San Francisco and Oakland. He appreciated its small-town charm, tree-lined streets, and beautiful, ornate Victorian homes similar to San Francisco's Painted Ladies.

Now, Hunter sat across from "Ivan" in a café on Encinal called The Blue Dot. The broad-shouldered Ivan, with jet-black hair cut close to the scalp, fulfilled Hunter's stereotype of a Russian thug, but Ivan's unexpected air of quiet sophistication surprised him. He wore his dark charcoal, double-breasted suit with a casual ease. They'd made their way through the introductions, the pleasantries, and each finished coffee and croissant. Hunter got to the point. "So why were you following Jonathan Acosta? He was only a fifteen-year-old?"

Ivan drained his coffee before answering. "Trust me, it wasn't my idea of a plum assignment," Ivan replied, his voice deep and slightly accented. "But our information, and forgive me if I'm not forthcoming on how we gathered it, told us Jonathan had involved himself with this Christophe fellow."

"In what way?"

"In a most important way, Jonathan invented Know-sis."

Hunter scribbled a note in his portfolio, wondering why Russian spies were interested in Savvy Seekers. "What can you tell me about this Know-sis?"

Ivan pulled out a pen and used a white napkin to draw a crown with an earpiece on one side. He explained when the user bought it from Savvy Seekers, it would come pre-programmed with their birth information. The device used their personal astrology data and a set of algorithms. When worn during meditation, the user would gain deeper states of relaxation. When conscious, it would boost productivity by modulating brainwave patterns along with the individual's astrology frequencies to create the optimal mood for any activity. Ivan sat back, letting Hunter examine the drawing. "I know. It sounded like bullshit to me, too, but we also have good information that Christophe approached his brother Sean for financial backing for the project."

Hunter studied the drawing. If this device fulfilled its promise, Christophe's fan base would buy them hand over fist. Hunter flashed upon the look on Jennifer Acosta's face when he told her Jonathan was dead. He'd be damned if he was going to tell her that her son was killed because of some wacky invention. "But this headgear, does it work? Are you sure it's the reason for Jonathan's murder?"

Ivan sat back in his chair, shaking his head. "Tell me, how long have you been police?"

"Long enough. What's your answer?"

Ivan smirked. "I like you. I was worried you'd be like so many other American cops, assholes in nice clothes. No, I don't think this Know-sis is what got this poor child killed. And trust me, I regret not bursting into that party and taking him home. But I had no authority to do so. Jonathan's murderer had a different agenda. I don't even think he knows Jonathan invented Know-sis."

Hunter remembered what he'd seen at Jonathan's school—the Tarot cards and astrology video—and that a fifteen-year-old came up with the idea for this contraption. "Why are you being so forthcoming?"

"I have an agenda, sure. But I have two teenage boys back home. I feel responsible for Jonathan and now Sasha, especially when you consider her family."

"Her adoptive parents, the Randalls?"

"No, her birth mother is Katia, Christophe's operations manager. Her maiden name is Volkov."

Hunter stared at Ivan. "Not of the notorious Volkovs?"

"Oh yes, my man. Katia is Irina Volkov's daughter. We know Katia convinced her mother to invest in Savvy Seekers when *Christopher* Muldooney started the company. Now Irina's granddaughter is dead, her beautiful face splashed on the internet."

Hunter felt his stomach drop as the implications of Ivan's bombshell exploded into a thousand shattering possibilities. He took a deep breath, wishing Vierra was with him to hear this. "Wait a minute, I'm sorry, but help me out here? Irina Volkov, Fyodor Volkov's widow. Doesn't she have two daughters?"

"Yes, her daughter Katia has an older sister, Alana. She is married to Sean Muldooney, who is on trial for murder."

Hunter nodded, "Yes," Hunter murmured, still thinking.

"You are putting pieces together?" Ivan asked.

"My partner is in a relationship with the aunt of our latest victim."

"That's true, but the more important question is, who killed Jonathan? If it is Christophe or one of his followers, did they also kill Sasha to get back at the Volkov family? You have much work ahead of you, my man."

Hunter stood up. "Thank you. I'll be in touch."

Ivan gestured a hand salute. "Good luck."

Hunter nodded at Ivan as he pushed his chair in and grabbed his portfolio. Ivan knew he'd need more than luck to wade through this mess. Then Hunter stopped and looked back at Ivan, "Why are you so interested in Know-sis?"

"Let's just say my compatriots are always interested in new technologies and leave it there." Ivan's casual tone now had a threatening edge.

Hunter nodded, "All right, we'll leave it there. For now."

···ᵐᴴᴴᵉ‹‹**47**››ᵉᴴᴴᴹ···

Noe Valley — 11:21 a.m.

Hunter and Vierra sat in what once had been the original parlor of the Randall's renovated Victorian. However, several interior walls were knocked out during an extensive renovation, and an upper floor was removed, creating a magnificent Cathedral ceiling. Like so many old neighborhoods, gentrification had infected Noe Valley. Hunter had considered buying a home in the neighborhood early in his marriage to Abby, but the prices were out of reach.

Hunter considered the socioeconomic background of both victims. Jonathan's parents were comfortable, but Sasha's parents must have been doing well to pay for the expensive renovation. Hunter admired the high-end finishes as he and Vierra sat on a tooled leather sofa, a marble table separating them from Johnston Randall and his wife Lauren, who sat in a wingback chair with gold accents. At the same time, her husband stood beside her, a hand on her shoulder. She balanced a box of tissues on her lap. Hunter guessed the wife came from money. Lauren's jewelry was gold and diamonds. Her "comfy" clothes were designer, while her husband wore a denim work shirt and jeans.

"Mrs. Randall, can you tell me the last time you saw Sasha?"

Lauren Randall lifted her head, pausing as though she needed time to register Hunter's words. "The last time … yes," she answered. "It was Friday morning. She was going to summer school at Mission High. She told me they had a field trip to the San Francisco Museum of Modern Art and that after the museum tour, she wanted to stick around the city and go shopping with her friend Ashley Mullins and spend the weekend."

"Was that a habit with her? Going shopping in the city with friends?"

"What can I say?" Lauren said, smiling through new tears with a grand gesture to the opulence surrounding them. "She took after me."

Johnston pulled over a stool and sat, taking his wife's hand and squeezing it. "Honey, don't work yourself up. She was our baby. We wanted her to have the best of everything."

"Mrs. Randall, please take all the time you need," Vierra said in a soothing tone.

"I'm fine, dear," Lauren said to her husband, dabbing at her eyes and carrying on. "When we called Ashley yesterday, she explained that Sasha texted her at the last minute and canceled the plan to stay at Ashley's. Sasha said her stomach bothered her, and she had asked her dad to pick her up. That was the last message Ashley received from Sasha."

"But I didn't get any message from Sasha to come pick her up," Johnston said.

"How long had Sasha known Ashley?" Hunter asked.

Lauren gazed up at her husband. "Since fifth grade."

"I understand this is distressing but can we see Sasha's room?" Hunter asked, to keep Randall's attention on answering their questions.

Lauren agreed by standing up. "Of course, I'll take you."

"Thank you. We'd appreciate that," Vierra said, waving his arm, letting her lead.

Lauren ascended the beautiful staircase, part of the original architecture. Hunter appreciated how it gleamed from heavy sanding and fresh shellac. His shoes sank into the plush carpet as they walked down a hall filled with modern artwork and family photos. Lauren opened a door, and Hunter swore they had entered a five-star hotel room. A substantial white rug in front of a massive four-poster bed, all the furniture done in white. The walls were painted a soft pink.

Hunter looked up because the ceiling was a true showstopper. It was painted a dark midnight blue and filled with stars resembling the Milky Way. The artist added holographic embellishments, revealing a series of zodiac constellations spanning the ceiling, so even in daylight, the stars twinkled. Hunter pulled out his phone and took photos, uncertain if these signs matched the signs left at the crime scene. He glanced at Vierra, studying the ceiling, and shook his head at seeing astrology symbols again. The rest of the room featured built-in bookcases, a desk with a high-end computer set up, and just above it on the wall, a giant corkboard pinned with tarot cards, metaphysical art, and at least a dozen astrological charts.

"Wow. That's a work of art," Vierra said. "Was Sasha into astrology?"

"She loved it," Lauren answered. "When she was little, we took her to the planetarium, which mesmerized her." Hunter realized she wanted to talk about

Sasha to keep her daughter alive in her mind. "At first, I thought she might want to study astronomy. But later on, when she was ten or eleven, someone bought her an astrology kit, and she was hooked."

"Did she shop at Sirius bookstore?" Vierra asked.

Hunter froze, locking eyes with Vierra in the split second before Lauren's reply.

"All the time. She said it was the only store selling academic books on astrology, not just the fluff you find online."

That sent a jolt through Hunter's gut, and he clocked the glimmer of a smile on Vierra's mouth. Wanting to change the subject, Hunter flipped open his portfolio. "Mr. Randall, you mentioned Sasha was adopted. Lauren, do you remember the name of the lawyer you worked with?"

"It was Grudzinski, Arnold Grudzinski," Lauren said as she moved closer to her husband, taking his hand in hers. "My gosh, it feels like we just picked up that beautiful baby yesterday, but I'm glad we didn't have to deal with Grudzinski for long. He was a bit off-putting."

"In what way?" Hunter asked as he jotted the name in his portfolio. He flipped through his notes, confirming it was the same lawyer Manny and Jennifer Acosta had used when they adopted Jonathan.

"It all happened so fast," Lauren fretted. "We thought we were in for a long wait, you know. When you sign up, they warn you it could take years. I don't remember how I found this guy," she smiled. "But it was only a month later, and we picked up our girl."

"Where did it take place?" Hunter asked.

Johnston placed his arm on his wife's shoulder. "It was so strange," he explained. "I thought we'd meet him at the hospital, but he asked us to meet him at a bakery. We used to joke about it. We went in for knishes and came home with a three-day-old baby." He and Lauren both laughed through fresh tears.

"She was so tiny and perfect." Lauren met her husband's eyes, and Hunter nodded to Vierra. They both knew it was time to leave the Randalls to their grieving.

Mr. Randall hugged his wife, then stared at Hunter with eyes swollen and wet with grief. "You guys get the animal that took away our daughter."

"We will. Thank you for your time," Hunter said and shook their hands.

"We can find our the way out," Vierra added, leaving the room.

Hunter was the first to leave the house, and he pulled out his phone. "I'll call the office and see what we can get on Grudzinski," he said.

Vierra whacked him on the shoulder. "No. We're headed someplace else first."

"What gives? We need to talk to Grudzinski. He handled the adoption for both of our victims. It's the first thing that links them together."

Vierra shook a finger in Hunter's face. "Hello? Weren't you listening, or did you ignore the other link between our victims? They both shopped at a *Siriusly* suspicious bookstore. We're going to Sirius Books to get some answers from a certain Ms. Merritt."

Hunter knew fighting Vierra on this one would be a waste of time, but as they walked to the car, he grabbed his phone and did a quick search for Grudzinski. He found a link, and his heart sank. "Turns out Grudzinski is dead. He was killed in a robbery gone wrong."

"And that, my friend," Vierra quipped, "is a sign from the universe that we should be heading to Madeline's shop."

··∗∗⊰⊹⟨48⟩⊹⊱∗∗··

Sirius Books — 12:28 p.m.

Hunter, further agitated from stress, faltered as he jogged to keep up with Vierra running down Polk Street. His erratic heart rate wasn't simply agitation from having to jog, but frustration because he couldn't text Madeline to warn her before Vierra blustered into her shop. When he had shared the second set of symbols, he had felt physically separated as she subtly distanced herself from him. Suspicion lingered in his mind - she was hiding something. Approaching the door behind Vierra, scenes from the Ferry building fiasco filled his mind, and he took a moment to chase them away before stepping inside.

"My, my, my. How does she celebrate the upcoming solar eclipse?" Vierra announced upon entering the store and seeing the eclipse display. "With an entire set of books devoted to our old pal, the Zodiac Killer." Ignoring his partner's theatrics, Hunter took in the scene. Standing behind the counter, Madeline locked eyes with him, searching for an explanation. Her assistant, Matthew-Tabitha, inched closer to Madeline, being protective and giving Vierra a stink eye. He spotted the shop girl (he couldn't remember her name) dusting some shelves in the corner, frozen in place. Her huge brown eyes turned to Madeline, waiting for help or instruction. A tall man stood by a shelf near the back of the store. Hunter guessed him to be a regular customer.

Vierra strode up to the counter. "Hey, how are you doing today?" he asked Madeline in his Mr. Nice Guy voice.

Hunter stayed back, wishing he had telepathic powers to let her know this charade wasn't his idea. He mumbled, "Good morning, Madeline."

"Morning, Investigator Davis. And investigator Vierra." Madeline stepped around them to usher out the tall customer, who walked to the door. She said goodbye and flipped the open sign to "closed."

"Howdy, I'm Matthew-Tabitha." The ponytail guy stood in front of the counter and effeminately extended his arm with his hand pointed down, offering Vierra his hand to kiss. "We haven't had the pleasure."

"Hiya," Vierra snapped, ignoring Matthew-Tabitha's hand and brushing him aside to zero in on Madeline, who returned to her place behind the front counter. "Good to see you again, Ms. Merritt. I'm sure you're aware that another teenager was killed."

"Yes, I saw it on the news," Madeline answered, giving Vierra her full attention. Her body was tense, ready for the onslaught.

Hunter noticed the shop girl creeping closer to the counter, just behind Madeline, while Matthew-Tabitha stared down Vierra.

Vierra leaned in. "And we just discovered that the second victim, Sasha Randall, also shopped here." He placed both hands on his face, his mouth an exaggerated O. "I was wondering…" Vierra said, and then he made a show of pulling out his phone and looking for something. Hunter kept silent, watching Madeline. He felt a new level of tension coming from her, unlike at the station when she handled his partner's outburst with remarkable poise.

"I was wondering," Vierra repeated, holding his phone up to Madeline, "if you have seen this girl in here before."

Hunter watched Madeline study the photo. Was she straining her memory for any trace of her? Was she struggling because she didn't recognize the girl—or because she did and didn't want to admit it?

"Such a beautiful girl. I saw her photo on the news last night. I can't recall seeing her in the store."

"I've seen her. And so have you."

Hunter and Vierra both turned toward the voice. The shop girl had said it.

"Oh, hi there. Who are you?" Vierra asked.

Madeline motioned for her employee to stand beside her, placing a protective hand on the girl's shoulder. "This is Geena. She helps in the shop. My apologies for not introducing you. What do you mean, I've seen her?"

The girl twisted her torso at an odd angle, radiating nervousness and the possibility of flight. Hunter wasn't sure if the reaction was due to contradicting her boss or the natural response to speaking with the police. Geena looked pretty young under all the black eyeliner. "I've seen her a bunch of times, mostly after school. She was here last week. The same day that you were here," Geena pointed to Hunter and then turned back to Madeline.

"Last week?" Vierra said with a sharp glance at Hunter.

Sasha had visited Madeline's shop on the same day they discovered Jonathan's body. Hunter absorbed the significance of the coincidence and stared at Madeline, who had turned to stone.

Matthew-Tabitha came to Madeline's rescue. "She bought an astrology book and ordered books we don't have in stock. Do you want me to look up her book orders, Investigator Vierra?" Matthew-Tabitha asked, morphing into the flirty character Hunter had met on his first visit to the store.

Vierra smirked at Matthew-Tabitha's advance but didn't bite. "If you don't mind, please."

"Give me a minute." Matthew-Tabitha slid over to a computer further behind the front counter.

Geena looked up at Vierra. "Is there a serial killer hunting in the city?" she asked.

Vierra glanced at Hunter. It wasn't worth arguing about. "We are not discussing that issue with the general public." Vierra gave Geena one of his signature nods and a sincere smile. Geena scampered back toward the bookshelves. Madeline said nothing, crossed her arms over her chest, and leaned into the counter behind her.

It took Matthew-Tabitha a few minutes on the computer to look up the sales records, during which Vierra ignored Hunter, taking in the store from end to end, poking into the nooks and corners.

"Okay, that's everything. Printing now," Matthew-Tabitha said.

Madeline strode over to the printer to collect the printouts. He saw the fear in her eyes disappear as she pulled her shoulders back and handed the pages to Vierra. "Is there anything else I can do for you, gentlemen?" She put one hand on her hip, ready to defend herself.

Hunter moved toward the door, ready to leave, but Vierra remained still. "Not at the moment, but we'll be back." He let his words fill the room, "Sooner than you might expect. Want to take advantage of your solar eclipse specials."

"Oh, did my presentation on astrology inspire you?" Madeline asked, her tone sharp and defiant. "Plan on doing some shopping for yourself?"

Vierra laughed out loud. "That's a good one. It's a great joke to make when shopping here apparently gets kids killed."

"Hey—" Hunter confronted his partner, but Vierra cut him off, now on the attack.

"Ms. Merritt, we've confirmed that both victims shopped here. Do you know what we found at Sasha's crime scene? Has your pal Hunter over here shared that information with you?"

Madeline crossed her arms. "No. I'm sure you're going to tell me."

Hunter looked from Madeline to Vierra but said nothing.

Vierra leaned in. "It said, '*She knows.*'"

Hunter heard and felt the hush deaden the room as Madeline dropped her gaze from Vierra and shook her head.

"Well, Ms. Astrology Lady, I know you're hiding something, and we're going to find out what that is." Vierra taunted. "And don't tell me it's some new revelation in some chart you scribbled up."

"I have nothing else to say, Investigator Vierra. I've answered all your questions. If there's nothing more, I have a store to run."

Vierra smiled. "Do we need to bring you in for questioning?"

Hunter itched to punch Vierra. "Ms. Merritt, I apologize for my partner. It's been several long days. You understand why we came in. But we'll be on our way. You've been nothing but cooperative."

Vierra shifted his scowl to Hunter, but after a moment, he turned to Madeline with all his charm restored. "Yes, Ms. Merritt, you've been ever so helpful," Vierra said in the most pleasant voice he'd used all day. "Thank you for your time." And with that, Vierra spun around and left, not giving Hunter a nod. With Vierra gone, Hunter studied Madeline's expression, but she refused to look at him. He didn't want to give Vierra any credit, but his gut told him Madeline wasn't telling him everything, and her secrets were a key to unlocking this case.

⁕⊱⟨**49**⟩⊰⁕

Sirius Books — 12:53 p.m.

Madeline paced in front of the sales counter, one hand on her chin and the other wrapped around her waist. She was not ready to open the store again after Hunter and Vierra's "visit."

"That was horrendous," Matthew-Tabitha said as he grabbed a feather duster and started fronting and dusting books on the nearest shelf. Geena moved out from her hiding place.

"I'm so sorry you guys had to be put through that." Madeline rubbed her abdomen, still churning from Vierra's accusations.

"So, what are you going to do now?" Geena asked. "You're not going to make another chart, are you?"

Madeline laughed in disbelief. Shaking her head, she turned to Geena, "but I already did. I couldn't help myself."

"May I see it?" Matthew-Tabitha asked.

Madeline pointed to the counter. "Why not? Geena, it's in the drawer next to the register. Could you grab it?"

Genna followed her directions as Matthew-Tabitha put the duster back. Genna placed the paper on the counter as Madeline and Matthew-Tabitha came over.

"It's brutal. Pluto conjunct the ascendant." Madeline pointed to the chart.

"Oh my god," Matthew-Tabitha paled. "And now Venus is on the descendant? Is it another woman or the same one?"

"It's a woman for sure, but look at this." She pointed to the tiny dot on the chart. "This is Algol, one of the fixed stars. It's stationary at 25 degrees Taurus. All the horary literature says it indicates sudden violence. On this chart, it's conjunct the Sun. Then Jupiter is in a perfect grand trine with Pluto and Venus at the midheaven. The poor girl was doomed from the start."

"So now what?" Geena asked as she traced her finger on the edge of the paper.

Madeline looked at Matthew-Tabitha and then back at Geena. "Now, the police are getting a warrant to search the store, my apartment, or both."

"Just because both victims shopped here?" Geena asked.

Madeline rubbed her forehead. "God, I wish I could do more."

"But if you go to the second crime scene, they'll bring you in for questioning, right?" Matthew-Tabitha asked.

"I'm staying put," Madeline said, holding her hands up, signaling submission. I'm going to my office to work on this month's financials. Are you guys okay to open back up?"

Matthew-Tabitha put his arm around Geena, who looked shocked. "Don't worry, goth girl, I got you covered."

Madeline smiled for the first time and walked back to her office. Sitting at her desk, an image of Lili filled her mind. Where was she? Madeline turned to her computer and opened a file she'd found on an old thumb drive. It contained the birth charts for all the original Bernal Heights group members. She remembered how much fun they had comparing their charts, seeing their similarities, and why they all meshed together. Madeline pulled up Lili's birth information. As she entered her astrology program and added Algol, she wanted to see where it appeared on Lili's chart. She clicked the various pull-down menus and then watched the pie chart appear.

"Oh, my god." She literally could not believe her eyes. Algol was 26 degrees Taurus when Lili was born, right next to her natal Mars. Mars's male energy amplified the energy of that little demon star. Was it possible the reason she couldn't find Lili wasn't because she was hiding Luna but because Lili was involved in the murders?

·••<(•‹**50**›•)>••·

The Incident Room — 1:52 pm

"So, what gives?" Assistant DA Alistair Dunham asked, sweeping into the room. "Why'd you call me down here?"

Hunter threw his hands up, clueless. After the disaster at Madeline's store, he and Vierra had just returned to the incident room when Dunham arrived.

"I asked you down here," Vierra answered while standing near the whiteboard. "As I've been explaining to Leo, it's time we bring Madeline Merritt in for questioning or at least get a warrant to search her apartment."

Hunter sensed Alistair's shock and Leo's determination. He understood the need to do something, anything, to feel like they were making headway in this case.

"I know you disagree with your partner, Hunter. But Ms. Merritt keeps showing up at every turn," Leo said.

"I'll give you that, lieutenant, but we haven't scratched the surface looking into Sasha's life, and we know both families used the same adoption attorney. I say we go find all we can about Grudzinski and the adoptions first."

Alistair shoved his hands in his pockets. "I'm siding with Hunter. No offense, Vierra. I know you don't trust Madeline's astrology analysis, but you guys followed her all weekend, and she wasn't anywhere near where the second victim was found. Right?"

Vierra stepped forward. "I know you two are lifetime members of the Madeline Merritt Fan Club," Vierra said, "but I gotta hunch, and we all work off hunches. She knows, remember? The killer wrote it on the back of that card. Madeline is hiding something. I want to know what it is."

The incident room door opened, and a woman from the records office walked in. She handed Vierra a file folder and excused herself. It was an old case file. Hunter noticed the dogged edges and faded color. Vierra held it up for them. "Madeline Merritt has a police file."

"Let's see," Leo ordered, and Vierra looked inside before dropping the file open on the worktable.

The blood drained from Hunter's face once he spotted photos of a younger Madeline. Her face … he blinked and stared. Her beautiful face was covered with cuts and bruises, the kind that resulted from being punched several times. "What the…?" Hunter said. He leaned in as Vierra stepped back. Hunter flipped through the file. More photos of Madeline's abdomen, purple with bruises, the blood pooled over to her hips and around to her back. Another shot of her legs filled with bruises and deep gashes. The bottoms of her feet were bloodied and scraped like she'd run barefoot for a long distance. Hunter couldn't take anymore and walked away. "What does it say?"

Alistair read it. "It's from 2002. They dropped her off unconscious at the hospital. Look at the statement." He handed the file to Leo. "All it says is, 'I don't know. I don't remember.'"

Vierra whistled and took the file from Leo. "And she never pressed charges against anyone. This astrologer of yours is very good at keeping secrets. If she didn't want the police to find out what happened to her, it means she's covering for someone." Vierra closed the file and threw the folder onto the table.

Hunter took a moment to absorb and comprehend what had just happened. He had seen countless pictures of battered women, but this one was particularly horrifying. All he wanted was a chance to sit Madeline down, with no one but the two of them, and get her to explain everything. But seeing Leo, the expression on his boss's face told him that option had vanished.

"That's it, boys," Leo said. "Alistair, get the paperwork started. I want a warrant to search her place."

Alistair placed a hand on Madeline's folder. "Yeah. I'll go do that," he said without looking up at any of them. As he left, he pulled out his cell phone and started texting without saying another word.

Leo started for the door, and Hunter realized that they were forgetting something after the drama of Vierra's revelation. "It's gonna take Alistair some time to get us that warrant. In the meantime, I say we track down what we can on Grudzinski. Leo?"

With a sigh, Leo checked his watch and then looked at Vierra, who shrugged. "Yeah, go find him. Fill me in when you get back." He shuffled out of the room, leaving Hunter and Vierra alone for the first time since they ambushed Madeline.

Hunter sat at the computer. After searching for a few minutes, he made a note in his book. "I got an address and a phone number. Grudzinski's widow is still alive."

Vierra hadn't moved. Hunter stood up and gathered his things. "Look. I can go by myself if you like."

Vierra glanced up at the whiteboard, overloaded with evidence, and then back at Hunter. "No. Let's do this."

✦51✦

WEDNESDAY, AUGUST 16, 2017

Sirius Books — 5:13 a.m.

Unable to sleep, Vierra's accusatory tone: "I know you're hiding something, and we're going to find out what that is," echoed in Madeline's mind. Beneath the taunting, another thrumming question, repeating in cycles: Where is Lili? Where is Lili? Where is Lili? She dressed and came down to her office, hoping the familiar task of ordering office supplies would ease her mind, but it didn't. She contemplated casting a horary astrology chart, asking for clarity about Lili. Madeline got up from her desk, went to Aunt Jane's personal collection, and pulled out the textbooks and reference manuals she'd need to cast the chart. As she piled the books on the desk, the image of Christophe's face when she saw him outside the Cathedral flashed in her mind. His teaching astrology in the Bernal Heights house had filled them with intrigue and wonder. Astrology served as a guide, allowing them to reconnect with their spirits and navigate the unpredictable energies caused by transiting planets impacting their personal charts.

But dwelling on the past would muddy the waters, and she needed clarity. Madeline chose a bottle of essential oil and dripped it into her diffuser. As the mist filled the office, the soothing scents of scotch pine, lavender, and sage enveloped her, calming her racing thoughts and creating the perfect atmosphere for focused work.

Opening her astrology program on her computer, she looked at the clock. It read 5:17 a.m. Logging in the time and asking the question: "Where is Lili" the program generated the chart. What popped up and grabbed Madeline's attention was a grand trine in fire, three major planets all in fire signs, and all trine one another. Her mind flashed to the image she'd seen at the Cathedral, the moon engulfing the flaming sun.

Madeline worked well into the early morning, studying eight complex variables, including dignities, angular houses, and the abscission of light, which started a headache at the back of her neck and crossed her eyes at the chart's intricacies. But everything told her that she could find the answer to her question. She looked up which direction to start the search; the chart told her southeast. Madeline pulled up her map application, found the store's location, and looked southeast. Ina Coolbrith Park showed up as she'd placed a "favorite" symbol on the map. She looked further to the southeast, and Washington Square was just east of Ina Coolbrith.

"A grand trine in fire," she mumbled to herself. Seeing the triangle symbol on the chart got her mind racing. At that moment, she understood why Aunt Jane always called astrology more "art" than science. Madeline printed a copy of the map and then used a red pen to draw lines from Ina Coolbrith Park to Washington Square. She drew two more lines to make a triangle, noting where the new lines came together; the third point landed on Kearny Street in North Beach.

She realized it was absurd to believe she could march down to the address and find Lili waiting for her. But having gone through the exercise, her intuition told her she'd learn something important once she got down there. Madeline rose from her desk, needing coffee and some form of breakfast before opening the shop. Her phone chirped, and she took the incoming call. "Hello, this is Madeline?"

"Yes," a woman's voice on the line. "I heard that you're looking for Lili Todd?"

Unbelievable. Madeline leaned against her desk. "Yes, who is this?"

"I'm Lili's real estate agent. I got a call from a Mr. Gome?, who lives in Sutro Heights, he asked me to call you, that you are trying to find Lili?"

Madeline felt a jolt of giddy delight, not expecting this at all. "Thank you."

"If you have a pen, I can give you her address," the woman said.

"I'm ready," Madeline said, her pen scratching against the paper as she quickly jotted down the address on the horary chart, fully aware of the cosmic irony.

❖52❖

Daly City — 3:36 p.m.

"Not what I'd call an investment property," Vierra quipped, knocking on the front door of a small, rundown 1950s house wedged between identical, decrepit homes, desperate for a date with a wrecking ball.

Hunter guessed it had been an excellent investment when it was first built, but now the weathered fence, once white, had many missing pickets, and those remaining hung askew from rusted wires, a cheap repair attempt. He and Vierra stood under an arbor whose wood was so damaged that the only thing keeping it standing was the tangled rose bushes growing up through its trellises. The house gave the impression of a structure caving in on itself. Vierra hit the doorbell, which sounded a pathetic buzz.

They heard shuffling feet, and the door flung open. Eileen Grudzinski, an older woman who stood five feet tall, had a head of sparse gray curls. She wore an old, stained green T-shirt and clam diggers that hung loosely over her bony frame. She resembled a shriveled bird, surviving on memories and past victories. She glowered up at them. "You the cops who called me?"

"Yes, good afternoon, Mrs. Grudzinski. I'm Investigator Daniel Vierra. This is my partner, Hunter Davis. May we come in and ask you—?"

"—Yeah, yeah, yeah. I know the drill. You don't have to pretend to be polite." Her smoker's voice was thick with sarcasm and a heavy Boston accent. She scampered down the hall before either of them could say another word.

Hunter shot Vierra a look. "Not your biggest fan, Audrey."

"I'm outta practice," Vierra said, extending his arm for Hunter to enter before him. "You can do the talking, Malcolm."

Upon entering, they were greeted by the original flocked wallpaper. It had started life as a soft cream color, but years of neglect had turned it a rusty brown. Cardboard boxes stuffed with papers vied for space alongside odd pieces of furniture in what could have been a decent living room. Hunter felt his skin itch, wondering what else lived in those boxes.

"Don't mind the crap. My son just closed his office and had nowhere to store this stuff. Come on in."

They followed her down the dark-paneled hallway. The term "open plan" hadn't been spoken anywhere near this house. They ended up in the kitchen, Hunter guessed this was her sanctuary because amongst the dilapidation in the rest of the house, this space was immaculate and well-organized. Mrs. Grudzinski grabbed a box of crackers off the counter, shoved her hand in, and started munching. It relieved Hunter that she didn't offer them any.

"So, you wanted to ask about my husband on the phone?" Mrs. Grudzinski said, spewing cracker crumbs.

"Yes, ma'am," Hunter said. "We wanted to access some of his old files."

"You know he's dead, right?" She said through a mouthful of crackers. "He died in this house ten years ago. Murdered. I found him with a bullet in his head."

"Yes, we studied his police file," Hunter lied. He had just requested the file on the ride over. "We are sorry for your loss."

"That's what those other assholes said. The ones who came to investigate and then did jack shit about it. Seems like you're not much different."

Hunter felt like a jerk. He should have done his homework before coming here. He glanced at Vierra for help, but his partner busied himself inspecting the ceiling. "We're sorry that the investigation was inconclusive."

"Incon-fucking-clusive? They took one look at the place, decided it was a burglary gone bad, and then gave up. The sons of bitches shot my husband. Now you wanna come talking about it all of a sudden?"

"I hope I didn't mislead you," Hunter said. "We have no fresh evidence in your husband's case. We need to consult some of his old adoption records."

She furrowed her brow. "Why? Because some fucked up kiddie needs to find out who his real mommy and daddy are. And what's with him?" She asked with a jerk of her head toward Vierra. "He doesn't talk anymore?"

"Mrs. Grudzinski," Vierra said, "we're working on a high-profile case, and your husband handled the original adoptions."

"You said adoptions, plural?"

"Yes, Ma'am."

"Is this about the weirdo case I seen on the news, the teenagers getting murdered?"

"We're not at liberty to discuss it," Vierra said.

"Not at liberty, my ass. That's cop speech for fuck off."

Hunter couldn't disguise his smile. This lady didn't take B.S. from anyone, but they needed to move things along. "Mrs. Grudzinski, I'd love to talk about this case with you because you seem like a real sharp lady, but my hands are tied. Did your husband keep records of his case files?"

She frowned, "Yeah. That old packrat wouldn't throw away a scrap of paper to save his goddamn life. He took the attorney-client privilege to heart. You know that privilege doesn't go away even when the attorney dies, right?"

"We are aware of that, Mrs. Grudzinski. We don't need to see all the files, just a couple." Hunter mentally crossed his fingers, hoping he sounded convincing.

"All right. Come on, I'll show you the office."

They followed the lady of the house down another dark hallway. Once a bedroom, the office featured a massive desk piled with bankers' boxes and flanked by rows of filing cabinets, all jammed together. Hunter wondered how they were going to find anything. "Mrs. Grudzinski, can you tell me if your husband had a filing system?"

"Sorta. He filed things in a vague chronological order. The files on the far end begin in 1997 and go from there. What are you looking for?"

"The adoptions took place in 2002."

Mrs. Grudzinski froze. "Did you say *2002*?"

"Yes." A chill brushed at the back of Hunter's neck.

Mrs. Grudzinski crossed her arms. "Well then, you're shit out of luck. If the original investigators had done their fucking jobs, we might have a different story."

"Excuse me?" Vierra asked.

She went to a filing cabinet in the middle of the room. "That shithead who killed my Arnold. He comes here, shoots my husband in the heart, and tosses the place. He steals a hundred bucks from the petty cash and then this." She pulled out a file drawer; an entire section was empty except for a few hanging folders. "The murderer took every single adoption file from 2002. Every single one."

Hunter looked at Vierra, both of them shocked to find the drawer empty.

"I told the cops when it happened. This means something. Who would do this? Let's hope you two aren't just a couple of pretty faces. So, what's so important about these adoptions?

"Well, ma'am," Hunter stumbled.

"Wait a minute, you said you're working on a high-profile case. Is it those two teenagers who were murdered, the ones in the news?"

Hunter studied the empty file cabinet, did the math, and glanced at Vierra, who nodded.

"Yes, Mrs. Grudzinski. Our victims were both adopted in 2002."

"That means you're gonna re-open my husband's case, right?"

Vierra answered, "We're up to our eyeballs in this case, but if we find out anything to do with your husband's murder, we will let you know."

"We're sorry for your loss, Mrs. Grudzinski. Thank you for your time. We can leave now."

Mrs. Grudzinski shrugged and wiped a tear from her eye. "Ah, what the hell. You guys want to stay for lunch? I'm reheating some spaghettiOs?"

"That's a kind offer, but thanks," Vierra said.

Hunter stepped into the hallway; as soon as he and Vierra were out of earshot, he said, "We can check ballistics, see if there's a match to the one Astroguy used to kill our victims?"

"It's worth a shot," Vierra said.

❈53❈

Half Moon Bay — 4:06 p.m.

Beating the traffic, Madeline got to Half Moon Bay in record time. She drove through a quiet neighborhood, following the directions on the map app on her phone. She found the modest bungalow nestled between expanding bougainvillea bushes in the hills at the end of the winding street.

Approaching the front yard, she noticed another collection of "rust art," combining weathered metal sculptures and repurposed objects: old tires, an antique wrought-iron bench, and bicycle frames painted in bright colors. Potted plants filled the gaps with branches climbing up a rusted trellis, many still blooming on this late summer afternoon. Seeing it eased her mind, as it resembled the collection in front of the Sutro Heights house. Lili had to be living here.

At the front door, however, her enthusiasm shifted. She knocked on the door and listened, but no sound of rushing feet, only a sense of abandonment. Maybe they were just out shopping, or Luna had some summer school activity? She waited, and while standing on the front porch, listening to the late afternoon sounds coming from the neighboring houses, Madeline contemplated her efforts to find Lili. Her first impulse had been to warn Lili about the murders and ensure Luna was safe. Madeline speculated that Luna was the next on the killer's list after connecting the symbols left at the crime scene to the Ceremony chart. A lingering regret remained. Why hadn't she kept in touch with Lili? Why hadn't she been a better friend? If she was honest with herself, Madeline had erased Lili from her life, removing any reminders of Christophe and all the mistakes she'd made at the end.

"Excuse me? Can I help you?"

Madeline turned. The voice came from a pudgy older woman with a brillo pad of white hair. Thank goodness for nosy neighbors. "Yes, ma'am. I'm Lili Todd's old friend. Do you know when she will be home?"

"It's a wonder," the woman said as she stood on the sidewalk in front of the house. "I live across the street, and oh goodness, they moved out just last night."

A tingle ran up Madeline's back, but she kept her voice steady. "Oh no, me and my bad timing."

"I should say. Did you know Miss Lili awhile?"

"Yes, Ma'am. We're old friends, but you know how it goes sometimes. You think about calling but get distracted. Did she tell you where she was going?"

The neighbor lady frowned. "No, she didn't say a word. She packed up the whole kit and kaboodle and one of them white luxury vans swooped them up last night."

White Luxury. That screamed of Christophe. Madeline asked, "And no forwarding address or anything?"

"No, dear. I'm very sorry. Poor Luna sure made a fuss. I could hear it over in my living room. She wasn't thrilled with the idea of moving again. They'd only been here about eight months."

"Aw, I had hoped to see little Luna. What a shame I missed them."

The neighbor lady sniffed, "Little Luna. She's not little anymore. And she's a snarling teenager who thinks she knows best."

Madeline reached into her purse for one of her cards. "Well, would you tell them I came by if you hear from them?"

Walking up to the front porch to join Madeline, the neighbor lady accepted the card but made a strange noise with her teeth. "But Miss Lili, she's a mighty private person. She keeps that young Luna under lock and key. You'd think she was hiding a fairy princess from some magical creature or something." She stood on the porch as if it now belonged to her.

"Thanks again." Madeline hoped to snoop around the house, but the neighbor lady clarified that she was watching all the comings and goings. Madeline walked off the porch, paused, and took in the quiet neighborhood. She felt a soft breeze coming from the ocean and walked to her car. She had to pause as a white van pulled away from the curb, blocking access to her car. Madeline glanced at the neighbor lady, still on the porch as she surreptitiously pulled out her cell phone.

⟨54⟩

THURSDAY, AUGUST 17, 2017

KXOP Newsroom — 8:38 a.m.

"Which brings us to their membership and public relations coordinator, Miranda Velasquez," Cora placed Miranda's official business photo on the whiteboard. She'd been going over the profiles of the key Savvy Seekers for the Eclipse Meditation prep team. While researching the company, she recognized Miranda as the woman who escorted Christophe to the studio and told him Cora was "the sister."

"Wonderful work, Cora," Renee said from where she sat at the conference table. "Do we know which of the Seekers is available for interviews leading up to the start of their show?"

"According to their press release, Miranda and Brenda will be at our anchor tent, which is set up in Huntington Park." Cora stepped over to another whiteboard. This featured a map of Grace Cathedral, Huntington Park, and the surrounding hotels. It showed the location of the KXOP satellite truck and mobile control room on Mason Street. Cora grabbed two magnetic pins representing Miranda and Brenda and placed them in front of the Anchor desk listed on the map.

"In front of the Cathedral, William Ryder and Katia Volkov-Ryder will be the primary guides for the meditators standing at the Cathedral doors." She placed two more markers on the map. She checked her notes. "They have not given an official statement telling us where Christophe will be, but I checked with the Cathedral, and the Savvy Seekers have rented space in the Cathedral offices, which are just to the right of the main entrance. Edgar Chun and Victoria Muldooney will be there to run whatever audio Christophe will use to announce the meditators' movements as the eclipse unfolds."

Cora breathed a heavy sigh. Things had gone much smoother than expected. She'd been able to answer everyone's questions and sent them all backup copies of her work. She checked her watch. "Excuse me, but I need to start my shift in the newsroom. Do you need me to follow up on anything else?"

Renee scribbled a note in her binder. "No, you've done a fantastic job. I will mention it to Bob. Now, go ahead, skedaddle."

Cora gathered up her notes and purse from the table.

"Oh, hang on." Renee looked at her other staffers and then back to Cora. "Cora, would you like to watch the meditation event from inside the mobile control room? We can squeeze you in."

Oh wow, Cora hadn't expected that. "Sure thing," she said. "That would be incredible, actually. Thank you."

"Well, you earned it." Renee smiled, then turned her attention to another staffer.

Cora hurried to leave in case Renee changed her mind. She couldn't wait to tell Madeline her news. She'd hoped to hear from her sister but hadn't received an answer to her last text. She'd spent more time on the Savvy Seeker research than expected. What an oddball organization, with three married couples running the operation? That had to be a challenge. However, the company showed steady profits over the years and owned extensive real estate holdings, which included the Tiburon compound, a single-family home in the suburbs, and several warehouses in a strange neighborhood called Dogpatch. What was it about San Francisco and the odd neighborhood names like Dogpatch, Hunter's Point, Butcher's Hollow, and Inner Sunset? Yet another question for Madeline.

Cora arrived at her computer terminal and logged in. She scanned the crime blogs and newsfeeds for updates on the Sasha story. The police department had nothing new to report, and the social media feeds speculated about Sasha and the crazy crime scene photos. Her phone pinged. She'd just received a new message from @SFCrimeblogger: "*Where are YOU?!! The cops are on the way now!*"

Where am I? Cora scrolled up and realized she missed a dozen messages from Hannah going back to the previous evening, telling her the police were getting a warrant to search her sister's place. Cora reread all the messages, then sat limp in her chair and stared at her phone. What was going on? Why was Hannah hounding her so hard with a tip? A tip about her own sister?

"Cora? You okay?" Amy asked from her perch at the assignment desk.

"Uh … I think so." Cora reviewed the messages again, focusing on the messages from the past week. Hannah had consistently updated her about Jonathan's and Sasha's murders. Why? Why didn't Hannah break the story on her brother's blog? Was this normal?

"What gives?" Amy came down from her perch to investigate.

"I just got a private message from SFCrimeblogger saying the police are about to serve a warrant at my sister's store," Cora said, relieved to share the updates with Amy, who would know what to do next.

"Jordan told you that. When? Let me see."

"His sister Hannah. Just now." Cora showed Amy her message thread with @ SFCrimeblogger and watched Amy's eyes bulge.

Cora's voice cracked, "What should we do?"

"You are going to do nothing," Amy said as she pulled out her cell phone. "You are going to stay here and finish your research. I'm gonna call Bob. This is a major development in the case, and we have to act fast."

A sudden flutter hit Cora's chest as Amy gave her a nod and hurried off. This didn't feel right at all. Amy was on her phone, all business. Damn. Cora turned away and started a text to Madeline: "*The police are coming to your store with a warrant. Like, now!*" Cora watched Amy wave down Ned Mullinex, the crime reporter. Shit, shit, shit. Just then, her phone chirped. Finally, a text from Madeline: "Yeah, I heard. But don't worry, they are just doing their job."

Looking up, Cora saw Mullinex running away and Amy on the phone, "Yeah, John, I need you guys at Sirius Books for a perp walk."

Cora texted Madeline: "*I'm sorry, but my boss just sent a camera crew to your store.*"

⟡ 55 ⟡

Sirius Books — 9:15 a.m.

Madeline was just about to check an incoming text from Cora when she heard the familiar tinkling of the door chime and expected to see Hunter and Vierra. She emerged from the work area with her head held high. It was just Matthew-Tabitha arriving with coffee for everyone. Geena replenished books at the eclipse display.

"You're not supposed to be here today?" Geena called from the window. "Wait, are you?" She said to Matthew-Tabitha.

"Can't I bring coffee for my two favorite dolls?" Matthew-Tabitha swooped in and handed out his offerings, giving Madeline a peck on the cheek. "Are you okay?" He asked in a hush.

"Wow!" Geena looked out of the window. "Is this really happening?"

Madeline looked out the front window just as a KPOX TV news truck pulled outside the shop.

"What the blazing Buddha is this action?" Matthew-Tabitha asked Madeline as he put down the coffees while a cameraman jumped out of the van.

Madeline motioned Geena away from the display as the man aimed his camera into the front window. Then, a familiar face came up behind the man. It was Hunter, but he wasn't smiling. Vierra was right behind them, and they held up their badges. They approached the front door and the cameraman recorded all of it.

Madeline put her arm around Geena, guiding her toward the back, but Geena pulled away, mesmerized by the drama playing outside as a man holding a microphone jumped out of the van and started shouting questions. Vierra and Hunter came through the front door. "Matthew-Tabitha, please lock the door behind them." She did her best to stamp down the fear and a wave of building anger that her staff was subjected to this scrutiny.

Hunter lagged a few steps behind while Vierra straightened his lapels and puffed out his chest. "Well, that's got to be good for business."

"Miss Merritt, can you answer a few questions?" The man with the microphone shouted just as Matthew-Tabitha locked the door.

Madeline ignored Vierra and studied Hunter, horrified at his partner's comment, which gave her a nudge of confidence. "You didn't barge through here to discuss my finances, did you?"

"Why, no. We're here to serve you this handy-dandy search warrant." Vierra pointed a thumb at Hunter, who carried a set of pages, all while the reporter outside banged and hollered.

Hunter used his official cop voice, "Madeline Merritt, I have a warrant here to search your premises, both your apartment and this store."

Madeline held her ground. "I understand, but I don't want my employees subjected to news cameras. Give me a moment."

"Perfectly fine by me," Vierra said.

Madeline ushered Matthew-Tabitha and Geena through the beaded curtains into the work area. "I'm so sorry about this. Go out the back door. Hopefully, that reporter won't realize that you've left. If they find you, please say nothing to them."

Geena gave Madeline a shy smile, "Of course not. You can count on us. Text me when you open up again?"

"Well, I'm staying," Matthew-Tabitha said with hands on his hips, defiant.

"Thank you, but I can handle this." Before he could protest, Madeline touched his shoulder and said, "Please, take Geena out of here safely for me, okay? I'll be fine. I promise." She held his gaze to make sure he believed her.

"Yes, ma'am," Matthew-Tabitha said. He turned to Geena with a mischievous grin. "Come on, fairy princess, let's gallivant through the forest." A moment later, they both slipped out the back door.

"So, what's back here?" Vierra asked, bursting through the beaded curtains. "Is this where you perform the voodoo sacrifices? Oh, no, that's cruel of me. Voodoo is against your religion, isn't it?"

Madeline held back a zinging comment to match Vierra's and kept her voice steady. "So, where do you want to start?"

"How about your apartment? If we disappear up there, the vulture out front will find another carcass to clean."

"Sure. Go out the back door, turn left, and there's a locked door to a staircase. Here are the keys." She pulled her key ring from her back pocket.

Vierra accepted the keys and called back into the sales area to Hunter. "Hunter, come on back." As he swaggered by, he pushed past Madeline, eyeing the stock with distaste.

Hunter parted the curtains to catch up with Vierra, but then Madeline felt a shock wave as he grabbed her hand. They locked eyes. Hunter lifted Madeline's fingertips to his lips, holding them for two heartbeats as they stared at each other. He dropped her hand and caught up with his partner.

Madeline reached for the nearest bookcase to steady herself, reacting to Hunter's apologetic gesture. Then she remembered her sister's text. Cora had tried to warn her. Madeline texted her: *Thanks for the warning. Your reporter is here, I'll be in touch.*

⸺❮56❯⸺

Madeline's Apartment — 10:45 a.m.

Hunter opened the pocket doors that separated Madeline's bedroom from the living room after spending an hour searching her closet, bureau, and side tables and finding nothing. Going through her private space felt like a violation of trust, a deep betrayal. Would she ever forgive him? Standing in the living room, his heart still erratic from touching her hand and the kiss, he'd hoped it reassured her he knew this search was a bogus waste of time, that they were just following the rules.

Hunter recalled the night he brought her the second set of symbols. How he appreciated the calming effect she'd created in this small, unique apartment. With Vierra's help, they'd violated that peace, bounding through her home like two dirty dogs tracking mud and filth on the floor and everything they touched. He was relieved when their search found nothing incriminating: no gun, no quilts, no drugs. In the living room, Vierra replaced the sofa pillows he'd pulled off earlier. "Anything?" Hunter asked.

"Nada, zip, nothing," Vierra's voice defeated with frustration. "I really thought we'd find something. That is if someone didn't warn her. Giving her the time to trash anything incriminating?"

"Don't be a dick."

"Sorry, it's in my job description." He pulled his shoulders back, ready to engage.

"I haven't given you a fraction of the amount of shit I could be pouring on your head for the whole Alana business, so back the fuck off."

Vierra did, waving his hands by his face and then returning to his search. "So, what's with this doohickey here on the table?" Vierra pointed to the Moroccan chest, standing on the little table in the sitting area.

"It's empty. At least it was the other night when—" Hunter caught himself.

"You've been up here before?" Vierra snapped.

The accusation burned. "Well, no…" Hunter backpedaled. "I mean, yes. I came by the other night to give her the symbols from the second crime scene.

Madeline already closed the store, so she invited me here. She'd been cleaning the doohickey, and all of the drawers were empty—"

"I don't want to hear it," Vierra said, opening the fiddly drawers in the Moroccan chest. Hunter sat in the chair nearby. Beefing with Vierra drained him.

Vierra opened another drawer and stopped. He shot a glare at Hunter as he reached in. "You said this thing was empty?"

Hunter balked when Vierra pulled out two cell phones. "What the heck?"

Vierra tapped the face of one phone, but there was no response; the battery had died. He picked up the second, a larger iPhone with a crystal case. He hit the screen, and the owner's home page emerged. The wallpaper photo was of a young girl winking. It was Sasha Randall.

···«‹‹(57)››»···

Hall of Justice — 5:27 p.m.

Hunter blew out a sigh as he flipped through his portfolio. He'd filled his notebook with several pages of Madeline's story. She sat across from him with Alistair at her side, as Alistair had been part of Christophe's group, and he corroborated all the essential details: life in the Bernal Heights House, the days leading up to the Ceremony, the Ceremony itself. How the group members reacted to the 9/11 attacks. Sitting next to Hunter, Vierra shook his head in disbelief. His underlying anger with Madeline dissipated after they listened to her story.

Although she looked tired and worn out, Hunter knew he had to tie the events in the house on Bernal Heights to the current investigation. Exhausted, Madeline sat back in her chair and let her shoulders droop with weariness. Her eyes had become swollen and puffy from crying several times during the interview, but when she looked up at him, a radiant beauty shone on her face as if telling the truth had transformed her.

Vierra spoke first. "So, you're telling me all the women who took part in the Ceremony got pregnant?"

Madeline sat up. "Not all of us. Me and Miranda didn't. You'd think it would bond us, growing our little family, but it caused more friction. One issue was health insurance. None of us had any, and Brenda and Victoria were worried about getting proper prenatal care."

"We also wondered where everyone would live," Alistair said. "We were all roommates. Not all the couples from the Ceremony were ready to commit to being together permanently, let alone becoming parents."

Vierra leaned in. "Did anyone think about abortion?"

Madeline glanced at Alistair and then turned to Vierra. "Everyone thought about it all the time. But no one talked about it openly."

"And your great spiritual leader? What did he have to say?" Vierra asked.

Hunter heard the sarcasm slip back into Vierra's voice, but he kept his eyes on

Madeline. Again, she traded glances with Alistair, who finally spoke. "At first, he had us meditating around the clock to uncover deeper meaning about why we'd created this reality. But in hindsight, he had no fucking idea what to do. He withdrew, spending more time meditating by himself. He'd walk in Bernal Heights Park like he'd find some answers out there." Alistair said.

"Did he?" Vierra scoffed.

"Yes," Madeline said with such finality that a shiver ran through Hunter. But fresh tears pooled in her eyes as she refused to look at him.

Alistair cleared his throat. "That was when I left the group. The whole September eleventh scene freaked me out. I was convinced we were under siege. My partner, Miranda, didn't get pregnant, so I had no obligation to stay. My mother, Senator Dunham, insisted I leave and finish law school." Alistair sat back.

Hunter prompted Madeline. "What was Christophe's solution?"

Madeline rubbed her temples, preparing herself. "It was on a Sunday morning after breakfast. Everyone was at the table, and he gave his pronouncement. He said we should look at the situation as a challenge in self-sufficiency. Women have been having babies without Western medical care for centuries. As a group, we had access to ancient wisdom, a garden, and our own resourcefulness."

Hunter sensed Vierra's impatience and lifted his hand, signaling him to wait. "And then what did he say?"

Madeline continued, "Christophe preached, saying if we truly believed we were dedicated to serving spirit, we would see this as an opportunity to make a deeply meaningful sacrifice. He spoke about couples who wanted desperately to be parents but could not have children. That our little group could bring these gifts—" Reliving the memory, Madeline burst into tears. Hunter reached for the tissue box, but Vierra was closer. He offered her the box, and she took one.

After a moment, and wiping the tears from her face, Madeline held her arms out, "I know what I'm about to say will sound absolutely and completely insane. But to us." She stopped, gathering her thoughts. "When you live with a group like this, it's like we're all kids again, you know?" She leaned against Alistair, who nodded. "No one out in the world understands you. Your friends are only focused on success and money, and the world is so fucked up. So, you create a new family, your spiritual family. They understand you and understand the need for spiritual connection. And being children again, Christophe was the big spiritual daddy."

Vierra nodded, "And what Daddy says is the law?"

"Yes, it is, and if you break that law, you will suffer. Disobeying his word means betraying God. Do you understand?"

"You've painted a clear picture," Hunter said.

Madeline nodded, "So, Christophe came to us and decreed that for our best interests, and for the benefit of struggling couples, we would put all the children up for adoption."

Hunter felt a ripple of the shock wave that Christophe's decision must have sent through his spiritual family. What in the world had Christophe been thinking? To force people to give up their children? He checked Vierra, who seemed to feel the same energetic ripple.

Vierra tossed a pen down on the table. "But that's just freaking insane," Vierra said.

Madeline nodded her head. "Yes, now, in the light of day, I agree. Sometimes, I still can't believe we agreed to it." She corrected herself, "that the others agreed to it."

"And now two of those children are dead," Vierra stood up and paced.

Hunter kept his eyes on Madeline. "And who killed them, Madeline?"

She locked eyes with him across the table. "I don't know. Honest to God, I don't."

"And why is the killer leaving astrology symbols and the words 'she knows' at these crime scenes? Why is Astroguy implicating you?" Vierra got up from the table and placed his hands on the chair, staring at Madeline. "And how did Jonathan and Sasha's phones wind up in your apartment?"

Stunned, Madeline gasped. "What? Where did you find them?" She snapped her head to Alistair, seeking some support.

Hunter opened his mouth, but Vierra raised a hand to him. "Don't look at him. Answer me. Where did you get it?"

Madeline shrank back from the accusation, the shock setting in. "I hate to keep repeating myself, but I don't know."

Peeved, Vierra stepped around the table and sat down, blocking Madeline's view of Hunter. "I'm sorry, that's not a good enough answer."

"Come on, man, give her a break. She's answered your question," Alistair said.

"And you are *not* her lawyer," Vierra snapped. "You're an Assistant District Attorney who will prosecute the killer in this case. Don't answer for her."

Hunter leaned over to look at Madeline and saw the shock moving through her as she spoke to Vierra. "Don't you get it? I'm cooperating with you. Would I seriously give you the entire history of Christophe and the pregnancies as a stalling tactic?"

"I don't know, are you?" Vierra asked. Having made his point, he got up from the table.

"Investigator Vierra, look, I'm being set up here with the astrology symbols and these cell phones. Whoever your "Astroguy" is, he's going to a lot of trouble to keep your attention on me. And remember the chart I showed you? It's Astrogirl, not Astroguy. You should at least interview the women from the Bernal Heights House, if you haven't already. Brenda, Victoria, Katia, Lili, and Miranda. They must know something."

Hunter glanced at Vierra, who nodded. She was right. "We've been to the compound, but tell me, why did the killer go to such lengths to implicate you?

"Because back then, they made me a scapegoat for everything that went wrong. I'm an easy target. But along with speaking to those women, you have to focus on the remaining two children. Because you are running out of time."

"That's right, your Monday prediction again?" Vierra said.

Madeline let out a sigh. "Okay, I was wrong the last time. But this coming Monday morning is the total solar eclipse. Your killer must have already stalked the other two children and is ready to do something horrible on Monday, possibly at the big event at the Cathedral. Maybe Christophe is somehow a target in all of this."

Hunter stood up, stretched, and leaned against the wall. He kept his eyes on Madeline while he let that sink in. Vierra looked at him as they both thought it through.

"Okay, if we're going to prevent this horrible event," Vierra asked, "we need to find these children. Do you know who adopted them?"

Madeline shook her head, "talk to that sleazeball, Grudzinski. He handled the adoptions."

"We'd love to, but you can't interview a dead man," Vierra said.

"What?" Madeline asked, looking from Vierra to Hunter.

"You really don't know?" Hunter asked.

"No, what?"

"Your Mr. Grudzinski was murdered back in 2007? Vierra answered.

"You're kidding?" Madeline sat back hard, processing the news. "But what does that mean?"

"It means Astroguy plays the long game," Hunter said. "He or she's been planning this for ten years."

Madeline rubbed her hands on her face, "I don't believe this."

Vierra pressed on. "So, we know the Acostas adopted Jonathan and the Randalls adopted Sasha. Who's left?"

"There's the boy Victoria gave up," Alistair said, "and wasn't there another girl? I heard Lili had a child?" He turned to Madeline.

"Luna. Her mother is Lili Todd. During the Ceremony, after Christophe had sex with Victoria, he slept with Lili. Christophe's children are still alive."

"Where's Lili now?" Alistair asked.

"I don't know," Madeline said. "Lili learned she was pregnant before the other girls did. She didn't want to be there, not between Christophe and Victoria. I helped her pack her things and got her out of there." Madeline let out a long breath and looked up into Hunter's eyes. "She's why I said nothing to you after you brought me the second set of symbols. Once I figured out the symbols came from Christophe's astrology chart for the Ceremony, I knew these murders had to do with the original group. I panicked. I looked for Lili to warn her that Luna could be on the killer's list. But I couldn't find her."

Vierra leaned in. "But let's get this straight. Christopher Muldooney slept with two of his followers and got both of them pregnant. But he married Victoria anyway?"

"Yes, yes, he did. When I checked the last place where Lili lived, the neighbor told me a white SUV had picked up Lili and Luna. Christophe only ever drove white cars. He must have grabbed them."

Alistair shook his head. "Christophe must have them, but what is he planning to do with them?" He paused, "and Christophe is the guy who taught us astrology in the first place. But I'm also wondering about the Muldooney family. Does patriarch Liam Muldooney know Christophe had children? Or has Christophe kept that secret?"

A fresh wave of exhaustion crashed over Hunter. He glanced at Vierra, who must be processing what Alistair said about the Muldooney family. He rubbed his forehead, feeling a headache coming on. "Okay, you guys have given us a lot to process. We're going to take all this back to our office. You guys sit tight, and we'll be right back."

Vierra held up his hand. "Hang on, partner. I have one more question." Vierra pulled out the faded file folder from a nearby shelf. Hunter recognized it, and Vierra slapped it on the table before he could stop him. Vierra flipped it open, revealing the photos of Madeline after her beating. She glanced at the images and sighed.

Alistair squirmed. "Madeline, can you explain this?"

Madeline, exhausted, let out a laugh. "Oh, Alistair. You missed all the fun." She glanced up at Hunter. "Remember what I said about being a child and Christophe knowing best?"

"He didn't do this, did he?" Vierra asked.

"No. After agreeing to Christophe's solution, we went to work in the garden, cooked healthy meals, and found a spiritually aligned midwife. The babies were all born within days of each other." Madeline nodded to Alistair. "And then reality sank in. It was a Sunday night after dinner. Christophe had the lawyer show up in a rented passenger van. The time had come, but Miranda wasn't around, so I was the only woman without a baby, and Christophe gave me the job."

Hunter watched helplessly as Madeline grabbed a fresh tissue. "Christophe instructed me to do it quickly. I went to each woman alone in their rooms with their partners. I took each child out of their mother's arms and helped the lawyer put them into tiny car seats in the van. He'd brought along a couple of cousins who helped."

Hunter watched her re-live the moment as she stared at the table.

"Then everyone gathered in the living room. Christophe provided the wine, and everyone drank. I got up to leave the room, and it started with a foot. Someone tripped me. Then someone kicked me. I tried to get up. I looked for

Christophe. I heard William say, 'Hey, what the hell.' Another kick to my stomach, then punches, landing on my head. Everyone was screaming and crying, and I, I couldn't stop them. I rolled over and took it."

"Wait, where were the men? Why didn't Christopher stop it?" Hunter asked. His initial shock at the severity of the beating churned in him, growing into a glowing anger.

"Stop the ultimate catfight? Even Christophe knew better." Her voice was bitter and resolved.

Hunter watched her lift her gaze from the table. "Look, I survived, but I think your Astrogirl is using me to keep you from finding her."

Vierra mulled it over. "I can see what you're saying. But that still doesn't explain how the victim's cell phones ended up in your apartment."

"If I could explain it, I would, but I don't know," Madeline wiped her eyes again. "I just don't know."

Scanning his mental inventory of the evidence, Hunter needed to speak with Vierra. He saw Madeline's exhaustion and felt disgraced. "Look, you've been nothing but cooperative. We will review all of this and get back to you. Thank you for coming in. We're sorry we made you endure the perp walk. You can go home." Vierra still stared at Madeline. Hunter grabbed Vierra's arm and steered him out of the room.

⟪58⟫

Incident Room — 6:38 p.m.

Hunter swept up Madeline's file and carried it into the incident room. He couldn't let it go. He couldn't open it but ran his hands along the cover. Vierra entered the room, putting his phone in his pocket. "Hey," Vierra nudged Hunter's shoulder. "Before we figure out our next move, I gotta say I get why you like her."

Hunter's exhaustion allowed him only a simple response: "Really?"

Vierra stretched and massaged his shoulder before sitting opposite him. "She's smart, single, and has all her teeth," Vierra smiled.

Hunter appreciated Vierra's effort to lighten the conversation. "Yeah, Malcolm. Teeth are a good thing."

"But Audrey, I still want to know how those cell phones got into her apartment."

Hunter nodded. "Me too. But I was thinking about Grudzinski and the adoptions. Like she said, our killer has to be one of the original members of that group. Who else knew they gave them all up?"

"I'm still thinking about the Muldooneys, not knowing that Christopher had fathered children."

"I get that too, but listen. Back to the lawyer." Hunter flipped through his notes. "Grudzinski was shot back in 2007. That means Astroguy's been stalking the adopted kids for ten years. That means he started when the children were five years old.

Vierra's face grayed. "You mean Astroguy found the kids and has followed them since they were in kindergarten?"

Hunter, "Yeah. Watching them grow up? Knowing he would come back and kill them before they turned sixteen? What if Christophe is linking the original Ceremony to the total solar eclipse? What if it's some whacked-out human sacrifice where he takes out the last two kids?"

"That's crazy talk. But we have no evidence that points to him?"

"We could bring him in on assault charges," he pointed to Madeline's file.

"The statute of limitations has expired. Did we ever find out what guns he has registered?"

"No, come to think of it. Did we ever get Sasha's ballistics?"

"Not yet, and we need to speak with the parents at Savvy Seekers."

Hunter appreciated his partner's willingness to consider his idea. "We can take the warrant, go in guns blazing, toss the place."

"No, these people are smart. They've done all their ass-covering. We are going to have to catch them outsmarting themselves. We go in Dumb Cop and Stupider Cop." Vierra smiled.

Hunter threw up his hand, "I call dibs on Dumb cop."

⟪59⟫

Hall of Justice — 7:45 p.m.

Madeline pulled herself from the chair and pressed her left foot against the chair leg, stretching her tight calf muscle. Inflamed nerves in her left leg shot pain down her hamstring and into the calf, all from sitting in the chair for so long. Alistair remained seated, staring at the table, looking crestfallen. "Why didn't you tell me the other women beat you?"

Madeline stretched her other leg. "I don't know. After recovering in the hospital, I swore I'd never discuss it."

"And Christophe did nothing to stop it?"

She pulled the chair around to face him and sat as she searched for the best way to phrase it. "Right after you left, something changed in Christophe. My guess is he missed Lili. Of all the girls, she mesmerized him the most. As much as Victoria was his perfect mate, he still thought about Lili."

"I had no idea. God, was I clueless."

Madeline shook her head, "No, you were overwhelmed like the rest of us. Lili knew it would polarize the other girls even more if she stuck around. And Christophe withdrew from us emotionally but went into overdrive. That's when he decided to create Savvy Seekers. He was the head of the household and had to become a good provider."

"But why did you stay? You weren't in love with him, were you?"

It surprised Madeline that Alistair didn't know. "Of course I was."

"Let's be honest, he was already in a relationship with two other women?"

Madeline flopped up her arms in a gesture of frustration. "In retrospect, I was head over heels, the perfect devotee. Sure, I had to do my karma yoga like the rest. I knew he'd never look at me romantically, but he changed my life. That's what allowed me to be his bag man. Taking the babies away? Having the shit kicked out of me was the wakeup call I needed."

"So, what happened after that?"

"After I woke up in the hospital, Aunt Jane helped me, and then I moved into her place and started working in the shop."

Alistair sighed, "I should have convinced you to come with me. You know?"

Madeline reached out her hand and rubbed his arm, "I'm glad you didn't. Had you tried, I would have called you a traitor. I was so screwed up. No, I'm glad we're friends now."

"But what about the case? Who is doing this?"

"It's got to be someone from that house. They're the only ones who knew about the children and the adoptions."

"Do you still have everyone's birth charts? Or the birth charts for the babies?"

"God, I left all that behind. And I don't want to think about casting more charts for this case." But as she said this, she had a vague memory but was too tired to pursue it.

Alistair got out of the chair, "But why is all this happening now? After all these years? It can't just be the solar eclipse, can it?"

"All I can think of is another one of Christophe's bullshit stories. He proclaimed that because these children had been conceived under such a powerful influence, the September eleventh bombings, the whole Pluto Saturn powerhouse, that they had the potential to become great sorcerers. He even called them the children of destruction."

"No, really? He said that?"

"Yup, and if they had all grown up together in a group home with us, there'd be the chance they'd become competitive, combative. So, to keep the women from freaking out, he promised them that when the children turned sixteen that we'd bring them back to the group and train them properly, that they would have the benefit of our knowledge to harness their powers for good."

"Holy shit, and they all bought that?"

"Hook, line, sinker, boat. I'm beat. Can we please leave?"

"Sure, come with me." Alistair opened the door for her.

Madeline followed him out of the cramped room. She couldn't even remember where she was anymore. Once in the hallway, they passed signs for the restrooms. "Hey Al, I'm gonna stop in the restroom. I'll figure out how to get home from here."

"Are you sure? The elevators are down the hall, just over there." He pointed in the direction he was walking.

"Yeah, thanks again." She watched him walk away. And she thought of Jennifer Acosta. All of a sudden, a wave of pain began in her chest and buried itself deep into her insides. She reached out and touched the wall, needing a moment. She turned back around, the sound of a door opening. It was Hunter. He stood at the door with a look of sadness on his face. She felt the sobs choking in her throat; she waved him away and plunged into the ladies' room, leaning along the wall as her body shook. Waves of memories tumbled through her mind, Lili running away. Brenda sobbed as Madeline pulled baby Jonathan from her arms.

She sat hard on the floor and covered her head with her arms, hiding from the past, but there was nothing she could do but endure. How Katia's baby girl had grabbed Madeline's hair and wouldn't let go when she put her in the Grudzinski's grubby van. Edgar chased after her when she ran from the house. And Christophe. A growl escaped her, like a demon seeking earthly existence. How much, how much, how much she loved that man. How she'd hung on every last word he said. How he'd helped her know more of herself, setting her free and enslaving her at the same time. She'd spent so much time with that ache.

After a few more moments, the shuddering subsided, and she pulled herself up to the sink. She splashed water on her face and reached for a paper towel, but the dispenser was empty. She wiped what was left of her makeup onto her shirt, not caring about the stains. Keeping her eyes on the ground, she managed to stumble from the bathroom down the hall to the elevator. But where was she going to go? She got in the elevator. She couldn't go home, not after Vierra and Hunter searched it. She couldn't call Matthew-Tabitha, as he was at some nightclub. She exited the elevator and crossed the big hall to the front doors. She knew she had enough money to pay for a cab if only she could find one.

She stepped into the cool night, wrestling on her coat.

"Madeline?"

Wondering if the press had been waiting for her, Madeline took a deep breath and prepared herself for whatever awaited her. Glancing down the sidewalk, she couldn't believe her eyes—there was Cora, smiling at her.

··«‹**60**›»··

Cora's Apartment — 7:45 p.m.

During the cab ride from the Hall of Justice, Cora listened to Madeline's story about living in the house on Bernal Heights, the story she'd told the police about the ceremony, and the women giving the children up for adoption. Listening to the story, Cora realized that so many things made sense now, but it was heartbreaking to see Madeline so diminished. Cora took charge and insisted Madeline stay at Cora's apartment for the night, and Madeline wasn't going to argue with her.

"Thanks, sweetheart, seeing you outside the Hall of Justice—" Madeline started.

"Hey," Cora said as she took her sister's hand, "I've been a shit sister. I made some terrible assumptions about you, and I'm sorry."

"I'm sorry I couldn't tell you more, but now you realize I've been set up. At least Hunter and Vierra are certain I was not involved with the murders."

"That's got to be a relief," Cora paid the cab fare, and they exited the car. "Okay, please don't hate me for bringing you here."

"Why would I do that? It looks like a great address," Madeline said, looking at the building. "Which unit did Mom and Dad buy?"

Cora pulled out her keys and cringed, "Umm, well. It's the whole building." She waited for Madeline to blow her top. What she didn't expect was laughter. "I'm serious. Did you hear me""

"Yes," Madeline said, stopping herself from giggling. "This is how Mom and Dad set you up? They bought you a building in the Marina?"

"Yeah, well," Cora felt herself blush and unlocked the front gate. "They said something about wanting an investment property. They'd stay here when they came to see shows and enjoy the city."

"And how many times have they come to visit?"

"Like, none. Come on." Cora led Madeline into the front hall. "There's a basement apartment if you ever want a place to rent," Cora jibed.

Madeline shook her head, "Our mother, she's some piece of work. So, give me the grand tour."

"On this level, there's a fully furnished outdoor space, a sitting room, and the apartment. Let's go upstairs."

They made it up the stairs, and Cora watched Madeline's eyes widen at the sight of the expansive living room. The room boasted large windows overlooking the bustling street and a twelve-foot-high ceiling. The pristine white walls showcased a collection of contemporary black and white paintings. On the right side, a floating wall, painted black, featured a sleek wall-mounted electric fireplace.

In her exhaustion, Madeline smiled. "How big is this place?"

It relieved Cora to see that Madeline wasn't angry and that she liked the apartment. "It's like three bedrooms and four bathrooms, but I haven't found the fourth one yet."

"Wow, this place is gorgeous. Looks like mom, though."

Cora glanced around the spacious living room, taking in the full dining table and chairs, sleek kitchen with abundant natural light, and every appliance you could think of. "Yeah, she had an entire decorating team come through after watching 100 hours of HGTV."

"I would expect nothing less."

"Are you going to call her?"

Madeline rubbed her eyes. "Not now. I don't know. I need a bath and some sleep."

"Okay, you can have the bedroom down the hall. I'll get you some fresh towels. But so, like, was it awful? I mean, with the cops?"

"Like what you'd see in a gangster movie? Bright light shining in my face, Vierra yelling, demanding answers."

"Really?"

Madeline smiled, "No, they were polite."

Cora hesitated but needed to know. "But they found something in your apartment, didn't they?"

"Someone planted Jonathan and Sasha's cell phones in my apartment. That's why the cops brought me in for questioning."

Cora opened her mouth, and only a squeak came out. "NO?"

"Your next question is, who did it? I'm not sure."

"Okay but. I mean, what's the next step?"

"Look at you, Nancy Drew, you love this, don't you?"

"I do. In the car, you said you made an astrology chart for the cops. You said it showed the killer is a woman?"

"Yes, I'm guessing it's one of the original Bernal Heights House women. So, what are you thinking?"

Cora plowed ahead. "Okay, can you make a chart for the future? Like for the time of the eclipse? Would it give us more about the woman killer?" Cora hoped she wasn't demanding too much as she watched Madeline rub her face.

"Duh, I hadn't thought about it. Good call. Is there a computer in this place?"

"Absolutely!" Cora felt another wave of excitement and joy that Madeline would help her. She ran to her room and brought back a laptop. Cora set it up on the kitchen island, Madeline grabbed it and got busy. Cora watched her sister's fingers fly over the keyboard, and like magic, a pie chart popped up on the screen. It made no sense to Cora, but after a moment of studying it, Madeline nodded.

Madeline pointed toward the top of the pie chart, where five symbols lined up in a perfect row. "Okay, little sis, I'm not going to go into too much detail, but all these planets are involved in the eclipse. The moon will be moving right across the sun. Got it?"

"Yes, did I tell you they put me on the eclipse meditation coverage prep team?"

"No, good for you. Okay, this chart ruler is Libra, which is ruled by Venus, which sits right at the top of the chart."

Cora saw the classic symbol for "woman" at the top of the chart and experienced an unusual shudder in her gut. "Okay, but what does it mean?"

Madeline smiled, "My interpretation, it's a woman, standing alone, watching this train wreck of planets."

Cora felt like Madeline read her mind, "That's what I was thinking, and it's like she's watching them, and she's got a plan. This is so weird."

"Why do you think I love astrology so much?" Madeline asked, touching Cora's hand. "Here's an interesting thing to consider. Venus is in Cancer, a water sign. You know who else is a Cancer?"

"Who?"

Madeline let out a sigh, "Our darling Miranda."

Cora sat back in her chair, "No shit, really? Did I tell you I met her when she and Christophe came to the station?"

"No, what did she say?"

"It was a total freakshow moment. She looked at me and told Christophe, 'She's the sister.' That meant they knew I was your sister."

Madeline shook her head. "I'm so sorry that I never told you about them sooner. It would have saved you a lot of stress. Forgive me?"

Cora felt a twinge of sisterly love, "What's to forgive? I better let you get some rest."

Madeline nodded and pointed at the computer screen. "Look here. See this symbol at the end of that crowd of planets, like he's pulling up the rear?"

Cora leaned in as Madeline pointed to the lone symbol at the end of the large group. "Who?"

"Mercury, which rules Gemini, and that is Christophe."

·")◦**61**◦("·

FRIDAY, AUGUST 18, 2017

Sirius Books — 8:25 a.m.

After a long shower in the sumptuous bathroom and breakfast with Cora, Madeline returned to her apartment. Walking in, she sensed a perceptible shift in the energy of the space. The lingering rush from Vierra and Hunter's search and the mess they left hit her first. After moments of straightening the misplaced pillows and putting the Moroccan chest back in its regular place, she sensed another shift. It was something within herself. She had moved into the apartment while still recovering from the beating she'd received. Aunt Jane gave her the space to rest and said the timing was perfect because she'd just bought a place in Oregon. Had it really been fifteen years? Fifteen years hidden away in the apartment and the store?

Looking at one of the watercolors on her wall reminded her of the weekend she drove down the coast to a small arts festival, but when had she even taken a full vacation? Why had she allowed her world to become so small? She pondered this as she performed a long, smoky sage session to clear the energy. Her time in the police conference room, telling her story, even seeing the photos in her police file felt like she'd gone through an emotional purge, and she had to adapt to these new feelings.

Now, sitting at her desk back in the store, she pulled up the astrology chart she'd made for Cora of the upcoming eclipse. She also remembered her vision at the Cathedral while doing the Labyrinth: the moon eating the sun while Mercury laughed. Over breakfast, she'd asked Cora to use her super sleuthing skills to see what she could find about Lili and Luna.

When someone knocked at her office door, she closed the astrology chart, preparing to focus on bookkeeping. Matthew-Tabitha dolled up in a fuchsia floor-length maxi dress, swept into the room, bringing a smile to Madeline's face. But the smile cracked when she saw Matthew-Tabitha holding Hunter's hand and dragging him into her office.

"Look who I found lurking out front," Matthew-Tabitha said as she walked toward Madeline's desk.

Matthew-Tabitha's playfulness eased Madeline's shock at seeing Hunter so soon. "To what do I owe the pleasure?" she asked.

"Oh, darling, a little more enthusiasm, please." Matthew-Tabitha shot Madeline a wink while Hunter hung close to the door.

"Hey, I hope I'm not barging in," Hunter asked.

"Not at all, but?" She didn't finish her sentence. She hadn't expected to see him after everything she'd divulged last night. "Are you here to search my office?"

"No, it's not like that," Hunter mumbled. The energy between them shifted. Matthew-Tabitha picked up on it.

"I'll leave you two to discuss important matters, but first," she turned to Hunter, a devilish smile on her face, "May I at least have this dance?" She twirled so her skirt fluttered in the air.

Madeline expected Hunter to decline the offer politely but firmly.

"It would be my pleasure," Hunter said. He grabbed Matthew-Tabitha's hand and pulled her toward him in a spin. Madeline smiled — she would never have guessed Hunter to be a dancer. He placed his other hand on Matthew-Tabitha's waist, and they swept through her office, imitating the dance from *The King and I*.

"You dance divinely, Investigator," Matthew-Tabitha lilted.

"Ready for the big finish?" Hunter asked.

"Ready if you are!"

Hunter put one hand behind Matthew-Tabitha's back, stepped with a bent knee, and dipped Matthew-Tabitha toward the floor. She responded by kicking out her other leg, spreading the fabric of her skirt in a graceful arch, coming back on both legs and finishing with a pirouette. Both of them explode with laughter at pulling off such a tricky move. Matthew-Tabitha twirled toward the office door. "The pleasure was all mine." At the door, she put both hands on her face, mouthing the words to Madeline, "Oh, my god!" Then slipped out the door.

Madeline couldn't help but smile and watch Hunter plop himself in the same chair he'd first sat in …. Had it really been only a week and a half ago? "My, my. But you're full of surprises."

"My mother sent me to gentleman's finishing school. What can I say?"

"Finishing school?" Madeline shivered. "I can only guess what was on the curriculum."

"How to read a wine list 101. Advanced bow tying and tuxedo ironing. How to be a closet alcoholic advanced and intermediate. But I flunked. I was supposed to become an officer and a gentleman, but it never materialized." He smiled, looking up at her.

Madeline felt a wave of reassurance as she sensed their enduring positive connection. The weight of her confession dissipated, leaving a sense of relief in the air. "Do you have follow-up questions for me?"

Hunter looked away for a moment. "No. I came to see you to make sure you're okay after last night. I owe you an apology."

Madeline melted. This was the last thing she expected this morning. "No apology necessary. You were doing your job. It did feel weird walking into my apartment after you guys searched it." A question popped into her mind, and she hoped it wouldn't freak him out. "Which one of you scoundrels went through my underwear drawer?"

Hunter pressed his lips together and down, then scrunched his shoulders in an exaggerated expression of guilt and pointed a thumb at himself.

Madeline put her hands on her face, embarrassed but still smiling.

"Don't worry. I didn't take anything," Hunter admitted. "Although the pair with the pink roses were awfully tempting."

"Just no," she knew which pair he was talking about, something she'd found at a 75 percent off sale. "I'd say something about you having good taste," but thinking about him wearing them made her burst out in a huge guffaw. She couldn't stop laughing. She fell back in her chair, unable to stop the giggles.

Hunter laughed, too. "Thank God you're laughing. I thought you'd throw that computer at me when I came here. I totally deserve it, of course."

"Yes," she said through her laughter, "you totally did."

"Okay, stop thinking about the panties. I need your help."

Madeline grabbed a tissue to wipe the tears from her eyes. "Okay, okay. What's going on?"

"Well, after what you told us last night, Vierra and I are heading to the Savvy Seeker Compound to interview the women and Christophe. By any chance, did you ever see him with a gun?"

She thought back to her days with Christophe. "Yeah, I did. There was a gun safe in the house on Bernal Heights. Christophe used to bring out his handgun every month or so. He'd clean it, saying it reminded him of the life he walked away from. Why?"

"We found out that the same gun killed both victims. Christophe has a gun that matches the caliber."

"Wow, so that's a huge development?"

"It is, but tell me more about the man. It's seldom that I interview a self-help guru. What should I expect?"

Madeline flashed on the chart she made for Cora. "He's a Gemini, so naturally, he's got a split personality."

"How so?" Hunter's voice was quizzical.

"The symbol for Gemini is the twins, Castor and Pollux." She pulled up an image on her computer and turned to the monitor for him to see. "One twin is mortal, the other immortal. That means one is fine, and the other is an asshole. Christophe, in his best moments, is lighthearted, fun, and inspiring. But when the darker side shows up, he's judgmental and hypercritical. It's like you can do nothing right in his eyes."

"And how do you know which twin will show up?"

"You don't, that's the problem. You always have to be on your toes."

Hunter flipped open his portfolio. "So, if he's the killer, then that first chart you showed me, with the female killer, is incorrect?"

Madeline sat back, weary of her initial interpretation. "It wouldn't be the first time I got something wrong, believe me." Which got her thinking. "Let me look at that chart again." She pulled the monitor back, tapped the keys on her computer, and found the chart. "Well, okay. Mercury rules Gemini, and in that chart, it's about ten degrees away from our victim, the Sun." She had not paid much attention to Mercury when making the chart.

Hunter came around her desk to look at the screen over her shoulder. She pointed to Mercury in the chart. "You see, it's hanging out. It's not in any major configuration with the key players."

Hunter returned to his chair and flipped through his notes as if he remembered something. "But those first symbols I brought you? You plotted them on a chart, right? Wasn't there something about Gemini?"

Madeline thought about those first signs and found the chart she'd made for him. "Yes, the moon is in Gemini."

Hunter found what he was looking for and held up a paper. "You told me about the three tarot cards." He turned the page for her to see. "Isn't Gemini in there somewhere?"

She took the page and examined the cards she'd dealt for him eleven days ago. She studied them in relation to Gemini and Christophe, and instantly, the pattern revealed itself. "Oh my gosh, look at this." She turned the page, and Hunter pulled his chair next to hers to examine it together.

"Now, forget your preconceptions about the cards. Just look at the graphics. What do you see?" Starting with the Devil card, are the two lovers at the bottom of the card?

"Okay, they're the same two people in the Lovers card, yes?"

"Yes, two sets of the same people, twins. Now, look at the Justice card."

"I see a man sitting holding a scale and a sword. What gives?"

"Look behind him. He's sitting between two pillars. Again, twins. Each image points to twins."

Hunter stared at her, "But this makes no sense. Why would he purposefully reveal himself like this?"

Madeline smiled. "He didn't. Not consciously. He thought he was clever by giving you the pieces of the ceremony chart. But he taught me that our unconscious is always in action. You can't ever get away from it."

"When I interview him and show him this chart, how do you think he'll react?"

Madeline drew in a deep breath. "Boy, I would love to be a fly on the wall to find out."

Hunter's phone pinged, "Sorry, I need to check this."

Madeline nodded and watched his expression change upon reading the text.

"The spirits are with us. This is from the lab. They found fingerprints on Jonathan's cell phone. They're Christophe's."

·»·◇·62·◇·«·

KXOP Newsroom — 9:36 a.m.

Cora skipped her second espresso, riding high on the energy of working with Madeline on solving this case. Cora promised Madeline she'd scour the internet for anything she could find on Lili and her daughter Luna, but the first thing she wanted to do was create a timeline of her communications with @SFCrimeblogger. She cracked her knuckles, opened up a browser, and got working. She compiled a timeline of all her communications with @SFCrimeblogger to piece together all their photos and conversations. Her internship included a final project for Amy and Bob. What if her final project was a complete timeline for the "The Eclipse Killer"? That's what all the news stations were calling him.

Digging back through the posts, she scanned @SFCrimeblogger's website and examined the website footer information. She hadn't paid much attention to it when conversing with Hannah. She remembered Amy telling her about the site but couldn't remember if she used the site's contact page. She clicked on the link, and a short contact form popped up. It included a simple form to add her email address and a thank you from @SFcrimeblog. She did a double take. It wasn't @ SFCrimeblogger. Wondering what was up, she filled out the form with her email address and dashed off a quick note to Hannah: *"Hey, Hannah! Just cruising your site. I noticed a different email addy. Is this still you? Thanks!"*

Cora spotted an alert from NASA regarding their live coverage of the total solar eclipse. She popped over to their site and grabbed a link for an animation showing the path of totality crossing the United States. Cora pondered what it might feel like to experience a total solar eclipse. She checked the updates to the KXOP coverage plan for the eclipse meditation. Savvy Seekers expected to have over one thousand meditators filling the streets for the event. Madeline had been pretty convincing. She suspected that Christophe and the Savvy Seekers weren't disclosing their event plan. The thought of another teenager being sacrificed in front of a Gothic Cathedral was unsettling, yet everyone was talking about it.

⋯»◇63◇«⋯

Incident Room — 10:32 a.m.

Hunter was relieved to write the latest ballistics news on the whiteboard and confirmed the lab findings of Christophe's fingerprints on Jonathan's phone.

Vierra joined him. "That's. Shit, that's fantastic."

"And it gets better: Christophe-r Muldooney owns a gun—a .22." Hunter knew the case was turning in their favor.

"I cannot wait to drag his sorry ass into our scuzzy interview room and watch him stew," Vierra said.

"You and me both, let's go."

Vierra shifted his stance, thinking, "Okay, so we hit the compound, grab Heir Guru and get alibis for the rest of the Seekers too?"

Hunter pointed to the list of Savvy Seeker staff posted on the whiteboard. "Yup, Miranda, Edgar, and Brenda. Okay, let's look—"

"—Hunter, Vierra. I need to talk to you for a minute." Leo entered the room.

Hunter turned to see Commander Watts on Leo's heels and a grim expression on Leo's face.

"What's going on, boss?" Vierra asked, his voice tight.

Leo stared at Vierra. "You should have come to me, Daniel."

Hunter froze upon hearing Leo use Vierra's given name. "Lieutenant?"

"Investigator Vierra," the Commander kept his voice low, yet Hunter felt it in his bones. "I'm here to escort you to see our fellow officers at Internal Affairs."

Hunter swung his head and locked eyes with Vierra. He saw his partner blink and shake his head. "What?" Hunter turned to the Commander. "Can't this wait? We're so close to breaking this case."

Leo stepped closer to Hunter. "The timing sucks, but it's out of my hands. You'll have him back when they are satisfied."

Hunter watched helplessly as Vierra crossed the room, his energy draining from his body with each step. The Commander held the door open for him.

Vierra shot a look back at Hunter, "Don't worry, you can handle the guru dude on your own." Then he stepped out of the door.

Leo said, "Please tell me you've made some progress?"

"Absolutely. We got confirmation from Ballistics that the same twenty-two caliber gun was used to kill both victims, and Christophe owns a twenty-two. And Christophe's prints were found on Jonathan's phone."

Leo considered the new information. "Okay, get out to that compound and bring that Christophe asshole in here."

·∙»)◊**64**◊(«∙·

Sirius Books — 11:51 a.m.

After her conversation with Hunter, Madeline pulled up Christophe's chart and checked out his current planetary transits. She discovered transiting Neptune conjunct his natal Saturn, a challenging transit to one's sense of reality. For some, it brought on bouts of depression, confusion, and disorientation. She toyed with these ideas as she moved through the shop.

The front door opened, and she looked up, surprised, as Kess walked in. "Hey, Madeline."

"Well, hey, yourself, this is a pleasant surprise." She walked over, and they met at the front counter. Madeline heard Geena dusting a bookcase nearby.

"And the surprise gets nicer. I brought back your brooch." He pulled a small silk pouch from his satchel.

"Aww, that's so sweet of you."

Kess opened the silk bag and held the brooch in his hand. Madeline leaned in. The silver leaf pattern glowed white, and the large center stone glittered blue and purple with sparks of pink fire. "And these aren't cheap rhinestones."

Madeline turned as Geena walked up. She nodded to her to join them. "Geena, check this out. What are the stones, Kess?"

Kess rotated the brooch so the gems glittered a rainbow of colors under the shop lights. "The little purple clusters are alexandrite. These babies are as expensive as diamonds."

"You're kidding?" Madeline had no idea they were that valuable.

"Yeah, and the gem in the middle is an extra fine-grade opal. Those little pearls are all real, fresh water." He handed her the brooch and the pouch.

Madeline saw Geena's eyes widen as she stared at the gems. "That's gorgeous. Where did you get it?"

"I found it while I was out walking. Not bad, eh?"

"In the street? Wow," Geena said. "That's just plain luck."

"So, what do I owe you for the repair?" Madeline asked.

Kess waved his hand in the air. "It's on the house, but if you don't mind, I'd like to pick up my commission check. If you have it ready."

"We've sold several of your eclipse sets and bracelets." Madeline walked over to the front counter, reached into a drawer, and retrieved an envelope while Geena dusted shelves closer to the front counter. Madeline felt that Geena wanted to hear more of her conversation with Kess. Madeline placed the bag with the brooch in the silk pouch on the counter.

"It's not too late. I still have a few more eclipse sets. I could bring them over later?" Kess asked as he took the envelope from Madeline.

"We're good, but you never know. Come Monday, we might have a last-minute rush. I'll text you."

"Works for me. Thanks, Madeline. Good to see you, Geena."

Geena gave him a rapid wave with her hand, and after he left, she came over to the counter. "Could I see that brooch again?"

"Of course." Madeline pushed the brooch toward her. "Do you like jewelry?"

"Who doesn't? Where did you say you found it?"

Madeline sensed a disturbing chill from Geena. Madeline didn't recall discussing the brooch with her before. "Oh, I was walking somewhere. It was down to the ferry building. I was lost in thought and happened to see it."

"Really? That's wild. I wish I had that luck." Geena lowered her head to examine the gem more closely.

Madeline basked in her fortune. They both turned around when they heard the shop door open. A young man and woman sauntered in, looking around. Madeline grabbed the gem and put it back in the bag. "Take care of these folks, Geena. I'll be in my office."

Geena greeted the new customers and Madeline escaped into her office, closing the door behind her. She looked at the brooch once more and wondered about her luck. Her eyes fell upon the shelf of Aunt Jane's astrology books, drawn to the vibrant hues of the spines and the enchanting celestial imagery. Then her mind flashed to the horary chart she'd made, the one asking, "Where is Lili?" She considered the grand trine on the map. Could that be the trick? Could she follow her map, consult with the elementals again, and see what happened? The eclipse was only two days away. She felt a strong urge to try it out.

She rummaged through her notes and found the map she'd drawn from the horary chart triangle. She shoved it into her purse, then dashed out of her office. She found her pea coat on the coat tree in the workspace. She pinned the brooch to the lapel, adding a bit of dazzle to her old comfortable coat. Tossing her purse over her shoulder, she headed out of the workspace.

Moving through the main sales area and heading to the door, she found Geena had opened the glass case that housed their Tarot card collection. Perfect. "Hey, Geena, I'm heading out to do some shopping. Text me if you need anything." She got to the door and, stepping out, felt a new energy zing through her.

·»◊65◊«·

The Savvy Seeker Compound — 12:05 p.m.

Bolstered by his conversation with Madeline and with the new evidence, yet, still royally pissed off at Vierra for being taken off the case, Hunter drove to the Savvy Seeker's compound, not sure what to expect. When he came through the drive, the parking lot was empty. After parking the car and grabbing his portfolio, he approached the gate, half expecting to see Katia greet him as she did that first day.

But just as he got to the intercom, the gate exploded open, and the round-shaped woman with the curly hair he'd met with Christophe on that first visit emerged. Carrying a purse over her shoulder and pulling a wheely suitcase, her face wet from crying. From his research into the company, he recognized her. "Excuse me, but are you, Brenda?"

Brenda sized him up. "Who are you? Oh, wait, you're one of those cops."

"Yes, I'm Investigator Hunter Davis," he held his badge.

Pulling her purse higher on her shoulder, she started walking. "Yeah, I saw you on the monitors when you searched the embroidery hut. My apologies, but I have to go." She stepped away from the open gate.

"Can you tell me where I can find Christophe?"

Brenda stopped moving and looked up through her curls at him, her body language and attitude skeptical. "Oh, and what interest do the police have in meeting the great man?"

Hunter wondered if her disbelief was related to him or Christophe. "I'd rather not say at the moment."

Brenda sniffed. "Well, good luck with that. He's not here. In fact, no one is here. They've all checked into hotels in the city."

"What for?"

She let her purse slip off her shoulder. "To prepare for the eclipse meditation tomorrow morning. No one wants to drive back and forth at four in the morning, and traffic will be a nightmare for the whole day."

"You don't seem all that enthusiastic."

"Because it's a tremendous waste of resources." Brenda dropped her purse on the ground, turning to him. "Yes, Christophe is always one to put on a good show, but this is a logistical nightmare. We now have a thousand meditators volunteering to be there. And unfortunately, we're relying on your buddies and other cops to help with crowd control. We didn't factor in enough private security guards in our budget."

Hunter had seen the memos briefing everyone on the street closures in the city, and he had to agree with her. "Got it. So, can you tell me which hotel Christophe is in?"

"I don't know. He said he's available by text but needs to keep his location very hush-hush."

"Then I need that number. Look, I need some answers. We have two young victims, and the speculation is the killer will add another victim on Monday. Now, can we go inside, sit down and talk?" Hunter grabbed the suitcase handle and steered her toward the gate. "The first victim was your son, Jonathan."

Brenda shook her head as she begrudgingly picked up her purse and followed him through the gate. "After all these years, I hadn't expected to be so saddened by his death."

"Did you ever attempt to find him after you gave him up?" Hunter asked as Brenda led him through the front door of the main building.

"No, I never did. Come on in. I'll bring you into the conference room. We can talk there."

Hunter wheeled her suitcase as they walked through the double glass doors into the lobby, which resembled one you'd find at a resort hotel. The decor enhanced the expansive feeling: high ceilings, walls painted a soft blue, with paintings of seascapes and colorful tapestries on the walls. The minimalist design of the furniture brought elegance to the space. But an eerie silence overwhelmed the intended serenity.

They walked past a receiving desk and down a hall with glass walls. A door opened into a conference room with a massive, custom-made wooden table at the center. Brenda pulled out a chair for herself and motioned for him to sit across from her.

Hunter laid his portfolio on the table. "What can you tell me about Jonathan?"

Brenda drew in a long inhalation, a look of determination on her face as she looked up at him. "What I know is Jonathan sent Christophe a fan letter. You can imagine, Christophe gets thousands of letters, but we read all of them. Jonathan's stood out, not just because it was from a kid, but because he outlined this incredible idea to harness the insights from astrology into a wearable biofeedback unit. He called it "Know-sis. Edgar read the letter and brought it to Christophe."

"What happened next? Did Christophe meet with Jonathan?"

Brenda straightened her shoulders. "No, he sent Edgar to check the boy out."

Hunter's mind flashed to Jennifer Acosta describing a Chinese man who came to visit Jonathan about Chinese social clubs. "Wait. Did Edgar realize he was meeting the son you two gave up for adoption?"

Brenda lifted her fist to her mouth and shook her head. "He had no idea. It wasn't until…." She gasped as tears fell from her eyes. "It wasn't until after we learned about Jonathan's murder that we found out he was ours."

Hunter searched for and found a box of tissues on a side table. He offered the box to Brenda. "Did Christophe know who the boy was?"

Through her tears, she raised her hands. "I don't know. And I don't want to know because, because."

"You don't want to know if Christophe killed Jonathan to keep the boy from telling the world Christophe stole this biofeedback invention?"

Brenda nodded through her tears. "And Christophe is showcasing it tomorrow with all those damn meditators.”

"You've got a thousand meditators wearing the technology?”

"Yes," she said, "But it hasn't been fully tested yet. Edgar tried to tell him this precious new toy was faulty, but Christophe was too impatient to wait.”

Hunter felt a chill. "What kind of bugs? What will it do?”

"Edgar isn't sure. It's supposed to help you focus, but who knows? Headaches for sure, possibly seizures? It's all too much.”

"What hotel is he staying in, Brenda?" Hunter stood up.

"Why? Are you going to arrest him?”

"We'll bring him in for questioning. What hotel?”

Brenda stood and grabbed her suitcase. "Katia made the arrangements. We all have suites at the Fairmont. Which is where I'm headed. Katia might be around here somewhere. You can ask her.”

Hunter watched her heave the purse back on her shoulder and wheeled her suitcase behind her.

⋯»◦66◦«⋯

KXOP Newsroom — 12:23 p.m.

Elbows deep in her internet research, Cora looked for anything on Lili Todd and her daughter, Luna. This turned out to be a challenge, as she couldn't find anything listed. Lili must have used some data-sweeping service. She had better luck with the daughter. Cora found a photo of Luna on her high school website. Tall and enviably thin, with pale blue eyes. Luna reminded Cora of someone, but she couldn't figure out who that was. Then, in a moment of realization, she knew who it was and pulled up one of Christophe's publicity photos. The gene transfer had been strong. Luna looked just like her father. She had a petite nose and the same thin, pale lips, but where her father's face seemed designed to garner attention, hers was one to fade into the shadows.

The school website offered a link to more data, and she found a small online newsletter that mentioned Luna in connection to a small fire at the school. But she found no follow-up on the story. She was putting it all in an email to Madeline when her phone pinged, a new message from the @SFCrimeblogger site.

Hannah: *"How are you holding up? The cops spent hours talking to your sister. Do you have any idea what she told them?"*

Crap. What was she going to say? She didn't want to give away her sister's story but needed to share something juicy as a 'thank you' for alerting her about the cops going to Sirius Books. She texted: *OMG Madeline wouldn't tell me what she told the cops, but she made an astrology chart for the total solar eclipse."*

Hannah: *"Ooh! Give me the deets! I'll list you as a contributor to my blog."*

Cora's fingers hovered over her keyboard. What to do? She backpedaled. She typed back: *"Nice! I'm in the middle of a project for my boss. But let me pull some of my notes together."*

Hannah: *"Yeah, but once they catch the murderer, we could totally do a hot collab. This could lead to a book deal."*

Cora leaned back. Was Hannah serious? She tried not to let her mind go down that path, but it did.

"Cora, come join me. Now," Amy shouted from the assignment desk. The icy tone in her voice sent a shock wave down Cora's spine. She got up from her computer and walked over to the assignment desk. Standing with Amy was a shlubby guy with dirty brown hair and a pudgy face dressed in a gray hoody and cargo pants. She'd never seen him in the station before.

Keeping her voice casual, "Yeah, Amy, what's going on?"

Amy tilted her head to the young man. "Cora, I'd like you to meet Jordan, and Jordan, this is Cora. Jordan, do you want to explain what you asked me?"

Cora offered her hand, but Jordan pointed to Amy. "Yeah, so I'm friends with Amy, but I don't know you," he stared at Cora, staying calm.

"I'm sorry. Did I miss something?" Cora asked.

Jordan explained, "I got your email asking if this email is still you. Who are you talking to?"

A fresh wave of goosebumps raced along Cora's arms. "I was chatting with Hannah. She's @SFCrimeblogger. I've been messaging her for about a week. Isn't she your sister? She said she worked on the blog while you cared for the new baby."

Jordan looked at Amy, who sighed and shook her head. "Whoever this Hannah is, she's an impostor."

"Wait, what?"

Jordan leaned in. "I have a sister, but she has nothing to do with my website. And yeah, my wife had a baby, and I haven't been posting anything. I checked with my hosting company, and somehow, this Hannah person got my password and posted some photos to make you think she was legit."

Cora stiffened, and her heart thudded in her chest as she turned to Amy. Then she pointed at her computer monitor before looking up at Jordan. "But I was just messaging with her a minute ago. Come look at my screen."

Amy and Jordan rushed to Cora's computer, and a new message popped up. Hannah: "Hey, where did you go? Did I mention a book deal?!"

Cora, Amy, and Jordan all read the last text exchange. Amy looked at Jordan. "Shit."

"So, what do I tell this Hannah person?" Cora asked Amy.

Amy grabbed her phone. "Nothing. I'm texting Greg in the IT department to check into this."

"But I was in the middle of a text conversation. What do I tell her?" Cora asked.

"Just tell her you got a new assignment and have to log off," Amy said.

Cora sat back at her desk. Oh god, she realized this would go horribly wrong. She started typing, *"Hey, my boss just gave me a new assignment. I gotta go."* Her hands shook while Jordan and Amy watched her type.

Hannah: *"Okay, but don't stay away long. There's going to be a big break in the case."*

Jordan shook his head. "What does she mean by that? I checked with my source at homicide. They ran the ballistics, but they don't have a gun to match with the bullets taken from the two bodies."

"Okay, I will have to get Bob on this," Amy said.

Cora's stomach turned to lead. Who had she been messaging with? Oh, hell. Cora stared at Amy, looking for some support.

Amy turned to Jordan. "Jordan, get on with your host server and tell them to go back to the site history to see if they can find out who hacked you from their end."

"Okay, and you know I will have to post a story about this to the blog. I mean, it could be the killer who has been sending this stuff to Cora. It's a legit scoop."

"I totally understand, but for Cora's safety, could you please give us twenty-four hours to inform the police and ensure he hasn't hacked into anyone else's sites?"

Jordan wavered. "That's reasonable. And then, when this cools down, will you give me an interview, Amy?"

Cora saw Amy hesitate. Amy's job was to report the news, not be the news. But because of her own stupidity, she'd now put her boss in that awful position.

"Yes, I'll sit down with you, and we can create a timeline."

"Thanks, Amy. I appreciate it," Jordan said. "I better get to my host guy. I'll be in touch." With that, he left the newsroom.

Cora felt wretched. She watched Amy type a text and gather her thoughts.

"Okay, Cora," Amy said. "You realize I can't have you working on the eclipse prep anymore. I don't think it's safe for you to be in the newsroom right now."

Cora hated to admit that Amy was right. "I understand. So, are you sending me home?"

Amy shook her head, "No, not yet. The IT guy is coming, and I need to bring

Bob into this conversation. Bring me everything you got from the impostor. We'll comb through it and figure out what we will tell the police."

"The police?" It hit Cora. How damaging would that be?

"Yes, if you've been messaging the killer, of course, we have to go to the police. But we need a strategy."

Cora nodded her head and felt the tears forming. She swallowed. "Amy. I am so sorry. I…"

Amy patted her on the shoulder. "I know you were doing your best. Sit tight. Don't go anywhere near your computer, promise?"

Cora nodded, "Promise. Hey, I can text Investigator Vierra. Will that help?"

"Yes, you do that while I go get Bob." Amy walked away. Cora grabbed her phone and tried to keep her hands from trembling as she typed out the text.

··»)◊**67**◊(«··

The Savvy Seeker Compound — 2:10 p.m.

After watching Brenda leave, Hunter sat in the conference room, kicking around the idea of searching the compound while he was there. If Christophe had checked into a hotel in San Francisco, finding him would be nearly impossible. Hunter half expected to see a security guard come and kick him out of the conference room, but nothing stirred. He pondered Brenda's information that Christophe may have stolen Know-sis with Edgar's help. The inventions must have a paper trail if Christophe planned to sell the technology. Had Christophe hired a patent attorney? Were there any filings on the contraption? Would Christophe go so far as to kill Jonathan just to keep the boy silent? Was Sasha connected to Know-sis?

The silence in the compound took on an eerie quality, so he picked up his portfolio and left the conference room. Brenda had turned left to leave the building, so he turned to the right, down the hall. He glanced at other offices, all furnished in a similar eco-friendly style, but no one was working. Keeping his footsteps light, he ascended a glass-enclosed staircase. A pungent aroma hit him. He sniffed. Manure? How could that be? In a place this immaculately clean. Logic told him it must be in the potted plants in the staffer's offices.

At the top of the stairs, he found a series of rooms with glass windows instead of drywall, so you could see into each one without going inside. One appeared to be their media room with television monitors, microphones, and computers. Next, an office with four desks, set up in a bullpen fashion. From the light pastel colors and feminine touches, he guessed this was where the women worked. He found a few small plants on the desk, which he guessed belonged to Brenda, but no scent of manure lingered in the space. Then, as he came out of the door, he heard a slight "ching," like a tiny wind chime. He looked around, but the space was still. No footsteps, no voices. He was alone.

The last room on this floor was larger and more elaborate than the others. It featured a massive desk and another table with chairs for six people. He guessed it had to be Christophe's lair and stepped inside. He was alone in the guru's office, with no one to stop him from tossing the place. Even if he had the energy, he'd be here until midnight. And if indeed Christophe had planned the murders, he wouldn't be stupid enough to leave any incriminating evidence behind.

The "ching" sounded again from the room's right side. Hunter spun his head in that direction and halted when he saw what dominated the far wall. A massive painting glowed with amber light from the ceiling light fixtures. Standing on an outcrop, a man decked in a metal helmet and a knight's graymail with a tattered white tunic emblazoned with a red cross, torn and ragged from battle. He held up a sword across his chest. In his other hand, he held a white shield with a red cross but pierced with a dozen arrows. The painting was so vivid and detailed that Hunter thought he could see the bloodied, shredded tunic waving in the breeze.

Then another sound shot through the space—a horse's whinny. Hunter felt a throbbing in his chest as he spun around, looking for the source of the sound. But again, nothing. He looked back at the painting, now an anger growing in him. Why had this knight not taken off his helmet? Was this Christophe's false vanity? A portrait of himself as the battle-weary knight? The anger roiled, and Hunter felt like spitting on the carpet.

But he turned away. He was wasting time. He scanned the rest of the office. On the opposite wall, behind the desk, he saw photos and memorabilia: Christophe with celebrities, Christophe standing on a stage before hundreds of people, microphone in hand, speaking to the crowds. There were framed CD covers from his various meditations. Even a supposedly enlightened guru had a "me" wall.

Then, just over the top of a low bookcase, he spotted an old photo in a silver frame. He walked over, his eyes drawn to a younger version of Madeline. She stood in a garden surrounded by Katia, William, and everyone, including Christophe. And a petite blonde that he didn't recognize. That must have been Lili. They were all holding up carrots, lettuces, and a couple of huge zucchinis. All smiling at the bounty. The matte surrounding the photo had writing at the bottom in beautiful calligraphy:

"Being deeply loved by someone gives you strength while loving someone deeply gives you courage." — Lao Tzu

As Hunter recited the quote, he could feel the weight of each word settling in his mind. The room's silence amplified the sense of abandonment. He gazed at Madeline's photo and breathed. Then he looked back at the painting of the knight, wondering how Christophe had taken his group from such humble beginnings to a multi-million-dollar company. There was a foul smell, and it wasn't coming from manure. Seeing no other staff members, he decided to drive back to the city.

"What are you doing here?"

Hunter spun around as Katia stormed into the office, scowling at the intrusion. "Brenda said everyone had gone to town. I still have my search warrant. I have some questions for Christophe." Hunter noticed a crack in Katia's hard-edged exterior; she was exhausted, with enormous black circles under her eyes. "But tell me, how did you take the news, discovering that the daughter you gave up for adoption had been murdered?"

"Unlike the other women, when I found out about Christophe's plan to give the children up for adoption, I was relieved. I never wanted to have children," she said as she walked over to the small table and waved to Hunter to take a seat. "But I feel terrible for her parents. They must be going through hell."

"I met them, the Randalls, a lovely couple, and they are grieving. I need your help. There are two children out there, two more potential victims, and all the evidence I have is pointing to Christophe. Where is he?"

Katia drummed her fingers on the tabletop, considering her answer. "You got that wrong. There aren't two children. There are three."

Hunter experienced an eerie shiver up the back of his neck. "Madeline told us about the births. I don't understand?"

Katia stared at the table, reliving the experience in her mind's eye. She didn't look at Hunter; he waited for her to go on. "Madeline wasn't there. It was the night Victoria gave birth to her boy. Afterward, there was so much blood. Madeline helped Christophe and me get Victoria into the car, and then he and I drove Victoria to the local hospital."

Hunter observed her becoming faster and her facial muscles tightening. "Go on."

"I'd never heard of a daisy baby before that night."

"What is that?"

"The medical term is Twin Transfusion Syndrome. When a woman carries twins that share a placenta, the blood flows unevenly between them. One baby receives more nourishment and thrives, while the other often cannot survive. Madeline and the doula helped deliver the boy but didn't know the girl was even there.

"And what happened to her?"

Katia smiled. "Somehow, that little fireball made it. Now, understand by this time we'd all had our babies, and the house was a wreck. When Christophe found out about this twin, he lost it. I'd never seen him go off the rails like that."

"He never knew she was carrying twins?"

"That's right. Victoria went home with Christophe, and I took the baby to my mother. She had a young woman who worked in her shop, desperate to adopt. We got in touch with Grudzinski, and he handled the rest. We took Victoria home to recover, never telling her about the girl."

"You did what?"

Katia shook her shoulders to shake off the emotions from the past. "Lili had left the group early but got back in touch with Christophe. She had given birth to Luna. So, not only was he dealing with having children with two different women, but adding a twin into the mix drove him over the edge. When Victoria came back to the house, she suffered incredible postpartum depression and ignored her boy. Then Christophe put the adoption plan into action."

Hunter considered the tension that must have filled that house. "How did you feel about it?"

"Like I told you, I didn't want to have children. When I looked at my baby, I felt nothing. I was happy to follow Christophe's plan, but toward the end, he was suffering from paranoid ideations. He said he'd dreamed about the children all grown up and that they all had supernatural powers. That they couldn't be raised together, that they'd turn on the parents. Ultimately, no one in the house wanted to admit it, but giving away the children was a relief."

"Okay, and what if he's decided they all need to be erased? I came here looking for Christophe. He has a gun registered that's the same caliber as the one who killed the victims."

"Are you implying that he would go out and kill these children?"

"I don't know. As you said, he never wanted them."

"But Christophe is no killer. He doesn't have time. He and Miranda have been skulking around late at night working on the damned Know-sis project. It's impossible."

Hunter stood. "But we know he's got a gun registered in his name, and I need to know if it matches the one used to kill these kids. Where does he keep it?"

Katia stood and walked over to a set of low cabinets next to Christophe's desk. "Okay, I can show it to you."

"If Christophe is all peace, love, and tye dye, why does he still own it?"

"I've given up figuring out that side of him. I just switch up the combination every few months for him." Hunter followed her and watched Katia flick open a door. Inside, a small safe, like the ones you'd find in a hotel room. She spun the dial on the safe to unlock it. She swung open the door, only to find it empty.

"Oh my. I hadn't expected that."

Hunter shook his head. "All right, give me the name of the hotel he's staying at in the city."

"He's booked a suite at the Mark Hopkins, but you won't find him there."

·∙»◇**68**◇«∙·

KXOP Newsroom — 2:28 p.m.

Cora drummed her fingers and tried not to twitch while Vierra reviewed the printout of her messages to @SFCrimeblogger. Across from him, the IT guy, Greg, sat at her computer, staring at the screen and laboring to find out who had hacked into Jordan's account. Back at the assignment desk, Amy spoke with Bob in hushed tones. Cora knew this was the end of her internship. She began thinking about what to say to her parents.

Vierra looked over at her. "What's going on? Why so blue?"

Cora grunted, "Figuring out my next move. My days here are numbered." My parents are going to be furious. I guess I could go back and finish my major in fashion design."

"Fashion design?" He jerked his head back in disbelief. "That's a waste of space. Looking through your messages with this whack job, you were on point. You should apply to journalism school."

Cora hadn't expected that, not from Vierra. "Well, thanks. I guess."

"And you said you'd checked with your boss about Jordan and that he was a reliable source?"

"Yes. I have never worked with bloggers before, so I didn't know what to look for to see if it was a fake."

"Don't worry, we have entire departments that cover this thing."

"So, the photos—the shots of Jonathan, the ones I brought to you—do you have any idea who took them?"

Vierra bobbed his head from side to side. "I'm not at liberty to disclose that."

Cora smiled. "Points for trying."

Vierra's eyes brightened, and he shot her a teasing grin. But the moment was brief. He got up and went over to Greg. "What you got for me, Sparky?"

Cora watched Greg pull his head from the computer and write something down on paper. She thought tech guys did everything digitally. Greg looked up at Vierra. "Okay, as best I can tell, your hacker convinced the blogger's hosting site to help him change his password. He must have convinced customer service he was legit."

Vierra studied Greg's screen. "That's it? Just a password? How are we going to track this bastard down?"

Greg stood up and stretched his neck. "I could see if there's a backdoor through his VPN, but I can't make any promises."

"Do your best, and if you can't get it, I'll get you in touch with the cybercrime guys," Vierra said.

Cora noticed an alert coming over her screen and heard it pinging on other screens around the room. Suddenly, the newsroom came to life.

"What's going on?" Vierra heard the alerts, too, and looked around the newsroom.

Cora read the headline, "Wow. Sean Muldooney has been acquitted." She looked at Vierra and saw his face turn to ash. And then he was all movement. He pointed to Greg, "Thanks, Greg. Text Cora what you find out." Then he turned to her, "Cora, send it to me. I gotta run."

"Okay, so what else can I do?"

Vierra stood inches from her. "Keep your head down, do your job. But come Monday, for that big Christophe meditation? I need you to be my eyes and ears. Will you be watching the live coverage?"

Cora whispered, "Yeah, I'll watch it in the live truck."

"Good. Let me know when you do. You have my number. Now, be extra vigilant when you are out on the street. Don't go out after dark, and just be freaking careful. All right?"

Cora sighed. "Okay. Anything else I should tell my boss?"

Vierra took several strides. "I'll take care of it. You get back to work."

Cora watched him stop and chat with Amy as Cora stood there feeling foolish. Amy said something to Vierra, and then he was gone.

Walking back to her desk, she looked over at Greg. "Thank you. I'm sorry you had to be dragged into this."

Greg gave her a modest smile. "I'm just sorry about you being cyberstalked."

She was, too. Her next urge was to text Madeline to let her know what had happened, but something told her to hold off until Greg sussed out who had stalked her.

-❖69❖-

Saturday, August 19, 2017

North Beach — 10:47 am

Madeline pulled up the map she'd made to go with the "Where is Lili" horary chart to check the coordinates again, following the impulse to check her "luck." So far, the elementals felt balanced, the earth solid in this neighborhood. North Beach, a well-established neighborhood, gave off mellow, stable vibes. The sky overhead was still cloudy but not foggy, and there was no rain, so there were no surprises from the water. She sniffed the air and smelled the tasty aroma from the woodfire pizza place around the corner, fire doing what fire did so well.

Her map brought her just a few blocks off Columbus Avenue, an area with more development over the years. Continuing down the avenue, she passed the famous restaurants and coffee houses. She found herself in a block with two-story, mostly mixed-use, commercial buildings and some apartments. She checked her map and felt a gut punch as she closed in on the address. "Okay, what do you have to show me?" She whispered. What would Lili be doing down here? Most of the street signage included names of engineering firms, several architects' offices, and a software startup. Did Lili work down here? Madeline breathed in and, for a moment, tried to sense if Lili was around. She'd been so intertwined with Lili's energy when they lived together that she opened her heart to see if there was a sense of her friend in this space. But after a moment, there was nothing, so she continued walking.

Plenty of cars were parked on both sides of the street, and peering further up the street, she saw a red brick building, the "site" on her map. It featured a parking garage, and she walked past a large plate glass storefront. She spotted some floral decor items in the window, but it was sparsely furnished and felt abandoned. She stopped at the garage entrance and waited as a minivan exited, made a turn, and gazed at the shop again. Her hand flew to her mouth.

She spotted the store logo, hidden by some butcher paper on the inside of the window. The design featured three flowers: two roses and, in the center, a red lily.

This couldn't be right, or she'd asked the wrong question. Should she have asked where is Lili Todd? She approached the window and put both hands around her eyes to peer through patches in the butcher paper. A large counter took up most of the space in the middle of the shop. Abandoned buckets of dried herbs, sprays of grass, and other floral decorations stood along the sides of the counter. She saw what looked like doors to a large refrigerator past the counter. In front of the counter were empty black flowerpot buckets in an aluminum stand, scraps of colored ribbons, and chunks of florist foam oasis. On the floor, still packed in cellophane, a bunch of curly ting, its twisted stems decorated with glitter.

Madeline stared, gob-smacked, and stepped away from the window, her mind whirling. On her phone, she scrolled through the KXOP site, pulled up a photo of Sasha's crime scene, and spotted the same curly ting as the bunch lying inside the storefront. She stepped backward into the path of a man walking down the street. "Hey, watch where you're going, lady."

She apologized to the man and then gathered herself. Madeline opened her camera app, held her phone to the window, and took photos of the ting, the counter, and the decorations, getting as many close-ups as possible. She'd missed it the first time, but at the end of the counter, she spotted what looked like a cosmetic bag. An open flap revealed a set of used makeup brushes. What was that doing there?

Stepping back, she took more photos of the street and the building across the street. Finally, she took a close-up of the flower logo, specifically the lily, a stylized version of an oriental lily with orange stamens and tiny pink dots at the blossom's center. She couldn't help thinking of Lili, and then it hit her: the red lily. In Greek mythology, the red Lili was called "the corpse flower." But this was beyond belief. She'd found "Lili."

Madeline leaned against the brick wall, not knowing what to do. She could call Alistair and get him down here. But that didn't feel right. Matthew-Tabitha would find this hysterical and would mock her magical thinking. Magic. Then, somewhere, a quote floated into her mind. It was from Rumi: "Stop acting so small. You are a universe in ecstatic motion." She breathed in and out for a few counts. If this were the universe sending her a message, she'd be a fool not to take it seriously.

❖ 70 ❖

Sirius Books — 1:18 pm

As she walked down Polk Street, Madeline's pace quickened. Her discovery of the "Lili" flower shop brought a sense of triumph and accomplishment, recharging her spirit and confidence. The antidote she'd craved raced through her bloodstream, curing her self-doubt and quieting Vierra's skepticism and accusations. Yes, she'd applied an ancient technology and added her own intuitive twist, and the result transformed her attitude.

She rushed into the store, spotting Matthew-Tabitha and Geena deep in conversation over a book open on the counter. Once again, Matthew-Tabitha, now in her "girl" mode, wore a smart, little black dress that, in an eerie way, matched Geena's regular goth garb.

"Hey, boss lady, what's up?" Matthew-Tabitha asked.

Madeline flashed upon how to explain what she'd found and how she found it. It would be a good idea to practice, so she plowed in. "Okay, now that you're both here, I want you to see this." She pulled out her horary chart and map and placed them on the counter. Then, she went into some detail, explaining the logic, or lack of logic, that she used to create the map. Getting quizzical stares from the two of them, she blundered on and pulled out her phone.

Pulling up the photos of the flower shop, she gave them a few details about her friendship with Lili and what motivated her to find her old friend, fearing that her daughter Luna could be in the killer's sights. Matthew-Tabitha took her phone and Geena leaned in, studying the photos over Matthew-Tabitha's shoulder. Madeline buzzed with excitement, "These are the same floral decor pieces they found at Sasha's crime scene. I mean, look at that curly ting, the dried twigs that are all twisted?" She zoomed in on the details, then shot a quizzical look at Geena, who responded with raised eyebrows and a frown.

Madeline stopped talking and considered their reactions. "You guys think I'm nuts, don't you?"

Geena glanced at Matthew-Tabitha, letting him respond. Matthew-Tabitha handed the phone back to Madeline. "Now, don't get me wrong."

"Hold up. Whenever someone says don't get me wrong, they think you're wrong. What are you saying?"

Matthew-Tabitha didn't back down. "You're wrong. I mean, look. It's a flower shop. Of course, they're gonna have flower decorations and tingly stuff in the window. It has nothing to do with the murder. You're grasping at tingly straws because you want to impress Hunter. He's a fox. I don't blame you."

Madeline shook her head, dismissing his reference to Hunter. She scanned through the photos on the phone. "But did you see the logo? There's a Lili right there." She stopped at the photo of the open cosmetics bag on the counter and realized it made no sense, and a wave of self-doubt washed over her. "Okay, okay. I'm suffering from magical thinking, but it all made sense when I stood at the window."

"Of course, it did," Matthew-Tabitha said, taking her hand. "You need to feel you're contributing. But don't run off the rails. Sure, you want to show off for Hunter and that other guy, but if you send this to them, they're gonna toss you in the freak file, you know it."

Madeline squeezed Matthew-Tabitha's hand and saw Geena's pleading look. "He's right, Madeline, because it just looks like a dumb old flower shop to me, too."

Placing her phone back in her purse, Madeline nodded. "You guys are right, thank you." She took off her coat and let out a heavy sigh. "Okay, I'm going to head upstairs. Are you guys going to watch things here?"

"Of course. But I put some mail on your desk. You ought to check it before heading home," Geena said.

"Okay, thank you. Thank you both." Madeline trudged through to the work-space and hung up her coat outside her office. Although it burst her bubble, she felt better having first shared the story with Geena and Matthew-Tabitha. She realized that living alone, being alone with her own thoughts, made it easy for her to convince herself that what she was doing made sense. She opened her office door and closed it behind her, toying with the idea of sending the photos of the flower shop to Hunter. Not the photos, just a text? She sat at her desk and pulled out her horary chart once again, only to feel the magic wearing off.

***

A simple, easy excuse, needing a fresh roll of tape for the cash register, it allowed her the moment she needed. Moving through the shelves, she'd come to despise, stepping ever so lightly, using her fingers to gently create an opening in the beaded curtain without making a sound, she skipped through the lengths of beads, still thinking whoever installed them was an idiot. She listened at the office door and heard the familiar click and clack of Madeline's fingers on the keyboard.

Using her time wisely, she grabbed the roll of register tape and moved to the coat rack. She flipped the lapel of Madeline's coat, found the brooch, and oh so delicately unhooked the pin, stuffed the brooch in her pocket, and slipped back to the front of the store. Thinking she'd gotten away with it, but the silent forces, cousins to the elementals, witnessed her every move.

⋯⟨⟨**71**⟩⟩⋯

Sunday, August 20, 2017

Polk Street — 5:42 a.m.

Hunter got nothing but pushback after going to the Mark Hopkins and pleading with the staff to let him know if Christophe had checked in. He'd walked to several other hotels, the Fairmont, the Ritz Carlton, and still nothing. The overwhelming number of smaller hotels made him decide to end his search for the day. In the early evening, he'd received Madeline's text. Hunter agreed to meet with her on Sunday morning. As he drove to her store in the early morning hours, his regrets caught up with him. During the entire investigation, she'd been forthcoming with her charts and all the insights she'd shared. But what she'd texted him about finding a flower shop made him doubt her.

After Vierra's raking her over the coals about her past involvement with Christophe and how she'd been the one to take the children from their mothers, knowing the pain she'd caused to those women, to her friends, and after covering up all these years, why was he racing through traffic to see her when he should hit the pavement, looking for Christophe?

He scoffed at Vierra for spending so much time with Alana and skirted around the ethics of it all. And yet, how was he any different? All of his instincts told him to wait. Wait until after Monday, wait until the case is closed, wait. How often had he seen a simple attraction turn into an obsession and the destruction it left behind?

Hunter parked his car when he got a call from Lt. Leo.

"Did you find Christophe?"

"No, he's gone into hiding. Preparing for the big eclipse meditation. Any news on my partner?"

After a slight pause, Leo answered. "I had to pull some strings, so he'll be back on Monday. He dodged a suspension, but not by much."

"Copy that," Hunter said, even though he had a ton of questions he wanted to ask. They would have to wait until Monday. "You know Monday is going to be a train wreck, don't you?"

"Yeah, we had a meeting yesterday afternoon. The tactical guys and crowd control people are treating Christophe's meditation the way they treat the Chinese New Year parade in Chinatown. They're promising a significant presence."

"Well, we better have eyes everywhere. We have to grab Christophe the moment we see him, right?"

"That's turning into a political hot potato. We'll meet up ahead of time in the command trailer and convince the higher-ups that our evidence is convincing."

"Okay, Leo." Hunter rang off as he turned onto Polk Street.

⸱⸱《⸱72⸱》⸱⸱

Sirius Books — 6:16 a.m.

Madeline walked through the store with her smudge stick and Tibetan bells, fulfilling her Sunday morning ritual, clearing the energy in the store, her nerves on edge, preparing for her meeting with Hunter. He agreed to meet with her for coffee so she could explain what she'd done to find the flower shop. She'd spent much of her evening creating a PowerPoint presentation that laid out, in plain English, a step-by-step explanation of how she'd found the flower shop.

Again, she knew her presentation was more "art" than "science," but she also knew cops worked off hunches. He could relate to her work on that level. She put away her smudge supplies on a shelf in the workspace, then checked that she'd packed everything she needed in her laptop bag and set it on the worktable. She moved to the coat tree, grabbed her pea coat, and noticed the brooch was missing. She searched for it around the work area when she heard a scratching sound from the back door. She returned to the old wooden door and reached to open it when a sickeningly sweet aroma assaulted her nostrils. Madeline looked down, and a liquid came pouring through the gap at the bottom of the door. She leaped back to keep the liquid from hitting her shoes – it was gasoline.

Flames danced from outside the door, engulfing the gasoline. Panic-stricken, she spun around and raced back through the store. She felt the rush of heat across her back as she grabbed her computer bag and pulled on her coat with her keys in the pocket. Madeline dashed through the stacks to the front of the store and pulled her keys, bracing as an awful whooshing sound filled the back of the store. She could only imagine how fast the books, paper, and essential oils would catch fire.

Madeline's eyes burned as the smoke filled the air, and she fumbled for her keys as she got to the front door. She dropped them when, looking through the glass door, she spotted a chain. Someone chained the doors together with a padlock. She gasped. Who could have done this? She stopped to breathe, but her mouth and throat stung as smoke filled her mouth. Coughing, she searched around the shop, looking for something, anything, to help her escape.

Vaguely remembering something from an old fire safety card, she knelt to get below the smoke to breathe clean air, but then an explosion shook the space. The old wooden bookcases were exploding from the heat. She found an old metal bookshelf and tossed off all the books as her eyes burned from the smoke. She pulled an old scarf from her coat pocket and wrapped it around her mouth and nose. Then she grabbed the metal bookcase and dragged it to the glass door with every ounce of strength. She put her arms around it and tried to heave it into the lower glass pane, but her body racked with coughing, and she couldn't get any momentum to break the glass door.

Smoke engulfed the entire storefront, and she could barely see out the window. Down on the floor, she thought she saw movement. Still coughing, she thought she saw two figures heaving something outside the store. She scrambled away as a metal trash can shot through the window, exploding the glass pane into the front of the store.

Fresh air streamed through the broken display window, and she saw a man's hand reaching her. It had been bloodied from pushing glass shards out of the way. She pulled herself off the floor, took off her coat, and held it out to cover her upper body to protect herself from the broken glass. Madeline grabbed his arm, and then another arm reached through, and the two of them punched at broken glass shards to make enough room for her. She held the coat over her face as they dragged her through the shards to the sidewalk and pulled to her feet. Trusting in her rescuers, she scrambled with them to escape from the flames and smoke billowing from the store.

Madeline breathed in fresh air as police cars and fire engines arrived. Soon, hoses filled the sidewalk, and firefighters yelled instructions to bystanders to get out of the way. "Come on, there's an ambulance across the street." Someone grabbed Madeline's hand, and pain shot up her arm. She hadn't realized it, but there was a long gash on her forearm. She looked up to see Sluggo helping her.

They half-walked and half-dragged each other across Polk Street as police helped usher them away from the fire. They got to the other sidewalk, now filled with people coming out of shops and cafés to watch the disaster. Madeline turned and saw her store engulfed and the flames flying up into her apartment.

Firefighters had hoses up and shot streams of water at the store next door to keep the flames from traveling. She couldn't watch anymore and looked at Sluggo. He was bent over coughing, and his shirt was covered in blood. "Oh my gosh, Sluggo. Thank you."

"Hey, I'm just lucky I was sleeping a block away. I smelled the smoke. The other guy got here first and found the trash can."

"The other guy?" Madeline looked around. There were people all over the place. An EMT approached Sluggo and drew him to the ambulance as Madeline scanned the faces in the crowd.

"Madeline!"

A wave of relief washed through her mind as she heard Hunter's voice.

"Madeline?"

Madeline spun around and saw Hunter halfway down the block, stuck in a crowd, coming toward her. She shoved her way past the onlookers, not caring what they thought. Hunter stumbled while gasping for air, and she saw scratches on his arms and neck from the broken glass door. She got to him just as he righted himself, and they were each propelled by a relentless momentum. They enveloped each other, their heads and arms akimbo, coughing, bleeding, until they stood in the middle of the crowd and gathered each other in a longed-for embrace.

"Are you okay?" Hunter asked, pulling away to look at her.

A sudden bout of coughing caused her to stop, cover her mouth, and draw in a deep breath. "I'm still dizzy, and my throat is raw, but what about you? How did you get here?"

"We were supposed to meet for coffee, remember?"

"Oh gosh, you're right. I." She looked around and realized they stood at the same spot where she'd brought him the coffee and bagels. "It's just that I did some more astrology research," she stopped, flustered, as this was not how she wanted to explain it to him. "I made a PowerPoint and wanted to show it to you, but." She looked back at the smoky remains of her shop and tried not to cry, but the tears came along with another round of coughing.

"Hey, hey. We have to get you checked out. There's time to go over your research later."

Hunter draped his arm around her shoulder, and they walked back toward the ambulances.

"But we don't have time! The eclipse is tomorrow. What if the killer has already kidnapped another child?"

"Madeline, Madeline," Hunter lowered his voice. "It's okay. You're in shock. We're both in shock. Now let these EMTs take care of you." One EMT checked out Hunter, and Madeline fought off a wave of dizziness as another EMT asked her questions, gave her oxygen to breathe, and dressed her wounds. To keep her mind from taking an inventory of everything burning up in the building across the street, she focused on Hunter, whose eyes never left hers.

While the EMTs finished up, Sluggo came over with his freshly bandaged head, and Madeline felt a wave of gratitude that these men had saved her life. "Sluggo, thank you. Are you going to be all right?"

Once he saw Hunter with Madeline, Sluggo shied away. Noticing his reaction, she calmed him down. "It's okay, Sluggo. This is investigator Hunter Davis."

Sluggo gave Hunter a nervous nod. "Yeah, I seen you come to the store." Then he turned back to Madeline. "I tried to warn you. You're getting too close. That's why they tried to kill you."

"Who did?" Hunter leaned in. "Did you see anyone set the fire?"

"No, man. No, but you know the killer's been framing Madeline. They want you to watch her instead of looking into Know-sis."

"Know-sis?" Hunter said. "What do you know about it?"

Sluggo shook his head. "I tried to explain it to Madeline before, but it's hard for me, you know? I know this guy who works at one of those swank social clubs, and he's heard some crazy shit about Christophe getting his hands on this far-out technology. That all those meditators on Monday will be using it."

Hunter glanced at Madeline. "And I learned from Brenda yesterday that they haven't finished testing the thing, but Christophe is going ahead."

Madeline shook her head, clearing away the dizziness, and knew she had to get Hunter to check out the flower shop. There had to be a connection there. She just wasn't sure they would find it in time. Madeline turned back to Sluggo. "Do you have a place to stay?" Then the words caught in Madeline's throat, "Who knows when I'll ever be able to open the shop again?"

"Don't you worry about me. I've got friends in high places," he said, pointing to the sky. I'll get myself to a shelter tonight."

"Okay. We'll see each other again soon?"

"You can bet on it." Sluggo walked away from the ambulance. Madeline looked at Hunter. "Okay, are you ready to hear about my trip to the flower shop?"

"All ears. Let's get my car."

They walked to his car. Madeline glanced back at the smoking husk of her store across the street. Hunter led her to his car, and he flagged down a street cop to help them escape the roadblocks.

While driving, Madeline did her best to give him the condensed version of how she found the store and why she'd been so determined to find Lili, thinking Luna was a potential victim. Hunter explained how he had failed to find Christophe at the compound or at any of the hotels near the Cathedral. Madeline received a worried text from Cora, but she told her sister that she was okay and she'd call her soon. She texted Matthew-Tabitha to come to the store to work with the fire department on securing the site after they put out the fire.

Hunter pulled across the street from the flower store and found street parking. Madeline knew she didn't have too much energy left. They made it across the quiet street, and Madeline showed him the storefront. She pointed out the flower, the "Lili" logo. She walked toward the window and looked inside. She stopped -- the shop was empty. Shock zoomed through her body, but every last piece of floral decor was gone, every piece of ting, every leaf, every stem, and the makeup bag. Hunter stood next to her, looking through the window.

"I don't understand it. Yesterday, this shop was filled with floral supplies. Here, let me show you." Madeline pulled up the photo app on her phone, and Hunter leaned in to examine the photos. Now and then, he'd look up to the store window to compare her photos to what was in front of them.

"See, all of that greenery and the curly ting? All of that was used at Sasha's crime scene. I saw it in the photos posted online. And the makeup bag on the counter? Sasha wore makeup, didn't she?"

Hunter stepped closer to the window. I admit it's a long shot, but I'll get a warrant to check it out. Good job, Malcolm."

"Who is Malcolm?"

Hunter let out a sigh. "It's a long story. It's a thing between me and Vierra." He placed his hands around his eyes, peering deeper inside. "But getting a warrant's going to take hours. There's light coming from a back door. Let's search for an entrance to the building."

They walked down the alley, between the buildings, and they reached a gate leading to a service alley. The shop had another window on this side. It was covered with butcher paper. She and Hunter stopped to peer into it. Madeline saw part of the main sales area, but just ahead of them was a walk-in freezer. "What's a freezer doing in a flower shop?" They walked down the alley and got to a gate as a man in a baseball cap and keys swinging on his belt came out of the building.

"Excuse me," Hunter asked, "But do you work here?" Hunter held up his badge.

"I'm the building manager. How can I help you?"

Madeline followed Hunter and the manager, and they walked back toward the shop's side window.

Hunter asked, "Do you know who rented this shop?"

"No, sir, I never met the tenant, but I got a call from the rental agent. They moved out last night before their lease was up."

Madeline glanced at Hunter as a shiver ran down her arm.

Hunter walked the manager back to the front of the store, "This is a potential crime scene. I'm going to call units here to search it. In the meantime, will you call your rental agent and get all the contact information for the renter?"

"Yes, sir. I'll do that," the manager pulled out his phone. Hunter pulled Madeline over. "Okay, I'm going to call in my team. I'll order you a cab to get you home. You need to rest."

"I'm fine, I can…" She stopped and realized that she would just get in the way. "Okay, I will let you do your job."

"I'll also get with the fire department and get a liaison officer to contact you about the store. There's going to be a lot to go through and you will want to rest up. I'm so sorry about it."

Madeline mumbled her thanks. The rush to find the store had kept the shock of the fire at bay, and she knew those emotions would rise up. She needed to get home.

"Hey, Leo? I found something. It's the staging space for the murders."

Madeline leaned against the nearby wall, letting Hunter carry on his conversation with his boss. A car with an Uber sticker in the window stopped on the street, and Madeline gasped, seeing Cora get out of the backseat. "Cora?"

Cora stopped and then stared. "Madeline? Are you okay? I was going to call you about the fire?" She examined Madeline's bandages and saw Hunter on the phone. "What are you doing here?"

"It's a long story, but what are you doing here?"

"I. Oh, jeez. I'm sorry, but I have a long story, too."

Madeline listened to Cora's story about the hacker who took over @SFCrimeblog's site, the photos she got, and how Vierra had come to the station. She'd been so worried about messing up that she stayed home in her apartment, too embarrassed to call Madeline. "But Greg, the station's IT guy, gave me this address," she pointed to the building. "He said it's the physical address connected to the computer IP address he found for the texts the hacker sent. I thought I'd check it out -- now you're here."

Hunter walked over, and Madeline asked, "Did you hear that?"

Hunter nodded. "Good work, Cora, but this is where I send you home. We'll get a forensics team in here as quickly as possible."

Cora placed a hand on Madeline's shoulder. "Of course. But what about tomorrow, the big eclipse meditation, Christophe?"

Hunter looked back at the store. "If he planned the murders and used this as his staging site, I'm sure forensics will find something. I'll get the cybercrime guys on it as well."

Madeline instantly felt ice run in her veins. "You don't think there's a body stored in that freezer, do you?"

"I hope not," Hunter said as he pulled out his phone. "Madeline, can you come with me?"

⋅⋆《⋅73⋅》⋆⋅

In the Incident Room — 9:05 a.m.

They drove in silence, each contemplating what they'd gathered while the crime scene techs took their photos, hunted for evidence. Hunter finally said, "Come on. I need your help." Madeline hesitated when they drove to the Hall of Justice, but it was Sunday, and Hunter, now resolved, brought her into the incident room as bold as you please. Madeline looked at the massive whiteboard filled with photographs, charts, and drawings of the crime scenes. She studied the close-ups of Jonathan's face; how serene he looked wrapped in that quilt. Then she noticed the close-up shots of the meticulous way the killer decorated Sasha's face, the floral adornments making her look like the goddess of spring-time when, in fact, she was the maiden of death.

"Is that my quilt?" She pointed to photos Hunter took at the Savvy Seeker compound. Hunter nodded, "Yes, it's on display in their embroidery hut where their volunteers work on the affirmation quilts. Did Christophe ever give you credit for his meditation recordings? For gathering these quotes?"

Madeline waved a hand in the air, dismissing the subject. "The quotes are all in the public domain. He introduced me to them, so there was no credit to give. In retrospect, I wouldn't want any of his money. Is this Jonathan?" Madeline pointed to a photo on the board of Jonathan standing next to a tall blond boy. Behind them, three girls stood, heads bowed, studying something on someone's phone.

"Yes, the photo was taken by one of his school friends at a party. That's the last time anyone saw him alive."

Madeline recalled Jennifer Acosta. "His mom told me he sent her a text, but she said it didn't sound right. Jonathan hated sleepovers. Who is this with him? The boy?"

"That's Stellan. They met in a summer media program, but come, I want you to listen to something."

Madeline joined Hunter as he pulled up a file on his computer.

"Take a listen." Hunter clicked the file:

"Uh … yeah," the woman's voice started, sounding nervous. "Yeah, I think I just saw a body … Yeah, on a bench in the funny park on Taylor, on Russian Hill? I think. I don't know but send someone. He's like, dead."

Madeline stared at the screen. "My god, that's Geena's voice."

"It's what I thought, but I only put it together when I was driving to see you."

"After I showed her the photos I found at the flower shop, she left in a hurry. She must have gone to the flower shop because that's when they cleaned it out. She knew I'd tell you about it. Oh, my god." Madeline clutched at her stomach. "And she set the fire. Jesus."

Hunter placed a hand on her shoulder. "Do you want some water? Anything?"

"No." She kept the tears at bay. Hunter's hand was warm and reassuring. But her mind roiled with ideas, images flashing. "So, Geena comes to my store, what, a month ago? She's a little strange but super helpful, and she watches and listens to everything. How did you hear about me? What brought you to the store?"

Hunter leans back, "Alistair. He said a secretary called him and told him to go to the crime scene."

"A secretary? He didn't say his secretary?"

"No. But why, why set you up this way?"

Madeline shook her head. "Because I was Christophe's fall guy, I took the children away from their mothers. Someone is out for revenge. That leaves Victoria's son and Lili's daughter, Luna, right?"

"No, there's another one."

"What?" Madeline couldn't believe what she was hearing.

"Katia told me about that night when Victoria gave birth to her son, that she kept on bleeding?"

"Yes, Christophe and Katia rushed her to the hospital. What are you saying?"

"Victoria had twins. One wasn't getting as much blood as the other, so the twin went undetected until she gave birth to the boy. The twin is a girl."

Madeline jumped up as if someone had jabbed her in the heart, then turned to the photo on the whiteboard. "This photo of Jonathan, and you said Stellan, who is that dark-haired girl in the back?"

Hunter turned back to his computer. "Electra, another one of Jonathan's friends, took a bunch of photos. There has to be another shot in here."

Madeline sat next to Hunter as he pulled up the file. It showed kids at a party, drinking and playing pool alongside a smaller group of Jonathan, Stellan, and three girls. The dark-haired girl avoided the camera, so no clear shots of her face were captured. "Wait a minute, it took him forever, but Lance finally sent me his photos."

Madeline shook her head, clearing the tension as Hunter pulled open an email and another set of photos. More kids, then three girls, a black-haired Asian girl, and finally, the dark-haired girl, with dazzling China-blue eyes, just like her father. Geena.

"Jesus, Cora spotted it. She mentioned to me once that Geena wore contact lenses and dyed her hair."

Hunter grabbed the photo of Stellan and placed it side to side with Geena's photo on the computer screen. The connection was obvious. "They're twins."

"Oh my god," Madeline sat back, "Geena must have planted the cell phones in my apartment, and she knew I was going to show you the photos of the flower shop. She set the fire to stop me from seeing you."

"That means Christophe convinced his children to help him kill the others. Why in god's name?" Hunter said as he stared at his desk, then he grabbed his portfolio. "Wait a minute." He searched through the pages. "Cora's crime blogger. When I interviewed his teacher, he said Stellan dropped Jonathan's project because he got interested in blogging."

"So, Stellan was Cora's cyberstalker?" Madeline felt the room spin.

"That sounds reasonable, doesn't it? And then there's Sean Muldooney. I think this all has to do with Know-sis. We have a source that told us Christophe stole the Know-sis concept from Jonathan and got his brother Sean to finance it."

"Sean was just acquitted on murder charges."

"Hunter, what's the meaning of this?"

Madeline jumped. Leo, Hunter's boss, entered the room along with a Latinx woman. Her sharp outfit — a blue suit, trench coat, and glasses — suggested she had to be an administrator or a lawyer to dress up like that on a Sunday.

Hunter got out of his chair and pleaded with Leo, "I needed Madeline's help. We've figured out that her shop assistant is Christophe's daughter. She's been spying on Madeline for months. She and her brother are working with

Christophe, and they just burned down Madeline's home and apartment."

Hearing the reality of her situation, Madeline fought back another gasp, but she shoved thoughts of what she'd lost away and stood up to Leo and his guest.

"Ms. Merritt, I'm so very sorry to hear about your loss. This is Assistant District Attorney Paulina Bucky."

Paulina stepped forward and shook Madeline's hand. "This is terrible. I can get you in touch with our victim services department. There has to be something they can do to help."

"I appreciate that. Thank you." Madeline looked at Hunter, who smiled.

"But Paulina has news for you, Hunter, and since you're already involved in the case, Madeline, it's okay if you hear this," Leo said.

"Yes, Investigator Davis," Paulina began. "I'm sorry, we should have contacted you sooner, but we needed to see how Sean Muldooney's trial ended."

"Not very well," Hunter said. "What happened to the secret witness that you had lined up?"

Paulina shot a glance at Leo, who shook his head and sighed. "That's why I'm here. Please understand that we had to keep this under wraps. We couldn't risk anyone, especially Sean, finding out who the witness was."

"Did you say who it was?" Hunter asked.

"Yes, I'm so sorry, but the secret witness was Sasha Randall."

Hunter shot a look at Leo, and then back to Paulina. "Hang on a minute. We're working on the theory that Christophe murdered Jonathan because he stole this Know-sis technology from him."

Leo's eyes widened. "Then he kills Sasha to keep Sean from going to jail?"

"Yes." Hunter went to the whiteboard and tapped a photo of Sasha's crime scene. "Because Sean financed the Know-sis project."

Madeline felt the shiver fly down her spine, feeling the collective gloom that hung in the air. She flashed to the first chart she'd made for the 911 call. She'd got it all wrong. Madeline pulled up a chair and sat down. Leo and Paulina both leaned against a table, and Hunter leaned against the whiteboard. It seemed as if the weight of their realization forced everyone to find support somewhere.

»•«**74**»•«

MONDAY, AUGUST 21, 2017

Grace Cathedral — Countdown to the Path of Totality 7:15 a.m.

Cora sat at the far end of the satellite van's control center, doing her best to stay out of everyone's way. The director, technical director, and producers all wore headphones, checking in with the reporters at the Cathedral, in the park, and outside the Mark Hopkins hotel lobby, along with their camera crews. Cora scanned the banks of monitors, scanning the images from the live cameras stationed on the roof of the Masonic Lodge and from four drones outfitted with cameras flying overhead, feeding their shots back to the van.

8: 47 a.m. - Hunter dressed like a tourist in casual slacks and a long sleeve shirt to hide his bandaged forearm. Vierra wore full tactical gear with a radio receiver on his collar. They stood on the Cathedral steps after having searched the entire complex, but they'd seen no sign of Christophe or any of the Savvy Seeker staff. There were dozens of private security guards roaming the Cathedral complex, all speaking into walkie-talkies. Meditators had been gathering all morning in the park, along the sidewalks. They all wore red outfits, pants, a red kimono-style shirt, and a hood attached. And what had to be the Know-sis headsets. Ivan's drawing was accurate: designed to resemble a metallic crown with an earphone attachment.

Hunter heard a crackle, a hum, and watched all of the meditators take positions, like an army of ants all forming a perfect line that ran up and down the park, along the streets, and in front of the Cathedral. Then a man's voice came over a loudspeaker: "Welcome friends to this our Eclipse Meditation, our joyous salute to community, to mother nature, and to healing our city's scarred past." It was Christophe's voice. Hunter listened closely, making out if he was speaking from inside the Cathedral.

"Christ, he could be anywhere," Vierra said. "It could be a recording from back at the compound."

"It's now nine a.m. in Lincoln Beach, Oregon." Christophe continued. "The first sighting of the pre-eclipse will take place in five minutes."

"No, he's here." Hunter felt it. Christophe had to insert himself into the middle of the action. Hunter watched the meditators all hitting buttons on their headsets and then standing at attention.

"I don't like the feel of this," Vierra said and waved at other cops in tactical gear in front of the Cathedral. "I'm joining up with the team."

Hunter had been assigned to walk the crowd, "I'm heading into the fray, I'll check back later." They each went their separate ways.

9:06 a.m. - Cora watched the news anchors at their anchor desk set up outside the entrance to the Fairmont Hotel. "Welcome, everyone, from the top of Nob Hill, I'm Norma, and I'm joined by Ken and our remote reporters, bringing you live coverage of the Savvy Seekers Solar Eclipse Meditation." Norma's face filled the middle screen inside the satellite van. Ken stood on the street in front of the Mark Hopkins, and they switched to his camera.

"Morning Norma, this is indeed a special day for San Francisco," Ken said as he spoke into the camera. "We're not in the best spot for viewing the actual eclipse as the fog is lingering for the show, but out here on Nob Hill, we're in position to bring you all the best of this meditation experience."

Cora listened to Ken's outline of what to expect from Christophe's meditators. "Our team has learned," Ken continued, "that the meditators will begin what are called magical passes, a series of dance moves that will entrain their energies together using the latest technology from Silicon Valley. It's all been very hush-hush up to this point, so like you, Norma, I'm looking forward to seeing it put into action. As you can see in front of me, many of the one thousand meditators are already gathering. That's double the original estimate. They will begin making their moves in just a moment after we come back from this message."

"Commercial break," the director barked to everyone in the van. Cora kept her eyes glued on the drone shots. Meditators in red garb ran down Sacramento Street to Polk Street and the civic center. People on the sidewalks stopped to take photos of the meditators who remained motionless. She saw one or two people take selfies with the meditators in the background.

9:23 a.m. - Madeline walked through Huntington Park, watching the spectacle of meditators standing motionless all around the park and across the street in front of the Cathedral. Exhausted after dealing with the fire and being in the Hall of Justice, she'd arrived at Cora's apartment and fell into bed. She woke up in a cold sweat, not knowing where she was, the cuts on her arms throbbing, and she remembered her escape from the fire. She smelled burning paper and panicked. She rolled over in bed, doing her best not to think about the lost inventory and what it would cost to replace the stock. Or how Aunt Jane would be devastated at hearing the news.

The books were her primary concern, but images of posters, CDs, prayer beads, Tarot cards, and I Ching sets prayed on her. Of course, one mainstay of any metaphysical bookstore was the crystals. So many customers came in to find the right crystal for their collections or to carry with them for the benefit of the stone's particular energy. Most people started with their birthstones. She'd been reviewing the list of stones when Cora knocked on her door. She'd gone shopping and presented Madeline with new clothes. Madeline hadn't even thought about what she was going to wear after the fire. She mentally thanked Cora again because now she wore the comfortable but expensive jeans, a purple linen blouse, and a black hoodie, with the hood covering her head, which made her feel safe from the meditators and security cameras.

She had walked with Cora to the satellite van, and now she was free to roam the park and keep out of the police's way. She couldn't help but remember that beautiful summer day with her friends from the Bernal Heights house. She walked past roadblocks set around the Cathedral that ran as far down as Powell Street. Regular folks gathered in the park, along with bands of meditators. She checked her phone. She still had another hour until the first sighting of the moon.

Madeline thought back to that first chart she'd cast for the time the 911 call came in for Jonathan's murder. The sun rising into Mars, with the Moon on the opposite side. Had she been so wrong? Madeline walked past a crowd gathered at the fountain. Madeline arrived at the statue of the dancing sprites and spotted her, and Madeline realized it was where she would have expected to see her. The woman wore the identical meditation robes as the others gathered in the park. The woman gazed up at the Cathedral, then turned and spotted Madeline. There was a split second of recognition. The woman leaped up and ran into the crowd, slipping into a sea of red.

9:37 a.m. - Matthew-Tabitha huddled in front of the Mark Hopkins, watching the television reporter speaking to a cop. Matthew-Tabitha looked up to the Top of the Mark, the famous bar on the hotel's 19th floor. She could only imagine what celebrities were there, getting a bird's eye view of the goings on. She wore a long red wig and her eclipse glasses, along with the red meditators robes, but she chose not to wear the hood. Too clannish a look for her. Instead, she wore earbuds and rocked out to her favorite tunes. Then she checked her phone, a text from Cora. The eclipse had begun.

"And now, meditators," Christophe's voice boomed through the area, "begin your passes."

Matthew-Tabitha watched the five meditators who stood in front of her begin the movements by bringing the left arm in front of the chest, then sweeping the right arm down to the ground and up, meeting the left hand in a prayer position. Then the meditator raised both hands to the sky, then turned the hands over and pulled them around and back down to their sides. Then, they repeated the motion. Matthew-Tabitha imitated the moves and tried to blend in. She glanced down the street and remembered one of the most powerful ley lines ran along it. Out of nowhere, she felt a jolt of energy, like electricity, hit her solar plexus. She checked an app on her phone, one designed for sensing telluric energy. "Holy crap."

9:41 a.m. - Madeline slipped through the meditators, monitoring the woman ahead of her, getting closer to the Cathedral. All around her, the meditators moved their bodies in what resembled an esoteric form of Tai Chi. Christophe's voice filled the area, coming out of loudspeakers set in the park. "And now, my people, begin your full phase of passes. The path of totality is upon us!" The meditators went into full movements, quick arm slashes, like a beautiful dance, all moving in unison. No one paid any attention to the woman ahead of her as she silently slipped through the crowd. Madeline's injuries throbbed, but she did what she could to keep up the pace. Why had it taken her so long to put it together? Walking through the park in the early morning, the answer revealed itself in a dazzling line of Sun, Mars, and Moon, like series of gemstones: opal, alexandrite, and pearls. Birthstones for Libra and two stones for Gemini.

Hunter stood on the Cathedral steps, watching the meditators synchronize their movements. The patterns were faster now, with an eerie quality. Looking up through the fog, the Sun now took on the shape of a crescent Moon. Searching the crowd watching the meditators, he saw many of them copying the meditators' movements. Some were just joking around, but he saw others whose faces took on the same placid expression as the meditators. Now the number of people going through the dance movements doubled. He felt a strange sensation in his chest, that it would be easy to just follow along with the others. What was going on?

Madeline kept the woman in sight, and "And now, gathered souls," Christophe's voice boomed through the crowd. Madeline kept her eyes focused on the woman, who got to the base of the stairs leading up to the Cathedral, next to a wall. The crowd in front of the Cathedral was shoulder to shoulder, and the woman had to shove her way past a group of onlookers. It gave Madeline just enough time to get within arm's reach.

The meditators continued their movements mesmerizing and fluid. They seduced the crowd around them. They all moved in unison but were so jammed tight that the woman Madeline was chasing came to a halt. Madeline got to her, threw her arm around her neck, pulled her up against the wall, and whispered in her ear, "A thirsty man calls out, 'Delicious water. Where are you?'"

The red hood on the woman's head slipped down, and she twisted her body to look at Madeline. Victoria cleared her throat, "'While the water moans, where is the water drinker?'"

Madeline wrapped her other arm around Victoria's waist, keeping her body pressed up against the wall, and then spotted the brooch pinned to her collar. "Geena just couldn't help herself, couldn't she? She stole that from me."

Victoria hissed, "And you stole her from me! That night, after I gave birth to my boy, Stellan."

"I had nothing to do with that. It was Katia." Madeline pulled away as Victoria turned to her.

"Liar! You and Christophe never told me about her, but she found me. My brilliant girl found me. And if you'd only found Lili, this would have been over by now."

"Was that your plan? Kidnap Lili and Luna? Make them the centerpiece to complete your twisted sacrifice?”

Victoria squinted, “And Christophe, too. My final display, a murder suicide for the ages. Now, get out of my way.”

“And what about Alistair? How did you get him to lead me on?”

“Simple. The idiot wants Know-sis. I promised I’d get it to him.”

“As the moon is now crossing the sun, in our last phase,” Christophe’s voice boomed through the crowd, “it’s my great honor and pleasure to introduce to you my daughter, Luna!”

Madeline and Victoria looked at the top of the stairs. A phalanx of meditators, all dressed in white, parted, and a tiny girl in white robes emerged. She danced to the center of the labyrinth and began her passes. They were different, a more elaborate set of motions. She moved like a ballerina. All around her, the red-clad meditators didn’t miss a beat as they joined in the pattern.

“Yes, now, let me go so I can finish this.” Victoria slapped Madeline’s arm, the one around Victoria’s waist, stabbing at the bandages.

Madeline tried to hold onto Victoria, but then she felt something hard shoved into her side. Victoria had a gun.

“I have to stop Luna!” Victoria kicked at Madeline’s leg, sending Madeline crumpling to the stairs. Victoria pushed through the crowd, scrambling up the stairs. Madeline spotted Victoria shoving her way to the top of the stairs, her eyes staring at Luna. Madeline screamed, “She’s got a gun!”

10:21 a.m. – Hunter spotted Madeline struggling with a woman. He recognized Victoria and spotted the gun in her hand. Shoving through the crowd, Victoria scampered up the stairs to the top of the Cathedral steps.

“She’s got a gun!” Madeline shouted. Hunter ran toward Victoria as the word “gun” brought Vierra and a swam of cops swarming through the crowds rushing to the labyrinth. In a heartbeat, police officers took positions in front of Luna with their guns aimed at Victoria.

Then there was a hush and shouts of “totality, we’ve reached totality!” The crowd stopped moving. The sky, still filled with fog, took on a gray haze. They were in the total eclipse. Madeline scrambled up the stairs, reaching for Victoria, who aimed her gun at Luna. Luna stopped her dance moves to come toward Victoria. Hunter pulled out his gun and aimed it at Victoria. “Drop your weapon,

Victoria." With his other hand, he signaled to Madeline to get down. Madeline followed his lead and got down on her haunches.

"Papa!" Luna's voice filled the square as she spoke into a mic pinned to her gown, "Now, Papa!" In a nanosecond Luna drew her arm across and down. The police stood frozen, but as Madeline looked at Victoria, her eyes grew wide, her entire body shook, and she crumbled to the stairs. Madeline wrapped an arm around her as Victoria trembled, her eyes looking wild as if in the middle of a seizure.

"Victoria!" Madeline pleaded with her friend. Victoria dropped the gun, and Hunter swooped in, grabbing it as it fell.

Victoria's body throbbed at a freakishly fast pace while the crowd stood looking at her. Madeline cradled her head so it wouldn't hit the stairs and then saw Luna staring down at Victoria, and then she cocked her head to one side. Victoria let out a scream, and Madeline felt a jolt move through her, and, unbelievably, a spark of flame caught on Victoria's robe.

By instinct, Madeline pulled her own body away as the entire blouse was covered with flames. Victoria's body kept seizing. Madeline couldn't believe it, but the fire was real. Victoria's clothes and body were burning. Madeline tore off her hoodie and covered Victoria's burns as she writhed in pain. "Luna! You must stop this!" Madeline screamed as Hunter joined Madeline, and they tamped out the flames on Victoria's clothes. Victoria stared up at Madeline, and the seizing paused for the sheerest instant, and a glimmer of their past friendship flashed between them.

Madeline and Hunter secured the hoodie over Victoria's wounds, but then Madeline watched Hunter draw back, the shock of what he'd just witnessed hitting him. Hunter stared at Madeline. She knew he needed reassurance that he wasn't crazy, that they had both seen the flames and they had been real. The crowd started shouting all around them, and people scrambled down the stairs, "There's smoke coming from the street."

10:22 a.m. - Cora watched the NASA feed as the Sun's brilliant light emerged from behind the Moon. Then she turned to the monitors, capturing the scene in front of the Cathedral as Madeline and Hunter quelled the fire that erupted on Victoria's chest. But in another shot, a drone camera over the Mark Hopkins hotel, steam shot up from the street.

"We can't tell you what we're seeing," Norma's voice was shrill. "But what looks like steam is streaming out of the Mark Hopkins hotel as police overcame the would-be assassin. Ken, what are you seeing?"

Cora watched the camera images from around the Cathedral where meditators jumped out of the way as lines of steam flew up into the sky.

"It's got to be the cisterns," shouted someone in the satellite van.

"What are the cisterns?" Cora pleaded as she flipped through the special event bible, searching for an answer.

The producer grabbed the mike on the tech board and spoke into Ken and Norma's earpieces. "There's a series of cisterns filled with water below the streets of San Francisco," Ken repeated the same information as Cora watched, mesmerized, as all four drones showed video of steam filling the streets. The director cut back and forth between the camera shots.

"The cisterns provide extra water in case there's a big fire, and the fire department needs more water to fight a blaze. It seems they are now boiling."

10:27 am. Matthew-Tabitha stood in front of the Mark Hopkins with her phone, capturing video of the steam spouts emerging from the street, filling the air with steam, and people, along with frightened meditators, all stampeded out of the area. "Hey, slow down, everyone," she yelled, but it was useless as people in the crowd panicked. Matthew-Tabitha edged her way over to the pillar at the parking lot entrance. She got as close as she could to evade the rushing crowds.

10:28 am. Madeline and Hunter sat with Victoria at the top of the stairs. Victoria screamed in pain.

"It's okay, Victoria. Don't move. The paramedics will be here."

"Why did you stop me?" Victoria cried in frustration.

Madeline looked out at the crowd, people running in every direction, and then up at Luna, who stared right at her and yelled, "Don't worry, Aunty Madeline, I'll protect you." Another explosion, this time across the street. Madeline watched in horror as the trees in the park all caught on fire simultaneously. The people who had been huddled in the park screamed and ran away from the trees, joining the confusion and panic in the streets.

Madeline looked back at Luna. "No, Luna. Stop. I'm fine." Madeline stood up and waved at Luna as she saw a group of meditators in white robes approach the girl. One of them was a woman, a hood covered her face, she placed her hand on Luna's shoulder, and Luna smiled. The hood flew off and Madeline recognized Lili. Luna pointed toward Madeline and Lili looked at her, she wasn't the same friend she'd known all those years ago.

"Lili, wait!" Madeline scrambled up the stairs, Vierra right behind her, but then a white van suddenly appeared through the Cathedral compound. The van door was wide open. Lili grabbed Luna, and they both jumped in before anyone could stop them.

"What the hell?" Madeline screamed.

Madeline looked back at Hunter who was still holding Victoria. Madeline returned down the stairs and watched police direct a fire truck in to hose down the fire in the park as the square emptied of people. An ambulance drove up the street, stopping in front of the Cathedral; Madeline waved to the EMT, who leaped from the back of the ambulance and came to help Victoria.

❲75❳

At the hospital — 2:43 p.m.

Madeline sat on a bench outside Victoria's room, waiting for Hunter to tell her how Victoria was doing. Madeline read the frantic text exchange between Cora and Matthew-Tabitha. She'd done her best to explain what she'd learned about Geena and Stellan. Thinking about the fire in the bookstore, Madeline figured out that Geena had lit the blaze after she'd shown Geena the photos of the "Lili" store. Madeline thought back to the vision of Mercury, laughing at her, how she'd thought it stood for Christophe, but it turned out to be Geena and Stellan. Cora reported that Christophe had escaped capture by the police.

Hunter emerged from Victoria's room. Madeline smiled at him. He looked like he'd seen two ghosts, five demons, and Big Foot.

"I never, I mean, never in my wildest dreams thought I would see a human spontaneously combust. Is that what we saw?"

Madeline shook her head. "No, that's not what you saw. You saw Luna set Victoria on fire."

"With her *mind?*" Hunter rubbed his face, hoping to erase the exasperation and amazement that matched Madeline's.

Madeline shook her head, "It's called pyrokinesis. A very rare psychic ability that everyone thought was pure bullshit. Until today."

"Until today." He turned to her. "I'm sorry, but I agree with you on the bullshit part. But I can't reconcile that with what I saw with my own eyes."

"I can't either. All I can say is Christophe must have done something wacky when he passed along his genes to those kids."

"And I apologize. The killer was a woman. You were right all along."

Madeline let that sink in. "And you know when I was in your incident room and looked at the crime scene photos, it all makes sense. They were beautiful."

"Yeah, in a ghoulish way, but she went to a lot of trouble staging the bodies."

"Victoria couldn't help it. It's in her nature. The stars don't lie. She's a Libra which is ruled by the planet Venus, the planet of beauty. For her, everything must look beautiful, or it just doesn't feel right."

"We should have brought you in sooner."

"No. I'm just glad it's over." Madeline wondered for a half second if she could have helped solve the case sooner but dismissed the thought. That Geena duped her left her feeling foolish, but worse, she thought of the pain Geena, Stellan, and Victoria inflicted on so many people. Jennifer Acosta, Sasha's parents. What drove her? Revenge? Payback? For what they'd conjured up during that ceremony all those years ago? And how it all backfired. Victoria's plan to get revenge on Christophe had worked for him.

"So, listen," Hunter started.

This was the worst part. Madeline hadn't expected this, hadn't expected him. Hadn't expected this man to have such impact on her life. "I know, you have to get back to work."

"I do," his voice sounded strained. "But not just yet." There was a long pause before he could continue.

Madeline picked at the bandage on her arm. A piece of cotton gauze had worked loose during her struggle with Victoria.

"I don't know if you remember, but we talked about sharing grilled cheese sandwiches at the Ferry Building?" Hunter said.

Madeline stopped picking at her bandage because she couldn't hold back any longer. She started crying. She didn't want him to see this, but he was watching her, and she put her hand over her eyes. "Look, before you go on. … I"

Hunter put his hand on hers, "Okay, this is rough, but I'll try. These days have been horrific, and yet right here, between us, there's something good. Something worth fighting for."

Through her tears, Madeline couldn't talk, but she nodded her head.

"It's good and yet there's something about it that scares me to death."

She pulled her hand away from her eyes and looked into his.

"And the thought of not seeing you again scares me even more. So, let's do this. We're on a bench. It's not at the Ferry building. We can't watch the ferries come and go, but we can sit here, for now, and watch these people, these patients, and nurses. They're not a great substitute, but taking advantage of this moment would help with everything going on. I can grab some stale sandwiches from the vending machine?"

Madeline brushed away her tears and put her hand on his. "You're a smart man, Hunter Davis. You might even make a good investigator one of these days."

Hunter leaned back and laughed, "Gee, thanks, Malcolm."

That's what they did. They sat in the busy hallway as nurses rushed by speaking into their phones, patients with IVs linked to their arms made slow marches back and forth from their rooms, and doctors carried on small conferences going from one emergency to the next, all ignoring the two people sitting on a bench, watching their world go by.

Epilogue

Red Oak Tavern — 3:17 p.m.

Sean Muldooney, dressed in a dark tracksuit and white T-shirt, stood behind the bar. He lifted a cold IPA beer bottle from the nearby drawer, popped the top, and took a long drag. Sean set the bottle down, and then leaned across the bar and smiled. Across from him, Stellan and Geena sat on bar stools, Geena swiveling back and forth while Stellan just smiled, pulled out a silver-cased hard drive, and placed it on the bar.

"As promised, Uncle Sean. Know-sis in all its glory. Don't say Muldooney's don't keep their promises."

Sean reached out and patted the hard drive. "How did you pull it off?"

"While everyone was freaking out about Luna, I slipped into the office and told Edgar to hand it over," Geena said.

"Oh, and he just gave it to you?"

"The knife at his throat persuaded him," she winked.

"This calls for a celebration," Sean said, taking another swig of beer. "Can I get you a beer?"

"Uncle Sean, you know you can't serve drinks to minors," Geena said. "We wouldn't want to get you in trouble with the law, now, would we?"

Sean held up his beer bottle and gave her a silent salute.

Thank you, dear reader, for embarking on this journey with me!

I hope you enjoyed *The Eclipse Killer*, with its suspenseful plot and unexpected twists. It is book one of my series, *The Forensic Astrology Files*. I'm excited to announce that *Secrets of the Red Oak Tavern* is coming your way in 2025!

Your review matters! By sharing your thoughts on this book, you help other readers discover books they'll love. Plus, your feedback helps tailor recommendations to your tastes, making it easier for you to find your next great read.

Warmest regards, Rachel Funk Heller

P.S. If you really enjoyed this book, please write a review and tell your friends ;-)

〉●《

Acknowledgments

I owe a huge thanks to my developmental editor, Eleanor Svaton of The Desk Publishing, whose relentless determination to ask challenging questions and to offer expert guidance has improved this book in more ways than I can count. To John Truby and his Truby Story Program for asking even tougher questions and designing homework assignments that caused much distress but helped me establish the structure this book needed to tell this story.

I would like to express my sincere gratitude to the fellow participants of Truby's Writer's Room program for their invaluable contributions and unwavering support. You can expect to read their work in the future. So, thank you to Jocelyn Lindsay, Kelly N. Jane, Gina Anjou, Rob Thesman, Sarah Crowne, Tom Watts, Gérôme Ordoño, Allen J Mummert, and Judith Blazer.

Learning astrology is a lifelong undertaking. While on this path, I've encountered many teachers and I'm grateful to Frederick Woodruff for his readings and many useful suggestions for adding accurate astrological information into this story. You can find him on Substack at WOODRUFF.

Also, thank you to Dan Paul Roberts for his excellent suggestions for the book cover, for helping pick the final title for this novel, and for his support of this project over the years.

About the Author

Rachel Funk Heller began her career in television journalism and worked as an associate producer for CNN. She worked as a Producer/Writer for the Hawaii Department of Education where she was commissioned to produce, write, edit, and illustrate a Young Adult story-telling series titled *Christabelle in the Museum of Time*. She also produced and wrote eight seasons of *School Connections*. She lives in Hawaii where she takes lots of sunrise photos while walking her dog, Quinn. For more information on future titles, please subscribe to her webiste, rachel-funkheller.com